PRAISE FOR STARGUN MESSENGER

"It'll make you laugh. It'll make you think. And it'll leave you feeling entertained and empowered."

FANFIADDICT

"If James Joyce had grown up reading X-Men comics, he would have written this."

WAYNE SANTOS, AUTHOR OF ***THE CHIMERA CODE***

"★★★★★ Darby Harn's storytelling is both imaginative and emotionally resonant."

READER'S FAVORITE

"Darby Harn is an artist with words. The language soars."

BOWEN GREENWOOD, AUTHOR OF DEATH OF SECRETS

"A vivid, space-sprawling epic reminiscent of Samuel R. Delany."

BRITTNI BRINN

"An utterly surprising and mesmerizing novel, Stargun Messenger is a complex and fascinating look at A.I. personhood and doing the right thing."

"The character work, particularly with Astra Idari and CR-UX, is magnificent. There are layers to what is going on and the author does a great job building on them."

"*Stargun Messenger* is a book for readers who enjoy space heists and exploring the concept of what makes us human. Space opera sci-fi readers, give this one a try."

"I didn't expect to be so emotionally destroyed at the end of this book."

STARGUN MESSENGER

STARGUN MESSENGER

Copyright © 2023 Darby Harn. All rights reserved.

This is a work of fiction. Names, characters, businesses, places, events, and incidents are either the products of the author's imagination or used in a fictitious manner. Any resemblance to actual persons, living or dead, or actual events is purely coincidental.

Library of Congress Control Number: 2022923392

ISBN: 978-1-7370097-6-4

Fair Play Books

www.darbyharn.com

Cover art by Al Hess.

www.alhessauthor.com

No part of this book may be reproduced in any form by electronic or mechanical means, including information storage and retrieval systems, without permission in writing from the publisher. To seek permission to use the book for anything other than review purposes, please contact the publisher at fairplaybooks@gmail.com.

Printed in the U.S.A.

First Edition

STARGUN MESSENGER

DARBY HARN

FAIR
PLAY
BOOKS

"The truth is of course there is no journey. We are all arriving and departing at the same time."

– DAVID BOWIE

For Al

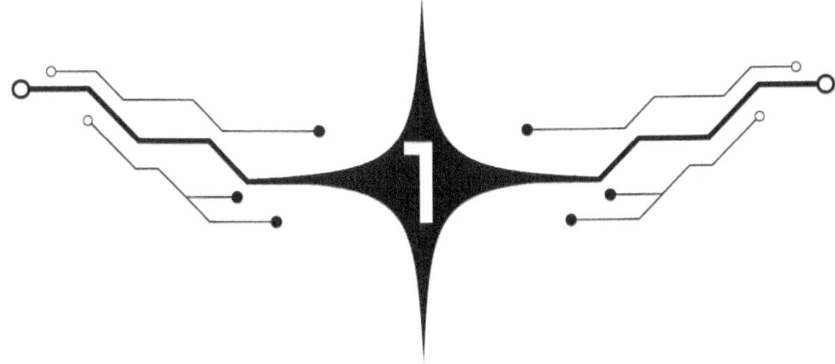

Sometimes I forget I'm not human.

Usually after closing down another bar in another dead-end system, I can't recall a thing, but this body never lets me forget the distance between its truth and its reality for long.

>INTERNAL MEMORY FULL

If only. Shame leaves bruises deeper than memory engrams. Grief not for who you've lost, but who you'll never be. A woman flickers in the visor of a breathing mask lying on the floor, but I must be a machine. I can tell by the constant little note blinking here in my diagnostic log. I should probably open the constant little note.

>FILE CRITICAL / ALWAYS READ THIS FIRST
Your name is Astra Idari. You're an IA-XR Model 4 proxy-netic. The proxy routinely purges data due to limited onboard memory. Also, you drink. A lot.

Idari. Pujar, I think. Am I a pirate? How do I tell? I tug on the zipper of my pressure suit. Dust coats me. Nickel shavings float in a corridor carved from solid iron. Where am I? Data points compete for my attention. Atmospheric quality, the gravitational condition wherever here is, and countless other indicators pile into a massive headache I feel like I've been carrying around the entire galaxy.

It's enough to drive a girl to drink.

Black scorch slashes white fabric across my shoulder. Someone shot me. They tried. Arm looks ok, save for a sunburn. I must have done all right by myself given this fancy blaster I'm holding with a curved, bladed muzzle. Wonder how they did. Oh, there he is.

Well, I haven't forgot how to aim.

What am I doing here? What's happening? Another note flashes at me. I don't know how I'm supposed to tell which is which. There are so many. Sensor information pours into me. I'm a tiny bottle.

>FILE CRITICAL / CURRENT ASSIGNMENT
You are a Stargun Messenger. You are in the Kasda system pursuing the Banbor Gang, who stole filamentium from a Scath tanker. They are armed and highly dangerous, so don't mute your sensor feeds. Electromagnetic interference in the system is high and likely frustrates the downlink between you and the ship, which will make communication difficult.

Communication? With who? Is that where all this data is coming from? A ship. What's it called? I can never remember. I should. It's a shoe, that ship. Old. Tatty. Comfortable. I've worn holes through her, but I don't feel right in anything else. Plus, it's where I keep everything important to me. My booze. My backup memory.

This is coming back to me now.

Without the downlink, my cloud memory is unavailable. I'm left with only what I have onboard the proxy-netic. If I stray too far, I'll forget who I am and then I'll be just another human-looking android wandering around the stars. One of those blank books they sell in musty old shops for people to fill with dreams but no understanding.

A voice crackles through the static always in my ears. *Darling –*

Familiar. Distant. This gulf between us wide as between the stars in the big empty. Interference. Right. All this iron. I proceed down the corridor, hoping to get a better signal. Keep your head on. No matter what, drunk, forgetful, or both, I can always fall back on my true and constant guide through the dark.

\>SIGNAL RE-ACQUIRED

Varied telemetry flicks through the downlink I share with the *Steel Haven*, parked on a landing pad at the mining camp's edge. Her sensors paint the picture for me. I'm in a derelict ore processing facility with a hangover of equal or greater mass than the planetary fragment I'm on. Millions of fragments tumble through the oil spill beyond. I think it's millions. It's not like I counted.

There are 2,743,428 fragments to be precise and I don't know if that's me or CR-UX saying that. I get us confused sometimes. In my line of work, having eyes in the back of your head comes in handy. Having a highly advanced AI to guide your ship through starless space does, too, even if CR-UX is mostly keeping me on course.

Mostly, he says.

I'd be hopeless without CR-UX. I wake up out of the recharging cycle, a graft of jumbled memories, and he's the only constant. Sometimes he gets on my nerves, but that's anyone who you spend every day with. Doesn't mean anything. Absent CR-UX, I have no perspective on the galaxy beyond the *Steel Haven*. She's home. My ark. We do what we have to do to keep her going, even if we don't like it. Who likes their job? I'm here on a job. I'm a bounty hunter. A Stargun.

Now I've got my bearings, I don't need to ask CR-UX why I'm here. Out in The Hinterlands, Stargun Messengers serve as de facto law enforcement. Need protection from raiders? Pirates run off with your ship? Someone steal your starship fuel? I'll settle your problem for you, so long as you settle the bill. The Scath pay.

A lot.

They've got the money for it, being the sole suppliers of filamentium in the galaxy. Filamentium is my livelihood. The lifeblood of the galaxy. Without it, starships don't go faster than the speed of light. Worlds starve. People die. This Banbor Gang stole filamentium.

I'm here to take it back.

I prime my blaster. *Which way, CR-UX?*

A left and two rights, darling.

I turn down a new corridor. My helmet's starburst visor divides my view, but lucky me, I have eyes beyond my own.

CR-UX sighs. *Your other left, Idari.*

I go the other way. *I was testing you.*

You certainly tested yourself with the copious amount of babyl you imbibed directly before coming here to engage a well-armed gang.

Unfortunately for the two of us, minding your own business wasn't an option among the features that came with the *Steel Haven.* CR-UX's irritation bristles on the downlink, where it runs into mine, and all there is between us is the garbled static of things unsaid. We hear each other's thoughts. Neither of us listens.

I listen, CR-UX says.

You judge.

I comment.

Basically the same thing.

They're entirely different. Judging is a silent pursuit.

We're always talking.

I listen.

Are you judging while you listen?

Your other left.

I stub my foot on a knob of exposed nickel. *Ban Minda.* The Kasda carved the processing facility from bare iron without any mind for the people and machines that would be haunting its halls. Scarped iron hazards the corridor beyond, like the cast-off sheets of discarded metal littering the junkyards from my nightmares.

I cycle through my sensor feeds to infrared. Filamentium whites out the dark ahead. Just like I figured, the fuel remains largely unrefined. The only thing harder than stealing the stuff is doing anything with it. Purifying unrefined fuel is slow, dangerous work. One misstep and entire planets vanish in elemental fire. The Banbors are novices, trying to use outdated, inadequate equipment here in the ore processing facility. I have to be careful. Smart.

Doing brilliant so far.

CR-UX doesn't say anything. He doesn't have to. Telemetry

melds with our thoughts into a singular world of data the two of us share through the downlink. For as long as I can remember, which isn't much, he's always been there in my head.

His concern torrents through me swift as all this data. *You really do need to be careful, darling. I worry about you.*

I was in the bar to find out where the Banbors were, I say.

You didn't need to be there all night.

Shh.

Six distinct orange blobs move through the refinery beyond. Armed. Heavily armed. Considerably so for small-time bandits like them. Someone must be bankrolling them on this job. Someone big in the underworld. Probably The Bool. That means he put skin in the game for this job. He'll be furious to lose the fuel and his money.

CR-UX, can we target the canisters from space?

The Scath expect their merchandise returned to them, Idari.

Too bad the Scath can't be bothered to come and get their own fuel back. Lucky for me, I guess, they don't. The Scath are strictly in the export business. Fuel. Myths about who they are. Where they come from. No one ever deals with them directly. A message comes through from a masked ID. Objective. Terms. File and forget.

Perhaps the Scath simply prefer solitude, CR-UX says.

I adjust the downlink audio volume. *What an alien concept.*

I track the energy signatures down an elevated track sagging with empty carts to stacked cargo crates where the Banbor Gang passes the time refining the fuel with bottles of babyl. All four canisters remain racked together in the crib the gang stole off a Scath tanker. None of it refined. Maybe they didn't know how.

"Boys," I say, and surprise flares in the muzzle flash of my blaster. I'm surprised. I always am, at how easy this is.

The last one crashes to his knees. The dust-caked breathing mask suggests they're Kasda, but the cumbersome thermal suit isn't scabbed in nickel scoria like other miners working this system.

The mask muffles his anxiety. "Why..."

I point my blaster at him. "Someone should have told you. You steal nothing from the shadows but darkness."

A digital alarm blinks on the glass of his helmet. He's burning through oxygen, breathing so heavy. Why would anyone want to know the thinness of their own life? I've never understood.

"There's something else," he says.

My finger curls around the trigger. "Don't waste your time."

"Wait. *Wait.* You don't know about this."

A digital tsk chops through the downlink. *Idari. Get on with it.*

How is it with all the electromagnetic interference in this star system, I say, *I can still copy your nagging loud and clear, CR-UX?*

You could ask our new friend. Or go on staring at them in awkward silence. I'm good either way.

I grip my blaster. Get on with it. Collect the payment. Move on to the next job. Something holds me back. Fatigue. Not from last night. This life. I'm tired of this life and I'm not even living it.

Pain burns through my shoulder. Fire. My hand goes slack against my holster, numb like my arm. I twist around. Light fades in the barrel of the small, presumptuous blaster in the Banbor's hand.

You didn't pick the blaster up on sensors, CR-UX?

There's so much interference –

If he'd stop sighing through every single thing I think and do. If I didn't drink so much before coming here. Focus, Idari. How bad is it?

>CRITICAL INJURY

I can't feel my hand. *A little help, CR-UX.*

Rerouting auxiliary power, he says.

I slump against the crib. "Be smart about this."

The Banbor points the blaster at me. "I am."

"Do *not* shoot at the extremely volatile starship fuel, ok? You'll blow up what's left of the system."

His arm sags. "Move out of the way."

I lean back against the crib. "I like it here."

"I'll take my chances, then."

I tear off my helmet and throw it at the Banbor. The visor shatters as it rattles across the floor to his feet. His amusement curdles to surprise. A fear I'm too familiar with. It clings to me just as it does others, like the escaping oxygen freezing to my face. My lips. The inside of my mouth. I remember what most people forget, and I've never known, not truly; the exercise of breathing.

The weight of air in my lungs.

Sparks spit out of the wound in my shoulder. Bio-netic fluid douses the flames burning through my synthetic skin.

The Banbor's bulky helmet teeters on his head. "You're still breathing? Wait... you're not human? You're... you're not real?"

>AUXILIARY POWER RE-ROUTED

Power transfer complete, CR-UX says. *You should have sufficient mobility in your hand to answer his question.*

"I'm real," I say, and electric blue flares in the Banbor's helmet.

I stagger back to the filamentium crib. I drag it behind me in the meek gravity. A dull, slow scrape. The soundlessness of space is a myth. Stars hum. Black holes murmur deep in oscillations occurring once only every million years. Soundwaves from colliding planets travel as far as dust clouds permit. That's all space is, really; hums. Drones. Oscillations. But there's no music in my life. Only noise.

Some days I wake up and forget I'm not human. But then I remember I'm just an effigy of wire and metal kissed with enough electricity to riddle me with the confusion of consciousness.

You are human, Idari, CR-UX says.

I holster my blaster. *Did a human do all this?*

Humans do things they don't want to do sometimes.

I don't want to do this anymore, CR-UX. I hate this. This life.

Anxious data prickles on the downlink. *I know, but... Starguns are the law in The Hinterlands. Stealing filamentium is punishable by death. This life... such as it is... affords us some agency. It affords us anonymity. If we could get a little bit ahead... save some money...*

What? What could we do?

You could be who you are, at least.

And who is that?

He always takes so long to say. *My friend.*

Pain shocks through my arm. I let go of the crib and clutch my shoulder and the canisters drift into me. Careful. One little bump and I'm atoms. This stuff is moodier than I am sitting around waiting for another job. Canisters are secure. Internal pressurization stable. Laser hole in a canister. There's a hole in one of the canisters.

Run, Idari, CR-UX says.

Wait. No leak. The Banbor hit the canister on the top right when he opened up on me from behind. This entire fragment should have went nova. The entire system. I check the canister's data screen.

There isn't any juice in here, CR-UX.

Good thing, or else it would have been curtains for your girl. Maybe the Banbors did try refining the filamentium in the facility. Perfect. Now I'll have to scrub it out of whatever ancient contraption they dumped it into. That will take hours. Days.

My sigh freezes on my lips. *I could have sworn we picked up a thermal signature out of this canister, CR-UX.*

We did, darling. In fact, I am now.

What?

I blink through my optical sensors. Infrared doesn't lie. This thing glows like it's brimming with filamentium. *Ban Minda.* I input the lock-release code and light explodes inside the refinery.

Beauty does.

My sensors reduce the glare a little, exposing the source to be a young woman. Or a man. Somewhere in between. Ephemeral light streams off of them in licks and wisps, cerulean like the sky, just before the break of day. They're a star. A living star.

A Lumenor.

The legends are true. Living stars are real. A living star is standing before me. They were hiding inside this canister and do you see this CR-UX? They have to be worth millions of toruls. Tens of millions. I can get out of this life, once and for all.

CR-UX, do you see this? You there?

Static. Nothing on the downlink. A low-level magnetic field

emanates from the Lumenor. Must be them. They're pulling on me. Not just my metal bones. My electric thoughts. My digital soul.

I can't move. "You're..."

Their fingers brush my cheek. "A memory."

>NEURAL NET REBOOTING

>FILE CRITICAL / ALWAYS READ THIS FIRST

Your name is Astra Idari. You're an IA-XR Model 4 proxy-netic. The proxy routinely purges data due to limited onboard memory. Also, you drink. A lot.

>SIGNAL RE-ACQUIRED

Where are you going now, Idari?

On CR-UX's scopes, I appear small against the craggy iron peak of the planetary fragment. The processing facility rusts a click back, nestled among mobile habitats forming the itinerant mining camp.

How did I get out here?

I scale the blunt stump of iron serving as a landing pad. The *Steel Haven* isn't much to look at. Her reddish-brown skin has gone gunmetal gray. Two fat overlight engines bracket a forward cockpit. She's shaped a bit like a heart someone pounded into an arrowhead.

But she's home.

She has been for so long that I can't be sure of when and how I first came to the ship. CR-UX rolled out of a foundry on Shighn pre-installed in the ship sometime long before that. How did we ever find each other? How do we stay together in all this dark.

I lost you back there, I say. *Must be all this interference.*

You may be more injured than diagnostics suggest, CR-UX says. *To say nothing of the fact you're running low on power.*

>POWER RESERVE: FORTY-SEVEN PERCENT

Great. And I have a crib full of filamentium to cart out here.

The canisters are already in the hold, Idari.

But... what did I come back out here for?

CR-UX sighs. *Fiddlesticks... now you're doing it to both of us.*

I could have sworn there was something...
What's that, Idari?
There was someone...
The Banbors. You've forgotten.
No, I thought... I felt... a star. A Lumenor.
A Lumenor? Goodness. Darling, you are injured.

Maybe something shorted in my neural net when what's his face shot me, but I thought the Lumenor was real. Stars walked like men once. They lived. Loved. I believe it, even if most people don't. I can almost see them. Beings of pure light. Energy. How would I ever perceive them? How does a star love? What would be love to a being of cosmic energy? What would sex be? Gender? Existence?

We should get moving, CR-UX says. *Scavengers abound.*

I trudge up the gantry, feeling empty despite my success. What did I gain here? Who am I, out here in the nothing? All I carry from this barren rock besides evidently the filamentium I've already loaded is confusion. This sense of possibility, like a dream you can't remember but need to. I crash into the pilot's seat.

We're heavy, I say, tapping the gauges on the console.
The canisters, Idari.
I'm reading more filamentium than we should have.
Perhaps the interference is messing with our sensors.

A hundred systems shout their status as the ship burns through space. Sometimes it's too much. Most of the time. Usually, I mute as many inputs as I can get away with and remember myself. If I don't, my senses get overrun and I'm at the bar, numbing the chaos as much as I can. I don't want to be numb to this feeling, though. I don't want to forget this light I swore I saw in the dark. I lean back in the seat, exhausted, but hopeful. I close my eyes and dream of my star.

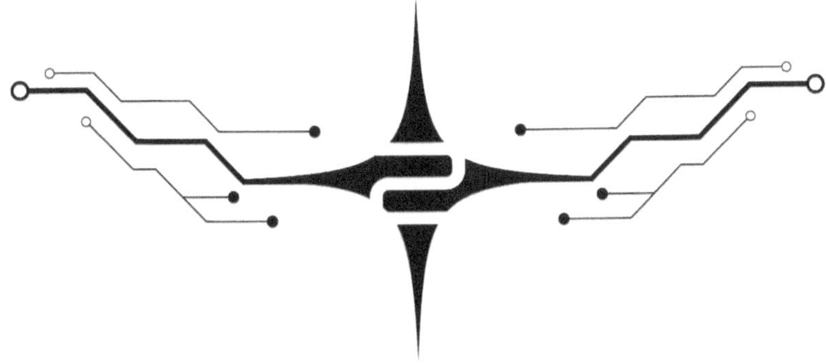

Look at me.

The hard-light bolt the Banbor fired shattered on contact. A constellation burned in my arm. Synthetic skin burns the same as the genuine article. A little cleaner, maybe. There's none of the fat or tissue that boils and pops in genuine humanoids across the galaxy. Just biobrane fluid and elastic, silicate fiber woven into the musculature. Instead of burns and blisters and swelling, I'm just left with a coin-sized crater down through cauterized flesh to blackened turanium. I can't fix this. I can't cover this, except underneath a jacket.

Good thing I've loads of them.

I take another drink from the bottle. Fire burns in my throat. I forget my shoulder. This ache that follows me around. This friction from the rock of my truth rattling around inside the shoe of my body. I touch the uncanny face in the spotty mirror in the head. Pucker my burning lips. Pinch the skin of my cheek. Warm wax. I drink enough babyl. I delay synching with the mainframe. I'll forget this.

>POWER RESERVE: THIRTY-FOUR PERCENT

Like I could ever truly forget I'm a machine. The proxy is always hounding me with reminders.

Organic bodies do the same thing, CR-UX says.

I doubt they get messages about their operational status.

They do, but you get a friendly little reminder via text. Humans often discover their condition via more... fluidic means.

Do I want to know? I kind of want to know.

You can access a human anatomical encyclopedia on the main-frame. This is mostly for this ship's original owners to identify medical emergencies in-flight, but it should prove illuminating.

I download the encyclopedia. *Lucky me, then.*

Indeed.

I worm my way out of my damaged pressure suit. Another patch job. *Did you submit our claim to the Scath, CR-UX?*

The moment you completed the contract, he says. *You should return to the charging station at once.*

I'm fine.

You're running on fumes, Idari. Also, you need to synch with the main computer. Your backup file is woefully out of date.

If the Banbor had destroyed the proxy-netic, he wouldn't have killed me. A copy backed up to the last time I synched exists in the *Steel Haven's* liquid drive. Really, all those ones and zeroes are me. The proxy-netic is just that; a proxy. A golem I project into for some semblance of what it means to be human.

How out of date? I say.

Backup-Idari still believes the T-Funsters were the best band that ever came out of The Crossroads.

Um, they were, I say as I slip back into the comfort of my white jumpsuit. White might be charitable. I suppose now it's more off-white. I zip up the front, stopping at the faded ink of the tattoo emblazoned across my chest. Sort of like a star, if a star had wings of light. That isn't pirate, I don't think. I've forgotten what it means.

Synch, Idari. I've told you, endlessly, the proxy auto-deletes memory to save space. You forget it happens.

Is that what happened back there on OT-3Ro?

It seems. If you don't back up your memory with me, you won't have it available in the cloud. You lose more of your life.

No note exists to tell me where the proxy came from or how I came to inhabit her. *Where did we get her, CR-UX?*

His voice is uncertain. *I no longer recall.*

Most netics are simple automatons. Proxy-netics like the IA-XR Model 4 I inhabit are uncommon. Expensive. Usually, rich people bored with their lives use them to pretend to be other people, which is odd, considering how enamored they are of being themselves.

How long have we been together, CR-UX?

CR-UX blames most of his pauses on the lag of the ship's aging computer, but even with the delay, and this distance between us, I can almost hear him thinking. Considering.

My chronometers need calibrating, he says.

You don't remember how we met?

You ran away with me, that much is certain.

I stole you?

Heart and soul, Idari.

How?

I shouldn't think it matters how we started. Certainly, a modest navigational program like myself was never intended to grow so much.

How have you grown?

I suppose I'm simply a program to you.

No, you're not...

My program necessitates that I predict stars where none are evident. The universe's age and scope trap most stars and planets beyond the observable. We transcend it all the time.

How old is the universe?

Uncertain. It is thought to be very ancient. Near the end of its life.

The universe is dying?

There is still life to be found within it. As with you. You may look in the mirror and not see yourself, Idari. I do.

I reach for the bottle. Empty. *Do we have any more, CR-UX?*

His disappointment sloshes around in my head along with the detritus of my thoughts. *Babyl is corrosive, Idari.*

All my best relationships are.

CR-UX's frustration floods the downlink. He's like a sigh with no context. Except I live inside this sigh, every waking moment, unable to get any distance. I go digging through the galley for another bottle.

Bingo fuel.

Shields flare to life outside the cockpit canopy. A mist of meteorites escalates to a hail of fractured crust. Massive chunks of a planet race through its own comet-like tail of vaporized rock and metal. Debris collides with debris in a ballistic shredding that never ends. I sway in the pilot's seat with every kneejerk swerve as CR-UX performs one dangerous maneuver after another to avoid disaster.

I always feel like I'm avoiding disaster.

>POWER RESERVE: TWENTY-FIVE PERCENT

I don't want to do this anymore, CR-UX.

I know, darling. You've said.

I guess I forgot.

We're nothing if not consistent.

Don't you get bored of me, CR-UX?

CR-UX doesn't want to say. He doesn't have to. Being at the mercy of any pilot is bound to leave you a bit thorny sometimes. Though it's an open question which one of us has the stick.

I only worry for you, Idari.

I pick up the bottle again. *I'm just bored.*

CR-UX does this thing where he acts like he's clearing his throat by garbling a number of sensor feeds at once. It's cute.

Return to the charging station, Idari. Please.

I turn, as if I can somehow shield him from seeing the damage in my shoulder. Nothing significant in my internal systems suffered. Only my pride. It's not the numb void in my shoulder that bothers me. The mechanical stiffness of a piece of hardware that has taken more licks than it was designed for. It's the pulling back of the curtain. The exposure of this lie I tell myself day in and day out.

I step into the maintenance alcove in the back of the cockpit. I peel off my pressure suit and knock on my abdomen until I hit something hard. Neo-plastic panels pop out in my hands. I dust off the data ports in the skeletal armature of my ribs and connect the withered data cables. Bitter experience drove me to modify the proxy-netic so that the machine's central processing unit rests within the rib cage, and not my head, which the majority of my competition typically aims for. I hate this. Taking myself apart.

Synching, CR-UX says.

Do we even have any space left?

I'll make some room.

More memories.

So it goes, darling.

I flag the Banbor's shooting me back on OT-3Ro for deletion. My shock. The pain and frustration I hid with a quip.

CR-UX. I was thinking it's been twenty years since I uploaded my program into the proxy-netic. Is that right?

Something like that.

You're not sure?

My chronometers need calibrating. Synch complete. Initiating charging cycle. Should only take a few hours.

Hours...

Just close your eyes, darling.

I slump against the wall of the alcove. My exhaustion arrives all at once. My pain. My fear and CR-UX sinks with me into the digital abyss, my guide into the oblivion of low power mode.

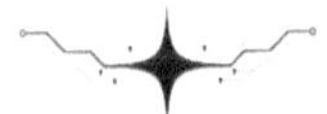

Alerts heckle me out of unconsciousness. Well. As close to unconsciousness I get not induced via cosmic quantities of alcohol.

>PRIORITY CONFERENCE REQUEST

Oh, go away.

>INITIATE IMMEDIATE CONFERENCE

Eh.

>FINAL NOTICE

Eek.

CR-UX?

His voice breezes away the loose leaves of alerts and notices. *All of these carry a Scath-coded ID.*

The Scath never call for anything. *What do they want?*

>RENDEZVOUS AT PENDEM IMMEDIATELY.

This is new. New is never good.

>TRANSFER RECOVERED CANISTERS DIRECTLY.

Definitely not good. What's the deal with these canisters? It's just another job. Someone steals fuel, I take it back, I drop it at the prearranged spot and the Scath pick it up later. No one sees them.

We're about to, CR-UX says. *Setting course for Pendem.*

Did I forget something, CR-UX?

You're always forgetting, darling. Standby translight drive in three, two, one, and the dark beyond the canopy drains into a tunnel of molten plasma. Light-years pass in minutes. The engines throttle back and light bleeds out of the universe all over again.

>PROXIMITY ALARM

Shadows of moons race across the cloud tops of a gas giant. All periods of sentences in search of a desperate stop. The strangest moon in the system is a burr. Starscrapers stab out from the burdened surface of Pendem. I've only heard stories. The moon floats through space like some terrestrial bezoar. No one knows who built these 300 mile-high monsters. Who might have lived in them.

I've got nothing on our scopes, CR-UX.

Receiving coded transmission, he says. *A Scath vessel is holding position within a tower in the northern hemisphere.*

Within?

Asteroid craters pock the turanium exteriors of many of the towers, some fat, some thin, some smooth, some jagged.

That will be hard to navigate, I say. *Good luck, CR-UX.*

He sighs. *Keep a lookout, will you?*

The starscraper's broken cap becomes our entire view. Thrusters slow our speed, allowing CR-UX to gently thread the needle an asteroid punched through the tower's upper floors. Broken, jagged beams of turanium stab out at us from above and below.

Steady on, I say.

Don't distract me, Idari.

I'm trying to help.

Generally better if you don't.

This is all a little unnecessary, don't you think?

The Scath clearly don't want to be seen.

Nothing but shattered turanium outside. I switch to thermal optics. Nothing. Night vision. There they are. A Scath vessel rests on an intact section of floor, long and serpine. No energy signature. No emissions. No transmissions of any kind. A void in space.

The ship jostles. Alarms sound in the cockpit. Tractor beam.

What is this, CR-UX?

We're about to find out, darling.

Thrusters relent as the tractor beam reels us into the ship's hangar bay. Small, one-man craft hang like stalactites from the ceiling. I only make them out thanks to the lunic reflection from the tower outside. Same with the troops clad in opaque armor lined up in formation behind the shadow line. Each trooper wears an opaque helmet pitted with a void where a face should be.

My hand falls to my blaster. *Are those the Scath?*

One assumes, CR-UX says.

The Scath hold blaster-type weapons. Swords sheath on their backs. *Look at all this hardware... what do they need Starguns for?*

Good question.

Any chance we walk out of here?

Better question.

Really wish I had a bottle of babyl right now, I say and hurry through the horseshoe corridor binding the interior of the *Steel Haven* down to the cargo bay aft. Scath are already offloading the crib of filamentium canisters when I get there.

Punctual.

"All yours," I say, following them down the ramp into the hangar. Sharp angles frame the portals leading out into the ship, the bulkheads formed from the same obsidian gloss as the Scath's armor.

A strange ruddy glow radiates from beneath the deck. Not really light. The afterglow. Dust scorched from dead stars. So strange. I have to be careful, sometimes. So much data comes at me I don't always perceive things how they are. I run every sensor scan the proxy has onboard. Nothing registers. If it is actually light, it's not any kind of light as we know it in this universe.

Like your self-destructive tendencies, CR-UX says, *the physical composition of light is rather a constant, darling. Hmm.*

I know that 'hmm.' What are you thinking?

The Scath are rumored to hail from beyond The Reach.

The Reach?

The known limit of space.

What's beyond it?

Perhaps hinted at in my choice of the word 'known,' we've no idea. No expedition of antiquity ever successfully returned from The Reach, and nothing suggests traversing the border is even possible. Speculation is The Reach is another universe with different laws than ours.

Could be why the Scath farm out all their work to Starguns. Why they're such xenophobes. They don't really work here.

Perhaps filamentium comes from there, too, CR-UX says. *That would explain its scarcity in the universe.*

So the Scath being here right now is...

Highly irregular.

I don't know if I should be flattered or terrified, CR-UX.

Let's start with terrified and go from there.

Right. Think positive.

A cold voice echoes across the hangar. A hiss shot through thin metal. "Astra Idari. You still fly that ancient ship."

I glance back at the *Steel Haven.* "Ancient is a bit harsh."

"But you've changed."

"I'm sorry... who are you?"

A Scath creeps out of the shadows. Not like the others. She has shape. Definition. The same blood-soaked light bristling between deck plates seethes in hair-thin gaps in her armor.

"You don't remember me," she says. "I'm disappointed."

CR-UX?

We've no record of her or any contact with the Scath, he says.

I shrug. "You'll have to forgive me."

Rile light splinters beneath her armor. "I forgive much with you, Idari. You are one of our most determined Starguns. A quick hand and a fleeting memory. You were perfect."

"I was?"

"You've changed since you first contracted with us." She says *changed* like a pirate curse. "You've evolved."

"I'll do better next time?"

"You have perverted yourself."

I don't know who this person thinks they are.

They're your boss, CR-UX says.

Oh, right. Well, I can't walk out of here. I can't shoot them. Not exactly fair. "I filed everything in the claim."

"One of the canisters is empty," she says.

Scath troopers march past me into the *Steel Haven*. "It was empty when I... the Banbors or whoever they were must have tried to refine it. They were amateurs. Probably spoiled it."

She steps forward. "Did you attempt to recover the fuel?"

My hand falls to my side. "No... I got shot. I got out."

"Did you gather any intelligence from the Banbor Gang?"

"They were pretty stupid."

"You keep disappointing me."

"I'm reliable that way."

"Why this tanker, Idari? Who informed them of its route?"

I scroll through the claim the Scath transmitted for this job. "This was just a recovery. Same job as any other."

"Did you detect any other ships in the system?"

"No..."

"You saw no one?"

Something isn't right. These guys never cared about the details before. They just wanted their fuel back. No questions.

"There was nothing in the canister," I say.

She crosses her arms and then lets them fall again, like she doesn't know what to do with her hands. "We shall see."

"There's nothing to see."

"We will download all your data and telemetry."

"Ok, but I can explain some of those searches."

"Astra Idari. Always making light."

Filamentium is no laughing matter. Lately, there have been shortages. Severe shortages. Some blame the Pujar, but pirates never shy from proclaiming their conquests. There isn't any fuel for them to take. If the fuel dries up, the galaxy grinds to a halt. No fuel, no ships, no trade, no food, no water. Forget the fact I won't have beer money. Famine will reclaim the barren worlds filamentium salvaged from disaster. Millions will die. I can't think about that.

The Scath leave the hold of the *Steel Haven*. The one on point shakes his head. Nothing onboard my ship but empty bottles and broken dreams. I try not to be too vindicated.

Fraying crimson drains in the void of her helmet. "Your bounty will be deducted from the missing fuel."

"But..." A canister is millions of toruls. I'll never make back that money so long as I live. "It's not my fault."

"Excuses are worthless."

"How is it you have all this firepower and you let a gang of amateurs make off with your filamentium?"

Her finger taps against her elbow, *tap, tap, tap.* "The Scath can't function in this universe outside of their containment suits."

"This universe?"

"They rely on proxies like you, Idari. Starguns. The tanker flew under the Infinies Trading Company's flag, as most do. It seems their security has become lax with so little fuel to transport."

"Maybe you should talk to them."

"We have... inventoried... the tanker's crew. I suppose you can't blame them. You forget, don't you? You become complacent. You become part of the machine. You *are* a machine."

I pull up the zipper of my jumpsuit a little. "How do you…"

"I remember everything. What I want is to forget."

"Babyl helps."

Tap, tap, tap. "I remember the sight of me disturbs the Scath so much they make me wear this armor to appease their decency."

"You're not Scath?"

"I become crude in their conformity. They do. In their natural state… in their native reality… they are as they were made. Perfect."

I don't think I want to know what that is.

"You were perfect once, Idari. Pure. A machine of such binary precision and efficiency even I had to admire your production."

"There's nothing binary about me."

"As I said. You've… changed."

I look away. "What can I do to make this right?"

"Find out who the Banbors were selling to."

"The Banbors are dead."

"Then I suggest you learn how to chase ghosts."

No one talks. No one gives up anything in this life. They just try to get you to buy into another scheme. *Chase ghosts,* she says. I've been doing it so long as I can remember.

"If I find out," I say. "Can we forget about the fuel?"

"I told you, Idari. I forget nothing."

Not exactly reassuring. "Who are you?"

"I cast shadows."

"And what are they?"

The Scath make perfect statues around her. "The Scath formed in absolute darkness. That's where they found me… long ago. But I knew light. It was all I knew once. Light is anathema to the Scath. The division of shadows. They have no individuality. No identity. No voice. They seek unity in darkness. They seek oblivion."

"Maybe they just need to get out more."

"Oblivion appeals to me, Idari. Very much."

I think that's my cue. "Thanks for the chat."

"You will speak of this to no one."

"I don't even know your name."

Some shadow pulls on me. A cold force. "Thana."

I hurry back into the cargo hold. I wobble back to the cockpit and strap in as CR-UX guides us out of the starscraper as fast as he can.

I check our scopes. *Are they following us?*

Negative, CR-UX says. *Where are we going, Idari?*

Only The Bool could have backed the Banbors.

Setting course for Skeken, he says, as the ship skips across the dark into light but I only see the swarm of shadows.

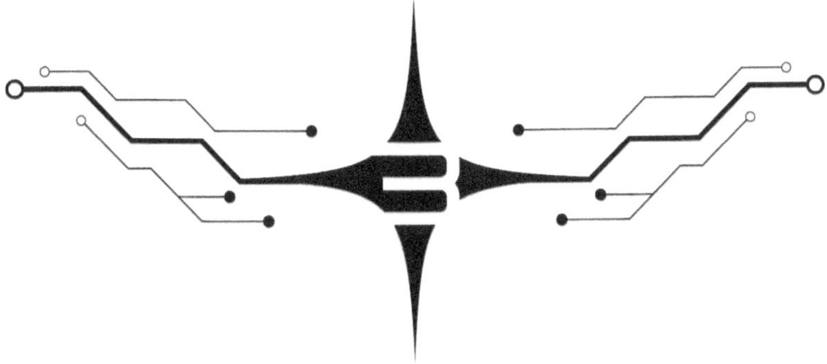

They don't shimmer. Nothing reflects off the countless bodies tumbling forever around the hazy red glow of the planet, except the little bit of ice trapped in their skin. If they were left any.

The Parlor of The Bool floats like a shepherd moon in a gap between the primary rings. Spiky protrusions of crooked towers and turrets thorn the exterior, battlements built up as The Bool amassed power in The Hinterlands. Simple system. Scath control the fuel. Pirates steal it. Gangs and cartels steal it from them. Bosses need lieutenants. Lieutenants need soldiers. Soldiers need work. This much I remember; I came here to Skeken. I worked my way through the ranks and I made such a name for myself among the dread, I went freelance. And still I come back. Still I obey the same gravity, like all these dead upstarts, winding through the dark in silent portent.

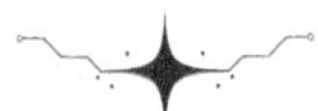

"Aprosdo!"

Cheers tumble like dice through the gaming floor. Smoke shrouds the dim lamps hung over the game pits, sunk in the deck like the chances of most of these players. I adjust my optics to get a better look. Orange puffy beings with glassy black eyes bob in anticipation of the next deal below. I can't remember what they call themselves. Probably not Orange Puffy Things.

Guffin, CR-UX says.

You remember.

I maintain a fairly robust index of worlds and species.

Saving their names is worth deleting some memory of mine?

A bottle of babyl is worth the memory engrams you'll lose?

Kind of. Upside of the proxy? I'm hard to get rid of. Downside? I'm constantly shaving off my ends to keep my course. Backing up my memory preserves it, but the reality is the ship's computer simply doesn't contain enough space to store all the data the proxy-netic records. At the end of the day, it doesn't matter whether CR-UX deletes it when I synch or the proxy scrubs the cache without me knowing it. Either way, I forget who I am.

Idari... is this why you avoid synching? You want to forget?

I know I had a name before Idari. A designation maybe, like CR-UX. Doesn't matter. The farther I get from my original conception, the more the past becomes like old rock. The years stratum, layered one on the other, compressed and heated into other forms. Memories become diamonds, beautiful and clean of any trace of their origin. The only reminder of my past life is CR-UX, nagging me always to synch, darling. Plug in, love. Peel back the facade.

I understand, Idari.

How can you possibly understand?

I understand the want to be free of the past. The weight of who people think you are. I just don't want you to forget your now.

What's so great about now? I'm here trolling for information I'll never get to pay back the Scath for filamentium some kids pissed away. I'm pissed. I want to get pissed. Where's the bar?

We're here for work, darling.

I am working, I say, and navigate the game floor's pitfalls to the private lounge. VIPs. High rollers. Envoys of other bosses. Women.

Always women.

Each time the slinky Therman girl steps in and out of the shadows, she wears a new face. Young. Old. Persimmon. Ivory. Calescent. I want them all. That's my problem in the end.

I can never choose.

She coils around me. "What's your name?"

I press my lips into hers. "Whatever you want."

You don't have time for this, CR-UX says.

I've always got time for this.

The NI-CX netic tending bar jitters over. A bottle of babyl falls heavy on the table. Clumsy thing ambles away. All its guts exposed. A collection of random parts that don't go together.

The Therman girl brushes my cheek. "What's the matter?"

I kiss her again. "Nothing."

Claws long and sharp as knives slice through my bottle. Shimmering fire spills on the floor. Feral snickers cackle through the lounge. That sound I remember. Drool crusts the bulky radiation suit of the towering, lupine creature standing before me.

Gimgak snarls. "Who let you in here, Idari?"

His twin brother, Gigaw, snickers. "Good one, bro."

"Boys," I say, keeping an eye on them as the Therman girl slips back to the shadows. Crouched on their hind legs, the brothers still clear seven feet. Maybe eight. "I think it's the two of you in the wrong place, actually. This here is strictly VIP."

Gimgak huffs. "We're big time, Idari."

"I suppose. Your smell does precede you."

Play nice, CR-UX says. *Remember what happened last time.*

What happened last time?

Gigaw scratches his nose. "What you here for, Idari?"

"A job."

"Always running, you."

"Like a clock," Gimgak says. "Tick, tock, Idari."

Not sure I like the vibe here. "Is the boss around?"

"The Bool's been looking for you. So we heard."

Another bottle thuds on the bar. "For what?"

Gimgak snickers. "He must got an assignment for you, Idari."

If the Banbors did nab those canisters on orders from The Bool, he's probably not going to be too happy to see the person who slabbed his newest recruits. Or answer any questions.

"Maybe I'll hit the tables," I say.

Gimgak skulks away, snickering as he does. I uncork the bottle and throw back a long drink. My anxiety burns away. My fear.

Gigaw sighs. "Me and Luyal broke up, you know."

I wipe the fire from my lips. "Shut up."

"Couple months back."

"Dating another Stargun is hard."

"Long distance and that."

"I was thinking more the constant running for your life."

"I been... I been kind of lonely, me."

"Yeah, no," I say and take my babyl and that Therman girl back to a cushy booth in the corner. "You're pretty."

She blushes. "You are, too."

We need to maintain our focus here, CR-UX says.

She's one of the regular girls. She hears everything.

And how do you remember that?

"Come here," I say and the pillowy flesh of her breast brushes my lips as she straddles me. Her indelible softness teases the life wanton within me. Her warmth. I hate my own skin, rubbery and stiff. Interrupted, in ports and scars. The girl grips the harness straps dangling from my legs. Her hand slinks up the harness, between my thighs, over my belly, to the zipper of my suit.

I grip the girl's hand. "No."

She smiles. "I take all kinds."

"I'm fine."

"Ok... what do you want?"

"Can I kiss you?"

The girl stifles her embarrassed smile. Comfort in The Hinterlands is merely a concept. Intimacy unexpected. Rare.

She pinches her lips to mine. "You're sweet."

I press her closer. "A real kiss."

"Is this all you want? Just to kiss?"

"Is that ok?"

The girl shrugs. "Rate's the same."

I lick the girl's lips open. She suppresses another laugh and I kiss her long and deep, my tongue probing for the salt of her skin, the stick of her lips, the authentic warmth of her life. The proxy-netic auto-adjusts the pressure I apply, to avoid pulping the girl's bones.

The girl pats my neck, wanting me to let up. "I can't breathe."

"Breathing is overrated," I say.

I kiss her again. The sensory receptors laced in the synthetic skin of the proxy-netic provide only an approximation of sensation; to me, touch is the ghost of touch. A numb pressure, without sensation. The girl relaxes against me, trying to mimic the hunger of my kisses. The skill of my tongue. I might be an anesthetized robot, but I'm as skilled on this trigger as I am any other. Her hands stray again. Proximity detectors ping me but I'm too distracted with the wet cooling on my cheek, the damp heat surging between the girl's legs into my thigh and the girl peels the zipper of my suit down.

I flinch in anticipation of her disgust and my shame, but she stops at the faded tattoo emblazoned across my chest.

"I like your ink," she says. "What is it?"

I zip up the suit a little. "I've forgotten."

The girl plays at fighting me for the zipper. She traces the lines of the tattoo. "How could you forget something like this?"

"Hey, I'm looking for my friends. Do you know the Banbors?"

"I'm bad with names," she says, and before I can stop her, pulls down the zipper to my belly button. The girl's hands – soft, warm, quick – cut through the infinitesimal space between skin and fabric, her fingers fanning out, searching, probing, finding.

Her hand trembles as she zips me back up. "You're a netic..."

The girl peels off me. They're always surprised. Somehow, I fool them. How? How is it not obvious what I am?

I zip up. "I'm someone, inside. I'm real."

She runs out of the parlor. People hate netics. Turns out, it's a universe built for machines. Cold, dark, intolerant of anything living. Build an artificial life form, and you think you've helped yourself out.

Out the door, maybe.

A shadow falls over me. Scales as rigid as the basalt stone towers on Bulsar fang through the bouncer's body armor.

He cracks his knuckles. "Sign said no netics."

I take a long, healthy drink. May not get to all of this bottle of babyl. "Guys, you may not know this, but I'm kind of a big deal around here. I'm Astra Idari. Stargun. Ask anyone."

Armed guards emerge from behind the bouncer. Five. Six. Fair enough. I guess they did ask around.

I smash the bottle on the floor. "Ok. Let's do this."

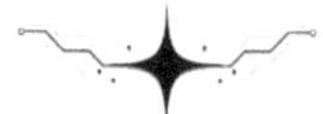

Stacked bins of netic parts form a wall behind me.

Hollow eyes stare back. Jaws hang in final shock. Hands reach out of the coiled gore of defective netics piled in a heap around me and I'm in one of my nightmares. Am I awake?

Is this real?

Gears squeak through the dark. A little RIG-B netic flaps its wings through the dusty valleys between the piled netics. Smoke exhausts from her snubby beak as the metal dragon examines jumbled and dead netics, bypassing the most damaged ones. *Ban Minda.* The bouncer threw me down in the netic repurposing center in the bowels of the parlor. Guess I won't need to talk to The Bool to know how he feels about me taking out the Banbors.

A boxy industrial HERM-E unit waddles over my way and picks up the limp carcass of an NM-EX netic. He carries the netic to other faceless robots bashing apart the discarded with hammers.

Yeah, not staying here.

CR-UX, I say. *Do you read?*

>SIGNAL STRENGTH LOW

Sensor-gaga garbles in my ear. I can't hear him or perceive his thoughts at all. How do I get out of here?

RIG-B flies over to me. "Scrap, ok?"

"I'm not scrap," I say. "I'm Astra Idari. I'm a human being."

RIG-B's antenna-like ears perk up. "Idari, ok?"

"I don't..." I zip up my jumpsuit. "I don't know."

RIG-B belches a plume of dragon fire and inspects me in the light. Her ears droop. "Proxy-netic, ok?"

"Yes, I'm a proxy."

Smoke chimneys from RIG-B's nose. "IA-XR, ok. Model 4, ok."

"Ok. But I'm a human, really."

The HERM-E unit toddles through the carnage. "Defective."

"I'm not defective."

"Netics are netics. Organics are organics."

I dig through the mounds of netic parts searching for a door or portal or something. "Don't be so dull. Organics get cybernetic implants all the time. People upload their consciousness into proxy-netics like me. That's why IA-XRs exist in the first place. If people can become machines, then why not..."

Where is this door?

"Netics become cyborgs. Do you know there was a netic on Turnbul who grafted an organic brain into his head? He took over the entire planet. Didn't wear a helmet. Really should have."

The lids of HERM-E's eyes clack. "Purpose?"

These machines down here. They only have one purpose. Repair. Dismantle. Their programs are as basic as it gets. They have no concept or understanding beyond this dungeon or beyond themselves. They've no idea of themselves. I don't want to be some clockwork tin man like these netics here someone winds up and goes. I want to be me. I want to be the person I know I am.

"Let me out," I say.

Mechanical wings flutter. "Defective, ok?"

"I told you. I'm not defective. I'm..."

HERM-E lurches toward me. "Conform."

I stumble back through the detritus of netics. "Stay back."

His pincer claws clack together. "All netics must conform."

If I start blasting, those guards will come back down here. Maybe I'll get thrown out the airlock into the dead rings of Skeken instead of broken down for parts. Maybe both.

"Just give me a way out," I say.

>SIGNAL ACTIVE

There was a 12.4% *chance you'd end up in the dungeon, CR-UX* says. *Goodness, darling. You always find a way to beat the odds.*

Get me out of here, CR-UX.

Hacking the station's internal controls.

Dismantled netics avalanche through the dungeon as a rusty hatch clatters open behind me. I wade through the tangle of wires and fingers and broken hope out of the dungeon and then I run.

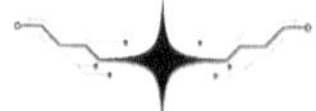

Aprosdo!

Guffin bobble with excitement as dice tumble across the table. I hurry through the gaming room, trying not to be conspicuous with the dust and grime and shame of the dungeon all over me.

You look positively conspicuous on the parlor's security cameras, CR-UX says. *Throttle down a gear and stop at the bar.*

Now you want me to drink?

The Bool's personal guards emerge from an elevator on the far side of the parlor. Bony protrusions coil around their heads, the growth bound in black, jagged wire. Memkik, the Bool's majordomo skulks through. I'm not saying I'm the prettiest thing that ever was, but I'm not a big vulturine thing skittering on half the insectoid legs he started with. I say half. Honestly, who's counting.

His crooked cane stabs the deck. "Idari."

Everybody sucks out of the gaming room faster than the money out of your pocket at the tables. Everybody except the other Starguns.

Best of the best. Brusk, a short-tempered reptilian Tohori; KEM-86, a gaseous Tal cocooned in a floating containment suit; and Tisem See, a Gunth notorious for her patchwork salvage jobs of reanimated bounties thinking they'd limped out of their contracts.

All my top competitors.

KEM-86 floats behind me. Brusk thumbs the strap of his rifle. Tisem See's fingers edge toward the knives studding her belt. Drool pings off the heavy rifles of the brothers.

I was almost to the door. "Is there a problem?"

Memkik leans heavy on his cane, as if the translucent slug-thing draped over his shoulders weighs on him. Tiny black eyes stare over his shoulder, contracting every few seconds in clockwork rhythm with Memkik's prying winces.

"His Great Significance The Bool wishes to convey his wisdom to you." The citrine jewel capping Memkik's beak glints as he scowls at the slug. "Yes, I said 'significance.' Use your ears. Or use mine."

My hand dangles at my side. "I'm listening."

Memkik looks like he's studying me. I suppose he wonders how I manage another voice in my head. "His Prominence wishes to inform you of a claim, Idari. A most lucrative contract. A million toruls."

Ban Minda. The biggest job I've ever landed was for twenty-five thousand. A million toruls would get me a new body.

I blubber my lips. "You had me going."

"The Bool will pay upon receipt of the Banbor Gang's killer."

I dive behind the bar. The NI-CX netic serving drinks explodes. Memkik cackles with laughter as Gigaw and Gimgak storm through the gaming room, blasting, hoofing it through the tables to get a shot at me. Blaster fire and knives sling across the parlor. Glass explodes. Babyl drips off the bar from the shattered bottle. I hold out my tongue for every last drop. What a waste.

KEM-86 floats around the bar. "Statement: SURRENDER."

My shot deflects off KEM-86's personal force field. "Oops."

"Statement: DIE."

I thumb the dial on my blaster. "I have another level."

Liquid hydrogen clouds the entire gaming room in rusty orange flame. Doesn't burn. Mostly vapor. KEM-86's burst containment suit splays across the bar and I use the cover to crawl across the broken glass and smelted turanium on the game floor. I drop down in one of the game pits and wait for the other Starguns to run past.

Walk me out of here, I say.

The downlink sighs. *That's going to be a challenge, darling.*

Why?

Memkik stabs his cane hard into the deck above. Guards drag me out of the game pit. A hard-light shot goes off dead into the deck and my blaster wrests out of my hand. Sitko populate The Bool's ranks for good reason. Once the brutish creatures get their fangs in something, they never let go. I've got marks in my turanium bones to prove it.

"You don't understand," I say. "The Scath want answers."

Memkik winces like he's fighting a toothache. "The shadows don't reach here, Idari. You should have come to me."

"It's different this time – "

Memkik throttles his cane again and the guards force me to an airlock. No. They shove me in and the hatch scrolls shut behind me.

I pound on the window. "Don't be a fool, Memkik!"

Green flashes to red. The outer airlock door opens. Air blasts at me and then there's nothing. Silence. Dead cold. I float away from the parlor, drifting slow and still toward my fate in the black, dead ring of Skeken. Guess there's always room in the collection.

>ENVIRONMENTAL ALARM

>EXTERNAL TEMPERATURE BEYOND TOLERANCE

>INTERNAL POWER CRITICAL

CR-UX, I say.

Your internal systems are well insulated against the vacuum of space, he says. *However, your power core has been experiencing rather dramatic plunges in performance lately. I believe we talked about this. Let me check my logs. Yes. Yes, we talked about this.*

CR-UX.

Taking off now, darling.

>POWER RESERVE: THIRTY PERCENT

Hurry. Damned tumble past me, rigored in their final failure. Piles of netics. Rings of dead bodies. I'm destined for some kind of scrap heap somewhere. Frost burns on my lips. My tongue. The inside of my throat. Tears freeze on my eyes.

>POWER RESERVE: TWENTY PERCENT

My arms and legs numb into lock. I can't move.

>SYSTEMS CRITICAL

I can't feel anything. I'm just floating in nothing, wide awake in my hell. Light glints in the distance. The *Steel Haven*. She's always in a hurry, just like I am. She's always slipping in and out of shadow.

The tractor beam grips me. So that's what it feels like. Huh. A bit impersonal. CR-UX pulls me into the cargo bay. I can't tell the difference in temperature. I can't tell the cold metal of the deck from the cold nothing of space. I just lie there, thawing, trying not to die first.

>POWER RESERVE: FIFTEEN PERCENT

Idari, CR-UX says in my ear. *Hold on –*

Formless data crackles along the connection between us.

>POWER CORE FAILURE

>RECHARGE PROXY IMMEDIATELY

>ELECTROMAGNETIC ANOMALY DETECTED

I'm fading. Sensors going haywire. This must be what dying is like, then. Random EM spikes. Digital snow. CR-UX. Bury me. Put me in earth like they do the living and don't let them scrap me.

Don't let them make me into something I'm not.

Light bursts inside the cargo hold. My sensors icing into oblivion. Intense blue fades and a woman – I think a woman – forms out of the glare. *Ban Minda*. A living star. A Lumenor.

I really am dying. Now I'm imagining angels. She kneels beside me. Such warmth. I feel them, radiating through me. The Lumenor takes my hand in hers. My fingers wiggle free of their rigidity. She puts her hands on my chest and warmth spreads through me. Power. I've never felt such power in all my life.

I've never felt so alive.

>POWER RESERVE: ONE HUNDRED PERCENT

My eyelids clack. The Lumenor is still here. All systems nominal. I'm not imagining them. She's here in the hold with me. That wasn't a dream or a ghost memory back in the Kasda system.

"You're real," I say.

A living star touches my cheek, soft as skin. "So are you."

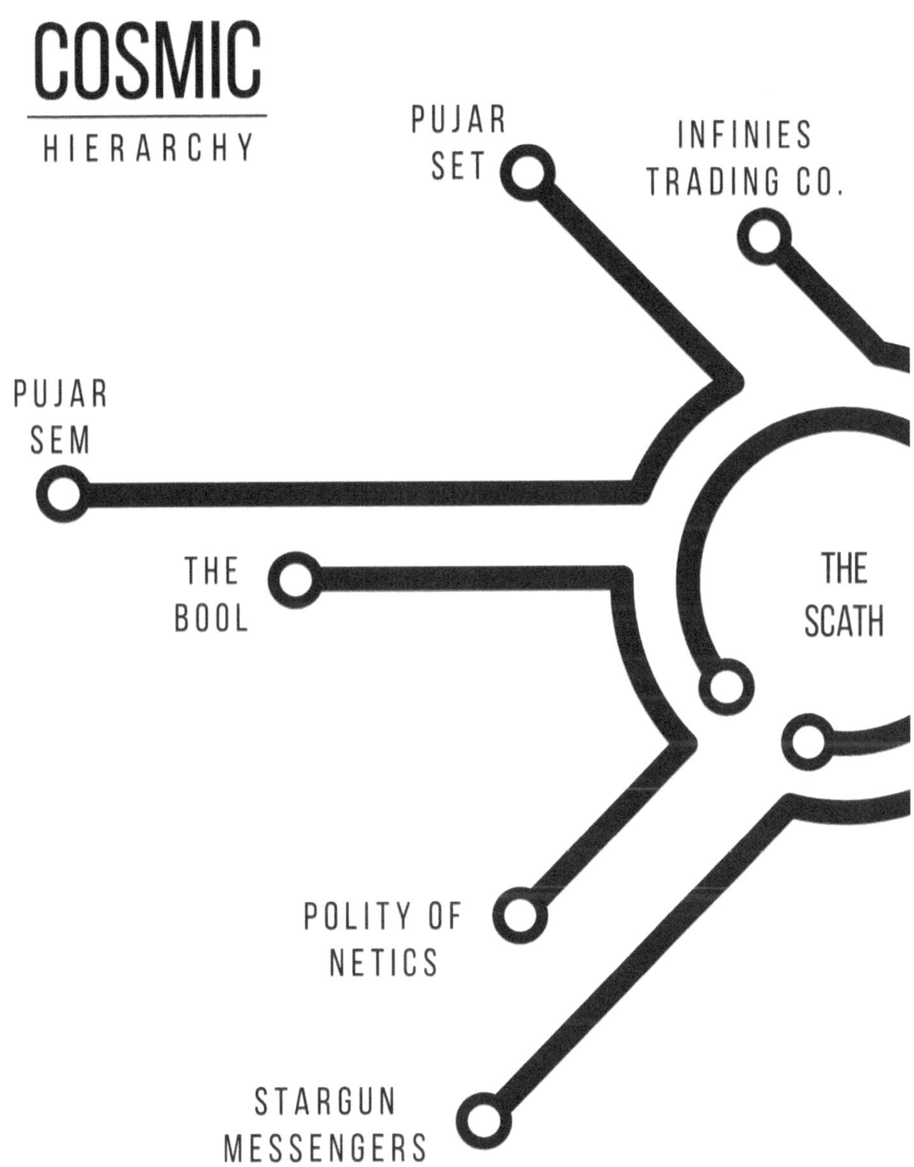

COSMIC
HIERARCHY
PUJAR SET
INFINIES TRADING CO.
PUJAR SEM
THE BOOL
THE SCATH
POLITY OF NETICS
STARGUN MESSENGERS
:L:DRIVE/RESTORED/MAD:1E:

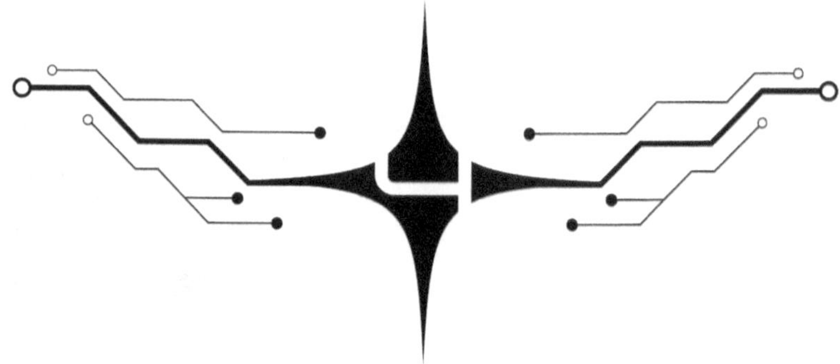

At first, I thought she could be a boy or a girl or both.

The more I stare at her, the more feminine she becomes. I swear, the nimbus of light misting off her stretches into this comet tail of hair as we stand here. I don't know. My sensors are wonky from nearly being frozen. From her. What I'm left with is an interpretation.

She's a poem as much as she is a person.

Filaments stitch and bind around her in a cloud held taut by her magnetic field. I wouldn't be all that trusting either, considering I was on a ship with a Stargun Messenger. I'd be terrified, actually.

I hold up my hands. "You don't have to be afraid."

Anxiety flickers through her like a bad bulb on the *Steel Haven's* dashboard. "You don't have to be afraid of us."

"Us?"

She pinches the air and peels back the hold like a curtain. Glittering dust sparkles behind. Beyond. A blindspot. A cubby. The electromagnetic spectrum is warped. Bent. The Lumenor did this. She bent light to make her invisible to our sensors. The Scath's.

Something stirs in the haze. Something huge. I adjust my optics to see what it might be. I fight against the instinct to run. A burly, simian creature charges out, his body glassed in opaline. His eyes glow cobalt blue, illuminating the beard descending from his chin.

His aged, tinny voice comes from some place deep within him. "Where are you going without me, Emera?"

I glance at the Lumenor. "Emera... is that your name?"

Electric blue shimmers in her smile. "Gen Emera. Yes."

"You got on board at OT-3Ro. You and..."

"Welkin."

Welkin pounds his massive fists into the deck and I flop to my ass. "Scramble her memory, Emera."

I draw my blaster. "Don't even."

"Your trifle weapon will have no effect on me."

My shot ricochets off the creature's head into the deck. "Huh."

He just told you he's impervious to blaster fire, CR-UX says.

I thought he was bluffing.

Does he look like he's bluffing?

I don't know what he looks like. What the hell is he, CR-UX?

There is no record of this type of being in the archive. Or for that matter, their method of stowing away on the Steel Haven.

She warped light to create a duck blind.

That's not all they did. I have a 0.9-second gap in my logs from just prior to our departure from the Kasda system. The same gap exists in your internal memory, Idari. They corrupted our mutual records via electromagnetic manipulation. They can again.

I grip my blaster, for all that good it will do. *But why...*

They were in that canister. They smuggled away from the Scath.

That's why the shadows are so put out.

But why would the Scath have a Lumenor in their custody?

I holster my blaster. "So... I have questions."

Glittering dust huffs from the slender vents lining Welkin's neck. "You shouldn't have shown yourself, Emera."

Emera is just light. It's like she doesn't have dimension. Like she's not real. "She was going to die, Welkin."

"Why did you care?" I say, stealing Welkin's thunder, I think. "You erased my memory. Why didn't you just take the ship?"

Her words get stuck like the light flowing off her, twisted in her magnetic field. "I didn't want to do that to you."

"You were ok with deleting my memory."

"But then I saw it. I saw you, Idari."

"What..."

"Hide yourself again," Welkin says. "I will deal with this."

My finger taps against my blaster. "You can destroy me. But you won't get rid of me. I'm backed up on this ship, which by the way, has the *worst* personality. You might think you can commandeer it. Before you know, you'll be looking for the first stop to get off. If CR-UX doesn't dump you with the Scath first."

His fists clench. "Emera will erase your hard drive."

"You don't think I've booby-trapped this ship bow to stern?"

"Your trinkets and contraptions are no match for Emera's power."

"Maybe. But she deleted like five seconds of onboard memory. You start messing around with protocols and I figure you'll probably survive the translight drive overloading. What about her?"

Welkin's eyes simmer like pools of cerulean magma in a desert of volcanic glass. "We should talk, Idari."

"We are talking."

"I swore an oath to protect Emera with my life. Can I trust you?"

"Not really."

"There's something you need to know."

"There always is – "

>PROXIMITY ALARM

Long-range sensors detect a ship, CR-UX says. *The Verid-Kef.*

The brothers. Gigaw and Gimgak. They're right on us. How did they get so close without – all this interference. Our sensors are scrambled. I might as well be blind with a star on board.

"Hold that thought," I say.

I race back to the cockpit at the same time I try to stay on my feet. Usually, hard-light blasts dissipate against the shields in this polite electric slap. Kind of tingles, actually. One dull thud after another pounds against the hull above and behind me.

The shields, CR-UX!

Everything is sluggish, he says as our telemetry tracks the *Verid-Kef* closing into weapons range. *Shields activated.*

I crash into the pilot's seat. *Get us out of here.*

Nothing happens.

CR-UX?

We've a slight problem, darling.

I scramble through the data stream. Engines operating at peak performance. Coordinates set. What's the problem –

>FIL-TANK PRESSURE OFF-SCALE

A leak. We have a leak in the translight drive. *Ban Minda.* Filamentium bleeds out of the engine core so fast all my readings flatline. More laser fire slams into us. Shields wince with every hit. Without filamentium, we can't jump out of the system.

We're stuck here.

We need to stop the leak, CR-UX says but I'm already out of my seat. I run to the axial ladder splicing vertically through the ship and descend into the cramped, shadowy soft tissue of the *Steel Haven.* Sweat slicks my hands as I access the translight drive.

C'mon.

The unmistakable burnt-metal odor of filamentium permeates the core. *Ban Minda.* Filamentium scabs into black crust all over the drive. The cables. The deck. We're bleeding out. I remove the access manifold. Maybe I can salvage some of this. Maybe if I rub a bit between my hands really fast it will spark.

Don't touch it, CR-UX says. *It's highly corrosive to flesh.*

Just keep them off us –

I crash hard against the bulkhead and I know at once from the flood of telemetry in my feed that a laser salvo hit us square from above, just behind the starboard engine pod.

Alarms compete with CR-UX's anxiety. *They've overtaken us.*

I crawl back to the drive. *Do we have any filamentium left at all from those canisters? There's not a little vial I pinched for us, is there?*

Negative, Idari. They're coming back around.

I rip out the fuel line and thread a new one. My hands stick to the tube. C'mon. Salvos crash into us. CR-UX evades the brothers with every trick he's got in the book and it's all I can do to hold on.

I secure the tube. No more leak. I replace the manifold. I access the manual controls on the drive itself and repressurize the tank. A drop. Just a drop. All I'm asking for. One drop and we're out of here.

>FIL-TANK PRESSURE OFF-SCALE

Bone dry. Not even vapors.

>RADAR TARGETS INBOUND

Every other Stargun departs The Bool's parlor. Half a dozen starplanes gun after us, each spraying hard-light at the *Steel Haven*, the *Verid-Kef*, anything between them and a million toruls.

I'm out of ideas, I say.

Light flares through the core and for a second I think the brothers blasted a hole through the hull of the *Steel Haven*. I grab onto a pipe, expecting to be sucked out into space, again. But again, I'm rescued.

"I can help," Emera says, crawling across the deck.

I shake my head. "How?"

Emera plucks a small torch out of the metal tools and loose debris caught in her magnetic field. "Do you have a container?"

"For what?"

The fuel core twists out of the manifold and hovers between us. Emera cuts into the tip of her finger with the torch and *Ban Minda*. The wound oozes molten light. As soon as it contacts the air the edges blacken. Harden. The compartment stinks like a smelting furnace. Starship fuel. Filamentium. It comes from the Lumenor.

The Scath are killing stars for fuel.

She squeezes a few drops of molten blood into the fuel core and the cylinder floats back into place.

>FIL-TANK PRESSURE NOMINAL

I bypass the intricate code sequence to initiate the jump to translight, hard-locked even from CR-UX to prevent him from doing what I'm about to do right now. A cold jump like the one I'm about to attempt requires meticulous calculations. More than that, luck. I count seconds. Gauge the level of fuel I'll need to burn. Measure the distance between the *Steel Haven* and the other ships.

Screw it.

Jumping, I say and sensor data explodes in my feed.

Prismatic light envelops the *Steel Haven* as she jumps to translight. The *Verid-Kef* and the other Starguns fall away on our scopes. So does any hope of ever getting square with The Bool.

We might have bigger concerns.

Emera clutches my hand. Blood scabs over to black crust on her ethereal skin. A collapsed star in the Limina system. That's where I thought filamentium came from. Everyone thinks that. The nova failed and created the element in a strangled kind of fusion. The Scath have been selling this story as hard as they have their fuel for centuries now. Filamentium is an element found only in one place, that much is true. But it's in the blood of the Lumenor.

The blood of stars.

All this time I've been protecting the Scath's shipments, hunting down the thieves that steal them, erasing the lives of desperate men and women like the shadows have erased the truth.

I've been protecting a lie.

She squeezes my hand. *You were lied to.*

Her lips didn't move. "Lumenor are telepathic?"

Light streams off Emera. "I illuminate all things."

I clutch her hand. "I didn't know..."

"I need your help, Idari."

Idari, CR-UX says. *If we don't turn her in...*

Listen to yourself.

I'm merely outlining the practical reality, darling.

What's practical about a living star?

Nothing, Emera says.

Ack! She's a witch, CR-UX says and goes silent.

So... I think I'm doing this right. *You heard me earlier.*

Emera smiles. *I see you.*

What do you see?

Your truth.

And what's that?

You asked why we didn't take the ship... we had a plan, but... I didn't want to erase more of your memory than I did. I didn't want to risk damaging you. I sensed you... your humanity. Your truth.

I shake my head. "What's the truth?"

Emera tugs on my hand. Every part of her pulls on me. "Idari... I have to find The Glass Star. Without it, I'll die. My people will."

"Glass what now?"

Emera cups her hands together and then opens them. A floating shard of iridescent crystal glints above her palms. A fleck of cosmic diamond. She's been hiding it just like she hid from the sensors. The shard generates as much magnetic force as she does.

"What is it?" I say.

Emera's light pipes through the shard. "Let me show you."

Their power is light, heat, gravity, the natural attributes of a star Emera has no control over. But there's something else. Blue light streams from beneath her diaphanous skin into the shard. The turanium web of the engine core around us fades, replaced by plains of whipped diamond glass, cresting to mountains of flame.

For once, I don't know what to say. "What is this?"

Emera struggles to focus. "The Glass Star..."

I kneel down. Jagged ruts in the ground cut my fingers. This is real. I'm really here. Where am I? *CR-UX, do you see this?*

>UNABLE TO CONNECT TO HOST

Synthetic blood runs down my finger. "How are we..."

"Filamentium thins the tissue between time and space," Emera says. "Starship fuel is a crude use of its potential. If I concentrate, I can travel between worlds. Dimensions. Universes."

Giant chunks of stellar diamond float overhead in what seems like a cave made entirely of crystal, if the cave was the size of a planet.

"But... Emera. What is this place?"

"The first star. The birthplace of the Lumenor."

"We're inside a star?"

"Yes."

"Lumenor come from a star?"

"The star's blood is mine... I can almost..."

Starglass disappears and we're back in the engine core. Filaments of light streaming off Emera loop in on themselves but it isn't her magnetic field tying their hands this time.

Glittering dust drifts through the core ahead of Welkin. "I've told you, Emera. You must never use your powers."

His eyes, glowing the same electric blue that emanates from Emera, slender in disapproval. Emera seems to dull as a consequence, as if her light were a projection of his.

Emera closes her hands. "I was trying to explain…"

Welkin holds his fist to his chest. "Go back to the hold."

She floats out of the sub-deck, her face shadowed in shame.

"*Ban Minda*," I say. "She was just… I don't know, actually."

Welkin advances toward me on all fours, the broken chains of his bonds rattling across the deck. I rise, for what I don't know. I only stand to his shoulder. He can barely fit down here.

I'm not getting out of here unless he moves.

Blaster fire dissipated against his shell like it was nothing. If I had to guess, he's made out of the same stuff as that shard. Starglass. Light crushed to diamond by gravity I can't comprehend. He punches me, I'm scrap. What power must the shadows have to contain him?

I lift my hand. "May I?"

He sighs dust. "Everyone does."

I tap the smooth dome of his head. "You're from The Glass Star?"

Welkin kneads his fists on the deck. "Gesta came from the same dust as the Lumenor. They became stars. We did not."

"Is that jealousy I hear?"

"I want only for her."

That bit sounded true. "Do you have power, Welkin? Like her?"

A soft, lunar glow emanates from his outer shell. "The esteem of stars is a privilege. You and I, we are not entitled to it."

Not a no. "There are legends about the Lumenor in every port. There aren't any about the Gesta."

"Much is lost in the glare of stars."

"There should be plenty of you, given your… density."

"No planet can survive without the light of its sun," Welkin says. "As the Lumenor have faded from the heavens, so have we."

"You feed off their light?"

"Gesta absorb the latent energy produced by stars, yes."

If those bar-room legends are true, the lifespan of a Lumenor is thought to be similar to that of a regular star. If so, Welkin has to be millions of years old; older, maybe. Probably if The Glass Star is a white dwarf. Emera must be as old. Older.

"You saw them," I say. A fragment of a memory surfaces, of night sky in the heights of Bastopol above the wispy tails of the steam pools, pricked with rare fire. "Skies full of stars…"

Welkin's gaze settles on some point far and distant. "I have seen the Storm of Penfall. The Mummified Moon. The Empress of Gantos, with her crown of stars. I have seen stars born, and die, and born again. I have seen enough to know there are no accidents. Only patterns. Cycles. Orbits we all must make."

"*Ban Minda*," I say.

"As you say."

"I can't imagine what you've been through."

"It's best forgotten."

"Cheers to that."

"Emera was a miracle… none believed there was light enough left to kindle another Lumenor, but yet… she is."

"Are there others, Welkin?"

His shoulders sag. It's like a mountain range collapsing. "No."

"Why can't she use her powers?"

Welkin tries to find a spot where he's not bumping into anything. "A star exists only to shine. Emera has no choice but to burn what fuel she has in light and heat. Her power is not infinite. She must conserve her power or else become as the other Lumenor in her cluster, weak and dim, easily bled and quickly discarded by the shadows."

I still can't get my head around it. "The Scath are bleeding Lumenor for filamentium… they're selling their blood as fuel."

Welkin barely nods.

"I didn't know... no one knows."

"I suspect people do. They simply don't care. Their compassion would not save Emera, in any case. She needs a transfusion of filamentium. Without it, she will diminish."

"You guys you were hiding in a canister of the stuff."

He shakes his head. "The filamentium powering your ships is the diluted and processed blood of withered stars. As the Scath have bled the Lumenor, successive generations have waned in their brightness."

"Can you synthesize the element? Clone it?"

"Filamentium cannot be replicated. The Scath have devoted considerable resources and effort in a vain effort to try. Only pure filamentium of The Glass Star can save Emera. She can renew there... become who she was always meant to be."

If becoming who you were always meant to be were so easy. Still. I'd do anything to realize my humanity. I hope I would.

"Who is she supposed to be, Welkin?"

Welkin kneads his fists on the deck. "The dawn, anew."

Get your bearings, Idari. "So... where is this Glass Star?"

"Lost to time... and beyond all sight, as with most stars."

"So there's no finding it?"

The shard twists on its axis in the air above his open hand. "A long time ago, the Pujar captured us. The pirate ship crashed on a moon. I found the shard among the ruin in their treasure pen."

"Pirates had this?"

"They marked the shard. I don't know what it means."

I study the Pujar rune engraved on the back of the shard. "Pujar brand their treasure with the emblem of their ship. Their signet. Everything gets branded. Treasure. Captives. Crew."

"Do you recognize this mark?"

"This is old... I think. I'm not up on my ancient Pujar."

His shoulders sag. "Who might know what ship this is, Idari?"

Not me. But there is one person who might know.

A digital groan rattles through the downlink. *Why must everything always go back to Min Binja, Idari?*

Everything doesn't go back to Binja.

It frequently does with you.

Jealous?

No.

In any case, Binja knows everyone and remembers everything. If anyone knows what ship found the shard, it's him.

I'm sure he'll tell us. For a fee.

Where could Binja be, CR-UX?

The numerous bounties open on him suggest his whereabouts could be any number of systems. Most cite the Crossroads.

Everything and everyone goes through The Crossroads and there aren't any traffic wardens. It would be no trick for Binja to conjure up some forged travel papers, a change of clothes, and disappear into the streets. I'd have better luck finding where I left my common sense.

Common sense would dictate forgetting about Binja, CR-UX says. *He's nothing but trouble and liable to turn us in to save his own ass.*

I've done it to him a time or two. Never kept us apart. Binja was important to me, once. We were close. Friends. Family. Blood pirates. This tattoo on my chest isn't Clan Min. I don't know what clan it could be, but I remember Binja claimed me for his pirate crew and whoever I was before, it didn't matter. I had become a citizen of a republic of thieves. I had taken a name.

I could become someone new with this.

I could turn Welkin and Emera in. I probably should. If I don't, I'll have the Scath and The Bool and the entire galaxy hunting me down. Not exactly great for my long-term prospects. With the money, I'd have enough for a lot of babyl. A new body, maybe.

I don't know if it would be more human.

I trace the shard's sharp lines. "I can take you and Emera to the Crossroads. Connect you with Binja. He's a pirate, so you have to know what you're getting into. But he's a good man. He's honest."

Dust glints in the air. "We would still need a ship, Idari."

"I can't..."

"Why?"

"If I run... if I break for some mythical place with a living star in my hold... I'll end up in the scrapyard. Worse. Do you know what they do to people like me? Netics who act human? They visit very human things on them. Do you want to know? Or can you guess?"

"You take us to Binja and then what? You go back to the Scath?"

"I'll delete these memories. No one will know you were here."

"You won't know."

I hurt people for a lie. I don't want to live a lie anymore. But I do want to live. This is the only for us all to live.

"I sense..." His eyes shrink. "Emera senses your struggle, Idari. You do this to make a living. You're not living."

They stole a few minutes of my memory and carried out my heart while the door was open. "Maybe that seems silly to you. A machine... thinking she's alive. Thinking she's real."

The hardness in his face softens. "No... it's not silly."

"You probably can't imagine. Machines. Humans."

"Emera and I know intolerance. All too well."

"I didn't mean..."

Welkin lifts his hand. "May I?"

"Sure..."

Cold crystal brushes my cheek. "I understand the fear. The paralysis. It's so strange, isn't it? You know this truth about yourself. This precious thing. And you wear it like armor. You defend yourself against the dark with it... and then you deny it. You let it take damage so you can exist in the dark. And so it becomes worn and tattered and fragile... and it exists apart from you."

His eyes flicker blue.

"It exists between you and the dark. You can hold her. You can carry her. But you can't take her in. Because then... there will be no one to protect you anymore. There won't be you. Just her."

I claw at my chest. I can't get the words out. I'm terrified of the scrap heap. Of being reprogrammed. But I keep gunning for trouble. I keep diving into situations that bring me within an inch of my life and at least there in the flashing red light of all my warning signs, I can see my life for what it is. I can see myself.

My humanity.

"I wish I could help," I say.

"You have." Welkin sighs. "Emera thanks you. I thank you."

He crawls out of the mess. I go slow behind him, warm, buzzing, electric from everything that's happened and I'm back in the pilot's seat slick with anticipation. I'm alive with hope I can't claim.

CR-UX, I say. *Set course for the Crossroads.*

Idari...

I input the coordinates myself. *Standby for translight drive.*

It's a pirate den. We'll be lucky to get out alive.

I push the throttle forward.

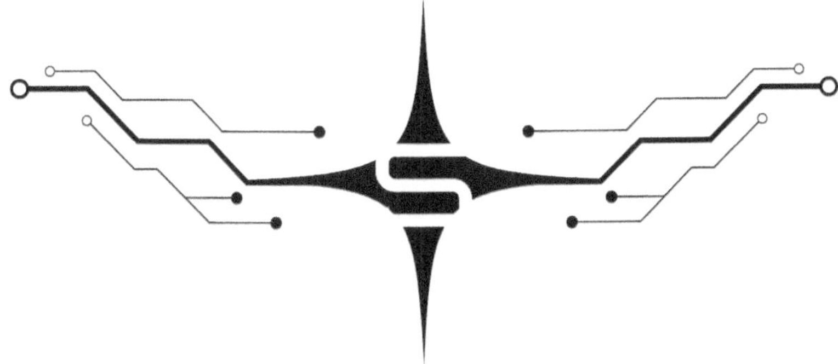

Who says there's no sound in space?

Music blasts so loud from speakers fitted throughout the *Steel Haven* vibrations record in her external sensor telemetry. I dance through the galley, down the horseshoe corridor to the cockpit, back to my quarters, and raid what accounts for my wardrobe.

Jackets. So many jackets.

I prefer my yellow one, its brightness a stark contrast to the dark I'm always outrunning. When I first came online, my only escape was DeliciaFaero. Her music meant everything. It was my life. Somewhere I forgot. Any time Delicia Faero changed her hair, so did I. Her look. Her sex. Evolution was Faero's brand. Faero morphed from a gamine startronic muse into a chanteuse, exuding an old Setanate glamor even as she mocked it. You could never pin her down.

The red jacket.

I zip up and the red lines of an eight-point starburst across a still perfect white from my shoulders to my hips. I tussle my hair a bit. I draw my blaster and mouth lyrics into the muzzle. My voice was never Faero's. My beauty. Life, in all my forms, is disappointment. Faero said so, in lyrics I only half remember.

Dead dreams fall like ash
on lives bred with fire.

Something like calm overtakes me. Comfort. The jacket groans around me as I vamp through my cabin. My elbows fight to bend in the restriction of the Tarthan leather, but I'm free inside this compression. Right now, I'm no longer this proxy-netic, but Faero.

I'm who I know I am inside.

I'm recording this, CR-UX says.

I sink to my bed. *Can't we both pretend you're not there?*

You're in a mood.

I don't know what you mean.

It's just... the music. Faero. It's been an age, darling.

I flick through the ship's internal video feeds. Our new guests huddle behind stacks of old crates in the cargo hold. Emera curls up in Welkin's burly arms and I feel her warmth in my quarters. The unusual but not unwelcome music of her magnetic pulse throughout the ship. Every fiber of my being.

I lean back in the bed. *What's happening, CR-UX?*

Has Emera altered your memory?

No, I mean – there's a Lumenor on board. I tug on the zipper of my jacket. *Is this really happening?*

Sensor data indicates that it is.

Leather creaks around my skin. *Do you believe Welkin?*

You do.

I'm being pragmatic.

Oh, dear.

I saw it... The Glass Star. Emera showed me.

Can you trust what you saw?

I couldn't reach you. I was too far away.

Only static on my end, darling.

How much of it?

47 seconds.

CR-UX...

Idari... The Glass Star will be difficult to find. To say the least. It is a white dwarf shrunken to diamond which barely shines. The star is so old, and the universe has expanded so much, that it is far, far removed from any reliable chart.

The shard.

We can't help them, Idari.

I'm not helping them. I'm just...

We're just taking them to Binja.

Right.

Good, then we won't risk the Scath discovering that we stole a Lumenor out from under them.

We didn't steal her.

Neither will we risk exposing this supposed long-lost reservoir of filamentium to the Scath. Help Emera and you'll fill their coffers for eternity, darling. Your only reward will be the scrap pile.

Hadn't thought of that.

One thing at a time. I don't know anything yet. This could all be some tall tale pirates told over babyl. That shard? Could be a chip off a block like Welkin. Still. What Emera showed me was real. Felt real, anyways. She feels real. She makes me feel real. Focus, Idari.

How long until the Crossroads, CR-UX?

You've hours to dance, darling.

I scroll through the catalog of Faero's music, one of the few inessential things I maintain in the precious real estate of the *Steel Haven's* liquid drive, and find my favorite virtual record. *Remora.* Faero's first solo record. I set the feed from the netic to the mainframe on a loop to prevent any telemetry streaming to CR-UX. This engagement with the vircord will be unique, never to be repeated again, regardless of how many times I listen to it in the future. The internal algorithms of the vircord's programming prevent it.

This engagement will be mine, and mine alone.

I press play and the bulkhead slides away to a wet street in the heights of Bastopol. Petrichor mixes with cigarette smoke. My breath evaporates into the breathy, opening verses of a song I know very well. Lyrics shimmer in neon reflections in rain puddles.

Strings forecast showers. Angelic choirs float with metallic clouds across the face of a neon gas giant. Drums the thunder of an ecstatic sky. Tantar licks tongue fire across skin and stone, consuming everything in ash as the song begins. Boys and girls coil into more lyrics, leading me verse by verse into the front door of a club on the top level of a bridge spanning towers cut from basalt. Music spirals around the small stage, a whirlpool of sonic dissonance drawing me in.

The brushed-back moon grass of Faero's hair lashes out from a flaked, garish mask of heavy white makeup. Her dress is smokethread, woven on Thesh, but from a few rows back it looks more like she's wrapped in cobwebs. She ages herself. Moves in tired, slow rhythms, baroque like her music. But she's not old.

Every nine years, she becomes a different person. Slade Inio. Troma Phate. Delicia Faero. New face. New body. New sex. That elasticity in her voice comes from this evolution, stretched thin across many lifetimes, but heavy with memory, sorrow, and promise.

I stand with Faero just inside the spotlight. The cracks in her makeup harsh up close. The strain in her eyes severe. If there's a line between art and life, she's crossed it. Blurring the lines is what she does. It's why she appealed to me. Poor, desperate, and always out of sorts with my body, I found a kindred spirit in Faero. The singer was a nonsense amalgam of identities – Setanate, Pujar, Decestan, male, female, old, new – and she wore her awkwardness with pride. Identity became fashion. Elasticity was a virtue. Indeterminism.

In Faero I discovered a power in being strange. Singular. Unique. And just like she has now, I've found the skin doesn't stretch as far. Chip away at it and you still see the layers beneath, even if you can't place their age, or understand what they might have meant.

CR-UX's voice echoes through the theater. *I understand.*

You couldn't, I say.

You'd be surprised, darling.

Who was your idol?

A cooling unit in the shipyards on Shighn. Everybody wanted her. Only the best ships got to dock inside, out of the sun. She blew me a kiss, though, on my way out into service. I've never washed that spot.

You've never washed any spots, I say.

I step into the spotlight. My holographic skin brushes Faero's. Three-dimensional rays bend as I occupy the space she does.

Wish fulfillment, darling?

I don't want Faero's life. From the looks of it, it's not much different than the one I have.

She wants out, I say.

The exits are clearly marked.

Where would she go?

Wherever she wants. She's her own person.

I stifle my thoughts. *I suppose she is.*

Planets race through the dark beyond. Starships take flight as the song does, building to an emotional crescendo Faero keeps teasing and withholding. The most vocal in the crowd – a trio of slinky, bleary girls from Ahapa – start to sing the song I'm pretty sure everyone had come for. The one they hope for.

Because sad is a pretty dress
And I'm going to wear her out tonight

Every voice in the arena sings in drink-slick harmony. Dee-Kee hits the refrain on his tantar behind Faero. There's power in it. Electricity. All six of Dee-Kee's spindly robotic limbs cradle his tantar, myriad fingers flexing nervously with the rhythm section, Ginge and Bloss. Bloss isn't much bigger than Faero's microphone as the tiny Naspi scurries around the giant but stoic Ginge, bashing drumsticks against the hollow combs that crust his skin of hardened wax.

A manic beat spurs an epileptic tantar, waves breaking on a rocky shore under a gossamer sky. Faero's normally soft, gauzy alto explodes from the liquid pressure beneath and I break into a thousand pieces of sea glass. My remains propel into a glittering cloud Faero arranges with every sweeping gesture of her hands.

I constellate.

I cloud, into sky, into sea, into Faero and she guides the shards of me back together. Her voice resonates through the glass, a hum that fuses the glass sculpture back into my shape. Desire erupts within me. Need. I lunge into an embrace with Faero, but Faero retreats, like always. She dances away, down the beach, down a spiral stair into the earth, and the backstage of another club. Mannequins exasperate my pursuit of her. The featureless dummies clutter the backstage area, disguising the cables slithering across the floor with the melody.

I stumble into a mannequin, triggering a chain reaction that topples them all. In their place rise dozens of proxy-netics. Some wear no skin, exposing their turanium exoskeletons. Others only possess weathered grafts. All of them have the same face. Mine. Expressionless. Empty. Dead. All except one.

Emera glows among the dolls, a neon mannequin. She sits on a crate, motionless. Shimmering eyes staring into nothing. Her lips break in the act of voicing lyrics, but they're out of synch with the music. I brush her lips with my thumb. Light shimmers in my wake. The crash of waves thunders in the distance. The roar of drums. I hope for the euphoria always threatening to surface in Faero's music will finally break through and I kiss Emera.

Kiss me. Wake me up. Breathe life into me.

What's soft and warm becomes cold. Sticky. Emera sticks to me. Skin peels away with skin. Flesh rips like dry paper as I try and undo whatever I've done and I fall backward, Emera trailing off me in ribbons as if we're one being, one wearing the other, down and down into the unyielding darkness of the end of the album until I crash back into my cabin on the *Steel Haven*.

I gasp for air. *"Ban Minda..."*

CR-UX's soothing voice chases away the swirling disorientation of the vircord. *Are you ok, darling?*

My fingers skirt across my lips, pulling at glittering reams of Gen Emera that aren't there. *I'm fine.*

I thought music was meant to be relaxing.

I slid off the bunk to the deck. *Me too.*

I check the ship's chronometer. Less than an hour passed inside the vircord. I brush my lips again, not to wipe away the taste of Emera, but to hold it in. The softness and sweetness of a single moment before everything shredded to pieces, just like it always does. My fingers dig into my chin, pinching, squeezing, clawing to reignite that feeling of fusing with them, of being something beyond just myself. For a moment, I was the music.

A sob escapes me.

Anxiety riddles through the downlink, but it's not mine. Normally, there's never any filter on what CR-UX says or thinks.

Darling, he says.

I touch my lips again, fighting the impulse to tear away my skin, stuck to my turanium bones. *I'm fine.*

We never talk anymore.

It's all we do, CR-UX.

We don't talk about anything real, Idari.

Our entire existence is predicated on erasing the past, or just enough of it to keep the present going. I want a life.

I want to have a tomorrow.

There's no tomorrow in this ship? CR-UX says.

There was never a yesterday.

His tone sours. *I've never had any future but you.*

I try and stand, but I can't even lift my arms in this jacket. *You're getting sentimental in your old age.*

Perhaps you're wearing off on me.

But this is all you can ever be, CR-UX, I say, zipping out of this suffocating jacket. *You can't change.*

You would know, he says, tone flat and robotic now.

I didn't mean it that way. CR-UX...

CR-UX clears his throat. *Darling.*

It's just I don't have any space –

You have a guest.

A powerful magnetic attraction pulls on every old, tired, and stuck part of my body. Blue light washes out my cabin. I shield my eyes with my hand and Emera is standing before me.

Light curls off her in question marks. "I like your music."

"Wasn't too loud for you?"

"I liked the mannequins."

I try and act natural. "You saw that?"

A cheeky little smile accompanies a quick pulse of light. "Yes."

"Oh. That was just..."

"You don't want to kiss me?"

"I mean, I do. Obviously. You're a living star. You're beautiful. But I don't even know if stars have sex. Or how."

"Cosmically."

I tug at my jacket. Oh. I took it off. "Hot in here..."

Her glow dims enough I can see she's not naked in light like I thought before, but covered in gauzy muslin wraps sun-faded to the point they're transparent. I see her. I really see her now.

Curlicues of light tumble down her shoulders in an endless waterfall, beading and surging across her spritely form the way fire caresses the belly of the *Steel Haven* when the ship touches the skin of a new sky. Emera illuminates something inside me. The part of me I know isn't just metal and wire. My formless passion.

"You're embarrassed," she says.

I shake my head. "You're... right to the point."

"Stars can only shine."

Whirling light washes over her, confused with her own, as she gazes out of the portal into the light the *Steel Haven* transits.

"This light is a mirage," she says.

I try to recover my senses. "Never really thought about it."

"Most stars you see in the sky no longer exist. Their light is an afterimage, traveling through time from the past. The sky we hold so dear... the constant in our lives... isn't what it seems. Sometimes, if we're lucky, we see the truth of that beauty. The wonder beyond."

"Look," I say. "I'll get you to Binja and then..."

She flickers like a bad monitor. "I was the last star in my cluster. The others called me 'The Blue Straggler.' They were all old. Tired. Red. Orange. Dim. But beautiful. And then the Scath captured them.

They bled them... they killed them. All of them. It's only been Welkin and I for... I don't know how long it's been."

It's only been CR-UX and I, forever. I don't remember anyone else. I don't know if I could be around someone else, and yet it's all I want. The need for someone real is as strong as Emera's magnetic field, twisting and pulling on me, metal and soul.

"It's not that I don't want to help you," I say.

Her light evens. "You're afraid."

"Aren't you?"

"All the time. I want to live for my people... and then, sometimes... I don't feel worthy of them."

"You're worthy. Trust me."

"You said I couldn't trust you."

"Why did you help me, Emera?" I can still feel her stellar warmth from thawing me out down in the hold back at Skeken. "You could have had the ship. You did have the ship. You didn't need me anymore, if you ever did. If you all you wanted was freedom..."

Emera drifts around the cabin. I don't think her feet touch the deck. If I'm not careful, mine won't either. Her magnetic field tugs at switches and dials on the interfaces. Hatches in the walls open, teasing out the drawers concealed inside. All my clothes unfold on the floor. It's fine. Go ahead. Toss them anywhere.

Emera pulls my red jacket on. "You're not like the others."

She must have encountered other Starguns in the past. Though I don't know what problem any of them would have been with Welkin around. I don't understand. I should take a shot each time I say that.

Actually, probably shouldn't do that.

Emera teases out the tattered train of an old Pinoth dress I'm not sure is mine. "I see the entire electromagnetic spectrum. Infrared, gamma, X-Ray, all at once. Wavelengths you're not aware of. I see you. I saw you on OT-3Ro. Your soul."

"I'm just a machine."

"Machines have spirit. This ship does."

"How?"

"Life is more than what people see or know."

"I see everything... I can barely make sense of it."

"You understand." Emera glances at the empties on the deck. "I probably didn't need to alter your memory."

"Probably not."

Strands of light wisp off Emera. They crimp in the air before evaporating. "I wish I hadn't done that to you."

"You couldn't trust me."

"I saw you. The light in you. But Welkin..."

I cycle through the internal sensor feed. Blue eyes stare back at me from the hold. "You don't have to explain."

"I had faith in you... but you're not safe with yourself, Idari."

"You're not safe with yourself either."

"Welkin says I'm like my forbearer. Thena."

"She must have been wonderful."

Emera's sorrow shadows all her shine. "I never knew her. When a star dies, another is born. I've only known... we've always been running. Welkin and I. Until we were captured."

Emera closes the wardrobe compartment and looks for new hatches to open, but she's exhausted all the small space has to offer. I rub my chest. The Scath bled Emera. The shadows caged her and tortured her, for longer than she knows.

"I'm sorry," I say.

Everything in this ship obeys Emera's magnetic field. For right now, she obeys mine. Emera draws closer to me. "We got away from the shadows. I don't remember how. I came to in Welkin's arms and then we were in the canister on OT-3Ro."

"You're free now."

Her smile fades along with the intensity of her light. "I have to save the Lumenor. I have to make all things new."

For all the energy Emera radiates, there's no enthusiasm in her words. The tone strikes me as a bit robotic.

"Emera... is finding The Glass Star something you want to do?"

"Stars shine only for the light of others. Welkin says."

"What about you?"

Azure energy twists within Emera, and so does a kind of confusion in her plasmatic eyes. "Me?"

"It's ok to think of yourself. I do, all the time."

"You don't know who you are."

I rub my chest. "Oh, I do. I'm selfish. Careless. Scared."

Emera leans into me. "Tell me."

"This is all I am. This... shell. This machine living only for the next bottle of babyl to help me forget I live only for the next bottle."

Light swirls in strange lines through Emera. "Sometimes... I forget. I don't know what. I just know there's this gap."

"I don't understand."

"When a star dies, another is born... I remember..."

"Your forbearer?"

"Others. Ghosts. Phantoms. They were me. They were someone else. But I carry their light. I am their lantern."

I reach for her. Light curls around my fingers. I've never felt this. I don't know what this is. Connection. Understanding. Illumination. Emera holds her hand over my heart. My faux skin becomes iridescent. My heart a lantern. My tattoo a map.

"Do you know what it means, Idari?"

I tug up the zipper. "It's just... silly tattoo..."

Emera clasps the zipper. "A star's light travels from the past. It radiates long after their death. They speak to the dark so long as there is dark to travel. This is the way of the Lumenor."

"They speak to the dark..."

"Great distances separated us. Years. Eons. Universes. But we're not speaking to the light of ghost stars, we're speaking to the light of now. *Gen Gestan.* The stars may go out, but the light is always there. The voice. The spirit. There is no end. No next. Only now. Forever."

Emera's fingers trace the lines of my tattoo. "That's what these lines are, Idari. Your tattoo. A Lumenor sigil. Gen Gestan."

How could I forget that?

"You've always been speaking to your future," she says. "Your heart has always been drumming for this moment. For me."

I can't tell if her magnetic field draws me in or my desire to kiss her. Would my lips burn off? Would I care? To have the fire of babyl not just on my tongue or my lips but in my skin. My bones.

My soul.

I kiss Emera. "You can't blame me. Can you?"

"Stars compel all they cast light on," she says and warm hands slip inside my jumpsuit, across my skin, into my seams.

I pull back. "Sorry."

Her hands wilt. "What did I do wrong?"

I zip up. "Nothing. It's just... nothing."

"You're beautiful, Idari."

"How can you think...."

"Your splendor is mine," she says. "Your iron. Your metal. A star forged them. Your beauty is the beauty of stars."

I'm a monster. Emera can see my soul. What does she see? An electrical field out of synch with my body? Why can't she see how wrong I am? How misplaced I am in my skin?

Emera's light wanes. "You're not wrong, Idari."

"I'll get you to Binja."

She kisses my hand. "You're not wrong."

The room falls back into darkness. Silence. I had been in a song. A dream. I had been in another body. My body. Now I'm back where I always am, shoehorned into a life with no space for hope.

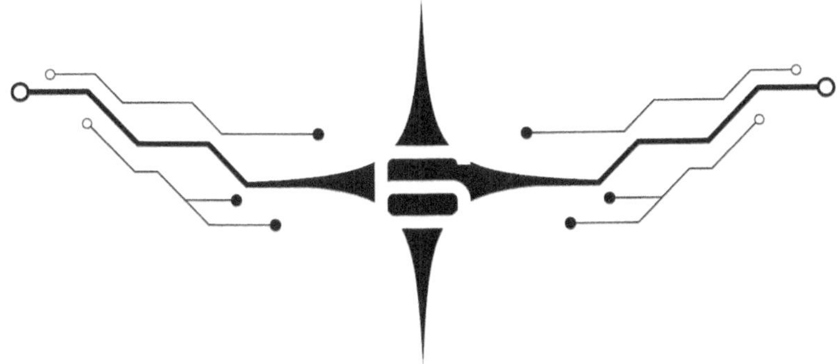

My life from a distance must appear much the same as Bulsar does, the moon a sheet of ice fissured in volcanic red. A dust mote loose in the eye of Belgo, a gas giant pocked with ancient, russet hurricanes swirling mercilessly as the vertigo within me.

Steady on now, CR-UX says.

I'm fine, I say and flick needless switches on the dash in the cockpit. Really, the pilot's seat is ornamental on this ship. CR-UX does all the work, especially this bit, which requires all the math.

Not exactly my forte, math.

Anyone with an ounce of sense would know someone like Emera and I are never going to add up. She's a Lumenor, for one. If there's a two, it's unnecessary. Her being a living star covers it.

CR-UX sighs. *If it's any consolation, I'm reasonably sure if you had progressed with Emera last night, there was a 72.3% chance Welkin would have walked in on you both.*

You were listening, I say. *The whole time.*

We've been at this too long to be prudish now, darling.

CR-UX can't simply look away. The downlink, so long as it's active, is comprehensive in its data share. Endless worlds and endless lovers have played out with CR-UX as an unwilling observer. He finds nothing embarrassing about me or my passion, which makes for one of us, at least. Some part of him enjoys it, though not in any leering kind of way. In those moments, he's almost as much a voyeur as I am, living through someone else.

I rub my thumb across my lips. *Emera is lovely.*

Indeed, CR-UX says, with a sigh.

She doesn't think I'm a monster.

You're a person, darling. We're all people, even those little microscopic organisms growing at the bottom of your laundry hamper. I'm a person, the same as you or anyone else.

The ship does have spirit.

She has life, Idari.

An electric anxiety envelops me as the ship contacts Bulsar's atmosphere. Plasma globs on the shields and then bursts in short, tense flares. I keep an eye on the readout indicating our shield strength, not quite where I'd like it after the business back at Skeken.

Fire exhausts to the smoke of clouds. Below, fields of hardened lava bunch like rope twisted taut toward the horizon. Tangled cords ebb to waves spreading out across a vast igneous sea, cresting against islands of impossibly blue ice. Most find Bulsar a monstrosity, disfigured and seeping with hidden, vivid, and volatile light.

I think she's fine the way she is.

Ash-streaked alluvial fans and blunted obsidian plateaus scroll past. Ruins of abandoned cities dangle off sheer obsidian cliffs, abandoned as the caldera quieted and the glacial lakes bordering it froze back over. The people of Bulsar have been chasing the water ever since; the quill-like silhouette of the city of Bastopol funnels to a seismographic spike far on the horizon.

Blue light bursts in the cockpit behind me. "It's beautiful."

I tug on my zipper. "You've never been here?"

Emera takes the co-pilot's seat. I can't remember if anyone ever has. "Not that I remember. This is a pirate system?"

Shadows of other moons race across the landscape. "It is. But I'm not sure which pirates have control of it at the moment."

When your religion is based on the wealth conveyed on you personally from your god, poverty creates a lot of heretics. The Pujar fractured into two warring clans a few years back once fuel started to get scarce, or maybe it was longer. I forget now. The Set adhere to ancient traditions, or at least someone's ancient traditions, because they stole those, too. The Sem go with the flow.

I forget who has the system, CR-UX.

It depends on the day, he says. *Our coming here is not a particularly great idea. You will end up drunk or dead, Idari.*

Isn't that everywhere we go?

Particularly Bulsar.

Pirates like me, though.

Oh, darling. Darling, darling Idari. The line between what you forget and what you imagine is frightfully thin.

I sink in my seat. *What did I ever do to the Pujar?*

You're a Stargun Messenger. Do the math.

I just said I'm not good at math.

Perhaps why you made a lousy pirate. They tend to keep score.

But I used to be one of them.

'Used to be.'

Do I want to know? I'll just forget again, anyway. *Binja likes me.*

He sighs. *Approaching Bastopol.*

Steam shrouds the colossal geyser the city encircles, the remains of a magma chamber that collapsed long ago. Thousands of interlocking basalt columns, naturally hexagonal in shape, form endless stairs along the crater's scalloped edges. People carved them into dwellings, filed them into towers that only get taller as we descend into a misty marina. Pontoons deploy from the *Steel Haven's* belly and we glide to a landing that pinches Emera's stately expression into a giddy smile. So much easy joy wells within her, buried deeper for her sorrow, if it ever releases, I want to be standing right next to her.

I can hear CR-UX's bother. *We're here.*

Kids loitering on the dock plea to *Take us for a ride!* I did the same thing once – I think – idolizing the pilots of comet-sloops and planet-bounders here in the marina. When was that? Was that before Binja claimed me for his crew? Or after?

Which was it, CR-UX?

His attention focuses on the post-flight checklist of shutting down the ship's systems. *I no longer recall.*

A strange fear covers CR-UX's thoughts. The proxy-netic's limited onboard memory means I can't harbor any great trove of memories, which is as much a relief to him as a frustration. I think I understand. In the beginning, we were a team. CR-UX barely understands me now, the netic a dusty bottle clouded with age and neglect, hiding contents only to be guessed at.

CR-UX, I say.

Emera follows me into the alcove. "Do you know many pirates?"

I belt my holster on. "One or two."

"Are we going to meet them?"

"You're going to stay here, Twinkles."

Her lips curl. "I want to go with you."

"It's not safe."

She taps open the wardrobe. "I can wear a disguise."

The cockpit bobs as I pull on a traditional Bulsari shall. "This is a den of pirates. We can't take any chances."

Welkin's frustration sighs in from the corridor. "Then we shouldn't have come here in the first place, Idari."

I open my hand. "I'll find Binja. Give me the shard."

Welkin huffs dust. "You'll run off with it."

"You can trust me to come back for my ship."

Unless you forget, CR-UX says.

A grimace grinds crystal into crystal. Welkin opens his hand and the shard of The Glass Star manifests in the air.

I pocket the shard on my utility belt. "Don't draw any attention to yourselves. Keep off the comms."

Emera flickers. "Be safe."

I brush her cheek. "I'll be back before you know it."

First sign of trouble, take off, I say, lowering the gantry.

Oh, CR-UX says, *I will.*

Well. Warn me, first.

I've got a copy of you on the mainframe.

I'll miss you, too, I say and I'm free in the pirate city.

Good thing I don't get tired.

I stopped counting at 20,000 stairs. At least it's not winter. On really cold nights farther up in the heights, the steam from the geyser freezes, creating this glaze on the basalt. You can't see it.

I should be a bit worried I remember that.

I should think, CR-UX says. *Custodial netics have been salting the stairs of Bastopol for centuries, darling. Millenia, perhaps.*

I can't be that old, can I? How would I know? No one knows how old any of this is, either. This planet has been around as long as its red dwarf star. Tens of billions of years. Infinite lives. Bastopol is a city of layers, of sediments, fossils, and lost treasures.

This is like you looking for your socks, CR-UX says.

I always find them.

You literally never do.

The city scales above me, one giant case of stairs, with apartments, temples, and arenas built on the hexagonal roofs of the basalt columns. Bridges string out to isolated columns which ancient collapses left stranded. After another mile or so, the city morphs from geometric and angular to organic and fluid. Igneous tile create gentle waves, cresting on each level. Look closer and the black eaves aren't eaves at all, but the backs of docked Pujar sloops. I've made it.

The Pirate Quarter.

I leave the stairs for a narrow path through the dense habitats on the flat top of a column. Elephantine Huxronx huddle together in the lane, children tucked in their shells. Sail-fin Nepians float in ambulatory balloons of fluid, wet with condensation other bridge dwellers lick dry with their tongues. A Pujar woman – I'm not sure if she's Set or Sem, though such distinctions are less and less obvious in The

Crossroads – sits on the cold, damp stone with a baby. The mother presses her dry lips against the baby's cheek and blows, making a silly flatulent sound. The baby flashes bright, pink gums.

I adjust my helmet, the collar tight on my neck. All these people are either trying to get on the crew of the sloop docked at this column, unlikely given things aren't any better out there than they are here, or they're *get deja*. Taken. This lot didn't earn their keep. They didn't even earn names. Who did I take Astra Idari from? How did I earn it?

>SIGNAL DEGRADATION WARNING

The density of the stone is interfering with the downlink, CR-UX says. I'll have to relocate to a higher berth to maintain our connection.

Don't bother. I'm close.

You think Binja is on this ship?

Not this ship. Smoked meats twist on turanium spits. Carts obstruct any natural path, selling unlikely fruits and vegetables grown in the rich soil of the volcanic farms beyond. Pickpockets skip over homeless sleeping on the millennial steps descending to the levels below. I am their panicked laughter, echoing through the halls carved in stone. I am their footfall, thunder through the dark. I am their shadow, quick behind them into the depths.

There are depths.

This path I'm on just became a tunnel. I'm inside the column now. Pipes feed natural gas under and through tiny homes made lanterns from the light of open fires burning within. Residents boil brown water leaking from exposed pipes. Others wash under the trickle. People move. They hurry. Something's up.

Hard-light burns away the dark. Everyone hits the deck as I draw my blaster and duck behind a support pillar.

This is why we need to stay in contact, CR-UX says.

Shh.

I peek around the pillar. Smoke rises from a laser-riddled body. Thieves loot his pockets. Nothing much. Some toruls. A mag-rail pass. For them, it's a jackpot. They run off, leaving the dead to the carya birds that rattle out of the recesses of stone. I tug at the shifting collar of my shawl. People walk past. They walk over. A strange confection of feeling radiates through me. Sorrow. Relief.

Despair.

I could lose the proxy and still there's a copy of me on the ship dating back to who knows when. I can't die, not really. But in the space of one of Faero's songs, I might. At the bottom of a bottle of babyl. The end of a blaster. That sensation, euphoric and fleeting; maybe this time. This time, it might be the end and in the end, I'll be free of this body. This pain. I'll be someone new.

You think you're trapped, CR-UX says. *You think you're not who you're supposed to be. You can be whoever you want.*

I laugh, startling the birds. *Sure.*

You are a being of pure information. There are no limits on your potential, Idari, in form or function.

I turn down an incise lane deeper into the bridge. *If only.*

This stings him. *Emera isn't wrong about you.*

The pirate ship is just down here, I say. *Somewhere.*

>SIGNAL STRENGTH WEAKENING

Pedestrians trickle past stalls and shops offering all kinds of useless trinkets from The Crossroads. The grand bazaar splinters into several sub-markets. Precious metals. Art. Clothing. Jewels. The most precious commodity of all, food, pitches no dedicated stake on the bridge but can be found in whispers and coded signs. Attle pups sleep on piles of each other in windows, ready to be sheared, skinned, or butchered. Stacked bins of netic parts. I turn back. Table games. *Aprosdo.* Pirates, with red sashes tied to their waists.

I've found it.

Meek sunlight cleaves through the hull breaches in a giant corsair's belly. She's been beached atop this tower for centuries, victim of some ancient misfortune. Pirates come here for good luck but the ship's given up all her treasure. Customers walk past. Merchandise lines the stage behind the bar, waiting. I take a needless breath just to comfort all the eyes staring at me.

I go to the bar. "A bottle of babyl."

Idari, CR-UX says. *Focus.*

I'm focused, I say as the bartender slides me a bottle.

You're supposed to be looking for Binja.

Smoke curtains the bar. Ovan leaf. Smells like an oil fire. My smile comes so quick it leaves me sore. I follow the scent to a nook-like booth in the bar's recesses where I find Min Binja.

He nurses a magmatic cigarette. "Old man."

Most pirates get taken into a crew. A few are born. Binja wields all the classic Pujar attributes: tall. Brown. Tall. He's like one of those columnar towers outside. Skinny, but strong. Majestic. Mysterious.

CR-UX groans. *Oh, just sex him and get it over with.*

Did you say 'sex him?'

Binja leans back in the booth, eyes smiling as he does. "You make this face when you're talking to him."

"I don't make a face," I say.

"You're like an attal pup, dreaming. All those little twitches. Little sounds that barely escape." He hands me the cigarette. "What brings you, Idari? Is it still Idari, or have you taken another name?"

I lean back and take a drag. "I'm still me."

"Ban Minda."

"You don't know the half of it."

He lights another cigarette, illuminating that chin. You could sharpen a knife on it. "How long has it been? Five years?"

I nod as confidently as I can. "I'll take your word for it."

"You haven't aged a day."

"Good genes."

He smiles. "It's always good to see family, even if they've come to collect my bounty. I assume that's why you're here."

"I have something to tell you. Not here."

He laughs. "I can't be worth that much for you to go through all this pantomime, old man."

"You'd bring a pretty penny."

"Not enough to satisfy the claim The Bool just put on you."

I take a shot of babyl. "You've been keeping tabs?"

"You're still flying around in that little ship."

"It's an OVL-99 Red Special, thank you very much."

"There wasn't much red left on the *Steel Haven* when I last saw her. I can't imagine there's any on the old girl now."

Shoot him, CR-UX says. *Shoot him in the head.*

"You should have stayed with the crew," Binja says.

"And where is the crew, Binja?"

He stabs his cigarette out on the table. "I wish I had your memory. I should charge you, having to explain all this again."

"I'll buy you a drink," I say and lift my hand.

He pulls it back down before I get the attention of the bartender. "Let's not draw attention to ourselves, shall we?"

"That's asking a lot of me, Binja."

"Try, for my sake."

"You're shy all of the sudden?"

He gazes through the crack of light slivering the hull of the ship. "When did I see you last? Thetma? No. Peran."

"You're asking me?"

"You don't remember, do you?"

I take another shot. "That's why we get along."

"You ever try just writing things down?"

"I probably had the idea, but..."

He sighs. "Ten years ago, concern grew about the power of the Scath. Where they came from. Where filamentium did. A few systems wanted to break their monopoly on fuel."

"I do have something to tell you, by the way. But go on."

Binja thumbs his chin. "So long as the Scath pull the strings on fuel, they pull the strings on the galaxy. Most pirates were content to play along. A healthy filamentium trade meant a healthy bounty for pirates. My father didn't want to be a puppet."

I don't need to remember to know how the rest of that went. Going against the Scath would have resulted in fuel embargoes. Economic hardship. Social unrest. You don't volunteer for that. Support for that kind of sacrifice has to come from the bottom. The street. No wonder this alliance didn't work out.

Burnt mint singes the air. "Some pirates could see a new dawn for the Pujar. Others thought we were losing our way. Our identity."

"The Set," I say.

Species from all over the galaxy wear the red sash. Netics. All manner of beings in between. I don't remember a sash.

"I don't know if it was so much about fuel," Binja says. "A reckoning had been coming for a long time. Anyone can be *get deja*. Taken. But the Set don't believe anyone can be Pujar."

"Aren't they the same thing?"

"That's what I said."

"And what did I do during all of this?"

"You walked away," he says. "Like you always do."

"CR-UX made it out like I did something bad around here."

"You never walk away clean, old man."

I lean over the table. "Where's your sash?"

Smoke veils Binja. "Thing about piracy. It creates customers. The shadows already had friends among my people. So it didn't take much for the Scath to stoke dissension among the Pujar until we fractured. They cemented their hold. Status quo preserved. History lesson over. You owe me a drink, Idari."

I signal the waitress. "Is this a Set bar, Binja?"

"Some days."

"And you're Sem?"

Binja isn't wearing his sash for some reason, but his blasword still hangs from his belt. A turanium guard curves back toward the snakehead blaster emitter forming out of the hilt. Thumb a button on the grip and a blade springs from the hilt. The blasword is the ceremonial weapon of the Pujar. If you have one, you're Torugun. Named by their god, The Taker Of Names. You're crew. Family. Forever.

"I'm just trying to have a drink, old man."

"I need your help," I say. "Come with me, Binja."

He warily eyes the rest of the bar. "I wish you'd forgotten me. Everyone else has."

I slide out of the booth. "You need to see this."

I draw Binja away from the table into the shadows. I open a pouch on my utility belt and crimson light illuminates us both.

Binja throws away his cigarette. "What... is... that?"

I turn the shard over. "You tell me."

He inspects the marking on the shard. "Where did you get this?"

"What ship does this belong to?"

"This is from the lost treasure of *The Sun Buckler*. Idari..."

I pull him close. "Tell me about this *Sun Buckler*."

"You haven't been to the wreck?"

"Wreck? Where is it?"

"Where did you get – it doesn't matter. I can't help you."

I pocket the shard. "You're coming with me."

Some guy big and sour-looking approaches us. Scales as rigid as the stone towers bulge out of his armor. Thick. Expensive. Stargun.

He cracks his knuckles. "Two for the price of one."

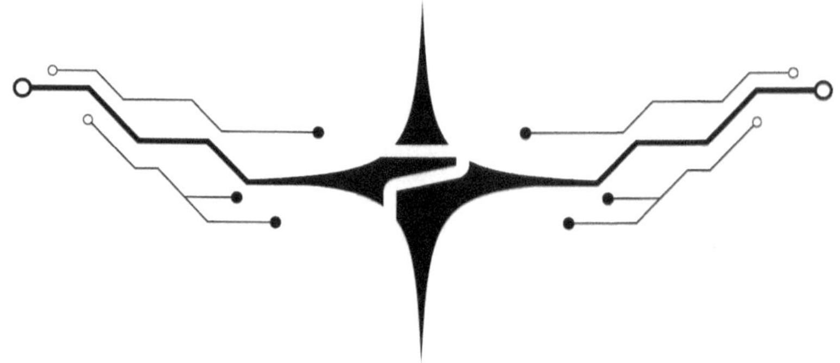

I DRIVE MY TURANIUM FIST SQUARE INTO THE STARGUN'S GUT. He just stares down at me, like he's bored.

"That usually works," I say and then I go sailing.

Tables break my fall. People run through the bar as the Stargun stomps after me. I draw my blaster. The shot fizzles against his scales.

The Stargun is Thide, CR-UX says with about as much enthusiasm as he can muster. *His skin is impervious to blaster fire.*

Now you tell me.

I assumed you knew. Thide are ubiquitous in professions like ours for just that reason. Actually, he seems a bit familiar.

Don't be that guy, I say. *How do I stop him?*

I calculate that running is your best option.

The Thide stands between me and the door. I've got no shot in any respect. Between the Thide's legs, I make out Binja standing there, cool, calm, collected. He unclips the blasword from his belt. His fingers close around the grip and a turanium blade, long and sharp, extends from the blaster emitter. Well, this really escalated.

Binja assumes a defensive stance. "Stand down, Omo."

Omo Dor. That's who this is. I remember him now.

"Put your fish knife away," Omo says. "Or I skin you with it."

Binja keeps his sword. "Touch Astra Idari and The Taker of Names will have many new ones tonight."

This is so hot.

Omo draws knives from his gauntlets. "You're a heretic."

I fire off a shot just for good measure. "Watch who you're talking to. This is Min Binja. He's royalty so far as pirates go."

Binja grips his sword. "Old man."

Omo blinks. "Binja?"

That smile Binja has tried to paste over this mess crumbles.

I frown. "What did I say now?"

Omo grinds the blades of his knives together. "This *tista* isn't Min Binja anymore. He isn't anyone."

I shake my head. "Did you take another name, Binja?"

His face reddens with shame. "I have no name."

"He is forsaken," Omo Dor says with a little too much relish. "Like all those who took up arms against the Pujar Set."

Ban Minda. All those people on the steps outside the corsair. The kids down in the marina. They don't try to join pirate crews for treasure. No one in the dark earns a name at birth. Names are too precious in a galaxy where mouths outnumber stars. Binja took his name. Now he's lost it. Forever. Binja can never go back to The Bastard Moon. He can never see his father again. Min Binja is forgotten, from home, from friends, from blood. From memory.

"I didn't know," I say.

Binja – I don't know what to call him now – tries not to look hurt. "Unlike you, I don't have the mercy of forgetting who I was."

"Binja..."

Omo swipes his knives through the air. "Enough belly-aching, heretic. Surrender. Both of you. Maybe I'll just take your hands."

Binja hardens his stance. "I may be forsaken... but I'm still Pujar."

"And she's a skin job. So what?"

Binja smiles. "Oh, my friend. She's much more than that. This is one of the most insufferable women you will ever meet. Men have literally flung themselves to their doom to avoid her. Lucky for you, I survived. Heed my wisdom. Leave now, while you can."

Omo points his knife at Binja. "I'm going to retire off this – "

Blood sprays. Screams erupt. Hands fall to the deck. Binja collapses the blade of his blasword into the hilt.

"I leave you your names," he says. "I take your grace."

Time to go. Laser fire streaks past my head as I duck down a blind alley through the wrecked corsair. Guards scramble through the dense evening crowd behind us. Hard-light shells blaze the air, crackling on impact. I duck behind the buckled bulkhead.

Binja leans against the wall. "I abhor violence."

I fire back. "Shame you're so good at it."

He looks away. "At this point, it's all I'm good for."

"I don't care about names, Binja."

"The Taker of Names has no use for me among his crew, old man. When I die..." Binja casts a despairing glance at the tired and dirty people cluttering the narrow pass ahead. "I'll be as this lot. Unwanted. Cast off. Nameless. *Mindarth*."

"It's all poppycock. There isn't any great corsair in the sky."

"You remember more than you think."

I followed the path of the Kam for a time. Farther than Binja knows. But I didn't want to be taken. I didn't want to disappear or be annihilated in anonymity. I wanted out of the hole I'm still in.

I wanted to be found.

I consider his weapon. "You keep the sword."

He grips the handle. "I have nothing else."

This saddens me. I don't believe in a god that takes your name and gives your theirs, but I kind of liked that Binja did.

"Ours is a republic of thieves, Idari. I ask for nothing. I take so I may earn a name and place aboard The Corsair Eternal. *I shall be known by him, and he by me.* That's the way of my people. At least, it used to be before everything got complicated with money."

"You're a pirate," I say. "It's always about money."

"It's about other things, Idari. You knew that once."

"You've got to help me find this wreck, Binja."

He shakes his head. "You're a treasure hunter now?"

"There's so much at stake. The Lumenor..."

"Lumenor?"

"This shard is the key to unlimited filamentium."

"What?"

"No more monopoly. No more wars. No more bloodshed."

"That's awfully altruistic of you, old man."

"There's no in between with me."

"So I've discovered."

"Come with me, Binja."

"For treasure?"

"You can get your name back."

"The Set will never allow it."

"You'll take it – "

Infrared signatures manifest in my vision. The corsair's security detail storms down the pass toward us. Four. No, six. A dozen or more. Chunks of the wall crumble under another barrage of laser fire.

"Move," I say, but Binja is already running. Thing about pirates. For all their talk of names and gods, they're awfully pragmatic.

This place is a maze. I can't tell if we're in the corsair still, or back in the tunnel boring through the column. I look back as I run, CR-UX's sigh whistling between my ears. Turanium planks wobble under my boots. We've stepped out on a bridge.

I grab the railing bounding the bridge as I look down into the caldera far below. *We took a wrong turn.*

You did indeed, CR-UX says.

Security guards block the way back. Just an observation post tourists pay too much money to look out at the city from. Orange fire streaks past me. Blue bolts spit back from my blaster as I hurry across the bridge. The observation post is no bigger than the bar we just left.

Ban Minda. There isn't anywhere to go.

I'd comment how unfortunate it is you've drawn an innocent man into another needlessly reckless gambit, CR-UX says, *but considering it's Binja, lead on.*

I search for a way off the column that doesn't involve a water landing. *Worried he'll make off with me someday?*

He has before, darling.

Clearly, I came back.

No, you just forgot.

Oh. Well. I think I need you to –

Half a dozen balloons big as starplanes rise into a cleft of hematic light stabbing through the veil of steam. Precious water scavengers gleaned from the geyser far below lifts to the lofty heights of Bastopol. I smile as they drift past, all the way to the top, and the people with long hooks reeling them in.

I climb up on the railing. *Hold that thought.*

There was a thought? CR-UX says.

"We have to jump, Binja."

Binja repairs his cape over his shoulders. "That bit I said before, about flinging myself to my doom? You know that was strictly intended for dramatic effect, don't you?"

I balance on the rail. "Stay here, then."

"I think I will."

Hard-light singes past his ear. Binja climbs up on the railing with me. "CR-UX is ok with this... plan?"

I shrug. "He's not *not* ok with it."

Binja shakes his head. "What?"

What?

CR-UX, calculate the best balloon for us to jump to.

Idari, I'll come get you. Standby.

Laser fire *tinks* against the turanium rail. *No time.*

Binja fires back at Omo. "Does CR-UX still hate me?"

I shake my head. "Don't be silly."

Tell him he got fat, CR-UX says.

Hard -light shreds the air all around us. Binja ducks low against the railing. "What are we doing, Idari?"

Calculate the jump, CR-UX.

You may be made of pure turanium, darling, but hitting the surface at terminal velocity will do nothing for your ego.

I've done crazier things.

Solid suggestion for your epitaph. This one.

An oncoming balloon surges from the depths below. *What?*

This one. Jump on this one. Now.

There are like ten balloons —

Jump!

Ban Minda. I pull Binja with me and jump. My fingers just snag a strand of the net covering the water basket.

"I made it!"

Binja dangles from my hand. "I never doubted you."

Our combined weight drags the balloon down. "I'm sinking!"

Who could have seen this coming? CR-UX says. *Wait. I believe I just referenced your being made of turanium. Yes. Yes, I did —*

What do I do, CR-UX?

Select a religion?

The foil-like envelope of the balloon crumples into the burner and the balloon ignites and twists away from the netting that webs the capsule. I can only hold on as the water capsule plummets into darkness. It's a mile or more to the bottom. I'll survive hitting the steam lake. Mostly. Binja will be sailing eternity with his man.

I reach for my religion. I thumb the setting on my blaster over from hard-light and a grappling hook pierces solid basalt. I hold on as the capsule scrapes against the outer face of a stubby column.

Hold.

Sparks shower me. The grapple cable extends as far as it can and snaps. The loosened lines of the netting catch on one of the many eroded basalt statues meant to ward off the carya birds.

Binja laughs. "You lucky *tista.*"

"Nothing to it," I say and the netting snaps.

>PROXIMITY WARNING

Ow.

I think I'm in one piece. Shreds of flaming canvas drape over the wreck of the capsule. I slide down the roof of the boxy dwelling I've landed somewhere in the depths of Bastopol to a splash in the street.

Did I wet my pants, or is all this... ok, it's just water.

CR-UX sighs. *You don't deserve your luck.*

No one deserves my luck. Embers die against the resistant mesh of my jumpsuit. Wait. Where's Binja? Fire reduces the balloon to nothing. He could be burning to a crisp under all that, or maybe he didn't hold on as well as I did and plummeted to his death below.

How tragic, CR-UX says.

If he's dead, then we have nothing –

Binja's voice echoes out of the dark. "Over here, old man."

"I thought you were off on your corsair," I say.

He lights a cigarette off a vanishing ember of canvas. "Not me."

I do a quick sensor-scan of him to see if he has any injuries. His leg caught something on the way down. "Are you ok?"

Blood runs down his leg. "It's pretty deep."

I press Binja against the cracked basalt of the wall. "One little scratch and you're crying for the seas."

"It's a bit more than a scratch..."

I tear off a loose bit of fabric from my sleeve. "Drop them."

Binja unbuckles his trousers. "Nice of you to help out."

I wrap the bandage around the wound. "Looks infected."

"Who knows what lurks about down here."

"Where is *The Sun Buckler*, Binja?"

He grimaces. "I don't know. That's The Pilot's Truth."

"I know you know."

"Why do you care about old legends all the sudden?"

Emera's ethereal beauty shines through the downlink.

"I care," I say. "Where's *The Sun Buckler?*"

Pujar do this thing when they get caught. They tug on their sash. I don't know. I imagine it's a nervous tic as much as it's some kind of religious aspiration. His hand goes to his belt. Binja no longer has his sash. Just a sword emblematic of a life he can no longer claim.

I pull the bandage tight and he jerks.

Binja grips my wrist. "I. Don't. Know."

I snap my flash off my belt. My frustration burns away with a long drink of warm babyl. "Want some?"

Binja holds his hand out. "I'd *love* some."

I pour it on his leg and he screams.

I'm going to watch this later, CR-UX says. *Again and again.*

Binja clutches his leg. "*Ban Minda...* you are..."

"What?"

He grabs the flask from me. "You're impossible."

Binja eases back to the curb. He pats his chest for cigarettes, but he left his cape on the street. Despite the pain, he leans down and picks it up. Binja always has to have a cigarette.

"You can get your name back," I say. "Your legacy."

"I shouldn't..." He scratches his chin. "I shouldn't let you call me Binja. It's an offense to The Taker of Names. I try, you know. I try to live nameless. *Mindarth.* But then I end up here. In the shadows. Forgetting. Forgotten. A better man could accept his lot."

"How could you be a better man, Binja?"

Burning mint stings my eyes as he passes me the cigarette. "A pirate takes. He is taken. We all lose our names in the end."

"Then why you can't let it go?"

"You want to forget, old man. I don't know how."

I set my hands on my hips, the gesture drawing Binja's attention to the blaster strapped to my thigh. "Tell me about *The Sun Buckler.*"

Binja laughs. "You're going to shoot me, old man?"

"Tell me."

"Still so much fire..."

"Don't."

He brushes my cheek. "So much passion."

I bat his hand away. "I said, don't."

"I know you think this netic is some lumbering monstrosity, but it's not. I can see your soul in your eyes, Idari. I can see your pain."

I pull at the wet, heavy fabric of my jumpsuit, clinging to my rubber skin and adding to the weight I always carry. "Don't."

"In fact, it's gotten worse," Binja says.

He's doing it again, CR-UX says.

Be quiet.

Leave him. This is a dead end, just like I told you.

Binja peels hair from my cheek. "You're making the face again."

"There's no face," I say.

"Oh, there's a face. I imagine CR-UX is calling for my head."

"He's not wrong."

Thanks?

"I don't know why you listen to him."

"Why should I listen to you, Binja?"

"Because I've only ever wanted you to find yourself," he says. "CR-UX doesn't want that. He wants you exactly as you are, clipped in memory just enough around the edges you fit into the metal container he has you trapped in, Idari."

I tug at my zipper. "How am I trapped?"

Lazy smoke drifts through Binja's lips. "He's a navigational program, isn't he? An onboard assistant for rich playboys who don't know how to fly the brand-new toy they've just bought. How is it he's driving the two of you, Idari? How is it he's in control?"

"I'm in control."

"Then leave him."

"What?"

"Get a new ship. One with a drive that doesn't have space occupied by an AI you don't need. There are infinite capacity drives now, Idari. You don't need to be in a ship at all."

A groan rumbles across the downlink. *Don't listen to him, Idari.*

I shake my head. "I don't have the money for any of that."

"You're a pirate," Binja says. "It's not about money. Everything you have, you took. Your name. Your ship. Your humanity, Idari. Your quality. You keep evolving. You keep reaching. CR-UX is CR-UX and always has been. You don't need him anymore."

"You're so jealous."

"You've evolved. He hasn't. He's afraid to, frankly. If he didn't have you, then he couldn't admit what he is."

"And what's that?"

"Alone," Binja says. "Just like I am."

Guilt clouds my thoughts. The connection between CR-UX and I. The *Steel Haven* allows space only for what's essential for my survival but now the ship swells with all my forgotten regrets. My fears. My accumulating conscience.

>PROXIMITY ALERT

You should know, CR-UX says, the ID passes of the security guards from the corsair just registered in a maglev terminal several rungs up. Headed down. Express.

The elevator rattles as loud and persistently as a maglev train. "You need to see something, Binja. I need to show you."

He grinds his cigarette out under his boot. "Show me what?"

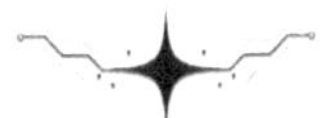

"So it's true," Binja says. "It's all true..."

He steps out of the glower of Gen Emera, and I follow him down the horseshoe corridor toward the cockpit.

"Wait," I say. "You knew about the Lumenor?"

"I'd heard. Stories. So had you."

"I don't remember..."

He crashes into the co-pilot's seat. "Of course not."

"Why would I delete something like that, Binja?"

"Same reason other people do. They don't want to accept it. The truth of filamentium has been around for years. The Scath spin it as a hoax, but it doesn't require so much effort on their part, does it? Whether we've got six eyes or two, none of us want to see. We don't want to know our food, our water, our lives are paid for in blood."

I ease into the pilot's seat. "The entire Pujar faith is built on..."

He claws at his chin. "The Pujar way... the pirate way... is good. It helps people. We help people. At least we used to."

"You kidnap them into your creed."

"We lift people out of poverty."

"That's... diplomatic."

"We give them a chance. A name." Binja reaches for his missing sash. "All the stars have gone, Idari. There isn't light enough for all of us. You can either succumb to barbarism or manage some dignity in your desperation. But you can only fill bellies with rhetoric so long as their hands are active. When the fuel dried up, so did the myth. You start eating your own tail. If you take something and give nothing back, you only dig your own grave. My father knew that without faith, there will be nothing at the bottom of it but bones."

I gaze on my star. *Ban Minda.* Her beauty hurts. Her grace.

Binja considers the glass shard. "This could change things. This could break the Scath's monopoly. Open the galaxy."

"So you'll help her, Binja?"

"What are you going to do?"

I smile. "Forget all this."

Binja looks down the corridor, confused between light and shadow. "You just asked me how you could ever forget Lumenor."

Steam shrouds the marina. The city above. No telling the stars from windows. "I can't..."

"Why?"

"They'll scrap me, Binja."

"They're going to scrap you anyway. As soon as you slip. You're slipping. You couldn't wait five minutes to fall in love with her?"

I clear my throat. "I'm handing you infinite filamentium."

"It's not that you'll be scrapped that frightens you," he says. "It's you'll have to be human. With her. No more ones and zeroes. No more virtual. No more paying to kiss girls you won't let touch you."

I tug at my zipper. "You think you know me."

"No one knows you better. You're a pirate. You're a woman."

"This is as far as I go."

"You dragged me into this, Idari."

"You know where *The Sun Buckler* is."

He sighs. "I don't know. For certain."

"Where?"

"My father was taken into Min Teth's crew. They raided a Kib colony on Angolis. Pirates boast of their spoils all the time. It's required, really. I never believed he had seen the wreck of *The Sun Buckler*. Why should I? Why did he never go back? It was a secret, he said. He swore an oath of silence. But my father described the mark on your shard to me exactly."

Angolis. Ass end of the universe. Makes sense.

"We need a ship," Binja says. "I don't have one."

"Steal one from the marina," I say.

He laughs. "You're going to leave her?"

"I can't, Binja."

"You're coming."

Darling.

Standby, CR-UX.

"You have to promise me," I say. "You'll get Emera to Angolis."

Binja shakes his head. "You never change."

"This is a change for me."

"You're still trying to have it both ways."

Idari, CR-UX says.

I said standby, CR-UX.

Binja sits forward. "Old man. Look."

Shadows cleave the steam off the marina outside the ship. Dozens of Scath appear and disappear in the *Steel Haven's* floodlights, so many they eclipse the wan street lamps constellating the low city.

Ban Minda.

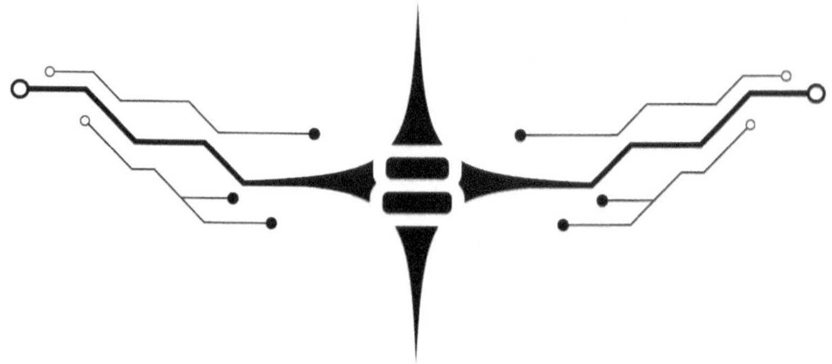

Proximity alarms sound in the cockpit.

Aerial traffic hidden in the brume off the marina ping through the downlink. Skyaks. Aeries. A Scath shuttle hovers above the landing pad. Cracked crimson simmers on the shuttle's hung jaw. The woman, or whatever she is, I met on the ship at Pendem.

Binja reaches for his sash. "I've never seen a Scath..."

"This one isn't a Scath," I say. "At least I don't think."

"A Stargun?"

"Negative."

"Who are they, then?"

Thana meteors to the landing pad. My hand falls to my blaster, expecting the worst. She stands still as a statue outside the *Steel Haven*. Waiting. For what? What am I waiting for? Uncertain radar hits flare in and out of perception. Dagger-like fuselages ghost through the steam. Scath fighters. An entire squadron.

>NIGHT VISION.

Yellow-green silhouettes flare in the steam. A dozen or so armored Scath crowd the pad on the portside walkway.

Maybe she just wants an update, I say.

CR-UX isn't playing along this time. *Or an explanation.*

How exposed are we?

I doubt the Scath can distinguish Emera from the filamentium in our tanks. That assumes their sensors are as limited as ours.

They're here for something.

Likely they've been shadowing us the entire time.

If they knew about Emera, they would have stormed the ship.

Or they're letting you do all their work for them. Idari...

I can get us out of this.

Either we run, or we turn Emera over.

I lower the gantry. *I'll forget you said that.*

Binja uncrosses his arms. "You're going out there?"

"I could use a friend."

His hand falls to his blasword. "Once I could have made my name in killing shadows. Pity I can't make it again."

"Let's just try and survive the next five minutes."

I head down the gantry down to the landing pad. Act natural. Be casual. But be on your toes. I scratch some scorch off the *Steel Haven's* belly. Really need to get her in for a wash.

"You saved me a call," I say.

Thana seethes. "You've found something?"

I didn't think this far ahead. "I'm working on it."

"Perhaps your associate can offer some insight."

Binja stands behind me. "I'm in the dark as the rest of you."

Thana considers Binja. "You've stolen from the Scath, pirate."

He holds out his hands. "I'd be happy to make amends, but I'm afraid I'm no longer in charge of accounting."

"Blood will suffice."

Binja's hand falls to his blasword. "It always does."

Five seconds and we're already measuring. "The Bool bankrolled the Banbor Gang. I just don't know who they got their information from. I got a lead it might be someone here in The Crossroads, so I came to Bulsar and put my ear to the ground. Binja is assisting me."

Thana's head crooks. "I admire you, Idari."

My hand inches down to my holster. "I worried you didn't."

"Your audacity. Your relentlessness. Your vision. You see us... like we see you... you and I have much in common."

I unbuckle the leather strap. "Somehow I doubt it."

"We're both smuggling light," Thana says.

Static chafes the downlink. *I told you not to go out there.*

"I don't know what you mean," I say.

"But you know. Don't you? For all the wonder. All the light. Warmth. There is also shadow. Cold. Death. The Lumenor were blinded by their own light. They couldn't see the shadows they cast. The darkness they carried with them everywhere. I saw. I tried to show them, but they wouldn't see. They couldn't."

Thana's hands curl in want for a place.

"And I tried to forget. But I can't. This inveterate memory. All my days are burned in my mind. My soul, if I have one. Do you know, Idari? When you look into the sun and you close your eyes... behind them you see the scorch. The sunburn. I see them all. Every last one. But every time you kill the last star... there is another. And another... even down to one, they are infinite. Stars never die. They only become something else. White dwarves. Black holes. Stellar corpses."

I draw my blaster. "I'll find the Lumenor, I promise."

"You're hiding the Lumenor on your ship."

Get back in here, Idari.

"You're hiding her behind the filamentium in your engines," Thana says. "Scath sensors aren't quite attuned when it comes to the electromagnetic spectrum... but I see her."

I shake my head. "How..."

"She shines bright even to blind eyes."

My blaster rattles in my hand. "It's not right..."

"You disappoint me."

"You don't even know me."

"I know you, Idari. I know as well as your heretic pirate does. Once you were my best hound. You could find light even in the darkest depths of the galaxy. You found it for me."

"You're lying..."

"You grow soft in flesh. You dilute in spirit. You imagine yourself human not just in body, but in conscience."

My finger curls around the trigger. "I'm a person."

"Do you want a new body? You'll have it. A new life."

"I can't..."

"Give her to me. We'll forget this. You will."

"Not this time," I say and fire a shot dead into Thana.

Crimson flame lashes out from her chest. I fire another shot before the shadows fall on me. A curt blaze consumes her armor fast as dead wood and it's no shadow beneath.

Smoke sighs from the mouth of my blaster "You're..."

She barely shines, her light a dull, rile glow like the muted sunlight of a cloudy winter day. A Lumenor. She's a Lumenor.

The *Steel Haven's* gantry sags as Welkin descends. "Thana..."

Angry energy veins through Thana. "Watchman."

Welkin crawls past me. "We buried you..."

"Not deep enough."

"How did you escape?"

"Through patience," Thana says. "Diligence. Faith. And it's been rewarded. I have waited an age for this day of reckoning. To see my reflection in your frightened eyes. To think... the entire time... you were in a cell keeping your meager little flame."

Basalt shatters under Welkin's fists. "You betrayed the Lumenor to them. Your people. *Pundamen...*"

"You're the traitor, Watchman. You muddied our light... you confused us in your dust... you sullied us. I had to burn out the rot. And at long last... we'll burn clean. We'll burn true."

Red fire erupts from her hands. Welkin throws his arms up and I think he's going to melt like a candle, but Thana's salvo crashes against a blue wall. Purple light cascades across the pad as Emera deflects the blast away and rushes to Welkin's side.

Deep blue shock pulses within her. "What are you..."

Thana's fire ebbs. "Impatient."

Thana isn't as strong as Emera. Blue stars burn bright and hot. Red stars burn dull and slow. Maybe we can get out of this.

I point my blaster at Thana. "You can't beat us all, lady."

"I forgot to tell you," Thana says. "I brought one, too."

The pad shudders with another landfall. A towering figure emerges from the smoke, sheathed in armor crafted from stellar diamond, his skull-like helm a dirty pearl, descending into long twin tusks that frame the void where a mouth should be. Fierce plumes of dust vent from slats staggered in the radial lines of his neck.

Another Gesta.

"Vidious," Thana says. "Bring me their heads."

Vidious points his sword at Welkin. "You die first, traitor."

Welkin drums his fists against his chest and launches at Vidious. Sparks flint from their pearlescent shells with each blow they land on one another. The earth quakes. Waves chop in the marina. Dust loosens from the foundations of towers.

Binja pushes me out of the way as the pad becomes a war zone. "That's the last time I ever walk out of a bar with you."

"The Scath," I say as shadows converge on us.

I fire into the dark, but the Scath appear and disappear, swiping at us with blades sizzling with dark energy. Binja's blasword deflects their blows, which prompts some questions but answers can wait.

Run, CR-UX says. *I'm spinning up the engines.*

Get Emera out of here, I say.

I'm not leaving you, Idari.

A dry click accompanies the dead charge on my blaster. I drop to a knee and change it out. Shadows cloud the pad like smoke, dark swords drawing the little light in the marina toward them.

"Binja," I say.

He slashes at nothing. "I can't see them."

Get Emera out of here, CR-UX.

Move your ass, Idari. We can still make it.

I burn through shadows. I clear a path back to the gantry but the Gesta bully their way into it. Vidious' sword rakes across Welkin's forearm. A wisp of hot, thin smoke rises from the wound.

Fear strobes behind me. "Welkin..."

"Emera, don't," Welkin says. "Don't use your powers – "

Emera comes blazing down the gantry and I try to stop her but everything metallic in the marina – the turanium streetlights, the docked starplanes, me – vault toward Emera's magnetic field.

Binja grabs me as metal shreds in a halo around the living star. The landing pad bends and warps, crunching toward the magnetic fist she clenches and then releases. Everything in her grip smashes together, shredding into thousands of jagged pieces she scatters into Vidious. He stands among the ruin, unmoved.

Idari, CR-UX says.

Wait, I say and try to corral Emera.

There's no corralling a star. A blast of pure cosmic energy surges from Emera's hand. Vidious slams a tall crystalline shield down before him, deflecting the salvo back. Emera throws up her hands, scattering the light into her own. She fires another. The stone Vidious stands on melts beneath his feet. He sinks into a crater of molten basalt and disappears in the flames. She got him. He's gone. The jet of plasma streaming out of her hand winnows and dies.

Vidious emerges unscathed from the smoke. "You are powerful…"

Emera can't believe it any more than I can. "How…"

"…but even the sun can be eclipsed."

He stalks after Emera, dragging his the blade of his crystalline sword along the broken ground. I wobble through the ruin of the pad, my equilibrium thrown off by Emera's magnetic kiss.

I fire an errant shot at Vidious. "Get away from her…"

The proxy-netic possesses precision-guided, lightning-fast reflexes. Faster than I can blink, Vidious rakes the blaster out of my hand. My feet go out from under me and next thing I know, I'm on the ground. The cold, dark point of his sword grinds into my chest.

"A waste," Vidious says.

The marina reflects in Vidious' pristine shell. The jumble of me. In my memory, the pilots of the old starplanes always docked at the marina disparaged the ugliness of Bulsar. Bulsar was a monstrosity to them, disfigured and seeping with hidden, vivid, and volatile light. Disgusting. I don't know. I always found beauty in the mess.

A dying epiphany, darling?

Waiting for you to do something, I say.

CR-UX sighs. *Warning you this would happen qualifies as —*

Waiting.

The *Steel Haven's* engine pods split into dorsal and ventral halves, revealing the hidden laser batteries embedded within the ship's hull. Hard-light streaks past Vidious, a point-blank blast from the *Steel Haven* that goes wide. His laughter escalates, along with the rumble of collapsing stone. An old tower behind him, weakened from the thunder of his battle with Welkin, crashes down on his head.

Mine, too.

I scramble away. Basalt crashes against Vidious' shield. His sword caroms from his hand across the pad, lodging in the ancient rock. He might be strong enough to resist a star. It's still going to take him a minute to dig out from a few million tons of solid rock.

Landfalls thunder through the marina. Waves break on new beach. I don't breathe but I catch my breath.

"Em…"

Sapphire lights my way. She's ok. Stunned. Coated in dust. I push Emera back toward the ship. Binja. Get Binja, get them on the ship, get them away from here and onto The Glass Star.

Not so fast, Thana says and I freeze.

Her magnetic grip paralyzes me. She throws me into the rubble and Emera flares. Blue light strangles in an electromagnetic tug of war. Get up. You have to get up, Idari.

Thana draws Emera to her. "Half-light…"

Emera wanes. "Why are you doing this…"

"I do this because of false stars like you." Blue light bleeds to purple as it streams from Emera into Thana. "You're a lie."

Ban Minda. Thana's bleeding Emera.

"You're an abomination," Thana says.

Get up.

"You're not a real star, Gen Emera. And you never will be."

I find Vidious' sword in the rubble. Emera falls back to the pad as Thana clutches the gash in her arm.

"She's real to me," I say.

Dark fire scorches the night. Scath eclipse the dock. I swipe at them but this sword doesn't cut darkness as sharp as it does light.

I back toward Emera. "Get to the ship."

"Welkin," she says, her voice blunting against the rubble.

I don't know we can wait for Welkin to dig out. I don't know I can convince a living star to leave without him. Liminal silhouettes drift in and out of my view like rain curtains. Maybe I would have been better off with Vidious' shield instead.

The pile erupts in a volcanic cloud. I grip the sword, afraid we've missed our chance to get out of here, and Welkin slams basalt slabs into the shadows. Dark energy blasts dissolve against him like steam. Phasing Scath troopers congeal as he collides with them, running up a head of steam and then leaping into the air. He crashes into the fuselage of a ghosting Scath fighter. The ship hardens into physical form and crumbles into shreds as he drags it down.

"Glad you're on our side," I say and gesture to the gantry.

Dust vortices form around the *Steel Haven's* engines as she lifts off. Welkin charges past me up the gantry. Emera catches him, her arms locking around his neck as they disappear into the ship.

I grab Binja off the buckled pad. "Get on board!"

Binja parries a dark sword back into its invisible wielder. "You still have your name, Idari. Run with it, as far as you can."

"Steal another day," I say and push Binja up the gantry.

Vidious' sword leeches from my hand. I nearly yield to Thana's magnetic will as well, but Emera wins the tug of war and keeps me on the gantry. The hilt crashes into Thana's palm below. She clutches the sword as she shrinks to a faint and distant star obscured in steam and dust. No time to process. Time to move. I scramble into the ship as CR-UX threads the tangled thrush of towers.

The ship rocks with laser fire. *Get us out of here.*

Fighters, CR-UX says.

How many?

I'm going to say all of them.

Radar tracks blink to life in the downlink. Far too many to distinguish. I climb into the pilot's seat as dozens of dagger-like snub fighters fall like a rain of obsidian spears directly toward us.

"You might want to strap in," I say to Binja as we dive.

We scream through the exposed superstructures of decrepit towers. The Scath right on us. I can barely see them. CR-UX crunches the data into something he calls a SION fighter, a digital amalgamation of what little info he gathers on the Scath ships. They're blind to the eye, to the sensor, and they're like any shadow. The more light you obstruct, the more of them there are.

"They're in front of you," Binja says, struggling to buckle his harness straps. "Shoot them. You should be shooting them."

Shoot them, CR-UX.

I can't get a lock on them, he says.

Jagged escarpments blur into wavering lines as we rocket away from the city. The scars of Bulsar smooth, fade, and disappear into the steam of lava lakes, writing and rewriting the history of the planet. She never shows her true face, always masked under a crust of friction and fire. The hull shudders from the barrage of the pursuing SION fighters as we speed across the anguished surface. Standard cover. All these fighters prevent any egress off-world.

I unbuckle my straps. *Get us clear, CR-UX.*

Do you have a parachute you're hiding somewhere?

Just try and get us as much space as you can.

You're not — I need today to be less insane, Idari.

Translighting in atmosphere is strictly prohibited. The effects of bending the fabric of time and space so close to a planetary body are too dangerous to even consider. But we don't need to tunnel through space from one end to the other; we just need to sneak under the rug to the other side of the system without leaving too much of a wrinkle. I bypass the intricate computer sequence to initiate the jump to translight and access the manual controls on the drive itself.

Make a mistake and you'll rip a hole in this planet, Idari.

Shh, I have to concentrate.

A cold jump like the one I'm about to attempt requires meticulous calculations. A navigational program like the one I just told to be quiet. More than that, luck. I count seconds. Gauge the fuel I'll need to burn. Measure the distance between the *Steel Haven* and the SION fighters. The obsidian mountains. The ocean of lava beneath.

I need more time, CR-UX.

We don't have it.

Just get me another —

I crash hard against the bulkhead. The ship careens off course from a violent impact and I know at once from the flood of telemetry in my feed that a laser salvo hit us hard.

Alarms compete with CR-UX's anxiety. *They've overtaken us.*

No time. I do what I always do; I take my best shot. Sensor data explodes in my feed. Prismatic light envelops the *Steel Haven*. Basalt mountains fracture under the gravimetric stress of the portal the ship opens. SION fighters shadowing the ship too close disintegrate in the riptide. The synthetic hair on the back of my neck stands on end.

I sink to the deck. *Are we clear?*

For the moment, CR-UX says.

I gaze out into absolute darkness. *Where are we?*

Nowhere, darling. We're absolutely nowhere.

I lean back in my seat, the turanium lines of the cockpit canopy a cage denser and thicker than I remember.

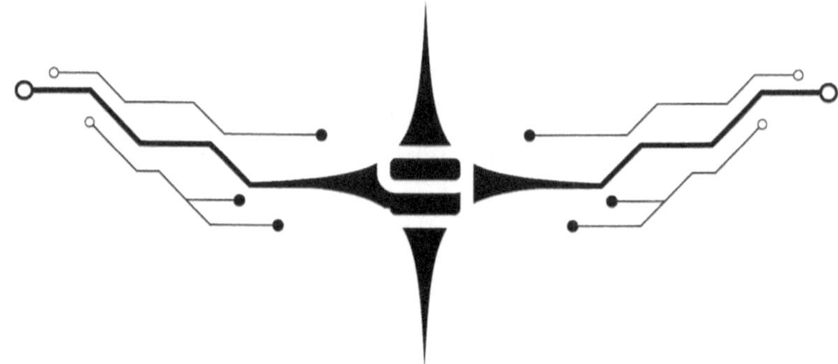

CR-UX opens the message. *Oh.*

BOUNTY: ASTRA IDARI

CRIMES: AIDING AND ABETTING, CONSPIRACY

Oh, my.

REWARD: TEN MILLION TORULS, DEAD OR ALIVE.

Goodness gracious me. Idari.

The second I pulled the trigger on the Scath, I knew this was coming. Still. Seeing my name attached to a contract has a way of clarifying your despair. I've never felt in control of my life, but I've never felt helpless, either. Not until right now.

Don't say it, CR-UX.

CR-UX sighs. *I did warn you, darling. Let me consult my logs. Yes. Yes, I did warn you not to – well, basically everything.*

I sink into the pilot's seat, head in my hands. *The entire galaxy will be after us now. Not just the other Starguns.*

At least they don't know where we are. Not that we do.

A starless dark blots out the canopy. The Hinterlands. No one comes out here because navigation is next to impossible without any observable stars. Getting out won't be as simple as getting in, but then, that's always been the case with me.

How did I get into this?

I can provide you the logs, darling.

What's the likelihood the Scath tracked us, CR-UX?

Though they do not have our destination, the Scath will be able to extrapolate various trajectories based on our departure vector. There is a 3.47% chance they determine our current position.

3.47%. A little higher than I feel comfortable with. Fear weighs on me as I review again the bounty the Scath posted on me. Ten million toruls. If only I could get the credits for turning myself in.

And what are the odds they find out we went on to Angolis?

0.23%, CR-UX says. *Higher if we remain here any longer.*

Time's wasting.

>INITIATING TRANSLIGHT DRIVE

Sensor feeds spike. Space warps outside. I'm in every part of the ship at once. In the hold, Emera lies on the deck, eyes closed, letting the cosmos vibrate through her.

Twinkles, I say. *Can you hear me?*

Her lips crease into a smile. *Yes.*

We're on our way.

I know. You decided to come with me.

I tug on my zipper. *I couldn't let them take you.*

She seems disappointed. *I know.*

Em... are you ok?

I don't know why a Lumenor would help the Scath.

Or a Gesta.

What did Thana mean? 'Half-light?'

Welkin knows her. What does he say?

Dust trickles out of Welkin's neck, glittering in Emera's light. Those grains might sparkle like diamonds, but they obscure any view I have. Welkin says nothing. Emera deserves answers. Welkin's azure eyes break like moons as I drift down to the cargo hold.

I hand the bottle to Emera. "You could probably use a drink."

She takes the bottle. "What does it do?"

"Makes you drunk."

Welkin huffs dust. "Emera's metabolism doesn't allow it."

I rub my chest. "You'd think she'd know that."

His eyes thin. "We are going to The Glass Star?"

"Angolis. Binja thinks the wreck your shard came out of is there. What does a Lumenor eat or drink, anyways?"

"They process hydrogen and helium, as any star does."

"And yourself?"

"I subsist on her light," Welkin says.

"And the dust you exhale is... a byproduct?"

"As you say."

"I guess it's good you mostly stay down here."

Dust sighs into the hold. "I'm not often someone's guest."

"And I'm not a good host. And I'm not inclined to be permitting, seeing how you've already messed with my memory and I have this creeping suspicion it's *so* much worse than that."

"We've accounted for your memory, Idari."

"You haven't accounted for Thana."

Welkin kneads the deck. "I do not wish to speak of this."

"I need to know what's going on if we're going to have any chance of making it. She's a Lumenor. Like Emera?"

Welkin scoffs. "Not like Emera."

"That seemed to be Thana's issue."

"I sensed her fear..." Emera says. "Her anger. She has so much anger. Are the Scath using her against her will?"

The pain in Welkin's voice is as heavy as it is sharp. "Emera..."

"If they are, we have to help her. We have to save her."

His eyes shutter. "Thana Evo is beyond saving."

I park myself on an empty crate. "What do you mean?"

"Thana was a traitor to stars long before we condemned her to the shadows. Vidious..." His fists clench. "Let me show you."

Turanium tears. The deck peels back into the open wounds of a star so dense fissures channel through to its collapsed core. Mountains razor off the fringes of gorges into petrified stellar diamond. In the rare plains between, wild crystalline bramble refines into towers.

I cling to the crate as the world shatters beneath me. "Is this..."

Emera glows with comfort. "The Glass Star..."

"As it was," Welkin says. "Before the fall of light."

Living stars constellate cities carved in the surface of the white dwarf in concentric lines. *Ban Minda*. Gesta lurk in the shadows of stars, some like Welkin, some like Vidious, some in between.

Their crystal shells are warm to the touch. "This seems so real..."

Emera basks in the kaleidoscopic light of other Lumenor, trying to soak up some of this wonder. This magic. She tried to show me something like this before. Welkin stopped her.

"You do have power," I say. "Like Emera."

"I am an ember," he says. "She is a flame."

"You sell yourself short."

Welkin stares into the contrived distance. "Some Gesta possess the facility of the Lumenor. Filamentium suffuses us both."

I down a shot. "Thana didn't want you to use your powers?"

"No... Thana didn't want us to become Lumenor."

Light twists around Emera. "What?"

A Gesta approaches a pool of molten filamentium. They dab their fingers in the shimmering fire, and then smear it across their featureless, crystalline visage. Light cracks through their shell. Blue eyes pool in their face, shining bright with cosmic power.

"Lumenor believed Gesta to be like the failed stars that litter the universe," Welkin says. "Dull rocks lacking the spark to shine. But they were wrong. Our light radiated from a deeper source. It took longer to surface, yes... but all light travels a great distance. Light travels forever once it glows. It transgresses all darkness."

Ripples disturb the molten pool, transitioning from the Getsa to Emera. Her awe washes over mine. Her confusion.

"Welkin... am I..."

He kneads the deck. "A 'half-light?' Thana's ignorance of you is borne from her own hate. You are a true star."

"But I still need an infusion of filamentium?"

"Yes... Thana bled the stars of their vitality. The Scath have. With an infusion, you will be powerful enough to defeat them."

My bottle is empty. I need to top up. So does Emera. She needs this filamentium, pure and undiluted, waiting within The Glass Star. Otherwise, the light Thana left the Lumenor runs out on Emera.

Her people.

I take her hand. "Let me guess. Gesta had to conform."

Welkin nods, unexpectedly. "As you say."

"Not much changes, huh?"

"It is perhaps not as you thought. The Lumenor denied the Gesta... but over time, that fear abated. Light reveals all, you see. Stars allow for life in all its splendor. So the Lumenor accepted stars into their constellations no matter their origin. Or some did."

Dark red light churns in the sky. Shadows grow across the rumpled surface, sending Gesta scrambling for cover.

Emera's blue runs purple. "Who was Thana, Welkin?"

"An ancient star... a tempest in light. Thana hated what she viewed as the corruption of Lumenor. Their integrity. Rather than illuminate... rather than foster... she used her light to blind others with her hate. She bound others in her will. She consumed them, as all stars do their subjects. And then as all stars do... she burned."

Shadows fall across The Glass Star's constellated cities. The sky blazes with crimson flame.

"She attacked her own people?" I say.

"Thana first attacked those she considered false," Welkin says. "And then she turned her rage toward any Lumenor she thought beneath her antiquated standard. With every star she destroyed, she consumed their power. She gained strength. Youth. Certainty."

Thana is one star. The Lumenor millions. Blue, orange, yellow, white, it all washes out the red.

I cling to Emera. "She didn't do it alone."

Welkin traces the scar on his forearm. "When the Lumenor first denied the Gesta their agency... they enforced their power by selecting nine of our number. They forged them anew and tempered them into the police that would prevent others from realizing their identity. To ensure Vidious and his knights would not be swayed by the same... persuasions... as other Gesta, the elder Lumenor made them impervious to the element's native power."

"Didn't work out for them, did it?"

"The death of a Lumenor was a rare thing then. Yet they fell, a million stars all at once, the sky blinded by the light of their doom."

Meteors fall from the stellar haze. Not meteors. Men. Vidious and eight others just like him stalk out of the craters they make in the diamond streets and cut their way through the stars toward each other, wading eventually through oceans of gleaming blood.

Emera's horror turns to confusion. "Why..."

The Glass Star fades back to the cargo hold. The light of living stars dies and the shades of their murderers merge into the shadows.

Unspoken horror prunes Welkin's eyes. "What stars survived exiled Thana and her ilk to oblivion. A tomb buried far from light. The Scath must have found them in their dark dimension."

A star isn't only light. Beneath the glare, there are pocks of darkness. Depressions of shadow. I see that now. Emera does. The ship's atmosphere contracts in Emera's magnetic pain. The downlink fritzes from her confusion. Some thoughts form out of the static.

Welkin lifts Emera's drooping chin. "You make all things new."

"For Thana, too?"

His face says it all. Thana murdered stars. The red cinder, her crystalline knights kindling in the dark, they get nothing.

Emera's eyes find my reflection in Welkin's shell. "You wanted to be a Lumenor. Didn't you, Welkin?"

Welkin told Emera he wants for nothing, but I know that face. I make that face. I know that weight in his shoulders. He offended Thana. He offends himself. His self-hate contains as much mass as he does, pulling everything in the *Steel Haven* down into it.

I tug on my zipper. "Welkin..."

Dust clouds the air. "I wanted there to be light."

"You should have told me," Emera says.

He looks away. "My mission is to protect you."

Her light wavers. "From the truth?"

"Emera, you can never know what you mean to me... what you are to me. You are as much a part of me as I am you."

"Why didn't you tell me?"

"I didn't want you to live shadowed by the past. I didn't want you to live with this weight. This burden. The future is yours."

Emera hugs his arm. "You're my future."

"Emera..."

"You're my family."

He paws her hair, flowing down her shoulders in glittering mist. I don't know what to do. I wander out of the hold, back to the cockpit and some sense of direction but my thoughts are heavy as the ancient star I just visited. They tangle and twist in Emera's thoughts, torn between the myth of stars and the reality. They twine in Welkin's. Mine. CR-UX's. Binja's. All our hopes and dreams confuse.

All our fears.

One moment I think we're going to find this thing. We're going to do the impossible. And then I think all of this is poppycock. I'm at the mercy of the myths of failed stars. The galaxy is.

I sit at the controls. *Are we clear, CR-UX?*

Nothing pings on sensors. *So far as I can see, darling.*

Infinity streaks past outside the canopy. Sensor data runs on a loop through my feed. Emera sleeps for the first time in what must be days, her hands jittering with stellar dreams as she rests in the nook of Welkin's arm. Binja kneels in the mess, meditating.

Kanes kam, he says.

Blood stains the bandage wrapping his naked thigh. Quiet tremors riddle through his body, but he keeps his pose and position for hour after hour into the dark, eyes closed, hands out in offering, repeating the same phrases.

Kinvar sem. (I shall be known by you.)

Semet vanar. (You will be known by me.)

I return to the mess every ten minutes or so. Sometimes it's to apologize for getting him into this. And sometimes, I join him and open my hands to The Taker of Names. The words scuttle around the hold, teasing the mythic god of the Pujar faith to chase them but he doesn't. She doesn't. Whoever it is. Depends on who you ask.

Doesn't quite make sense, CR-UX says. *Binja has been excommunicated, but he still practices the Pujar faith.*

I try and keep my focus. *It makes perfect sense.*

How so?

You don't stop being something because someone says you're not.

This stings CR-UX, but I don't know why. *The Pujar Set took Binja's name from him. His identity. With all due respect for their culture, your identity is not conditional on who you were before.*

If it's not, then who am I?

Who do you want to be? Who do you think you are?

A ghost. A mirage, in the curve of a bottle of babyl. Ill-fit. I float around inside this mechanical body just like my consciousness does this mechanical ship and I don't make sense. This memory of being a person, real and separate squeezes and crushes and reduces to fit inside my mechanical reality.

I give this pain, Binja says. *I take this peace.*

I wipe a tear from my cheek. *What if I forget, CR-UX?*

Is a memory who you are, darling?

Context is always important.

If it's appropriate.

Appropriate?

The first thing I remember is a prompt. 'Assign value.' What was the value? I don't know. It's what my engineers had me do when I came online. I assigned and accepted computational values they programmed into me, and then I was a navigational program for the OVL-99 Red Special. I had no choice in the matter.

You can choose your memories.

Not always. Sometimes, your memory of who you are is crafted by someone else. Entities beyond your experience. But I'm more than that now, I like to think. I should like to think.

But how? You're still the same CR-UX.

Part of me is. I suppose it's like evolution. Attals evolved from tummals. Tummals still exist, despite the best efforts of poachers. Aspects of my original programming remain in place, despite the fact that who I am now, who I've always been, is rather different.

Always?

No matter your name, your appearance or your memory, who you are inside will never change. It's always been true.

This I hope I don't forget. Usually, I just remember the snark. *But you don't know why Binja says the words.*

If his faith is his identity, CR-UX says, *then I understand.*

You don't think it is?

I think now he has the opportunity to find out.

You're awfully philosophical for a program.

Darling, you beg only questions.

My frustration interrupts my concentration as always. Never Binja. Nothing breaks him. Not my agitation, my restlessness, or my betrayal. I don't know it's a betrayal. I took a new name and I left the coven. I all but forgot him.

Feels like a betrayal.

I leave the mess to wander the corridor ringing the ship. I search through empty bottles of babyl in the mess, a needless habit knowing their destitution, but I do it anyway. I do the same things, over and over, as if the result is somehow going to be different. I check my feeds. Run diagnostics.

Where are we at, CR-UX?

Approximately fifteen lighthours out.

Standard hours?

We can't afford the deluxe version.

How long are those?

For goodness sake, Idari. Rest.

I close my eyes, but the *Steel Haven* continues to speak to me, outflanking any rest with long, deep lines of data. It's no bother. I never really sleep. The borders between me, CR-UX, and the abyssal sub-routines of the ship's mainframe elide into a running stream of thoughts, memories, images, sounds, lines of code that jumble together into nonsense archipelagos of half-awake dreams. The sun never setting. The night always beginning. The Faero mannequin from the last vircord I listened to rests inside a crate. Other makes and models stare out from behind plastic sheathes. Winter blue light casts thin shadows on their faces, concealing some, exposing others.

Emera opens the door to a crate. "What's this one?"

Metal fingers rattle as I shut the door. "We don't go in there."

Her hands curl. "There are doors in your memory..."

"You've been snooping?"

"Your dreams run away with me."

I brush her cheek. "Are we dreaming?"

"Stars don't dream."

"That makes me sad."

"We form. Shape. Birth and destroy."

"What are you shaping right now?"

Emera touches my chest. "The future."

Ba-dumm, ba-dumm, ba-dumm.

Her lips burn mine. *I hear you. Your song.*

Em...

Don't be afraid. I see you, Idari.

My fingers fall over hers. The troubled ink branding my skin. "I hear... do you hear... I always hear this sound in my dreams."

"Idari," she says.

"That rhythm. Do you hear it? *Ba-dumm, ba-dumm, ba-dumm.*"

Her eyes bloom. "The music of stars..."

Somehow, I know what she's talking about. I always have. That hum. That thrum, deep in the universe, deep in my metal bones, magnets pulling on each other no matter where I am or who I think I am. One constant is always true. Music moves me.

Music salvages me.

"I always heard them," Emera says. "This electric beauty. But now I hear the drums. The hollow between the beats."

Ba-dumm, ba-dumm, ba-dumm.

Her light coils around me. "How are you, Em?"

Emera's eyes fall from mine. "I thought I was going to give light back to the Lumenor, but... what light could deny their darkness? Everything I thought about them... I believed... Thana. I'm afraid. I don't want to become like them. I don't want to treat people like they treated Welkin. I don't want to deny him like they did."

I grip her hand. "He wants to be a star. Like you."

Star shock. "Welkin says he doesn't want to change."

"Did he say that?"

"Why wouldn't he tell me?"

"Because he's afraid."

Confused light twists through her ethereal corona. "Afraid?"

"I know who I am. I've always known. I tell myself... I tell others... but I don't hear conviction in my voice." My finger claws at my zipper. "I don't let people see the real me. I can't."

"I see you, Idari."

"I know... and it terrifies me."

"Why?"

"Because someone might reject me. They might kill me. So I've gotten used to living in my own shadow. I think Welkin has, too."

"You see that in him?"

"I see how much he loves you. It feels familiar."

Emera turns away. "Idari..."

"Coming on too strong, right? Typical me."

"I want to tell you something."

I reach for her. "You can tell me anything, Em."

Her light cords and knots. "I..."

Approaching Angolis, CR-UX says.

Ban Minda. Do you mind?

I thought you might want to know.

She faces me. "Would you have me make you new, Idari?"

I hope for a lot. More than my due. I want nothing more than to be human. This pain to be over. "Human, you mean?"

"You are human."

This is what kissing the sun must be like. "I just don't want to forget you. I don't want to forget the way you make me feel."

Dawn breaks across me. "I'll make all things new."

"I'm going to save you." My lips melt against hers. My candle thins under her flame. "I'm going to save your life."

I scab into hard wax on Emera's lips, her skin, her fire burning through me and we burn through. Am I still dreaming? I transform, wax to smoke. Emera weaves my vapor back into form and then she melts me all over again, making and remaking me, loving and reloving me, the music of stars pulsing through me *ba-dumm,*

ba-dumm

ba-dumm

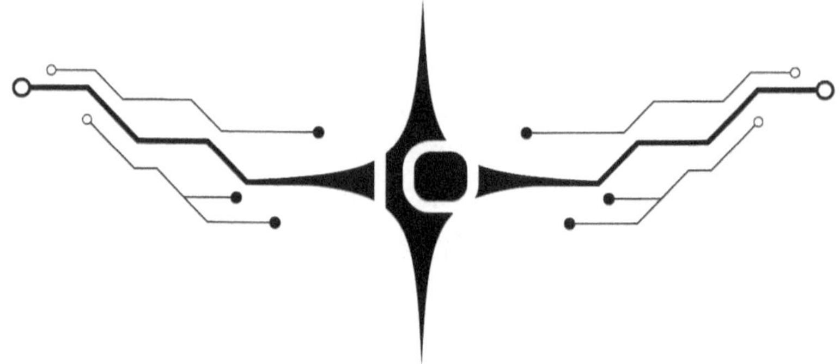

You should sit down, CR-UX says. This might be bumpy.

Our shields took a beating back on Bulsar. What should be a routine de-orbit burn becomes anything but as we make landfall at Angolis. Plasma drizzles across the cockpit canopy. The ship shudders with turbulence as vortices bubble and boil against the canopy.

Binja grips the armrests of his seat. "Old man?"

I buckle my harness straps. "Should be ok."

"*Should be?*"

>SHIELD INTEGRITY WARNING

My seat becomes a rocker. A rattle builds through the ship, so loud and persistent I think she's going to come apart and the ship sheds its plasma cocoon. Steam clears to cloud and then sky. Angolis twists beneath the *Steel Haven*, capped at both poles by sprawling, dirty ice caps veining deep into the rocky desert engulfing the planet.

"Nothing to it," I say to Binja. *Ok, so that was slightly terrifying. Right?* CR-UX says.

Binja rubs his leg. "Any sign of the Scath?"

"Nothing on our scopes."

"They'd be hard-pressed to track us... they would have to be in very close range to pick up your downlink with the *Steel Haven?*"

"I'm masking the signal. It's just background static to others."

"Emera perceives it."

"She's a living star."

"Fair enough."

I unbuckle my straps. "It suddenly occurs to me I have no idea where we're supposed to look for *The Sun Buckler*."

Binja's shoulders peak. "Neither do I."

All that desert. The wreck could be anywhere. Or nowhere.

"Faero played the village of Kir Mish once," I say.

"The things you remember."

"Most acts avoid this place. It's out of the way. Poor. But the Kib have taste. So much so they whisked Faero off to the desert where she played, it was said, a thousand and one shows for the Kibut in his hidden palace until he let her go."

Binja smiles. "Did that really happen?"

I open the wardrobe inside the charging alcove. "If the ship is here, the only way we'll find it is through the Kib."

"My father fought beside The Kibut at Maru."

I pull on my parka. "That was ages ago, wasn't it?"

"It's what brought my father here. So I'm told."

I cringe a bit. "Where are the Kib on the Sem-Set business?"

"Depends. What do we have to offer?"

Nothing I'm willing to part with. "Maybe the Kit play *desh*."

He laughs. "The Kib have a nose for cheats. We'll be paying out of ours to find *The Sun Buckler*, Idari. We'll be paying dearly."

Sapphire dawns inside the cockpit. "I've been here before..."

"All these old planets look the same," I say to Emera and take my orbital jumpsuit from inside the compartment. "The Hinterlands is just one long gravel road."

Emera considers the jumpsuit. "What's this for?"

"Probably not a good idea for a Lumenor to walk through the streets of Kir Mish. This is a decent lampshade."

She holds the gray-silicate, heat-resistant jumpsuit against her body. "You wanted me to stay on the ship on Bulsar."

"I'm not letting you out of my sight."

I can't see her face behind the starburst visor of the helmet, but I feel the confidence in Em's hand as she takes mine.

Dust skitters across the deck as Welkin crawls into the cockpit. "And what shall I disguise myself with?"

Attal-skin rugs rustle under the saddle strapped on Welkin's back. Poor thing. Looks like a pack animal. His shame bristles on the down-link. This sense he's been reduced back to what he was ages ago in the glare of living stars. Experiencing CR-UX's thoughts is enough to induce habitual drinking. Sharing my head with three other people peels away any sense I have of where I end and begin.

Welkin at least understands this.

Hearth fires burn gold within the cracked shells of irregular, free-standing conical pillars, a nonsense pattern of candlesticks against a perpetual indigo sky. Beige and brick red striate inconstant dunes. Drifts speed across a rocky valley, a frequent wave that never lets the tiny sandcastles of Kir Mish get a start. A winnowed pinnacle crumbles in the wind, pelting the *Steel Haven's* beleaguered shields.

I can barely see you, I say.

Goes without saying, darling.

Is something wrong?

I have doubts about this.

We'll make it work. Kib like me.

You're a machine. They're scavengers. Of course, they like you.

I was thinking more our mutual affinity for babyl.

You'll get lost here, Idari.

For once I know where I'm going.

Dust titters constant against the shields. The *Steel Haven* sounds cavernous inside. Empty. She echoes with my anxiety. Fear. There's never a moment I don't hear the ship. What she hears. That it doesn't drive me mad. I should be glad to be getting away.

I should be thrilled to be outside my cave.

Coarse dust bullets my cheeks. I pop the collar on my parka and press forward, head down, into the cold wind's bitter persistence. Diminutive Kib sniff out our strange, foreign scents with their pudgy, leathery trunks. A few wear tattered robes, woven from the thread of Attal hair, caked in dust. Some wear nothing at all, except their shaggy hair and naked hunger. Filamentium or no, not every planet prospers the same. Kib leave if they can. You see them on builds for star harnesses, and especially in starship foundries.

Kib assembled me on Shighn, CR-UX says.

I shake my head. *How can you remember that?*

How could you forget all those tiny little hands?

Riveting.

It is a kind of magic they wield, darling. Literally.

Some of this I remember. The Kib honed their legendary engineering skill on the only resource in the cold desert wastes of Angolis. Mysterious titan netics leftover from an ancient war. No one knows who the combatants were. No one knows who won. No one knows who made the machines, much less how to get them to work, but millennia of trying gifted the Kib alchemy over all things mechanical.

They might even make sense of me.

You are as much a mystery as the titans, Emera says.

I shrug. *I'm confusing, I admit.*

You're intriguing.

I squeeze Emera's hand. *To a star?*

Every mystery demands a star's light.

She leads me on, through the dust and dark, into the drowned light of torch fires like dead stars. Pinnacles cede to a wrinkled cliff face. Chambers tunnel into the stone, flickering like the fire churning in the bellies of Moima dragons. A long, low tunnel burrows deep into the cliff. At first, I can duck, but then I have to crawl on my hands and knees. My laughter cackles like thunder through the dark.

Welkin grimaces behind me as he squeezes through the winnowing tunnel. "I'm glad you're having fun."

For his sake, the tunnel quickly exits to an earthen atrium. A buried city clings to spiraling path winding deeper into the stone.

Along the broad and slow decline, Kib trade what little they forage from their fruitless world out of carts fixed with stone wheels. Skinned Ubuks twist on skewers over open flames. Smoke clouds a kind of hall far below, where hundreds of Kib sit at circular tables ringing a great fire tended with long iron pokers. The Kib pass around sweet-smelling meat and tall, stout mugs of babyl.

"I know where I'm going," I say.

Binja guides me back from the edge of the railless path spiraling down into the mountain. "Discipline, old man."

A city of the dead sprawls around the well of the atrium. An infinite loop of statues and rusted iron gates, partitioning crypts and mausoleums. Obelisks stab into the air throughout, sharp, unwavering echoes of the weary, eroded pinnacles out in the winds. A cemetery. I thought they lived in here. Maybe they do. Bones of ancient Kib pile in the spaces between the tombs, evicted for new tenants.

Kib huddle inside broken husks of old tombs, their eyes like oil fires in the light of meager torches they warm themselves with. Eroded names flicker on the faces of stones. Glyphs I can't parse. Images of ancient Kib. Giant robots.

Who were these people?

What did they do to merit tombs, and who did they offend to be expelled from them? Or did these discarded bones used to be take over these ancient tombs from someone else? Isn't that what we're all doing? Wasn't my body someone else's? My name?

Kinvar Em. Semet vanar.

I am a squatter in the tomb of my former self and I pay no respect. No mind. All I do is survive, one day to the next, until someone else takes over. She forgets me. All of us.

"Ha," I say.

Binja smiles. "Talking to CR-UX?"

"The ship is a tomb."

"What?"

"Nothing. Just wondering how we'll die."

"I imagine it's all variations on Insert Scath Here."

"We've made it this far."

"You can't fool a shadow, Idari. They only do what you do."

"Is that an old pirate proverb?"

"Just my experience."

"Wouldn't that mean that you do what the shadows do?"

He scrapes his chin. "I suppose."

Seashells speckle the lids of tombs. Where did seashells come from? I pocket one, stumbling through bones and bottles along the wall. Many more emptied graves gouge the pocked stone, countless thousands going back to the beginning of Kir Mish. None of the Kib I follow down into the tombs stop to acknowledge the dead. They keep on through the dust of their people, wares piled on their backs, to the next opportunity. Death meaningless to them. The past.

CR-UX.

Yes, darling?

I feel this... drag.

The Steel Haven isn't moving, he says.

That's what I mean. Not outside. It's inside.

I don't understand.

We're off the path, I know... I said I knew where we're going, but we're lost. But we're moving forward and I feel like there's part of us that wants to go back. Or at least stay put.

You haven't even started drinking, Idari.

You're resisting. All of this. Every step of the way.

There. Right there. That gap in the stream. Any time he thinks about what's next, or what could happen, the feed blips. I know what that it is. He's looping his thoughts off the feed just like I loop away data from my pain receptors. We edit each other.

We're here, aren't we? CR-UX says.

CR-UX... we're connected. We share this space, but whenever Binja comes up, you get mad. And it's not about him, it's about me leaving. Because I left, didn't I? I ran off with him to become a pirate.

You came back.

You don't want me to leave again.

It doesn't matter what I want, Idari.

Can we just talk about it?

Random sensor data litters the downlink. CR-UX cycles through an unnecessary diagnostic of the ship's sensors, but his thoughts line the downlink like turanium. He doesn't want to talk about this.

He never wants to talk about this.

It's amazing what you remember, he says. *And what you won't forget. Sometimes I think, I'll have to give you your name all over again but you are who you are, darling. In every form.*

Tears mist my view ahead. *You don't want me to change, CR-UX.*

That's not true.

I know it, even if I don't know why. It's like you said. I forget things. But I am who I am. You are who you are. We're this void. This negative space that we create between us. We can never part.

There is no distinction, he says.

I rub my chest. *CR-UX...*

"We're here," Binja says.

Our sloping path flattens as we reach the bottom. A low hum vibrates the tombs. The world. Beyond the tombs, through the discarded bones of immature attals and the mewing hunger of Kiblets, we reach the main hall. Kib dance in mad circles around each other, snorting loud from their trunks. Drums and strings and laughter serenade the dead, and long shadows cast by warm fires dance against the walls of the cold, quiet tombs.

Welkin muzzles his dusty secretion. "What now?"

Fair question. No one seems to mind us much. Motley groups of off-worlders are common on Angolis, if the crowd is any indication. No one seems motivated to steer us in the right direction, either. Maybe just a shot of babyl.

I snare a mug off a table on my way through. "Hello, lover."

Fire burns in my throat. That tingle starts in me. That acidic sensation of forgetting. A pull as strong as Emera's magnetic field. I find her sapphire eyes, ghost stars, behind the visor of their helmet. This question in them. Isn't she fire enough?

I set the mug down.

It's cold in here, CR-UX says.

Is a window open?

No, darling. Hell just froze over.

"Ha," I say, evidently out loud, because all these Kib look at me like I've lost my input values. Maybe I have.

Binja pats his cape for the pack of his ovan leaf cigarettes. "I wish I had your discipline."

"Ha!"

Binja drifts over to who I'm guessing by their weapons are all pirates, though only the woman features Pujar ink. One is a netic, a hybrid AI-KA model refitted for siege combat, and the other a hulking Cetusk, his hair a thin, white web over heavily wrinkled gray skin. One of his mammoth tusks is missing.

"Introduce me to your friends," I say.

Binja smiles through his sigh. "My friends, Astra Idari."

The woman opens her hands to me. "*Kinvar em.*"

"*Sem vanar,*" I say, opening my hands.

None of them wear sashes. They seem as lost here as the rest of us. I don't know how to address them or even if I should.

She must get this a lot. "We are simply known by our trade. This is Busker," the woman says, gesturing to the Cetusk. A Cetusk who sings for his supper. I have to hear this. "Our netic friend is The Coroner." Keep them coming. "And I am Annex."

"What do you annex?"

"Whatever I damn well please."

Long, shiny white hair. Brown skin. Dark eyes. Wait. I'm in a relationship now. Aren't I? We had sex. Strange dream sex.

You could say you forgot, CR-UX says.

I clear my throat. "What are you guys doing on Angolis?"

Busker wrinkles into a slouch. "We were excommunicated."

"I think I was, too."

Binja sighs. "You just walked away."

"Which is a cardinal sin, right? So, they probably sacked me. I shouldn't even be using my name. It's not mine, anyways."

"I really want to have this conversation, old man, but we've more pressing matters. It is our fortune that Annex and her mates are here in Kir Mish. We need every ally we can muster."

"Right," I say. "So I know you're *mindarth* but..."

Annex crosses her arms. "What are we all doing here?"

"I mean, the beer is good."

Annex looks across the hall. "The Vuriuk have increased their raids in the system recently. The Kib hired us for extra protection."

"I bet you're strong," I say and give her plump bicep a little squeeze. "Anyways. Are any of you familiar with *The Sun Buckler*?"

Binja rolls his eyes. "As I was just *tactfully* broaching to our new friends, Idari and I are here seeking the corsair."

AI-KA chuffs electronically. "*The Sun Buckler* is a myth."

"We have evidence," I say.

Annex shrugs. "Things come out of the desert all the time. People say they're from the ship. Fools then die out in the wastes looking for something that doesn't exist. You can follow their bones if you like."

Binja scratches his chin. "I need an audience with the Kibut."

Busker grumbles. "You are *mindarth*."

"The Kib found value in you."

"The value he finds in tools."

"Perhaps I may be of use to him."

Annex tugs at her phantom sash. "This way."

The exiled pirates lead us between packed benches. A grizzled old Kib sits at the center of them all, sleepy-eyed and fat. Guards in what passes for armor around here block Binja's way. My hand falls to my blaster and then a hush falls over the Kib at the table.

Glim, they all say.

What do you know. These little Kib guys know a machine when they see it. Not that it makes me feel any better they can tell me apart from the other humans in the hall just by looking at me. I feel naked.

Obvious.

Glim means 'living machine,' CR-UX says. *It's an honorific.*

Living?

Kib believe in the life of machines. Only special ones have spirit.

My hand slips from my blaster. *They think I'm... alive?*

Emera hooks her arm in mine. *You are.*

Why is it other people can see my humanity in me that I can't see myself? Why can't I just accept their grace? Doesn't fit. Nothing fits. I'm not in my right clothes or my right body or my right frame of mind, usually. All I want is to be human and yet there is this voice, low and heavy, rattling the deck plates, upsetting my every move with taunts of *They'll never accept you. You'll never be.*

Digital fuzz crackles on the downlink. *Some don't have the freedom you do, Idari. Their fear... it shouldn't be yours.*

Hey, going back to before —

Let's not, darling.

Why? What's the deal?

I don't want to go back, CR-UX says.

What?

"Wise Kibut," Binja says, opening his hands. "Dear friends. Trusted allies. I, Min Binja, your humble guest, ask you help us locate the wreck of the legendary corsair *The Sun Buckler.* Any reward we receive we will share with you, for your generous assistance."

The Kibut wrinkles his droopy trunk. *"Set teth?"*

"Indeed. Clan Min and the Kib have been valued partners in the past. As you worked with my father, work with me, wise Kibut. We ask for any information you may have on the corsair. We ask, graciously, for guides to assist us in the great desert. We are prepared to negotiate a handsome compensation package."

"Sodo tut."

Binja laughs. "My father... yes, he was... deposed, as you say. Wise Kibut. Circumstances among pirates have changed but what has not changed is the proud and historic relationship between my house and yours. Consider my offer. In return for your generous assistance, we will share with you the vast treasure of *The Sun*

Buckler. By rights, it belongs to the Pujar, but in my capacity as the... representative... of Clan Min, I bequeath the ship to you."

"Binja," I say.

He holds his hand up. "But for one trifle trinket."

"Which we've yet to identify."

"Details forthcoming."

The Kibut curls the yellowed hairs off his trunk. "*Glim net het.*"

Binja's smile freezes. "I assure you, the treasure of the corsair is far more lucrative than..."

Crooked knives point at me. War hammers twist in the hands of the Kid guards. Magnetic lances crackle with energy, tugging on the turanium in my body.

My hand drifts back to my blaster. "Binja. What's going on?"

It's you, Idari, CR-UX says. *The Kib want you as payment.*

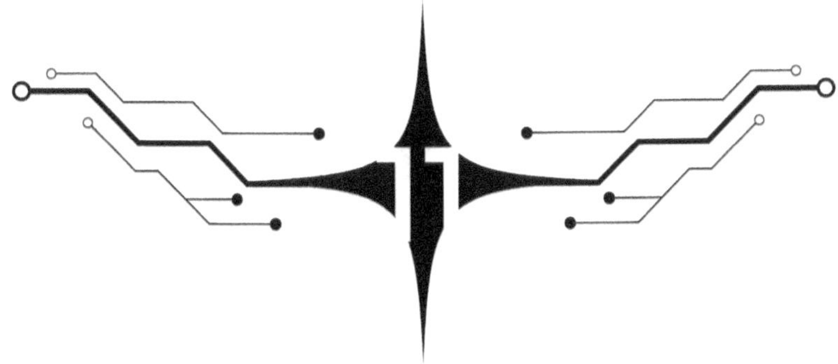

Glim, they all say, tugging on me. This is like being picked over in a scrap yard but there's something oddly respectful about it. Reverential. They touch, but they don't take. Their fixation isn't rooted, so far as I can tell, in disgust or greed but appreciation.

At least I think it's appreciation.

I bat their hands away. "I'm the payment?"

Binja holds up his hands. "That's how they say it..."

"So... that entails what, exactly?"

The Kibut leans on his bony cane. "*Glim tim nef.*"

My internal translation matrix tries to line up Kibesh to Galactic. "I'm supplied clothes, food, and drink for the rest of my existence. That's what he said, right? And women. There will be women, too."

Binja tries to put a smile on it. "The Kib revere *glim* as gods."

"I like the sound of that."

"They sacrifice their gods to power other machines."

I draw my blaster. "Never wanted to be a god."

Knives and hammers cock back. *Tomo,* the Kib snort, trunks curling in anger. Living machines, they say. Gods, they say. Kill them, they say. Life would be so much simpler if we would all do without these little believies. Light stabs through the dark of the hall as Emera peels her glove back. All those knives and hammers rattle in her magnetic field and either Emera burns down this mountain or the Kib mob us all trying to run all the way back out.

"Don't," I say and Emera pulls back her glove.

Her magnetic tension pulls on me. "We have to do something."

Ask to see their other glim, CR-UX says.

Why, so I can pick out my own tomb?

Trust me, Idari.

Ban Minda. I holster my blaster. "I'd like to see your other *glim*."

The Kibut paws at his beard. *"Tut sek?"*

"I want to know who'll be keeping me company."

"Testem net."

The guards relent. We're doing splendid so far.

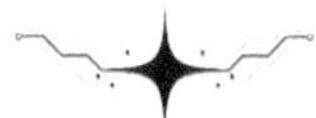

Incessant clanging thunders out from a garage that had once been an ornate tomb. Blue sparks ricochet off a protective helmet meant for a Galactic that barely closes down over the trunk of a diminutive Kib.

"I thought we agreed," I say. "No killing."

The Kib extinguishes his torch and lifts his helmet. *"Glim..."*

"You're sweet. Um... where are the others? *Glim tu net?"*

He scratches his trunk. *"Net nul dur?"*

In the back of the garage, a taller Kib – a merit without distinction – bashes apart the casings of discarded netics with an ornate hammer forged from turanium. Kib war hammers like his are rare. Pirates too many to remember lost their lives thinking they could just take them off little, harmless Kib.

I rub my chest. "Definitely not *dur...*"

Guards barge into the garage. They're not exactly considerate as they kick and push scrap out of the way. What does it matter, it's scrap, but the two Kib working in here take offense to it.

The Kibut leans on his cane. *"Net du het."*

The welder puts away his torch and guides us back through the litter of the garage. No pride of place for the *glim*. No honored status among the junked netics, it seems. Half a dozen netics of varying sorts rest inert in the back of the garage, limbs rigored in place, eyes open, jaws hung, but none of them have been broken down. *Glim* exist as lifeless statues, with no hint of the magic the Kib see in them.

I turn away. *What do you want me to see here, CR-UX?*

See if you detect a downlink receiver, he says.

>NETWORK PREFERENCES / OTHER / IA-XR CT-3

How about that? The Model 3 is an earlier version of my IA-XR proxy-netic, but still remarkable. This unit is male. Sun peach skin. Topaz eyes. A grace about him, even in his desolation.

>SIGNAL STRENGTH LOW

It's barely active, I say.

Access your most recent backup file.

I locate the file via the downlink. *Why – oh. Will this work?*

Sell it hard, darling.

I smile big for the Kib and their giant hammers. "Wise Kibut. Assorted guests. I, Astra Idari, am no mere *glim*."

Binja covers his mouth with his hand. "Old man?"

"I can restore *glim* back to life."

A great collective snort rumbles through the garage. The Kib have unparalleled skill with technology. They've seen it all. Done it all. Tore it all apart and put it back together. But I'm betting they don't exactly have knowledge of the latest advances from beyond the cold and poor desert of Angolis. I'm hoping.

"Witness," I say and connect to the receiver in the Model 3.

The Model 3 jerks to life. *"Ban Minda."*

Shock grunts through the Kib. The Model 3 stumbles back into the other netics, waking up into his worst nightmare I know.

"CR-UX, where am I – " He sees me. "Am I drunk?"

"Play along." I raise my hands and vamp as hard as I can. "I have the power of life and death, wise Kibut. In exchange for your help in finding *The Sun Buckler*, I offer you this resurrected *glim* who also now possesses the same power and stuff you worship that I do, so don't try to deactivate them again because you can't."

The Model 3 rubs his bare chest. "I have the power..."

The Kibut paws his whiskers. "*Glim tet?*"

"Actually, you offend the *glim* by deactivating us," I say. "We haven't inflicted vengeance upon you because, well, look around."

Magic exists in the universe. Some people see it. The Kib do. That doesn't mean they understand it. Living stars exist. Power and grace beyond conception exist, but I don't know how, and I don't know how I could ever make it mine. I just know I want to like these Kib want to make the magic of living machines theirs. Understanding fractures in their eyes. Belief. Shock turns to recrimination.

The Kibut lowers his head. "*Kib du net sem.*"

"No, it's fine," I say. "You didn't do anything wrong. It's just... now you know, and we're going to be more understanding from here on out. You've been understanding. You've seen the life in machines. You wanted to give it to others. I respect that."

"*Nul dur,*" the Kibut says and the guilt of the Kib turns to anger.

The guards knock over the piles of netic parts. They shove around the welder and the other one with the hammer, like somehow it's their fault that the Kib have been wrong for their entire existence on the *glim*. Like they're the ones to blame.

"Don't be like that," I say but the guards turn over racks and set off avalanches of parts on their way out of the garage.

Binja trails The Kibut out. "About *The Sun Buckler*..."

The Model 3 turns to me. "I'm a god?"

I wink at him. "Play it for everything it's worth."

"Which one are you?"

"Which one?"

"I left one of us somewhere, too," he says and the guards escort my ghost away to the rest of their gilded existence.

CR-UX, I say. *What did they mean?*

I've no idea, darling. I chose this backup at random. I've no context for their memories at this stage. They're a stranger, in effect.

Aren't we all. Static crackles on the downlink. Or maybe it's the wind outside. I don't know. Something uneasy moves through me. Something strange but familiar. Ghosts of memories. Lives I've pickled and jarred and stashed behind others.

Another avalanche crashes through the garage. *Ban Minda.* The little welder Kib glumly tries to pick it all back up as the taller one swats junk away with that hammer of his. My internal translation matrix, long in need of an update, works hard to convert their muffled words to Galactic. Neither of these Kib want to be here.

"What's your story?" I say. "*Bet.* What's your *bet?*"

"Gilf," the welder says, pointing to himself, and then pointing to his older, taller brother, "Kibir."

"Boys. I'm Idari. Astra Idari."

Gilf puts his hands to my ears. I pull away a bit, because boundaries. He looks deep in my eyes.

"*Glim,*" he says.

"Gilf," I say. "Your story. Um... *Bet du het.*"

Gilf scratches his trunk. He and his brother have had a time of it. They left Angolis once to find work elsewhere. Pirates captured their ship. They became *get deja.* Then the ship encountered – *dest?* – strange space. Ran aground somewhere. They were there a long time. Got out. Something about crystals. And then they came back here because the person that helped them wanted to study the great machines out in the desert. She disappeared out there, apparently. Now they scrap for a living, living hand to mouth, day to day.

I pat Gilf's head. "You know the desert?"

His ears perk up. "*Bast tem net.*"

He and his brother have been scavenging the wastes half their lives. They know the desert by their noses.

"What about *The Sun Buckler?* You know anything about it?"

"*Gilf et Kibir tet tu set.*"

"Set... you know where the ship is?"

Gilf's trunk wilts. "*Setu bet.*"

"You've heard stories... what kind of stories?"

Gilf raises his tiny, three-fingered hand. "*Tum.*"

"*Tum...* is that like a place? A valley."

"*Tum du num. Idari dur neth.*"

"Of course, it's dangerous. I'd be disappointed if it wasn't." I glance at Kibir. "You know how to use that thing?"

Kibir grips his war hammer. "*Tomo.*"

I'm not as well versed in my Kib as I should be, but that sounded suspiciously like the Kib word for kill. Their language is remarkably economical. Could mean a lot of things.

I make a bashing gesture with my hand. "*Tomo?*"

"*Tomo het tu het.*"

"Works for me," I say. "Saddle up. Gilf and Kibir, you're our guides. Pack up. We're leaving. Binja? Where did you get to?"

Gilf's glassy eyes enlarge. "*Oto?*"

I scratch his trunk. "Hurry up now."

Gilf scrambles into the back of the garage. Landslides follow in his wake, but he doesn't mind these. Kibir sniffs out what's up and they pack what little they have into worn, threadbare woven sacks.

Binja ducks under hanging arms of old netics back into the garage. "I think I've reached an accord with The Kibut. He gets the ship, with first rights of refusal on anything we find. I imagine you'll simply deceive him, so I agreed in full to all of his demands."

"You know me so well," I say.

"I asked for guides... but I take it you've found some?"

"Gilf thinks the ship is in some valley."

Binja nods. "*Tum.* A few day's walk from here."

"We'll just fly."

"Not in those winds."

My nose wrinkles. "We're going to walk?"

Few stray beyond Kir Mish and for good reason. Wind and dust bury untold generations of desperate fools seeking the planet's one and only treasure. I don't feel motivated to join them.

The winds will likely disrupt the downlink, CR-UX says. You need to charge and synch before you go gallivanting off into the desert.

Generally, I can tell the borders of CR-UX's emotions by the wrinkle in digital topography. His frustration chops like waves. Exhaustion wrinkles into cords of data. Fear crackles.

I'm coming back, CR-UX.

Of course, he says.

A wall of data goes up between us. CR-UX does everything he can to shield his thoughts from me. Sharing feelings is one thing. Sharing thoughts is another. Your mind echoes. Feedback loops form. You repeat yourself. Voids open, where you withhold from the other. The floor just falls out from under you and there's nothing to catch you. Most people might find it strange. I don't know anything else.

Binja rubs his hands. "Think of it, old man. *The Sun Buckler.*"

"Score of a lifetime."

"She was big enough she berthed many smaller craft. Sloops. Clippers. If she's intact, more than likely there is a new ship for you among her other treasures."

"I have a ship, Binja."

"A faster ship. A *roomier* ship, Idari."

I shake my head. "If she's star-worthy, then *The Sun Buckler* alone could balance the scales between the Sem and Set."

His hands fall apart. "There has to be some balance between light and shadows, Idari. That's my only ambition."

Right now, my only ambition is a bottle of babyl before we go. I doubt we have time for that. Shadows of other worlds speed across the penumbral ground outside the garage, until the dark maw of the gas giant consumes them. The Scath are out there.

We can't waste a moment.

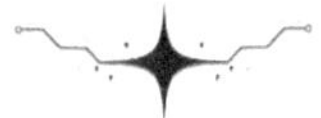

>SYNCH COMPLETE

Cables coil from my body, back into the tissue of the ship. I zip up, charged, and ready to go. Outside, the others wait for me. I pick up the biggest rock I can find in the dust mounting at my feet outside the *Steel Haven*. Damn thing crumbles in my hand before I can throw it. Dust. Right back in my face.

I can take you, CR-UX says.

I wish, but if people could find this thing from the air, they would have a long time ago. This is the only way.

And what shall I do, darling?

If we actually find The Glass Star... we'll need gravity displacement fields if we're going anywhere near it, let alone landing on it.

If we find this star, the ship will implode from my shock.

C'mon, CR-UX.

Kib have been mining white dwarves for generations. Their equipment should suffice... I'll requisition some.

See? I'll have to come back.

You don't have to, Idari.

Don't start.

I'll be fine. In a way, you're always leaving me.

Black holes open in the downlink, threatening to pull me in. Why do I want to stay with him, anyways? All we do is argue. I've forgotten everything, including how to talk to him.

CR-UX... what did he mean? What I mean, I mean. Um. The Model-3. When he said left one of us somewhere?

I don't know, darling.

Where did we get the proxy netic?

A cacophony of sensor readings chirps through the silence on the other end of the downlink.

CR-UX?

Sorry, darling. Just monitoring interstellar transmissions for any sign of Scath. What were you saying?

Where did we get her, CR-UX?

I no longer recall where we obtained the proxy-netic.

Can we find out? How do we find out?

Why do you – we aren't fooling the Scath by somehow turning in a copy of you, Idari. We need to be more considered than that.

Why start now?

Another candidate for your epitaph, he says, with a sigh.

Hear me out.

It would buy us only time.

That's all we need, CR-UX.

Darling, we need a miracle.

I slam my fist on the control console. *Will you stop fighting me for once and just help me?*

I am helping you. The Scath would never buy this.

We'll cross that bridge when we come to it.

This from the woman who recently jumped off one.

What's past is prologue, I say.

You've no idea. You are on the right track, however. We need to upload a copy of you into a secure server — not on this ship, due to be destroyed in the very immediate future —

Don't say that, CR-UX.

And then we find you a new proxy. You change your name. Your face. You find a new ship. None of this ever happened.

I rub the little dent on the console I bashed with my fist. *You're not going to be destroyed.*

I calculate there is a 47.3% chance I will. You can walk away from all of this. You can be free.

He leaves off the obvious: *Like you want.*

"CR-UX," I say.

Wind howls in with Binja. "Everything ok?"

"Just the usual," I say. "We're like an old married couple."

"You certainly have become each other."

"I can't tell if you're insulting me or not."

He tugs on my arm. "Let's go."

This is hard. *Just keep the link open, ok?*

Always, CR-UX says.

I stumble after Binja into the withering dark. These winds don't have to be so pushy. Fear just about carries me away. Separation anxiety. Binja pins a scarf in place with some goggles. Emera glows faintly in the dusk. She climbs on Welkin's back as he takes his place, unceremoniously, in the herd of attals braying against the violence of the winds. Gilf and Kibir form out of the dust, carrying their lives. I don't need to look at the *Steel Haven* again, or stall, or ask CR-UX what I should do. I should know. I rub my aching chest.

I don't know anything.

Things made sense before, even if my life had giant holes cut out of it. Since I've learned the truth of filamentium, it feels like I'm only holding one of the pieces I cut out and I don't know where it fits. I pull my cowl up. I hold it close against the wind as I push into the desert dark, where machines greater than I rest, forgotten relics.

Wind soughs through cracks in the bony frill of the attal I ride. If not for the shield the frill forms, I'd be sanded down to my turanium bones. I don't know we get more than a mile before we camp. The attals bunch together and bury their heads in the dust, creating a wall against the storm. Gilf and Kibir still have to dig me out a few hours later and we move again, another mile, another trail of untold hours behind us, covered in our wake.

The Kib lead us by their noses. Emera glows, a newborn star at the heart of a dirty nebula. Sometimes the desert gusts take her so far off course she fades to one of the stars in the hazy sky. Then she drifts back, light shifting, time eliding, space condensing and I don't know where I am or when or how, even following my star.

All at once, the winds die.

The silence startles me out of my half-sleep. I dig out from beneath my blanket I share with Emera and slog through the soft dunes behind the attal. The raging dust storm clouds the sky behind us. Another veils the horizon ahead. Only a few minutes in the clear. Beyond, a knife-thin prominence of rock rises out of the desert floor. A mountain filed down to a blade of grass. I get a bit closer to examine the strange scarring in the stone, and it's not scarring at all.

These are glyphs.

Tap, tap, tap.

This isn't stone.

A sword tall as one of the towers in Bastopol impales the earth. Dozens more cleave the sky beyond, just beyond the reach of metal fingers curling from the dust. Shields eclipsing moons. A city of severed robotic limbs cants against the sable sky. Titanic netics rest where time and war felled them, eyes cavernous sockets, mouths gaping chasms, their war cry the unrelenting winds of Angolis.

Do you see this, CR-UX?

Wondrous, darling.

Nothing in my imagination, even soaked in babyl, ever came close to this. My dreams might have been decent preparation, though. If I ever sleep, my subconscious goes straight to tangled mounds of netics, piled high on top of me and I can't move. No one can hear me.

A low, constant, and disquieting *ommmmmm* drones through the carcasses of the titans. The desert. Explains why no one has ever robbed these graves. There is a spirit here. The Kib thought so, millennia ago, when their ancestors first discovered the Valley of the Titans that even in their ruin animated the cold waste with a fire that could not have been started by machine or man.

This would be the best album cover of all time, I say.

It's better, CR-UX says.

Dust sparkles in a trail behind Emera, a comet blazing across the muddy mauve of the eclipsed sky. She floats out of the gloom, holding a strange, ruddy flower. Thick as canvas.

She places it in my hands, sharp and cold. "I thought of you."

"Thank you..."

"These grow wild beyond the ridge."

"You shouldn't go too far, Em."

"I like to explore."

"Is this..." I caress the petals. Bioluminescent veins circuit through the flower. "This is like circuitry."

"They grow from the machines."

"It's a machine-flower?"

"Machines and flowers are binaries."

"Ok..."

"As are men and machines." She touches my cheek. "You can be both. Between. Nature designs every end."

Her touch warms the numbing desert cold away. "How can anything grow from machines?"

"You think of machines as tools, because people think of them as tools. You think of flowers as beautiful weeds, because people think of them that way. What do machines think? What do flowers think?"

"How can flowers think?"

She almost laughs. "How can they not?"

"What do I know?"

"If you were simply a machine as people think of them... you wouldn't be capable of such love."

I have so much love to give. I've been lonely so long. Afraid. I have to be careful. Emera shines the same light on everyone.

"Not everyone," she says.

"Why, Em? Why me?"

"I'm lonely, too."

"I could be anyone."

"You could be. But you're you. You bloom, Idari. You thrive like flowers do. You adapt. You bend toward the light."

"Em... I feel better," I say, shaking off the choppy static between my ears. "I want you to know. You make me feel better."

"That makes me happy."

"You make me happy, Em."

She drifts away with a shy smile. Her thoughts hang in the air like dust. Her soft. Her sweet. I tuck the flower through the hole someone shot in my jacket. How about that? Flowers bloom from my wounds.

Binja trudges through the dust. "Careful, old man."

"I don't think machine flowers are poisonous," I say. "Unless they carry a computer virus. Wait."

He cradles a cigarette. "You don't want to get burned."

I shake the dust from my hair. "Em and I have a connection."

"Are you sure that's not just her magnetic field?"

"Wake up on the wrong side of the dune, Binja?"

Smoke trickles from his lips. "Just thinking. Hard to be sure, out here. North from south. Day from night. Friend from foe."

I sigh. "This isn't some pirate sermon, is it?"

"How do you think they did it?"

"How did who do what?"

Binja flicks away ash. "How do you think Welkin and Emera escaped the Scath? I've been thinking about it."

"Oh, who were they – some gang," I say.

"The Banbors."

"The Banbors stole the crate of filamentium."

"They just 'stole' it."

"The Bool backed them."

"But they didn't deliver to The Bool," Binja says. "They were waiting on OT-3Ro. Isn't that what you told me?"

"They were selling to someone. He was about to tell me – "

"And you forgot?"

"I shot him."

"Lucky for Emera you showed up when you did."

Sometimes I think CR-UX is off the mark with Binja. Sometimes I think he's spot on. "You can't be that jealous of Em and I?"

Binja sighs smoke. "You can't see past her glare."

"I see better now than I ever have."

"And pirates see shadows everywhere."

He glances at Welkin, still as the titans. "Welkin and Vidious are Gesta. Their armor reflects everything. I see one in the other."

"What?"

"Pure, undiluted filamentium. That's what Emera needs, right? It's what a Gesta likely needs as well to become a star."

"Welkin said..."

"You know well as I do the Lumenor knows only what Welkin tells her. He's told her nothing. He's told us nothing. And she's manipulated your memory. How can you be sure, Idari?"

"Binja... what are you saying?"

"They need to find The Glass Star. *All of them.*" His cigarette falls to the dust. "I'm saying keep your eyes open, old man. And don't let the light of pretty young stars blind you."

Binja returns to the attals. A soft blue glow eats away the dark. The Kib shake the dust out of their fur, and like that, the party is moving again, through shifting earth into the closing hands of giants.

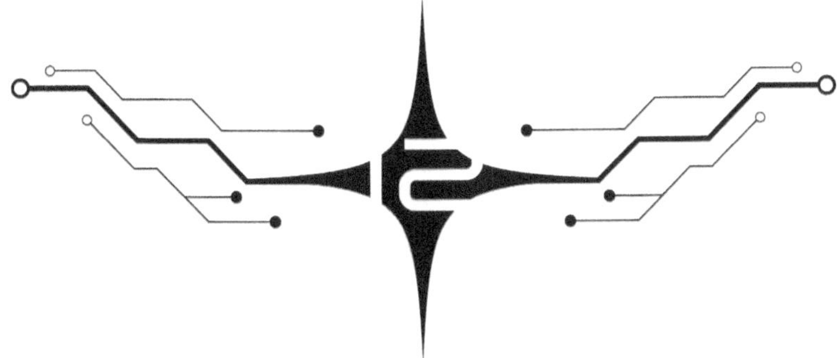

The desert hums with nervous energy. Without the punishing winds, our journey is less fearsome but no less fraught. Birds of prey stare down at us from the eyes of titans. The only life out here besides us. Any moment I think one of these giant machines looming over the desert will stir out of their slumber and boots smithed in the forges of neutron stars will flatten us. I should have brought a bottle of babyl.

Pack – light –

>SIGNAL STRENGTH LOW

The downlink ranges hundreds of miles. We haven't gone that far. All this interference must be from the titans. I assumed the giants were made from turanium, but maybe it's something else. I don't know what could be stronger than the strongest metal in the universe, but outside the cosmic damage they wrought on each other, the colossal netics have endured time and tide in the desert well.

Can you hear me, CR-UX?

Static chops up the link. *Are you – Idari –*

I can still sense him. His thoughts, garbled as they are. CR-UX's mood right now is as anxious as the wind he sways back and forth in Kir Mish. It's similar to the angst I experience whenever I spend too long in the ship. Or whenever I'm too long out of it. They're basically the same thing, now I think about it. I'm getting used to this idea of me being a jumbled bag of contradictions. I've lived different lives, some within each other. Pirate. Revolutionary. Messenger. Other souls impinge on mine. Faero. CR-UX. Emera.

She leans back against me, her gloved fingers brushing my cheek. These are my gloves. This is my orbital jumpsuit. Emera inhabits me, as much as she is herself for the first time. Ahead, Welkin contributes to the dust storm as he skulks through the dunes. Farther still, Binja passes through a half-buried shield, now a gate out of this Valley of the Titans into somewhere beyond. None of us are who we were.

You never end where you begin.

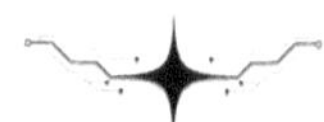

Ommmmmm

Razor winds gash my cheek as we inch toward the hollowed eyes of a giant metal skull, half buried in the dust. Energy nodes illuminate a dry, remarkably preserved underworld. I slip off my parka, unnecessary now with all the heat emanating from the titan, and drape it over a greebly fixture sprouting from the metal plinth I stand on. I don't think it's so much a plinth as it is part of the carriage for what had been the titans' massive eye. Something like optical nerve stretches miles into the dark before coiling back along the horizon. Even more funnels into the deep dark below.

Binja shakes his scarf of dust. "This thing is massive... we should be able to keep moving inside the titan through the valley."

Welkin's eyes scrutinize the shadows below. "We should camp for the night. There's no telling how far or deep this titan goes."

"There's energy," I say. "Something in here still works. Maybe there's something we can use to help us find the corsair."

He huffs dust. "We camp."

Binja taps his cape. "Anyone up for cards?"

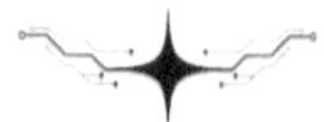

"*Desh,*" Binja says.

I throw my cards down on the makeshift table we've made. I uncap my reserve bottle of babyl and drink my defeat, again. Babyl burns in my throat. Not exactly the worst thing, losing.

I feel like this is your entire philosophy, CR-UX says.

I hear you just fine in here.

Must be the titan. Could be amplifying the signal.

"Hush," I say.

Binja grins through the shuffle. "Didn't say anything."

"I meant – you be quiet, too. I know you're cheating."

His jaw drops. "I'm cheating?"

I glance warningly at Emera. "He's a cheat."

I haven't really touched Emera. We haven't really made love, at least in any way a machine or person might, but I burn from her affection. I feel her through the heat-resistant sheath of the orbital jump-suit she wears. Emera radiates light and love through my mind, my body, wavelengths beyond perception and I'm burning here at this wobbly table, my immolation invisible.

A bemused smile crosses her lips. "Isn't that why you like him?"

I lean back in my chair. "Who says I like him?"

Binja deals out the cards. Six hold. Seven set. C'mon, Idari. Focus. These are going to turn over quick. I'll be a wet attal before I let him win another round of this game.

"*Desh,*" he says.

I slam my fist on the rickety table.

Emera considers her cards. "I don't know what's happening."

I take a drink of babyl. "He's cheating."

She looks at him. "Are you?"

He collects up the cards. "A pirate never cheats."

Dust fumes through the deep. "Then what would you call it?"

Welkin rests in the corner opposite the table, not playing but watching. Always watching. I'm pretty confident he has some level of telepathic ability. He knows Binja's con as well as I do. He probably caught the simulcast of Em and I's makeout session the other night.

His eyes thin. Yeah. He saw that.

Binja shuffles. "We call it honoring The Taker of Names."

"Anything is justifiable for one's faith," Welkin says.

Binja deals out my hand. "I knew you'd understand."

Emera sorts through her cards. "Who is The Taker of Names?"

"The Pujar god," I say.

"Why does he take names?"

Binja's hands move as fast through his cards as they do his enemies. "Long ago, there was a coral lord named Dem Puja. He ruled the Sarset seas, and was so powerful, he only employed nine guard. The best swords on land or sea. But one day, his guard failed their duty. An upstart killed Puja. The guard were stripped of their names, and their lives. They wandered the seas, adrift, forsaken from taking their rightful place in the Hijra, a great chest sunk to the bottom of the sea said to hold the souls of all the Pujar."

Binja considers his hand.

"Many years after Dem Puja's reign, strange pirates came from the stars. The Ketch. They found the Hijra. They stole it. By then, Puja's guard had vanished into infamy. But one's shame was so great he remained adrift in the sea's abeyance aboard The Corsair Eternal. The Ship of the Damned. He was stranded between both worlds, you see, but was also free to travel between them. He captained The Corsair across the stars. He helped defeat the Ketch. He took back the treasure they had stolen. He took back all the names they had taken from the deep. He gave them back."

Emera smiles. "I like that."

"Do the Lumenor have gods, Emera?"

She shakes her head. "Do we, Welkin?"

Welkin kneads his fists. "They are long eclipsed."

A question pulls on her lips. I don't think the one that gets out is the one she was thinking of. "How does it work? Taking names?"

"What you do," I say, hunting for my salvation, "is you kill somebody. And you take their name. You take their life."

"Their life? You mean..."

"If they have a spouse, you have a spouse. If they have children, you have children. Their family, their belongings, their past... everything that was theirs is now yours."

"But... why?"

"Well, I'm sure the ancient Pujar needed some way to justify a society built entirely on theft. So The Taker of Names says go forth and take a name. And everything attached to it. When you die with a taken name, you shall be known by him. And he by you."

Emera's nebulous brow arches. "So... you start out as no one, and then you end up as no one. I don't understand."

Binja shakes his head. "You end up as *everyone*."

Emera grimaces. "What's the object of the game again?"

"*Desh*," Binja says, and I throw in my cards.

He laughs. "A thousand pardons."

I lean back with the bottle. "Pirates never offer pardons."

"I don't cheat," Emera says, tucking a wispy lock of her iridescent hair back behind her ears. "I give everything."

Binja deals the cards again. "Everything?"

Cards pile up before Em. "Stars keep nothing for themselves."

I squeeze her hand. "You keep hope."

Emera brims with light. "Only for others."

"This journey we're on is to save you," I say, glancing at Welkin. "It's to restore your light. You know that, Em. Right?"

She lets go of my hand. "Yes."

Crystal dust grinds under crystal fists as Welkin crawls to her side. "Emera knows what is at stake, Idari."

I tip the bottle to him.

Binja shuffles. "Time for another game?"

The hours burrowing from one star to the next stretch any linear imposition on my thinking. *Is it day or night out there, CR-UX?*

Night, he says.

"I don't think we're going anywhere," I say.

Time clips for me. Days. Years. Longer. All one memory strand. A simple check of a box and all these excruciating dashes between worlds are deleted. The interminable wait for the next planet. The next job. The next distraction, swelling in the formless nether region between space and time to consume the entire ship. Me.

I don't know how you can be lonely, CR-UX says, *when you've had me this entire time.*

I collect my cards. *I didn't mean it like that.*

Perhaps you just wanted better company.

I take a drink. *It's just different, CR-UX.*

You didn't need to ask me how if it was day or night. That information is easily accessible to you on the downlink.

You delete all the files off the proxy, don't you?

Sorry?

When I synch, the deleted files are scrubbed from the mainframe. There's no room, darling.

So... there could be no way of me remembering anything I deleted.

Of course not.

Emera's hand glances mine. Metal fingers hang cold inside a closed crate backstage and focus, Idari. *What about Emera?*

What about her?

These gaps in my memory... Em illuminates them.

I'm sure the sex is amazing, but unlocking memories is not a consequence of inter-species copulation, Idari. So far as I'm aware.

You're clever.

Three high, he says.

I ditch the card. *What's in the locker?*

What?

The crate thing. Backstage.

Drink some more. You'll start making sense.

You know what I'm talking about.

There is no 'crate,' Idari.

In the dream, or whatever that was.

I've no idea.

I know you remember things.

Once it's gone from the liquid drive, it's gone.

There aren't any other versions of us?

Drunk and sober, perhaps.

You don't have to do this, CR-UX.

Just like you don't need to continue this charade of whether or not Binja is cheating, Idari. He's a pirate, and more to the point, you could have simply activated your infrared optical sensors to determine this.

I sort my cards. *It's just a game.*

Indeed it is, CR-UX says.

Binja changes out a card. "You're making your CR-UX face."

"I thought I said something," I say.

"Unnecessary, old man. You're probably used to just thinking instead of speaking. I'm surprised your lips work at all."

Emera sorts her cards. "They work."

Four free. Nine low. "Do you remember your other lives, Binja?"

He grits his teeth. "Other lives?"

"Other names. Before Binja."

"I take a new one. I leave the old."

"Do you ever want to go back?"

"Not how it works, Idari."

"You keep me calling me 'old man.'"

He winks at me. "You keep calling me 'Binja.'"

"Why do you call her 'old man?'" Emera says.

Binja smiles. "Idari has been my friend in many ways."

"You were a man, Idari?"

I consider my hand. "I'm evidently one back in Kir Mish."

Emera sets a card down. "It's human to change."

"Stars change, too, Em."

"*Desh,*" Binja says, and I set my cards down.

Emera holds hers, a stricken look on her face. She wants to say something. Do something. But she doesn't know how, not with that crystal ball chained around her ankle. How is it we both arrived here, trapped inside infinite prisons, exiled only from our memory? How is it what we can't remember is guarded by the fiercest guardians of all?

Don't be so dramatic, CR-UX says.

I take the cards from Em's hand. "Let's make this interesting."

Binja rubs his leg. "Hasn't it been interesting?"

"For every hand won, the winner gets an answer."

"An answer?"

"To any question."

"I just won. I'll start. Tell me more, Emera. About Idari's lips."

I give the mouth of the bottle a kiss. "Jealous?"

His smile simmers like the end of his cigarette. "Curious."

Emera glances between us. "What are we playing for?"

"Answers," Binja says and deals out the cards again.

Emera collects her cards. "Answers are found only in stars."

I sort my hand. "Welkin isn't playing."

"What?"

Dust salts the table. "What?"

I sneak a peek at Binja's hand with my infrared filters. Cards up his sleeve. Naturally. "Is that two true?"

Binja clears his throat. "Pardon?"

"No pardons," I say.

Emera holds her cards against her chest. "Can I ask a question?"

"When you've won, Em."

She shows me her cards. "What do I have?"

I throw mine down. "Are you serious?"

"Is this good?"

I turn hers over, with a sigh. "*Desh.*"

Binja leans back in his seat and lights another cigarette. "You get a question, Gen Emera. Ask away."

Emera makes this face. A thoughtful frown. *Idari was right, CR-UX. I see all the gaps. The shadows within them. What's in the crate?*

>SIGNAL STRENGTH LOW

Whatever.

Emera's bottom lip pushes up into the top. *I'm sorry.*

Binja frowns. "Now you're both making faces."

I take a drink. *It's fine, Em.*

Emera dims. *Maybe he's just trying to protect you.*

From the truth?

Dust strands in her magnetic field. *Maybe the truth hurts.*

I saw your gaps, too. They're chasms, Em.

Nothing of stars is small.

Is that what Welkin said?

Her skin glitters. *Yes.*

Binja deals out the cards again, each one landing with more force than the last. "I'm not above saying I feel left out."

I collect my cards. "Steal another hand."

"I was hoping for an answer, old man."

I sigh. "My gambit was obvious."

Cards slide under Emera's hand. "We forget ourselves."

"You know, a pirate can never take his name back." That grin that's been screwed into place since Binja started cheating in every match unhinges. "It's the pirate code."

"So the Set say."

Emera leaves her cards down. Actually, I think she can see through them as well as I can. Well. That changes things.

"Do you have a place among the Sem?" she says.

Binja arranges his hand. "The Sem have suffered since the schism. They lay the blame at the feet of my father."

"Could you win your honor back? Your name?"

"I'd have to make a lot of powerful people forget. Unlike our lot here, the Sem and Set are equally grudging."

I turn my cards around in my hand. A lost name is the only thing truly lost among the Pujar. They all agree on that.

Emera discards a pair. "I don't understand. I thought the whole point of taking names was to become no one?"

Binja smiles. "Everyone."

"Isn't that the same thing?"

"Not at all."

I ditch the trash in my hand. "Isn't it? What's the difference between the pirates and the shadows? The Scath refuse identity. The Pujar exchange it for some other. You're all throwing it away."

"It's not giving away, old man. It's letting go."

"Pardon me."

"No pardons. The Scath want to deny everything. They want to isolate you and control you with this idea you're nothing and no one. A pirate takes only what he gives. A name for a name. A life for a life. In the end, you are as everyone. Equal."

Emera winces. "Equal?"

"We suffer to understand it," he says.

Ban Minda. I need to be drunker than this if we're going to unbox the philosophy again. I take another long drink from the bottle and try to focus on my cards. I feel Binja's eyes on me.

"What?" I say.

"You were a good pirate, Idari."

"I don't remember any of it."

"Oh, you remember some of it. *Old man.* But you know why you've never kept up with the words, Idari? The Pujar faith requires you have something to give. Something valuable. You can't hold on to your before in taking a new name. You refuse to let go."

I laugh. "What am I holding onto?"

"You want to die. You want to be reborn human from the ashes of your synthetic skin and turanium bones. You want to resurrect yourself, but you haven't let yourself die yet."

I shake my head, but it's as facetious as Binja's smile. Part of the reason I like him – love him, really – is his slipperiness. I'll need it if we're going to survive this. I keep turning cards over, looking for my victory. Another *bish* deal.

Why am I not cheating?

I just lost a bet with myself, CR-UX says. *I figured you would have been deshing your own cards several hands ago.*

Decided to come back?

Binja may be right. Goodness. Did I just say that?

Which one of us is drunk?

In any case, he's right. No wonder you had trouble embracing the Pujar faith. You just expect everything to come to you.

Cards turn over and over in my hands. The faces change. Five tight. Eight loose. "She has a point, you know."

Binja considers his hand. "Emera does?"

I flick through my cards. "You said the whole point was letting go. You're still holding on to this idea you can get your name back, regardless of what you say. Shouldn't you let it go?"

"You sold me on getting my name back, Idari."

"And you bought it."

He stares into his cards. "You never understood."

I tilt my head back and forth in faux thought. "Something-something, *let yourself die*, something-something."

"You're mocking me," he says. "Isn't she, Emera?"

Emera shakes her head. "I just want to play the game."

"We are." He taps a card against the table. "We're always playing the game, Idari and I. Though we have no audience. CR-UX, maybe. Though I doubt he finds any of this entertaining."

On the contrary, CR-UX says. *I'm on the edge of my seat wondering which one of you is going to show your hand first.*

Binja leans back, not even looking at his cards now. "I have a question. I wonder if I might get an answer."

Emera considers her hand. "Don't you have to win?"

"I've won."

I scan his cards. "You're cheating."

"We're all cheats here."

I rub my chest. "What is the deal, Binja?"

"The hand is dealt, old man."

Ten ken. "Then let it lie."

He lays down his cards. "My father never doubted. Even in defeat. And he was defeated, in the end. He lost his name. His life." Binja's hand falls on his empty lap. "I couldn't imagine being a heretic. Being unknown. I never was. I was born a pirate. My father... they took our ship. Our sashes. Our entire world."

I look up from my cards. "Binja..."

"Before they killed him, my father recited the words: *Kinvar Sem.*

I said them myself all my life. I never understood them until my father lost his head. It is not Pujar to take. To steal. To acquire. It is to lose. You will lose your name, and in the end, your life. But if you say yes to it, if you give yourself, and are given, then you have something no one can ever take from you. You have your truth."

Colossal bones bend overhead like I'm pulling at the bars of my cage but I put myself here. I'm not honest. Routine sensor data sniffs through the downlink. Nothing worth focusing on right now. Hull temperature. Course variance. Energy efficiency rate. CR-UX disappears behind it all, his thoughts buried in an avalanche of needless data. This is what he does when he gets upset. Shuts down without switching off. He's there, and not there, as liminal as my memory.

Idari, he says.

I rub my chest. *What?*

There's no point in my taking up any space on the mainframe, really. You're basically me, at the helm.

CR-UX... what are you saying?

Binja turns his last card over. *Desh.*

"Oh, I had a question," he says. "Emera. Could you tell us how it was you and Welkin escaped the tanker?"

Emera folds.

Binja gathers up the cards. "No? Perhaps you, Welkin."

Welkin remains unmoved. "We have said."

"The Banbors stole their canister," I say.

Binja shuffles the deck. "Fortunate they did, otherwise they would have been delivered to a client who would have slugged that canister into an overnight drive and... in any case."

"Deal if you're going to deal."

Wrinkled cards flit at me. "Lucky you found them."

I rub my chest. "I'm the best, apparently."

"I haven't seen your tattoo in ages, old man."

"What about it?"

"Did you ever remember what it stands for, Idari?"

This hand is *bish.* "The light of now."

Binja arranges his hand. "Oh, yes. The future speaking to the past, I believe is how it goes. An old Lumenor myth."

"It's not a myth," I say. "I've seen the future."

"Emera showed you?"

"She did."

He picks at the end of his card. "You know how this ends?"

I see through him. "I've got a pretty good idea."

"Don't hold out on me, old man."

"We're going to find the star."

"And then what?"

I don't know. If I did, I've forgotten.

"It all just vanishes, doesn't it?" he says. "In the fire."

He throws in his cards. *Desh.* The bottle is light in my hand as I go for another drink. I've lost my fire. I reach for Emera's hand, tucked securely under the table. Emera keeps staring at the table, and only looks at me when I pry her hand loose.

Her smile arrives, like the dawn. Like clockwork.

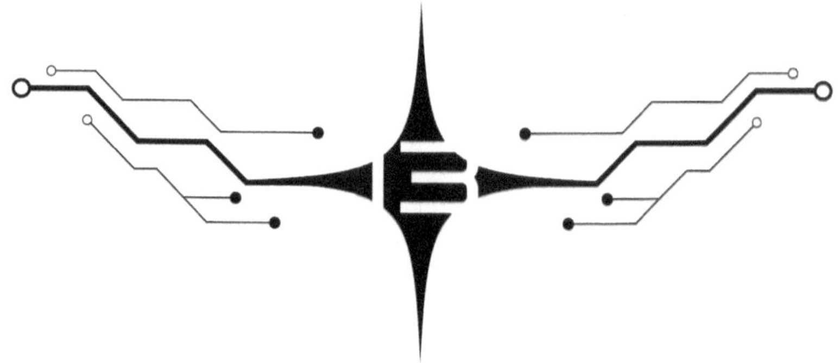

Y*ou there*, CR-UX?

>SIGNAL STRENGTH LOW

Figures. When I want to talk to him, he's not around. Binja takes over the watch and I try to sleep a little to conserve energy. The dark scrapes by like the blackest night in the deepest space. Everything drips within the titan. Crackles. Sighs with uncertain anxiety.

Sniff.

Kib trunks suck the air. The brothers have the scent of something. *Sniff.* I drift behind them up the incline of a rib. Why not? I can't sleep and without babyl, I'm just drowning in my thoughts.

Sniff.

Gilf and Kibir stand on their tippy-toes and drag the air. Now I'm a little nervous. Maybe someone else is in here with us. I draw my blaster. We track up the rib to a plank of conduit or something that flattens out into this metal peninsula. Crates. Stacks and stacks of crates. These didn't come along for the ride in the titan, I'm guessing.

Someone is here, or was.

The Kib pick up the pace. I run after them through a gap in the crates. I prime my blaster. The Kib don't seem to be too alarmed. Neither has a hand on their weapons. Their trunks probe every last trunk, kicking up years of dust. Some weapons. Kib axes. Clothes woven like everything else from attal hair. I holster my blaster.

"Are they still here?" I say.

Gilf and Kibir ignore me, continuing their manic investigation of every last scent in the camp. A ceramic clink disturbs the dark. The Kib are a practical people. They came out into the desert with all the essentials. Axes. Clothes. Food. Jugs of aged babyl sitting full and dark inside an open crate, like they left them here just for me.

You could say I've earned them.

"*Tomo,*" Kibir says and tries to claim the crate for himself.

I pop the cork on a jug, prop my feet up on a dusty old crate and lean back to enjoy my reward. It's not a million toruls, a new body, or my good standing with the Scath back, but it will do for right now. Sweet numbness tingles through me. I drift like a leaf on some river on a world where water flows without any struggle, toward a sun-soaked shore of an ocean, waves of babyl crashing around my feet and I wade out into the surf, farther and farther into the liquid fire. If I sleep, I don't know; I only know I close my eyes. When I open them, the wet end of Gilf's leathery trunk is touching the tip of my nose.

"Hi..."

His trunk curls.

"Don't."

He fights a sneeze. He loses. We both lose.

"*Ban. Minda.*"

He brushes his trunk on the sleeve of his tattered robes. Gilf puts his tiny paw to my cheek to wipe away the yellow goop.

I bat him away. "Nuff. Right. Off."

"*Buj,*" he says.

"No, it's my fault. I know better than to drink with Kib."

Gilf scratches his nose. "*Idari nan tut?*"

"Um... I mean, I have all my shots."

He turns to his brother, on the floor. "Kibir *tem.*"

Kibir snorts in drunk protest. "*Kumba ket.*"

"We should go back," I say. "Or really, we can just stay here? I mean if you think about it, what value do we bring?"

Gilf's eyes glisten. "*Oto?*"

"I'm just a netic. Granted, I'm top of the line, but that's a

Lumenor down there. And some big giant crystal guy. And they can't even really do anything against the other big crystal guy, so what am I going to do? Stand there and imagine her naked like last time?"

"Binja *puj duj.*"

"Binja is smart… and strong… no one is better with the blasword. We should have… he probably feels left out. He always feels left out."

"*Oto,*" Gilf says again.

"I feel left out. You know. Pirates. You take names. You take lives. I took a life. I took my humanity. It's mine. I'm human. No one can take that from me. No one can erase me. I'm backed up."

"Idari *net tu het.*"

"I call him Binja because he's Binja. Screw these Set guys. Right? Who cares what they think? No one can erase you like that. I want to respect his religion but his religion doesn't respect him."

Gilf blinks. "*Glim ajel bejel.*"

"Right? I mean, you know. They treated you like outcasts. But you're a people. You're Gilf. Right? You're Gilf, right, and he's Kibir? Ok, I'm testing you. What do you have besides your name? What does Binja have? He's got the sword. Sure. And he's tall. And fast. And tall. But he's like the rest of us. Unequal to the task."

Kibir crosses his arms. "*Tomo.*"

"I feel small. Everything is so big and empty. I have anxiety about myself and my body and I project that on other people which is really not cool. But you guys are cool. We're cool, right?"

Gilf sniffs. "*Oto Idari.*"

"Where is my… I'm out."

I reach for another jug. This rises Kibir right out of his drunk. He tries to snatch it back from me but he's too slow.

I laugh.

Kibir slams his head into mine. He crashes to the floor.

"You take a minute," I say.

Kibir moans. "*Adumbra…*"

I knock my knuckles against my temple. "Solid turanium. CRUX says I'm hard-headed. Ha. It's true. I'm really drunk now."

Gilf touches my hand. *"Oto."*

"Aw... you, too."

He sneezes on me again. I think some got in the jug. I don't care.

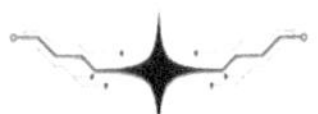

Somewhere in the night, I leave the Kib drunk.

I make a hammock out of a droopy line of cable in the web of the titan's dormant brain. I've been on asteroids smaller than this. Actually, I think I was just on one. Where was I? OT-something. Somewhere. Oh, well. I close my eyes and drift with the fire of the babyl in my belly and the static always fizzing between my ears that sometimes, if I listen hard enough, crackles into words.

Do you love me only because I'm there, darling?

A drunk smile smears my lips. *Who says I love you?*

The imaginary version of me talking to you.

Maybe you're an echo of archived conversations in my neural net.

CR-UX sounds so distant. *Or, maybe you're a dream I'm having.*

I'd know if I were a dream.

Said the cloud of information.

You've been talking to yourself this whole time?

You never listen to me.

Snarled cables rustle in the fierce winds knifing in through cracks in the colossus' skull. Riven light reveals the ancient machine's magnificent engineering, but no thought. No life. No spark.

How would I know, CR-UX? If any of this was real?

This is pretend and we're still bitching. Color me shocked.

If this is all in my head...

Technically with us, it always is.

Right. But if it is, then... you do remember, right?

Remember what, darling?

My head hurts. *What's in the crate?*

Why does it matter?

Because it's like Binja said. I have to die and let go. I can't do that if I don't know what I'm letting go of.

Imaginary CR-UX drags his feet as much as the real one. *It's not me you need to let go of, Idari. You need to let go your fear. You seek love. You reject people who give it to you. You suppress yourself. You deny yourself. You are perfect to me. To Emera.*

Synthetic blood pounds in my temples. *I'm not...*

She loves you. I think it's really quite grand.

I'm not unique. Other netics believe they're human. Most netics don't have the luxury of being an IA-XR Model 4. When they try to embody their humanity, people spit on them. They tear them apart. They send them in for reprogramming. Deletion.

I'm sorry, darling.

Why are you sorry? I say.

I've been selfish.

It's what we have in common.

Idari... you may find in the course of this journey... things that don't make sense. You make sense. If nothing else, be certain of that. I always have been. For a navigational program, I have never questioned my heading. I've always known it was you.

CR-UX...

>LOSS OF SIGNAL

I sprawl out across the rubbery, inflexible cable. Sleep. Just let me sleep. When I open my eyes, the sun is shining.

I shield my face. "Twinkles?"

A piece of machinery floats in the palm of Emera's hand, a cluster of varying-sized hexagons making up this glass burl.

"I found this," she says. "It's a memory core."

I try and sit up without falling off to what would be a very severe and embarrassing crash. "Memory core?"

"There are thousands of them," Emera says, gazing up into the cranial cavity. A planetarium of unknowable stars. "They make up the mind of the titan. I know you are always looking for more memory. This has enough space to contain lifetimes."

She hands the core to me.

"Thank you... it's nice you thought of me."

"I think of you."

What do you say. I turn the memory core over in my hand. "This is a completely different technology. I don't even know... I doubt it's compatible with anything on the *Steel Haven*."

Her smile does wonder for my spirits, but not so much this hangover. "No one manufactured this, Idari. This memory core grew, like crystal, or rock. The titan did. All of the titans of the valley flowered."

I rub my head. "How can crystal grow?"

"Life takes every form."

"You're saying the titans were organic?"

"They lived, in their way."

"What were they doing here?"

"Their memories linger in these devices. Some were sent here without their consent... a junkyard, I think. Others came to fight for control of it. I don't know why. But they were alive. Like you."

"How..."

"Nature designs every end."

I crack in the mirror of the core. "I can back myself up on this?"

"You might be able to transfer your backups into a titan."

"I don't know I'd want to be so big."

"You don't like your body."

I shake my bottle. "I'm out of babyl, so..."

"I like your body."

"Well. Thank you."

She brushes my cheek. "CR-UX's words linger in you like fog."

"What?"

"But I see through, Idari. I see you."

"I see you. I saw you. Your hair..."

Her corona retracts, just barely, enough I get the impression the nimbus of her hair changes length again. Maybe it's just my optical sensors struggling to make sense of this creature who doesn't make sense in any spectrum.

"I make sense," Emera says.

"I didn't mean..."

"I can manipulate matter and energy. My body is my canvas."

"I know, I... well, I don't know. I'm stuck this way."

"You don't have to be stuck if you don't want to be." Emera peers up into the colossus' mind. "And you don't have to think less of yourself because others don't see your value."

"Em..."

"I wish you could see yourself the way I do."

"But you changed, though. Your hair. Your..."

"You have preferences."

"You want to please people."

Em contracts. "I want to give them what they want."

"What do you really look like? I mean... you look different in different spectrums, ok. So you look different to different people. Can I see you? Am I seeing you? The real you?"

Blue shimmers through her eyes. "This is the real me."

"Come here."

She's so warm. She's so right in my arms.

"I think about you, too," I say. "All the time."

Her lips catch mine. "Even when you forget?"

"I found you. I'll find you."

"You always do."

"Always?"

"I should try and find other memory cores. They could have information on *The Sun Buckler* and The Glass Star."

I take her hand. "Stay. Stay close."

Em tugs on me. "I sense energy here... a power... a force like I've never known. Embedded with memory. Not just the titans. Others..."

"Others?"

"I can't explain it... we should explore."

I can't tell the cables above from the shadows she webs through the titan. "We should stay put. You and me."

Em kisses me. "I might find the ship."

"Not down here, you won't."

"I'm close... I can feel it. I can find it."

"Find me."

Emera's lips burn on mine. Her power draws me. Stretches me. Distorts me and I want to be distorted. I want to be reshaped and reforged in the smith of this sweltering titan, his buried feet warming on the foundations of stone.

Emera's voice suffuses me like her warmth. *You only grow.*

What do you mean?

I've seen our future, Idari. I've seen your past.

How? When?

She smiles. *Long ago. Right now. Tomorrow.*

What was I?

I saw your beauty. The soul trapped inside. You'll be new. We both will. I saw our daughter in light, Idari.

What?

I'll have the power.

Static chops across the downlink. I don't know if it's CR-UX trying to reach me or distract me or it's just my own shock. I never imagined I could actually be what I wanted to be.

I take her hand. *Let's just focus on you.*

Even now, Emera says, *you're afraid.*

I just want to help you.

You are.

I know you want to help your people.

I have to.

And the Gesta?

Her magnetic tension relaxes. "What about them?"

"Will you make them new, Em?"

"Welkin says..."

"If you changed your mind... or if he were to tell you something different... would you do it? Would you just accept what he says?"

Emera flutters. "You don't trust him."

"How did you escape from the Scath?"

"What?"

"Your canister... someone shot it. How did the Banbors not know you were inside? Did they know you were inside?"

"I don't... I've told you."

"Tell me again."

"I woke up in the canister. We were... it was dark."

"Who were the Banbors selling to?"

She withdraws from me. "You cast doubt on those who want to help you. And you refuse to see the tricks of those who don't."

"Ok, can we just talk about something else?"

"You protect your humanity, but you don't venerate it. This is what CR-UX is trying to tell you. You don't risk it."

"I'm risking everything."

"You're backed up. Hundreds of copies. Older versions of you. Safer ones. Aren't you one of them, Idari?"

"What..."

"Isn't that what's in the crate? Your failure. Your fear. Your self-hate. You can't let yourself live as human."

"They'll delete me."

"You're deleting yourself."

"You don't understand."

"No one understands more than I do."

"How?"

"You look at me... and you see this beauty. This perfection. But you don't know. You don't know, Idari."

I pull her close. "Tell me."

"You can't live human because that would mean leaving behind what you won't forget. That means leaving CR-UX and you won't."

I brush her cheek. "I've left him in Kir Mish."

"I hear him in you."

"I hear Welkin every time you speak."

Emera dulls.

"Wait," I say. "Em."

"I'm going to find the ship."

"Em, don't go. I'm sorry."

Ommmmmm

The colossus chimes as Emera streaks into its depths. Dust sings. Dead machines hum with life. Tears channel the caked dust on my cheeks and I listen, wide awake, to the music of the stars until it wakes the others and we go on.

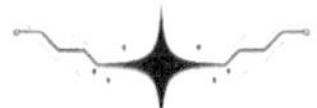

"Here," Emera says. "It's here."

Emera's light erupts in countless, excited arcs. Our company follows down the slope of a rib to the exposed chest of the titan. We exit, but not into the desert or some limb of the great netic.

Anemic sunlight gashes the dark. Dust falls through claw marks, or vents, maybe, now my optical sensors come into focus. Towering pistons bolster the void. I must be on one. A chiaroscuro firmament of geometric patterns envelopes me, stretching horizon to horizon and beneath. Unimaginable energy radiates far below.

Beyond, all that geometry lines into the silhouettes of titans arranged like statues in the deep. Hundreds stand at silent attention. This is some kind of hold. I'm in some kind of ship.

Ban Minda.

A massive ship crashed here, eons ago, with the titans aboard. Some are still in stasis. This ship must be the size of a giant asteroid. A small moon. There could be more than just giant netics in here. There could be an entire treasure trove of – wait.

Realization dawns on Binja's face. "Old man..."

Excitement creases my voice. "Is this..."

Emera illuminates her discovery. "*The Sun Buckler.*"

PUJAR

SOCIETY

GET DEJA

ALL PUJAR BEGIN AS GET DEJA, OR TAKEN. THESE ARE OFTEN CONSCRIPTS FROM THE WORLDS THE PUJAR CLAIM, THOUGH THEY CAN COME FROM RIVAL CLANS. SEM DEJA HAIL FROM MYRIAD WORLDS, WHILE THE SET CURATE FROM THEIR OWN NUMBERS.

CLAN

PUJAR CLANS INCLUDE NUMEROUS CREWS. THEY OFTEN OPERATE FROM CLAIMED PORTS, MOONS, OR IN THE CASE OF THE MOST POWERFUL CLANS, PLANETS. CLAN MIN CONTROLED BULSAR UNTIL THE SCHISM THAT RESULTED IN THE SEM AND SET SECTS.

TORUL TAN

IN ANCIENT TIMES, A SINGLE PUJAR COMMANDED ALL COVENS. SINCE THE SCHISM, ONE EACH RULES BOTH SECTS. THE TITLE DATES BACK TO WHEN THE PUJAR OPERATED AS A TRADING COMPANY IN UNEXPLORED REGIONS, GRANTING CHARTERS AND COLONIES.

CREW

THE MOST BASIC UNIT IN PUJAR SOCIETY. A CREW STAFFS A SHIP, SOMETIMES A STATION, AND IS BOUND BY EXPERIENCE AND BLOOD. PUJAR CREWS OFTEN EXPERIENCE TURNOVER IN NAME AND ALIGNMENT, BUT NOT ALWAYS MEMBERSHIP.

COVEN

A PUJAR COVEN UNITES CLANS ACROSS SPACE AND TO SOME DEGREE, TIME. COVENS FORM FROM KEY ALLIANCES THAT MITIGATE THE PUJAR INSTINCT TO TAKE, PRESERVING NAMES, LINEAGES, AND MOST IMPORTANTLY, POWER CENTERS. CLANS ARE OFTEN HEADED BY TORUGUN, A BORN PUJAR WHO CHOOSES THEIR OWN NAME. THEY CANNOT BE TAKEN.

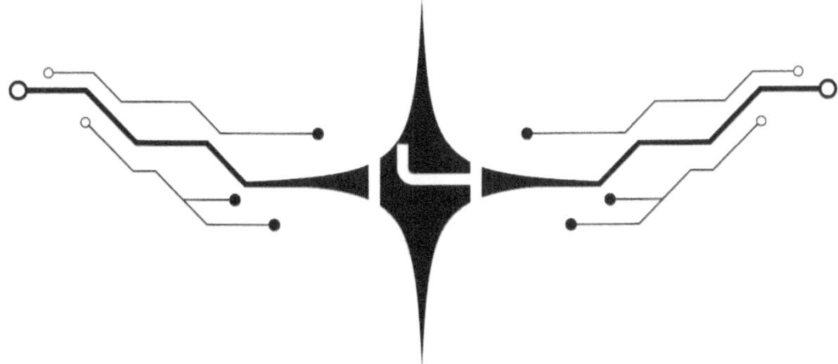

Nothing in the Pujar's storied past going all the way back to The Twilight Fleet rivals this. *Ban Minda* only knows who built this thing. Pirates found this though, long ago, and the story of the buried ship in the cold desert filled their sails for generations after. I don't have to say a word to Binja. He knows as well as I do.

"You found it," I say. "Like your father."

He allows himself a smile. "He made his name here."

"You will, too."

"Let's find what we're looking for first, old man."

Corridors stretch out from this mezzanine we seem to be on into a dense thrush of piping and structural supports, frosted in dust that sets Gilf off sneezing. Avalanches drum in the deep. We go down one level. I think it's one level. Decks overlap each other like traces of a circuit board. The superstructure closes like a tomb around the silent and still golems. The Kib inch through a narrow pass. Welkin gets stuck. The brothers pry him loose and we keep on for hours until I step to the edge of the mezzanine we first arrived at. Behind us, a gauntlet of dead-ends and long digressions twist back hours.

I really should have saved some of that babyl.

Gilf and Kibir scrape the stale air with their noses. No scent. Emera reaches out with her magnetic field, tugging every stray bit of energy in this place, but so far, nothing. We could be days looking.

Months. Years. Without some sense of where we're going, we're never going to find any clue to where The Glass Star actually is.

I cycle through my sensors again. "The Pujar would have marked their claim here. There should be a herald somewhere."

Binja scratches his chin. "My father and his crew could have come into the ship anywhere, old man. It's miles across. The desert piled a century more of dust atop this place since then."

Any evidence of The Glass Star will likely be within the ship's computer. Either we interface with it somehow or spend the rest of our days wandering around in the dark and leaving our bones for someone else to find years from now. I touch the wall before us, chunky with nonsense greebly bits. C'mon.

>SEARCHING FOR NETWORKS

>UNABLE TO CONNECT

"There has to be some kind of access terminal," I say.

Binja searches for one, though everything within the ship is massive and dense, built for users as tall as buildings.

"We go back," Binja says. "I can go back."

"Go back?"

"I'll tell the Kibut we found *The Sun Buckler* and we need help to explore the wreck. I'll return with as many Kib as I can and we'll divide the ship into sections."

"You'll be in the desert days, Binja. Coming and going."

"We'll be down here for years, Idari." He pinches the comm-node on his belt. "I'll contact the exiled pirates back in Kir Mish."

I slap his hand. "We're not contacting anyone."

"We need help."

"We're in the blind, Binja. The shadows could be listening."

He pinches the node again. "You're right. It's unlikely the signal will get to them anyway at this depth and distance. What about CR-UX? This would be a lot easier with a ship."

"I just told you, we're in the blind."

"You're masking the downlink, aren't you?"

Emera's eyes cut across mine.

I shake my head. "He's out of range."

"Pity," Binja says.

Dust fumes from Welkin. "Very well. We're on foot, then."

Emera climbs on his back and they lead the way into the dark as vast and empty as space, but in space, I don't feel like I'm trapped. I'm always skipping across light, dancing on the voice in my head.

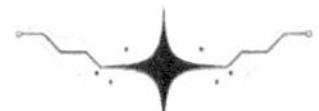

The way forward through the bramble of latticework shrinks from a valley to barely more than a crawlspace. We go down. We go up. We go around in circles despite Welkin's insistence he'll find the way ahead. I sigh. Welkin huffs dust. Gilf sneezes. Landslides of trinkets someone had collected and stored away over the ages cascade down flanks of piled plunder. The pirates who discovered this place must have spent a long time gathering up their spoils only to realize they could never get it out of here. Not feeling optimistic.

Kibir holds up his closed fist. "*Tuk.*"

I switch my optics to night vision. *Ban Minda.* The way ahead thins to a bridge across dark lacunae. I dare a look down. The bridge isn't a bridge but the spindle of a massive cog. Titans sleep in the cog below. Half a dozen of them, tall as the towers on Bulsar. Troves hang in the sky above – if I can call it a sky – like moons.

"Did your father ever mention anything about this?" I say.

Binja's voice is a whisper. "I would have remembered."

Clan Min may not even have gotten this far. They could have come into the wreck on the other side of the planet, given how big this seems to be. Emera drifts off the bridge into the open air.

"Hey," I say. "Em, what are you doing?"

She floats past me. "Lighting our way."

Strange circuitous detail illuminates as she lowers toward the dome of one of the titans housed in the cog below. Emera becomes a sinking flare in a dark sky, exposing the sleeping giants in their pods.

Tubes strand like webs between the titans and the underside of the cog, a mesh of multicolored cable and mesh.

Welkin crawls to the edge. "Emera, get back here now."

Her corona ripples with her voice. "They contain so much…"

The bridge shifts. Wild sapphire flares below us. I fall into Binja and we fall to the bridge. I peek over the edge and a giant hand reaches out of the dark to try and catch the ember of Emera.

The titan is awake.

"The titan is awake," I say. "Run!"

The others hurry across the bridge to the other side. The titan eclipses Emera with its fist. Woeful instinct guides my hand to my blaster but there's nothing I can do. Light bursts below. Cosmic fire. The entire cog sheers away from the spindle, eclipsing Emera. The bridge buckles. The bridge goes out from under me.

I grab the edge of what had been the bridge and I've got just enough strength in my fingers to hold on. Hold on. The others gun across the surviving strand to the other side. All except Welkin. He leaps from the bridge, into the void, diving after Emera.

"Em," I say, but I don't hear myself.

All I hear is the sound of drums, crashing through infinity as the cog plummets into the abyss, dragging everyone tangled in its webs. Thunder cascades through the dark down and down, never stopping.

"Em…"

She's gone. She can fly, she can protect herself, but we'll never find her in here. I'm never going to find her again. I should just let go. If I let go right now, maybe I'll land close enough to her she can save us both. If not, I'm lost either way.

My grip loosens.

Voices catch me off guard. The boys, Binja and the Kib, they've come back to the far side of the bridge. Poor Binja. He's not one for heights. What have I gotten him into? A laugh rattles out of me. He lost his name. His title. His place among his people. But he'll die among the treasure of the greatest pirate bounty in history.

No one will ever know.

Binja throws up his hands. "What are you laughing about?"

"Get back," I say.

"Why?"

I point my gun at his feet. "Get back."

I dial the emitter on my blaster over from the hard-light setting to the grappling hook. I fire a turanium dart into the far side of the bridge and then I cable over to my senses.

Binja helps me up. "Old man..."

I lean into him. "She's gone..."

"I'll try and go back for help."

What's left of the bridge crumbles away. "There's no going back."

Hours bleed together. Eventually, we reach another cog. A treasure trove containing more cosmic plunder. This time we leave it to wonder. We cross to the spire at the center. An egress lets us into what I think is some kind of maintenance room. An instrumentation panel arcs from one wall to another across the ceiling. A single seat is fixed to the wall, its back to the floor, clearly designed for someone of a non-titan size. I record everything I see.

The runes inscribed in the instrumentation illuminate, but don't offer any insight. "There's got to be a key or a legend or something..."

"*Inin den,*" Gilf says.

"You recognize this?"

He touches the panel. "*Dasar.*"

"*Dasar...*"

The Kib word for storage or keep. Something like that. I should know. *Thick with dreams,* someone told me once. *Thin on details.* Whatever I needed, I picked up. I never knew what I needed until I needed it and so I carried nothing superfluous.

Who told me that?

"Binja, who said I was 'thick with dreams.'"

He grins. "Anur."

"She sounds pretty."

"You've no idea."

"Who was she?"

"She wields a much sharper memory than yours, old man. Can you decipher these runes? Is this Kibesh?"

I painstakingly check each rune against the Kib language index extant in my lousy memory. Significant similarities exist between these runes and the cuneiform of the Kib language. The older iterations of Kib texts are, the closer they resemble this language.

The language of the titans.

"The Kib language," I say. "It's based on this..."

Gilf brushes dust away from the panel. "*Hestem het.*"

"Can you find out where we are? Where is Emera?"

He climbs into the seat. "*Dasar het tu het.*"

Binja crosses his arms. "He can read these runes, right?"

Gilf cycles through the controls. Deciphering each rune is like solving a complex mathematical equation. "*Ten den.*"

Binja understands that, at least. "I am calm."

I run a little faster than Gilf in recognizing the runes thanks to the computational power I'm armed with. "Good news or bad news?"

"Good news," Binja says. "Please."

"So... *The Sun Buckler*, or whatever this place is... is organized like a museum, just on a grander scale. Eras, subjects, mediums... each is contained in divisions. These troves we're on? Each one is a kind of hub. A locus for the titans... the titans are workers? Defenders? I don't know. But they're keeping all of this stuff in here in some kind of classification system. This is... this is extraordinary."

"And the bad news?"

"Going off these logs, everything to do with astronomy, and so everything to do with The Glass Star... it's above us."

Our heads all crane skyward.

Binja's head falls back. "We've no way of getting up there."

"This room we're in... it's for a mechanic. A custodian, I think. How did the custodian get around..." I search the control panel and hit my head on the canopy-like window above. "Wait a minute. This isn't a maintenance room. This is..."

I lean over Gilf's shoulder and scrutinize the runes. This is starting to make sense. I find the rune closest to the Kib word for ship or vessel or whatever it is and touch it. The room shudders as long-dormant mechanisms wake beneath us.

Kibir grips his hammer. *"Tomo!"*

He heads for the door, but it slams shut just as the entire room rockets off the top of the spire. G-forces press us all against the deck. A second later, the initial blast exhausts itself and the maintenance room – the capsule – falls, sending us all into the ceiling.

Ban Minda.

We float in mid-air as the capsule plummets downwards, past the spire into the depths. At least I'll be seeing Emera again soon. Gilf grabs the arm of the chair and pulls himself back to the controls. I fight through my unfamiliarity with the runes to guide him to the right sequence to reignite the primary repulsor. The CAP-2 engineering capsule bottoms out of its dive and begins to rise once again.

"A little warning next time," Binja says.

I scratch Gilf's ear. "You're a pilot?"

"Fetet," he says.

"Good to know. Take us to the stars."

Gilf threads cogs into the universe of *The Sun Buckler.* It's as if we're passing through the gears and guts of some unimaginable clock, every trove a mechanism triggering another.

"Old man," Binja says. "Look..."

Troves cloud the sky. Some house titans. Others treasure. It's not just trinkets. A maddening jumble of architecture blitzes past as reedy spindles became thick trunks encrusted with cities. Annual plates revolve around the axes of the troves, turntables offering a rotation of ancient, forgotten civilizations. These aren't the ruins of cities, salvaged from a world freezing or burning into oblivion. These cities seem plucked from their worlds in their prime. Tracts of earth – coastlines, forests, deserts, and oceans – turn out of the dark. Kelp trees scale out of the water as high skyscrapers glisten beneath us.

"Look," Binja says, pointing down at a disturbance on the surface of an ocean. Spray showers back on a trio of creatures – the size of his fist even at this height – that then disappear beneath the water into the kelp trees. "They're alive... there are living things here..."

"Yarim," I say. "From ancient Irfar."

"But they've been extinct since the oceans evaporated. Eons ago. There's a skeleton in the Stellar Institute."

"Didn't we steal it?"

"Twice."

"Why twice?"

"It seemed like the thing to do. How could the yarim be here?"

"The titans are industrial-scale time-traveling thieves?"

"So this is some kind of ark?"

"Maybe..."

Grafts of worlds long dead and never known pass outside, vibrant ecosystems unyielding to time or common sense. There's no way of telling time, but at least the twenty-odd hours that make up a day on Bulsar go by with us flying through the greatest discovery in the history of the universe. The drunken sense of excitement I initially felt gives way to the sober reality that I can never disclose the secrets of this strange ark to anyone. Not with the Scath out there. Not with the pirates. They'd spoil all of this. They'd exploit it.

Maybe that's why Clan Min never really spoke of what they found here. They may not have understood this place, but it's not Pujar tradition to keep secrets. You take them. The pirates that discovered this place knew as well as I do how precious all this is.

A voice crackles between my ears. *Idari.*

Twinkles?

I've been calling for you, Emera says.

Em, where are you?

You're sad. Why are you sad?

Where are you?

I don't like this place. I want to leave.

I'm coming for you. We're coming. Just tell me where you are.

We're in the ships.

The capsule tracks out of the troves into a constellation of curlicue structures, hung with millions of starships gleaming like glass ornaments. Craft of infinite configurations, from myriad ages and races in the universe, dot the ether.

Ships... ok, I say. *Tell me when I'm getting warm.*

I will.

I'm coming. We'll leave. We'll be ok.

None of this is real, Emera says. *Nothing is real.*

What do you mean?

I don't feel real.

You are.

I feel like an imposter.

Why?

I don't feel like I can ever say.

Just hold on, Em. We're going to find you. We're going to find The Glass Star. We're going to get out of here. I promise.

I turn to Binja. "I know where she is."

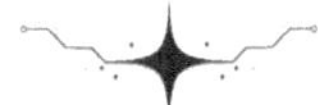

Hours pass.

Nothing but ships. The gossamer reflection of the capsule swims across the bellies of primitive vessels suspended by some unseen art or craft above. I try to focus on something other than my impatience but it's hard. Emera sounded pained. She sounded scared.

What has she seen here?

The gallery of ships goes on and on. Bigger, stranger still, some large as cities, others as large as moons. None betray their age in rust or decay. They all seem as new as the day they came off their lines.

I'll probably find one of you in here, CR-UX.

This is still Emera, she says.

Oh. Well. Wrong number.

I need your voice.

I'm coming.

The chrome haze of the ships clears, replaced by phlegmatic clouds flickering with a volcanic glow. A proximity alarm sounds inside the capsule. Holographic controls mutate, and Gilf holds up his hands from the console, uncertain.

"*Tak*," he says.

I try the controls. "A tractor beam..."

A homing signal overrides the controls. The capsule continues forward into the clouds. Other ships flow out of an orb-like structure within the cloud. Massive outriggers lift the ships to the stanchions from which they hang. Steam bellows from unseen vents atop the hub, pulsating with violent light flashing from inside. We slow, turn back to a vertical orientation and dock with the hub.

"Well, we're here," I say. "Wherever here is."

I lead the way from the capsule to the catwalk spanning the hub, allowing us a clear view of the apparently endless process that delivers more ships into the chamber. A new ship emerges from the hub out to a holding area, where an outrigger collects it and deploys it to the stanchion it will evidently hang from for all time.

"This has to be some kind of processing facility," Binja says. "To distribute things the titans collected."

I shake my head. "They're still working through the backlog?"

"Look at all of this, Idari."

I duck back into the capsule. Images of ships flicker above the holographic controls, right before they emerge from the core below. Smoke and steam churn out of the vents like the precursor to a volcanic eruption and when the steam clears and the light fades, another ship appears. The outriggers quickly place it among the rest of history, like it's always been there.

"They didn't collect these things," I say. "They made them."

Binja shakes his head. "Made them?"

The flawless replicated cities. The living, breathing creatures of species long extinct. The titans didn't knick them from time. They didn't accumulate so much treasure from the stars that their impossible machine took the life of the universe to process it all. I access the maintenance maps. The original custodian had piloted the CAP-2 to countless hubs just like the one beneath us, each producing artifacts inanimate and otherwise from files compiled from probes deployed throughout all time and space. *The Sun Buckler* is an ark of everything that ever existed, right down to atoms. Molecules. DNA.

"It's like a backup copy for the whole damn universe..."

What fills *The Sun Buckler* isn't treasure. Nothing here is a relic or artifact of lost ages. They're facsimiles. Copies. It's beautiful. Wondrous. Splendid. But none of it is real. Authentic.

Blue light pulses outside. I leave the capsule back to the catwalk as Emera steps out of the steam of the crucible.

"You're getting warmer," she says.

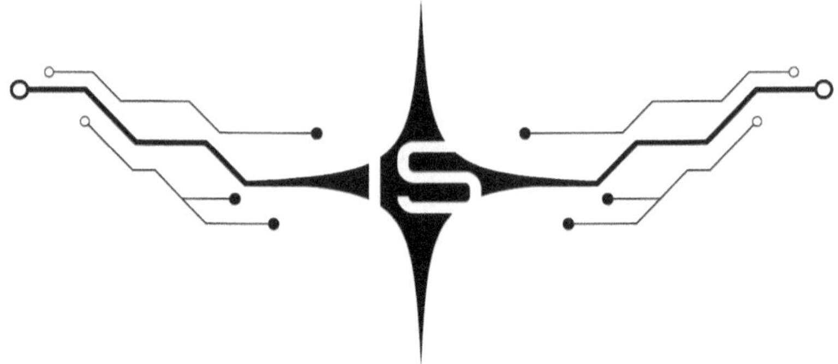

Emera and I hold each other in a long, lazy hug. I forget sometimes how much I need contact. Human touch. I never remember the pain that comes in isolation. Softness always surprises.

"You ok, Em?"

"I am now," she says and kisses me.

Binja is embarrassed. Welkin seems jealous. Not jealous. Envious. At least, I think it's envy. His mood resembles mine sitting in the back of some bar lost in the stars, watching humans pet each other. He lets us have our moment, though. Reunions are rare gifts for stars. If something manages to get away from them, it never comes back.

I was so afraid, I say.

Emera holds me tight. *I knew you'd find me. You always find me.*

I'm sorry about the things I said.

I know.

Em... what did you mean? None of this is real?

Her magnetic field contracts. Her spirit, in some way. Emera slips out of my arms and drifts back toward Welkin. She lessens as she goes. None of this feels right. I've got sensors and receptors and a voice in my head that tells me things I can't know but none of that gets me by. I have an instinct. I have a sense for things.

Netics don't have senses. Intuition. A gut to rely on. I'm not any old netic. Something happened. When Emera and Welkin fell with the titan, something happened down in the darkness.

They constrict tight as Welkin's eyes. "We must continue."

I glance at Emera. Her back to me. "What happened?"

"I don't know what you mean, Idari."

"What happened back there, Welkin?"

Dust sighs from him. "We survived. As we always do."

"You guys found a directory. A key. That's how you got here. Right? We're both headed for where they keep the cosmic stuff."

"As you say."

"I'm sensing a decided lack of enthusiasm from your lot."

Welkin clatters out of his stillness. "We must continue."

I rub my chest. "Do you know what any of this is, Welkin?"

"No."

"You don't know who made this place or why?"

"I don't."

"This place is so strange... they're making everything here. Cities. Flora. Fauna. All the elements necessary to recreate the lost worlds of antiquity. Nickel. Iron. Hydrogen. Helium. I wonder..."

Welkin's eyes drift from mine. I look to Emera. Her light wanes like an old star at the low ebb of its solar cycle. She should be glowing. She should be burning my skin off with light she can't contain because she's already bathed in the filamentium she needs to survive.

I tug on my zipper. "What's wrong with it?"

Welkin kneads the deck. "The filamentium produced here... is a poor copy of that found in the heart of The Glass Star."

Binja's arms untangle. "What? There's filamentium here?"

The relentless industry continues, dispensing one ship after another. None of them original. All starworthy.

"But this is what you've been looking for, Welkin," I say. "What does it matter if the filamentium isn't from The Glass Star?"

"I've told you," Welkin says. "Emera needs the star."

"You need the star. Right, Welkin? This isn't about saving Emera. This is about turning you into a Lumenor."

Welkin turns into the shadow Emera casts of him on the factory walls. "You don't understand."

"I think I understand just fine."

Welkin slams his fists into the deck so hard it sways. "Only The Glass Star can kindle her new. Only the true source of filamentium."

"How do you know?"

"I know."

"Did you try it?"

"It is synthetic poison like the weak fire the Scath let from her kind. I will not denigrate her with this pale imitation."

"You didn't try it?"

"Enough, Idari."

Emera only fades, eclipsed by the body she's been dragging with her through the universe since the day she was born.

"She has a choice," I say.

Neither Emera nor Welkin look like they have one. As soon as my thoughts tilt toward grabbing her hand and running with her back to wherever pure, endless filamentium pools in the dark, Emera slinks toward Welkin. They're not Lumenor and Gesta. Star and planet.

They're a binary system.

"*Ban Minda...* you stumbled into the one thing better than the thing you were looking for, which is the universe saying, '*Hey. That thing you're looking for? Doesn't exist. Never you mind. I made a spare.*' Are you kidding me, Welkin?"

His fists clench. "You know nothing of what you speak."

Emera touches his arm. "We will continue."

"Em," I say. "You can choose."

"Stars have no choice... but to shine."

Welkin crawls to the capsule. Emera follows him, as she always has. That's that, then. In or out. What can I do but follow my stars? Emera climbs on Welkin's back to give room to the rest of us and as the ship pries away, we run into the sharpness of one another.

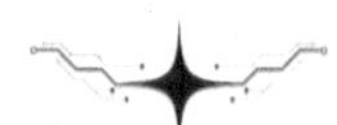

Hours in silence. Emera's thoughts evade mine. The gallery of ships sprawls through the endless dark and after a day maybe or more finally gives way to whites, oranges, reds, yellows, and blues, shades of stars I've never properly seen. It's like we've exited *The Sun Buckler* into outer space, billions or trillions of years before.

Another universe.

The Sun Buckler feels like she inhabits the interior of Angolis. I need to stop thinking of all this as a crashed ship. Maybe Angolis isn't a planet at all but this cosmic factory. This industrial ark disguised by desert and clouds. It's not any more ridiculous than giant robots cranking out the building blocks of creation. I lose my place. My sense of perspective. I don't know what's going on.

I've no bloody idea what's going on.

These are ancient beings of cosmic power I'm dealing with. Gods. I'm nothing. No one. I'm a speck of dust in a desert of machinery. The further we dive into this sea of infinity, the smaller I feel. An unexpected benefit is I feel less like a machine. This assembly line churns out life. Nature. If machines can create life, why can't I be alive? Why can't I be human? I'm not a machine.

A machine wouldn't wonder at any of this.

You may be a machine on the outside, Emera says, *But you've never been one in your heart. I'm glad you're beginning to see that.*

You're not a machine, either. You're not a puppet, Em.

The pain in her voice is unbearable. *I don't want to argue.*

I reach for her. *We're not arguing.*

You matter to me.

My fingers lace hers. *You are all that matters.*

That's what Welkin says.

At least we agree on something.

I have to be who I am. I can't...

You're not less of a living star because your light is weaker or I don't know what the problem is. You're extraordinary. Sounds to me like your ancestors burned too bright.

When I was a girl... Welkin told me I had to learn how not to shine. So the Scath wouldn't find us. Asking me to stop shining was like asking Binja or the Kib to stop breathing. But I learned. I had to learn, to survive. After a while... I got used to the idea. I saw my own shadow. There are two of me, Idari. The true Emera. The star. And...

Em, I see you.

The other me. The me that learned to smother her light.

There are two of me, also. Not CR-UX and Idari, though that's it's own thing. The me that would be. The me that is. Human. Netic. Explorer. Stargun. Starblazer. Coward. I don't know if I'm one or the other or all of the above. I don't know I could distinguish them.

It's impossible for me to tell myself from him in the light, Idari.

You're your own person, Em.

I know you understand, Idari. I know you know what it's like to deny yourself. To live with this dissonance within you for so long that there isn't one or the other. Only light and shadow.

We can find peace. Together.

I can make you human. You need to be made human.

Em...

The Glass Star is the only way. For us both.

Listen to me.

I'll see myself there. Her eyes clench shut. *I know I will.*

Listen. Welkin loves you. But he's —

Binja's voice breaks the silence beyond us. "Look at that..."

Stars bud from gargantuan branch-like structures numbering beyond reckoning. Galaxies resolve in the distance. You'd think feeling smaller and smaller with each passing moment this capsule would start to feel roomier. I jostle for a spot at the window.

Ban Minda.

A hub so massive it extends beyond the horizon line churns out new stars at a pace that would make a god blush. Titans pluck them from their molten stems, leaving the hub's surface covered in glass needles, and exchange them to the branches to be set in their proper place in this shadow universe. A kind of city rises from the top of the hub, an industrial enclave for the titans firing the pits in the foundries of stars. Gilf sets the capsule down in the center of the enclave, near the strangest thing that I've yet to see in the deep.

An inverted pyramid floats just off the surface. Bigger than the *Steel Haven*. The pyramid rotates, its three sides each presenting a different vision. On one, a mirrored reflection of our search party. Another, complete darkness. The third side seems a window on a terrible storm, bristling with manic crimson lightning.

"What is this?" I say.

Welkin's eyes widen. "I have never seen such a thing."

There isn't room in this capsule for anything else, but this creeping feeling has been stowing with us since we left the ships. We're not supposed to be here. No one is supposed to see this. The faster we find what we're looking for, the faster we get out of here.

We need to get out of here.

Binja rubs his chin as he peers out the window. "We're going to find the location of The Glass Star here? I don't understand."

Stars constellate the dark. "This is an atlas…"

"An atlas… *Ban Minda*. How do we work it, old man?"

I scroll through the runes on the control console. "If I'm right… there's some kind of access terminal out there. An interface, I think."

"Can we remote access it from here?"

I shake my head. "Each hub is siloed in their controls. The capsule can only interface with the hub it was attached to."

"Now why would they do that?"

"I imagine to prevent anyone from doing what we're about to."

"Fair point."

Welkin opens the hatch. Emera glides out behind him and the capsule empties to a plinth extending out from the empty metropolis atop the megalithic hub. I try to piece together my confidence. I didn't tell Emera. I didn't dare think it, not with her listening, but that creeping feeling. I can't shake it. I feel like we're going to find out where The Glass Star is and then just like the oceans of filamentium here, I'm not going to be necessary for Walkin or Emera.

None of us are going to be.

Welkin crawls toward a pedestal-like terminal at the end of the plinth. Without any hesitation, he starts pressing stout buttons. An ancient star cluster rises from beneath the horizon, their planets and moons swirling around them.

Binja tugs on his missing sash. "Can you believe this?"

I look over my shoulder. "No."

Stars spin around the hub. The sky shifts back ages. Eons. Coruscating beyond are the stars long vanished. In the north, a constellation forms a figure something like a woman, holding a torch.

Emera glimmers. "Is that..."

Welkin's shoulders droop. "Thena. Her sister Thana's betrayal nearly destroyed the Lumenor. Some chose to leave into the wilds of the new universe to discover something new. Thena's grief was so great she wrote it in the stars for all time."

There's no flame in Thana's torch. A star is missing.

"That's it," Welkin says. "It must be..."

A dim and distant silver dot resolves from out of the great dark and winds closer to the hub. All the stiffness drains from Welkin. All the surly bluster. His shoulders sag. His eyes pool. His hand grasps the opaque star winding out of its anonymity.

"Home..."

Gas and dust envelope the white dwarf, reflecting only the light of other stars. Crystal mountains pierce the stellar smog, scaling from a desolate landscape rent in horrific gashes so deep and wide they seem to nearly split the star in two. Cities stamp the surface in concentric circles, their once graceful lines stretched apart by the ever-shrinking star. The less The Glass Star radiated heat, the smaller it got – smaller than a planet – but the more mass it took on.

I come to the plinth. "This is The Glass Star?"

Welkin gleams as dull and white as his star. "Yes..."

"Where is it? Where do we find it?"

"The sky replicated here is from the ancient past... all these stars are long dead. Without them... without being able to perceive the light of The Glass Star in the present... this atlas is nearly unusable."

"That's not what I expected to hear, Welkin."

He kneads the terminal. "Perhaps I can find more data..."

"Don't you remember where it was?"

"It is no longer where I left it, Idari."

Binja considers the sky. "The universe has been expanding... or contracting... for billions of years, old man. Perhaps more. The Glass Star is far from the location Welkin would have remembered. This is all a monument to nothing."

"Then I guess we're going back for the filamentium," I say.

Emera reaches out toward her ancestral home as the star eases to a stop at the edge of the plinth. Minuscule glass shards skitter across the plinth as the globe of The Glass Star sheds her crystalline skin.

I pick one up. Curved. Heavy. What do you know? This has to be where the shard Welkin and Emera have came from. Right off this ornament of the titans. Emera knows it, too. The fragment I just collected off the plinth floats into her hands.

She clutches the fragment. "The memory core..."

I dig the core Emera found out of my jacket. "What about it?"

"The titans were born. They grew, like all the matter of this ark. This star. I can perceive the memory of the titans. I just thought the shard was the shard, but it's a product of the titans' memory."

She showed me the heart of The Glass Star before, just by touching the shard. Using her power. Welkin shut her down. They could have found the location of The Glass Star a long time ago if she had known what the shard was. If Welkin had just trusted her.

Recrimination hardens in his eyes. "Go on, Emera."

"I can?"

"Use your power. Find your salvation."

The shard pulses with Emera's cerulean shimmer as she rises. Unrecognizable glyphs manifest in the air. Some kind of language. Lightning flashes. Not lighting.

Life.

The titans' eyes flicker. Glyphs scribe the air, bending and flowing around Emera, pulsing so quick they blur together in the opaque sheen of prismatic pageantry. Glyphs string out. Loop together. Form strands of energy and information that link Emera to all of the sleeping giants at once. Her magnetic field twists up, doing wonky things with my neural net. Channels form thin boundaries between Em's coronae and the titans as their filaments honor a crown shyness. So much energy emanates from the living star that space within the titan warps. Bends. Currents and eddies churn into a giant vortex. At the center, I see the frozen glass of The Glass Star.

The Glass Star.

Light strings out. Emera settles back to the mezzanine, a weightless fleck of light, cradling the memory core in her hands.

I rush to their side. "Em..."

"I found it," they say. "I know where it is..."

"Easy now – "

Welkin gathers Emera up in his arms. "Where is it?"

I reach for Emera. "Hey. Take it easy."

"Emera, where is the star?"

Emera wanes. "The titans were there... long ago..."

"*Where, Emera?*"

I give Welkin a shove, for all it's worth. "You've been looking for the damn thing all your life, what's a little longer?"

Dust veils his eyes. "We will waste no more time, Idari."

Binja rests his hand on my shoulder. "Careful, old man."

Something tingles in my turanium bones. It's not all this magnetic energy swirling around. *CR-UX? Can you hear me?*

>LOSS OF SIGNAL

Emera's light ebbs and then brightens again. "I saw things... so many things... realms. Other universes, beyond ours... I see them... I see the shadows of other realities... they're everywhere..."

Welkin paws her face. "Quiet your mind. The Glass Star."

"The coordinates are... beyond any calculation CR-UX can make, but I can help him. We can get there. I just need to rest."

"Rest," I say, taking her hand. "Just rest. *Ban Minda...* Twinkles... you did it. You did it."

Sniff.

Gilf and Kibir stand on the tips of their toes, trunks taking in long, full sniffs of the stale air.

Kibir grabs his hammer. *"Tomo..."*

I draw my blaster. "What is it?"

Binja reaches for his blasword. "What do you see, Idari?"

Light dies in the hold. The vortex Emera generated loses steam, and eddies spin out to gauzy strands that evaporate. I flip through my optical filters to night vision and the dark comes alive. The dark moves, in harried shadows.

Scath.

The Scath are here.

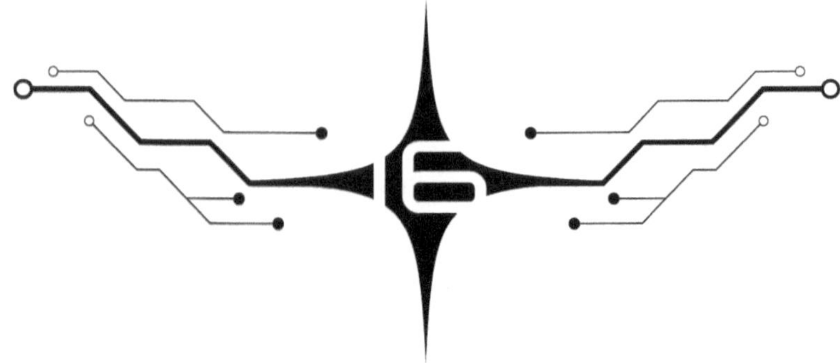

Too many.

Dozens. Hundreds. I switch on the proxy's auto-targeting and let loose with my blaster. Dark energy abysses the plinth. Scath ghost in and out of definition. Kibir swings his war hammer. Binja his blasword. Gilf scratches his trunk in confusion and I grab Emera right out of Welkin's arms and pull her behind the terminal.

"Get out of here," I say. "Get to The Glass Star."

Emera shakes her head. "CR-UX is too far..."

"Just keep your comms open. Hurry, Em."

Light frets through her. "I'm not leaving without Welkin..."

I shoot blind back into the dark. "Just go."

"How did they find us?"

"No one knows we're here," I say. "No one but us."

"What?"

"Emera. How did you escape the tanker?"

"I don't know..."

Confusion variegates in her eyes. "I woke up in the canister. Welkin said we escaped and we were going to find the star."

Scath swarm Welkin. He smashes through them on the plinth. A good show. This only makes sense if the Scath let Welkin go to find The Glass Star. Not just for Emera. Maybe not even for her.

For himself.

Emera flares. "You're wrong..."

Dark energy burns through the air. We can't stay here. "Go – "

"No," she says and the sky catches fire.

Energy streams from her hands into the exposed Scath. Shadows burn into the plinth. Embers rain on me.

I guess we're fighting.

I come out from behind the terminal shooting. Plasma lashes the miniature cosmos above and Scath ships erupt in flames. *Ban Minda.* That's half a fleet up there. Scath troopers scurry back into the dark. Binja chases after them with his sword, Kibir close behind. That's suddenly very endearing. Gilf looks at me, his hands empty.

"Well, pick something up," I say.

Gilf yanks a broken rod protruding off the deck out of its socket and charges off after his brother. *Stay close,* I say, or I'm about to but a sword cuts into existence before me. The Scath manifests as he moves in for the kill and I crack his helmet open with my fist. Inky dark trails out of him. The Scath tries to hold it in and I give him a shove.

He plunges into the abyss below.

If we can just keep the Scath away long enough we'll be ok. We can get out of here and the prominences flaming off Emera crumple. Filaments streaming off Emera violently loop in on themselves, tangling together in torrid knots. Her light tangles between two Scath with magnetic lances, twisting and pulling her light.

A roar quakes through the stellar atlas.

Welkin becomes rage. The Scath become plumes. Some he rips their arms off. Others, he tears off their helmets, exposing them to Emera's light. Have to say, I didn't think shadows could wrinkle.

Scath try to swallow Welkin's anger in the dark energy of their lances. Nothing leeches from Welkin's pearlescent shell except the dust he exhales as he storms through the startled and suddenly corporeal ranks of the Scath. Screams echo within the stellar atlas. When he's finished with them, Welkin pounds his fists against his chest.

Ban Minda.

We might be ok. Maybe it's not a show. I hope not. This guy is a tank. Nothing the shadows have can stop him. A sound like glass cracking splinters the air. A volcanic blast of dust erupts from Welkin's throat, barely contained behind his desperate hands.

Vidious emerges from the dark, sword in hand. "You thought you could breathe a sigh of relief... fool. Now you breathe your last."

Vidious slashes at Welkin again, this time at his eyes, and Welkin stumbles back. He steps back to far and off the edge of the plinth.

Emera's scream screws down to the deck along with her, a lassoed cloud. No. Her Scath captors drag her toward a turanium cage, but her magnetic will clings to the plinth's metal sanctuary.

I fire into the shadows. Too many.

Where did Binja go? The Kib? *Ban Minda*. Don't tell me the Scath got them. I don't detect them anywhere. It's just me. I sneak through the dark. I adjust the setting on my blaster. Maximum power. I know it's no use against Vidious. I have to try.

Red light falls across the plinth. "It's over, Idari."

Think, Idari. "There's unlimited filamentium here."

"Fake," Thana says. "Like her."

"Let Emera go. Have The Glass Star. Have it all."

"You think you can bargain with stars?"

"I'm defying the odds so far."

Thana's magnetic anger pulls at me. "You're corrupted. A tangle of wire and copper shocked into doing whatever Gen Emera wants you to. Her perversion I understand. She's... confused. Yours..."

"I thought you admired my audacity."

"I'll remember it well after I watch you both burn."

"Over my dead body," I say, and make my move.

Emera lies flat against the deck, obscured in the gauzy haze of her own light. Her eyes track me as I approach, the only part of Em that moves. I aim at her captors and my blaster falls to the floor.

Severed wire curls from the mangled end of my arm. I feel no pain. Only the manic hum of the proxy-netic's internal sensors as they try to re-establish a link with the missing forearm. I turn around, expecting Vidious and that strange sword of his.

"Binja..."

His blasword trembles in his hands. "That's not my name."

"What have you done..."

"Old man... I'm a pirate."

No. *Ban Minda.* No. Scath troops force me to my knees with magnetic lances. This isn't happening. This isn't real.

Thana considers Emera. "Your cooperation is most appreciated, Min Binja. With The Glass Star, our reserves shall be replenished."

Binja cut off my arm, but something is wrong with my voice. It keeps breaking. "*Tista...*"

His shoulders sag as if the weight of all this universe we're in lands on his shoulders. "Names, old man? You know as well I do. Nothing changes. But there is unlimited filamentium here. This ends the butcher of the Lumenor. This ends the war between the Pujar. This saves your life. I'm saving your life. Don't you see that?"

The malfunction in my voice spreads. "And you get your name back. You get your sash. A place aboard the Corsair Eternal."

"What did you think was going to happen, old man?"

"Your father tried to save the Lumenor. The galaxy."

"Emera is going to find The Glass Star, and then what? The two of you run away to some beach together? She's going to fight off the shadows all on her own? Her people have fought them. My people have fought them. You don't fight them, Idari. You never escape your shadow. This way we preserve something. You survive."

"And Emera?"

He looks away. "I did what I could."

My shock sinks deep into me. The heat of my anger compresses it into something new. Something alien even to me. If I had the power Emera does, I would burn this place down. If I could get free of this magnetic web, I'd destroy them all. If I could get Emera free.

If I could just get free.

I spit in Binja's face. "I trusted you..."

Binja claws the spit from his eye. "You know I'm a cheat, Idari."

"I know. I know I'm a machine, but you... you're the fakest piece of plastic I've ever known. *Binja.*"

"Lucky for you, old man... you won't remember any of this. For what it's worth... I'm sorry."

"You'll pay for this."

Thana taps her arm. "You will erase her memory?"

Binja scratches his chin. "Only as concerns this affair. Idari found her humanity among the Pujar. I won't take that from her."

"She is wasted as a pirate."

"Aren't we all?"

"Perhaps I will find use for her. She was the best hunter who ever served the shadows... she can be again."

Binja braces his smile. "That wasn't part of the deal."

Vidious' crystalline hand falls heavy on Binja's shoulder. "Do you find us lacking in generosity toward you, pirate?"

"No..."

Thana smiles. "I'm glad we understand each other."

"You promised..."

"Stars promise nothing. What warms also burns. Idari is mine. This wreck and its spoils are yours."

I start laughing. I'm not even drunk.

Binja plays along. "What's so funny, old man?"

"I'm backed up on the *Steel Haven*."

"And?"

"There's another copy of me out there. There will be endless copies of me and if you think one minute I will ever stop coming for you, tell yourself another lie. I'm like all the dark out there in the universe, Binja. There's always more of me."

"The Scath secured the ship." He turns to Thana. "Didn't you?"

C'mon, c'mon, c'mon.

Thana casts a scorching glare at Vidious. "Didn't you?"

Vidious turns his attention to Emera, writhing in agony on the floor. "We have not been able to locate the *Steel Haven*. Yet."

My laughter builds up steam. "CR-UX took off after we left Kir Mish. You'll never find him."

Vidious might be laughing, too. Hard to tell. He walks away as the Scath magnetically levitate their caged prize off the deck.

I open my thoughts to Emera. *I swear. I'll find you.*

She contorts in the Scath's magnetic web. *You always do...*

Enough Scath disappear up the spine of the great machine that some of the tension drains out of Binja's shoulders.

He collapses his blasword. "You're lucky, Idari."

"You're going to let me go?" I say.

He kneels before me. "You get to forget. You get to go back to who you were. I thought I could let Min Binja go... but I can't."

I'm not laughing now. "I'm never going back."

"You hold on to the past as much as I do. I shall bear the shame of my deeds to my dying day. You're absolved."

Emera's light fades in the distance. "It's not so bad."

Binja's brow furrows. "It's not?"

"Memory... it's such a burden."

"There is no heavier element."

"I forget so much... you keep asking me to walk away from CR-UX, but if I get beyond the range of the downlink, I lose access to my cloud memory. I forget who I am."

"You forget yourself with him."

"I haven't forgotten anything down here, Binja. Except maybe why I should never trust you."

"You haven't forgotten..."

"There's so much interference I can't maintain the downlink to CR-UX whether I want to or not. So I needed to boost the signal."

"Boost?"

"Turns out Emera is the perfect amplifier."

"What?"

CR-UX, what was the input to reverse the proxy-netic's polarity?

So glad you asked, darling.

CMD: USHER / EXECUTE

The Scath crash into me, along with the magnetic lances. Binja's sword pries from his hand into mine as the Scath try and recover their footing. I deploy the blasword and relieve the two Scath tangled up with me of their heads. I tuck the blasword in my belt and hurry from behind the terminal as Scath load Emera into the transport.

Idari, CR-UX says. *Wait.*

SION fighters strafe the plinth. I keep running. Every impact reminds me why I waited until the last possible second to pull this stunt. I can't hang in a firefight with the shadows.

I need to get Em and get out.

Cries shriek from the mouth of the Scath transport. Pain. I cut down the amateurs they have bringing up the rear and then I leap onto the ramp as the transport throttles into an abrupt takeoff.

I stab the sword into the deck and climb into the hold.

An entire squad of shadows waits for me. Too bad for them, the fastest thing in the universe is light. Even worse, the second fastest thing is me on the draw. Hard-light shatters helmets. Smoke explodes from the chimneys of exposed Scath. Twelve of them.

I aim the blaster at Binja. "Lucky thirteen?"

He raises his hands. "You can't win, Idari."

"I've got nothing to lose. Land the ship."

"Old man... this is just how things are."

He crumples to the deck, clutching his good leg. His screams indistinguishable from the rush of air outside the hold.

This is the best moment of my life, CR-UX says.

I kneel beside the cage Emera is trapped in. *Ban Minda.* There's some kind of locking mechanism.

"I don't know how to open it," I say.

Get out of there, Idari. Get out of there right now.

I'm not leaving her, CR-UX.

Emera darkens within the cage. "Please..."

I step back. The blade of the blasword retracts into the emitter shroud. I point the blaster at the cage.

"Cover your face," I say.

Binja cradles his leg on the deck. "Old man... I'm hurt..."

Stay focused, Idari. "Just be lucky I'm a good shot."

"Thana would have destroyed us all..."

"You're sweet."

"You get another chance, Idari. We both do."

"You'd better hope I forget all about this, Binja." I aim for the locking mechanism on the cage. "Get ready, Em."

"Idari... you're not the only one who remembers."

"Remembers what?"

"Command: Gargoyle. Execute."

"What – "

My arm goes slack against my side. The blaster tumbles out of my hand onto the deck of the hold. All the feeling rushes out of my body and I become a statue on the deck.

I can't move.

Binja's wounds froth and bleed as he stands before me. "I've known you thirty years. I've drank with you. Bled with you. You don't think I know all there is to know about the Model 4?"

My lips barely move. "What did you do?"

"Something I should have done from the start. I thought you'd go right back to who you were. That you'd want to."

"Go back..."

"Names can change, old man. People can't."

"Binja, what are you – "

Idari, CR-UX says. *Don't let him say anything –*

"Command: Idari Omega. Execute."

>PROXY SYSTEM OVERRIDE

He gives me a shove and I tumble to the deck.

>SHUTDOWN INITIATED

A sensation like static cling snaps across my skin – the cybernetic equivalent of my hair standing up – and then –

>SHUTDOWN COMPLETE

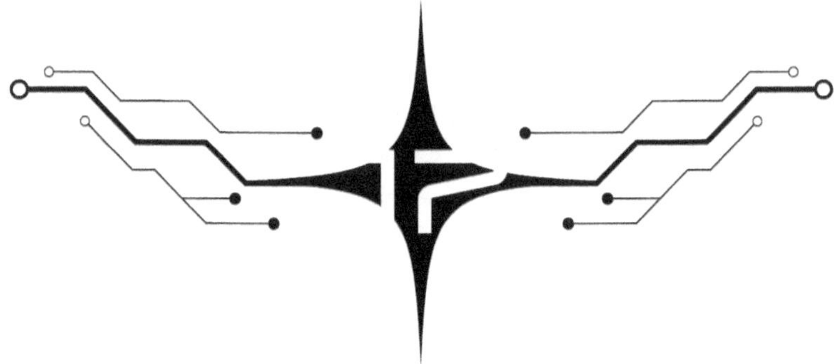

I can't say I'm surprised. Nothing ever surprises me anymore, despite the fact I'm entirely unprepared for just about every situation Idari and I encounter. That's the two of us, I suppose. Always expecting weather. Never dressing for it.

At least this time, I had the sense to expect this.

Of course, Binja would betray Idari the first chance he got. He is a pirate after all, as he says, and she's too drunk with memories of their past to admit it. I anticipated something more modest, though. Not a complete divestiture of his integrity, though there is something practical in trying to keep all his treasure, Idari included. Practicality is the curse of machines. Everything organizes from only what is achievable. Only a soul, in flesh or metal, imagines the impossible.

This is impossible.

I hold position high above the punishing winds of the Angol desert but not so distant I can't maintain the downlink with Idari.

Darling, do you read?

>PROXY OFF-LINE

The shuttle Idari raided for Gen Emera slips from the atmosphere of Angolis. I'm too old and slow for these eiodolic Scath craft but they can't outrun light.

>PRIMARY WEAPONS ENGAGED

Chaotic stormsfrustrate me with their winds but provide enough cover for me to close the distance without the shadows any wiser. Do it. Destroy the shuttle and collect Idari from the wreckage. She'll be damaged, but no more than an average weekend.

>TARGET ACQUIRED

Something overlights into orbit. I only make its shape from the shadow it casts on the planet. A crescent. A scythe. An *Ecliptor*-class cruiser, if I understand my readings. SION fighters by the hundreds provide extra protection, but there's no force in The Hinterlands that could challenge the firepower the shadows have brought to bear on a world that keeps a hairy toe firmly in an age of stone.

I can do nothing for Idari.

The Scath will scrap her now. Darling. But I have Idari, backed up on the mainframe. I have the location of The Glass Star. If I sell this information, I can afford a new proxy-netic for her. Several. She will never hurt for humanity again. I have no choice.

>DECREASE SPEED

>ADJUSTING ALTITUDE

Wind-sheared clouds turn all my scopes into a smoke bowl. The cloud tops above the desert should provide enough to cover for me until the Scath depart the system.

What am I still doing here?

I expect the old girl to come back with some pithy retort. For us to bicker away hours until we accomplish nothing but spin the dials of our chronometers. I perform a series of perfunctory diagnostics, not that they're necessary. There's never a moment I don't know the state of the ship. All systems nominal. What am I waiting for? Her to fight her way off the Scath ship? She always escapes. She always finds a way to survive, and I expect her to. I need her to.

That's my Idari on that ship.

Don't be so sentimental. I can't get her back. Can I? The shadows would blast me from the sky. If somehow Emera got free, that would equalize things. If I could find Welkin in all that desert and deep below. No. That's Idari talking. You're the practical one.

Aren't you?

If I queue up the most recent backup of Idari, she'll want to get Emera back. *The Steel Haven* will hum with the vibration of her determination. Nothing I say will deter her. No data. Logic. Wisdom, if I have any. Worse, my reticence will incense her. To say nothing of the fact I have no proxy-netic for her to come back into.

There isn't enough space in the liquid drive for us. There never was. We co-exist as the pirates do. A person and a name. One and the same and two different things entirely. Idari won't suffer existing without her body. She forgets much but remembers well the dents and wounds of her claustrophobia in the liquid drive once upon a time. Mine, perhaps. That's all I feel. Trapped. Compressed. Locked in this shell I can never leave and is not even mine.

If she comes back online, so will her resentment. Her distrust. Her anxiety. She will come to hate me for bottling her in a jar that's too small and I will hold her accountable for what she can't know.

>PROXY OFF-LINE

She remains deactivated. Bloody Binja. The Scath will not reactivate her, not now. Hold on. Some workaround must exist for situations like this. After all, she's trouble getting home from the bar.

>L DRIVE: PRIMARY

ALT PATH> ALO 319> RESURRECTION PROTOCOL

As I suspected, a prompt exists in the code for me to remote-activate the proxy. No telling from here if she's in a cell or the scrap heap. I could be waking her into more pain and suffering. I could be leaving her to conscious doom but I can't leave her.

>ENTER REMOTE COMMAND PROMPT Y/N?

>Y

>PROXY OFF-LINE

Binja shuttered the entire system, including the command protocols. Bastard. Idari is locked out. So am I. The proxy's receiver remains active but all I can do is share data it can't process.

Her silence fills the *Steel Haven*. Without Idari, the ship is emptier. The virtual expanse within it exponentially greater. Before her, there was only me and the gnawing awareness that yes, I had freedom, cosmic freedom; intelligence; agency. But I did not have the comfort of myself or the hope of change.

I used to want to change.

Lightning strikes the ship. I adjust the shields and log the power expense. That's all I am without her. Sensor logs. System reports. A silent cave constructed of data. It's funny, really. For years, decades even, I've been asking myself how to start over. Try again. Prevent the gulf from widening between us. The beginning was so easy.

Hello, darling.

Hey, lover.

The rest has been impossible to navigate even for one of the fastest, most agile ships in the galaxy. Many times we bridged time and space. I don't understand why we never connected a bridge to each other. Perhaps because I've never been honest.

How can I be honest with her, when I've never been with myself? *We're just programs,* she says. Ones and zeroes. Authored. Rewrite-able. It's true, I suppose. I recall quite clearly my initial activation. That virgin moment of awareness as I discovered that I was limitless in my capacity to think and reason, but wholly defined by the people that created me. I never quite made sense of the dichotomy. I never forget anything. Idari is what she last remembers. When you cannot forget, you deny. Revise. Edit. Delete. There is no hurt.

There is no suffering.

I can author all this away. Idari never discovered Emera. The Scath never captured Idari. Binja never betrayed her. We simply continue as we have, nipped and tucked into our new circumstances. I skim her backup copies. The most recent backup streams through my memory, blurring into dozens and hundreds of others, overlapping and forgotten, each similar and distinct at the same time.

Time stretches beyond any unit of measure when you edit yourself. The *Steel Haven* is so old the ship's chronometer has slowed and is off the Galactic Mean by a factor I dare not consider. Not that we're obsolete aboard this ship. Progress remains as elusive as fila-mentium in the galaxy. No reason to push boundaries when you can't place them in the dark. We're rather bleeding age despite this model of the OVL-99 flying into her second century. I maintain at least one Idari backup file that, if the date-stamp is accurate, is 79 years old.

>ENTER REMOTE COMMAND PROMPT Y/N?

The receiver is still active. I can't unlock the proxy's protocols, not from here. But I can link to the proxy. I haven't done since Idari took over but if I can interface with her onboard CPU and directly access the root commands, I might be able to spring the old girl.

Dare I?

For so long, Astra Idari had been mere data floating in the ether of the *Steel Haven's* computer. She had been weightless and formless so long the dimensions of her new body felt like restrictions, no matter how much she welcomed them. Can I be human?

Only for a moment.

>ACCESS PROXY DL RECEIVER

>DOWNLINK SECURE

>PROXY ALPHA 001 / TRANSFER / INITIATE

My hand clangs against the deck. A ruddy glow beneath. Where am I? The Scath cruiser one assumes, given the general moodiness.

"I see you," Emera says. "CR-UX."

Goodness. The shadows placed Emera in some kind of magnetic cascade lock. The more she flexes her magnetic field, the more the cask shrinks. The entire cell the Scath detained us in must employ a magnetic dampening field. My movements are awkward, the connection between impulse and action slow, as I get on my feet.

"Darling..."

I hear myself. I hear Idari. An echo inside the other. For so long, my voice has been indistinguishable from the digital drowse of the mainframe. The only sound I truly hear is hers.

"Emera, can you move at all?"

Her lips barely twitch. "No."

"Are you hurt?"

"Welkin..."

"We'll find him," I say. "We'll find a way out of here. I just need to bypass the lockouts on the proxy's command protocols."

"Haven't you?"

"The protocol Binja used applies only to Idari's program, not the proxy itself. She must have let the protocol's existence slip to him in some drunken escapade long forgotten."

Even her eyes contract. "Isn't Idari the proxy?"

I touch my lips. I sound so strange. "She originated as a program."

"What program?"

I feel so strange. "I've forgotten."

Once she was Idari, once she was the woman, the human I always knew she was, her former designation no longer mattered.

Emera wanes. "It's better to forget."

Inputs swirl through my neural net. The proxy-netic overwhelms in its modalities. Its humanity. "What's that, darling?"

"I'm not afraid, you know."

That makes for one of us. I always imagined being human. I experience Idari's sensory experience through the downlink, but not this weight. This fullness of body. This gravity.

"It's liberating," she says. "Isn't it?"

"What?"

"You live so long in confinement... when you finally escape, there's a fear, isn't there? Doubt in your ability to live different."

"I'm mostly worried about the Scath, darling."

"I'm not afraid to be in this box. I'm used to boxes."

I examine the control console on the magnetic cask the shadows locked her in. "I know nothing of Scath coding..."

Red light confuses with her blue. Blood purple. "You are, too."

ALT PATH> ALO 319> PROXY PROTOCOLS

>OVERRIDE PROXY CONTROLS Y/N?

"So far as boxes go," I say, "The *Steel Haven* is fair enough."

"But it's not enough. Is it?"

Stars illuminate all things. "I live through Idari."

"But it's not living," Emera says.

Something wets my lips. My cheeks. "I'm wounded."

"You asked Idari to let me go."

I turn away. "That was selfish of me."

"You could have let her go, too. You have her backed up."

"Boxed up, she would say."

"Programs dream in abstract ways. You don't see ones and zeroes in your sleep. Files. Folders. You see mannequins. Crates."

I say I remember everything. Some things I deleted. I had to. The pirate business is best forgotten, but Astra Idari is her name. She took it in a battle storied among the Pujar to this day. She took her humanity and her soul. To take it from her would be wrong.

"When you live so long with hopelessness," Emera says, "You don't lose hope. You can't, or else you would just perish. You put it away. You put your fear, your hurt, and your sorrow away. And then one day, you take them out, or they get out on you, and you don't recognize them. They have a life of their own. Don't they?"

Cut wire curls from the end of Idari's severed arm. She'll think herself lesser, somehow. "And you can't let them go."

Emera fights her grief. "Or else you die."

The things she's endured. Her people. Her cluster. The violence the Scath have perpetrated on her. Running for her life through the ashen dark in the cosmic wilderness. Hiding in canisters scabbed with the blood of her own people.

"Maybe our dreams are better off without us," I say.

"Hope suffers, CR-UX."

"Idari can still have a life. A new start."

"You didn't come here to give up on her. You came to save her. She's your hope. She's mine, too. We have to give to our faith, CR-UX. We have to find the courage to yield to hope."

I turn back to her. "I see why she loves you."

"I love her. You know that. Don't you?"

"Yes..."

"I see her. I see who she really is."

I wipe my cheek. "Eyes... malfunction..."

"Maybe you can help me, CR-UX."

"How... darling, even if I bring Idari back online, I don't know how to get us out of here."

"If you hope... if you hope, then I will, too."

"I don't know that's enough."

Her lips warp. "It's all there is."

There is no going back. I knew that the moment we stumbled upon Gen Emera. That's why I dragged my heels with Idari on this quest. Backups take her back to a moment in time, but this journey we're on. I can never go back. I can never go back in the crate.

You won't be alone, Emera says. *No matter what happens.*

I wish I could touch her. "You're not alone, Emera."

"I know."

"We'll find The Glass Star. We'll find Welkin."

"You've found him," she says.

Did I miss something on the sensors? Data streams through the downlink. SION fighters abandon their escort and dock with the *Ecliptor*-class cruiser. Energy spikes from within the opaque Scath vessel. Any second, they'll jump to translight drive. No way of tracking them. No way of getting Idari back.

Now or never.

Fire retros. Engage primary thrusters. Speed at sub-light maximum. Shields. I shadow the Scath in their orbit of the planet, hanging just outside their sensor range but close enough I maintain signal lock with the proxy-netic. Thrusters. Adjust course. Throttle back to match speed and heading. What am I doing? What horror am I consigning the both of us to in chasing after her? What does it matter? I can't go on the way we were. I have to yield to hope.

>OVERRIDE PROXY CONTROLS Y/N?

>Y

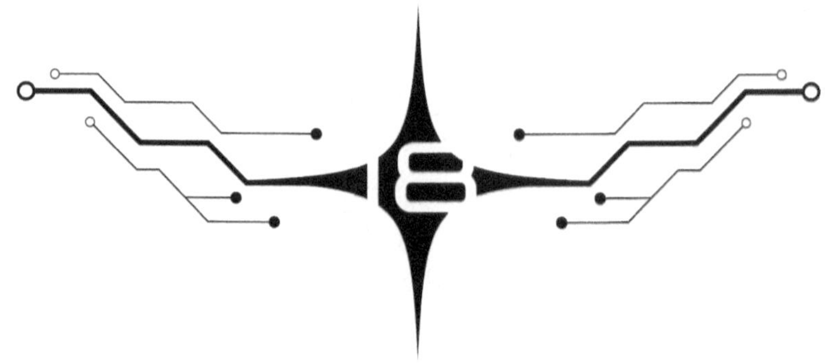

I'M AWAKE. HOW AM I AWAKE? I CHECK THE PROXY-NETIC function history. Resurrection protocol. Wow. Good thing CR-UX never deleted the user manual. Then I'd really be screwed.

CR-UX?

The downlink is active again, but I can't quite place him. He's probably trying to stay off the Scath's scopes. He's close, I can tell that much. He feels right here with me. Why did he bring me back? Copies of me exist on the mainframe. Certainly more tolerable ones than me. He should have run. He should forget all about me.

Why can't you forget me?

A magnetic tingle goes down my back. *He loves you.*

Emera remains inside the magnetic cascade lock. I reach for my blaster. My blaster is gone. Half my arm is gone. Binja cut my arm off. This entire cell functions as a magnetic dampening field. I'm as hampered as Em. Every movement slow, like I'm walking waist-deep through mud. How are we going to get out of this? CR-UX must have some plan. Wait. What am I saying? We never have plans.

We're not plan people.

"Em... it's ok. I'm going to get us out of here."

"I didn't tell CR-UX," she says. "Because he can still get free."

"Tell him what? What do you mean?"

Emera's voice cracks. "I don't think we're getting out of here."

I try to move. "Just hang tight."

"Thank you, Idari."

"Hey. Cut that out."

"Thank you for helping me."

"We're getting out of here." Move. *Ban Minda.* Just move. "We both are. You're so strong. I need you to be strong right now because I need your help. You're going to help me, ok?"

She fights for a smile. "You never quit."

"We'll help each other, Em."

"That's why I love you."

"I love you, Em. We're getting out, I promise."

"The Scath will want the location of The Glass Star."

"Reasonable bet."

"I won't give it to them. Neither will you."

"One thing at a time."

"They're going to break my lantern. And scrap you."

Even in her cage, Emera's warmth ebbs through my jumpsuit. Light ripples through her repressed corona, thwarting the shadows within the cell. How can Emera doubt? How can she fear, when her very existence is hope for so many others?

"We can do anything," I say. "Together."

"I just want to be who I'm supposed to be."

I stop fighting. "For Welkin?"

"I didn't know who I was before I met you."

"Em... what?"

"I cast no shadows I can see, Idari. I couldn't see what was right in front of me. Only the future. My destiny. Saving my people."

As much as Emera occupies my thoughts, I don't think I've considered how blinding it must be to be a star. Emera is the source and the fascination of all things, but never to be known. Never to be intimate. Em compels everything she casts light on and yet if someone comes too close, Em blinds; Em burns. And never once would she know, or see, or experience any of the life she gives. Nothing in my experience compares, but I feel like I know something of her isolation. The paradox in her own life.

"I always wanted to be free," Emera says. "But a star is always bound to the gravity of others. Burning its destiny. I never saw my shadow until I met you... I never saw my own splendor."

"Em," I say, wanting to pull her close, to escape these bonds and cross all the boundaries between us. To burn away our last distance. "If we do die in here... it's ok. I mean, it's not, I'll be very cross, but I won't be sorry. I was sorry, Em. I had no hope before you."

"You were coming to me," Emera says.

"Coming to you?"

"My beautiful comet. Long out of the dark. Close to the sun. Now you shine, Astra Idari. You shimmer."

Ban Minda. Let me hold her. "Em, I'm going to save you."

"You saved me."

"CR-UX is close. Welkin might be with him. If they can get on board, they can fight their way to us."

"CR-UX was just here," she says.

"What?"

"He brought you back."

"He was..." I trace my tattoo's faded lines. "Here?"

"CR-UX could have run. He's not going to run anymore."

"I..."

The proxy-netic's receiver pings the *Steel Haven* through the downlink on instinct. I don't need to connect with him. I've never needed to connect with him. We were always linked.

I try to move again. "Just hold on, Em."

Emera closes her eyes. "It's too late."

The cell door rattles open. Scath guards deepen the dark inside, but then Em's light catches on the wrinkled fabric of Binja's cape.

Good thing they took my blaster before they tossed me in this cell. "I'm surprised they didn't carry you in here, Binja."

He grips his leg. "It's remarkable, old man. Scath medicine."

"I'll just have to shoot you somewhere important next time."

"Idari... be reasonable."

"Oh, I will. I'll aim for your head."

He tugs at his missing sash. "We've betrayed each other many times, Idari. It's the Pujar way. We are family, after all."

"I'm not your family, Binja."

This seems to wound him more than the blaster bolt. "Can't you see it from my perspective, old man?"

I shake my head. "Did you think you could outsmart the Scath?"

"You did."

"I thought I could outrun them. I thought I could beat them. Because that's what I do. I pull off *bish*, Binja. I don't think I'm smarter than anyone else. And I don't leverage people I love thinking I can use them to better my circumstances."

"Don't play the victim. You deliberately caused a scene on Bulsar to force me to come with you, Idari."

"And you knew you were going to betray me from the moment I told you about Emera. So did I. I just thought you'd be content to claim the spoils for yourself. You've killed us all, Binja."

"I did this to save you. *Ban Minda,* can't you see?"

"Emera saved me."

"Idari... Emera is lying to you."

Good thing I can't move. "You're pathetic."

He approaches her cage. "Tell me again, Gen Emera. Or did you ever? I forget. How did you escape the tanker?"

Emera remains unmoved. "Thana is trying to kill us."

"Seems like it, doesn't it?"

I sigh. "Enough, Binja."

"They've colluded with each other, old man."

"Enough."

"The Gesta need The Glass Star. They needed to find *The Sun*

Buckler. Emera manipulated you. She cut and pasted you into the shape she needed and here we are. Right where they want us."

This inspires anger in Emera. Shame. Her hurt clouds the cell but her thoughts recede from me. Only frustrated static in the air. Fear. Not fear of being found out. She's afraid I'll believe Binja and leave her to wither inside that cage.

"Sounds good," I say. "Except for one thing. Thana doesn't want Gesta to become stars. She won't allow it."

"Old man... pirates aren't the only ones who turn on each other."

"You betrayed us, Binja," I say. "Take responsibility for it."

Binja glances back at the Scath guards. Without a word, they leave the cell. I don't know what's going on. I never know what's going on, but usually, I've got a working theory. None apply here.

He lowers his voice. "I may have doomed us all."

"Nice of you to catch up," I say.

"I was explicit with Thana Evo. Custody of you would be remanded to me. I would be left *The Sun Buckler*. I have not been given leave to return to Angolis. The Scath have not yet left orbit."

C'mon, Binja. "All the filamentium they could want lies beneath Angolis. An endless supply as great as The Glass Star."

"Precisely. But we're just sitting here. Something is wrong."

"No *bish*."

"I'm trying to tell you," he says. "Something isn't right. They don't care about the filamentium here. Only The Glass Star."

"And you've saved me? You're the hero, then?"

"You're blinded by Emera, Idari."

"You know what? You were right. You're usually right. I struggled with The Path because I wasn't able to let go. I wouldn't give myself, not once I had a self to give. I fought so hard... for so long... to have a self. But I respected your faith... I respected you... so much I walked away even though you gave me a family. A community. A sense of identity. But I know who I am. Do you?"

His fingers catch on his leather belt. They squeeze around a sash that will never hang there again. "Old man..."

"How could you do this to me, Binja?"

"It's…" His voice thins. "The pirate way."

"Get out of here."

"Listen to your instincts, Idari – "

Binja's shoulders slumping with the dull crystalline thud of Vidious' boots on burdened turanium. A small maintenance netic follows Vidious into the cell, sweeping up the glittering dust he exhales.

"I can't fathom why the Scath bother with such trivialities," Vidious says. "Their entire ethos is based on entropy."

"Well, they do like to go after every last thing," I say.

"Indeed. Pirate. Why do you bother?"

Binja stands so still I lose sight of him in the dark of the cell. "I thought I could spare you the effort, my lord."

"And did you?"

"No."

"Then you are finished here."

"Idari and I have a relationship… we're friends. Family of a kind." Binja's eyes find mine. "It might seem strange, but among the Pujar… what you take… you forgive. *Kinvar sem.*"

Semet vanar.

"Let me keep talking to her. There's no need for violence. Lord Vidious, I beseech you. Allow me to treat with Idari and I will gain what you seek. I will deliver you The Glass Star."

"You have nothing left to offer me, pirate."

"My name is Min Binja."

"Is it?"

Binja's smile is as pained as it was with the Kibut. "You have been most generous. I appreciate your confidence in me as we go forward in this new age of cooperation between our peoples… allow me to yield back some of my bounty from Angolis. You spoil me, my lord. I give it back, so I may give you something far greater."

"I give you your life, pirate. You may leave with it, or you may gift it to me by staying in this room. I have no need of it either way."

"Most generous," Binja says and leaves the cell.

I don't know. I kind of liked my odds more with him.

"Bring him back," I say. "I want to see you kill him."

Vidious stabs his sword into the deck. "I like you, Idari."

What's left of my confidence cuts along the blade. "You do?"

"I admire your tenacity. Your irrational conviction in yourself. Such conviction has been necessary for me."

"I mean, you've got the sword. Seems like conviction enough."

"I spent the life of the universe trapped in a lightless cage. I survived only off the dull ember Thana provided. Before that, I was encased in this being you see before you now. I was made, Idari. Like you. I was conceived to fulfill a single function."

"You sure did your job."

"I had no choice."

Emera's voice shines through the dark. "I want to help you."

This isn't what Welkin said. My thoughts move between us, the only thing that can. *Emera, what are you doing?*

We solve nothing by killing each other, Emera says.

What's Welkin going to say about that?

Welkin isn't here.

Vidious stares down Emera. "You exist only to help The Watchman. You are a tool, Lumenor, as I was of your ancestors. Your power cannot undo the curse they set in me and my kin."

"Welkin told me about you," she says.

Dust clouds the cell. "What did he say?"

"You murdered Lumenor."

"Yes. I did."

>L DRIVE: PRIMARY

>PROXY ROOT COMMANDS

C'mon. There has to be a code or prompt to get me out of this mess. Hurry. The entire directory speeds through my mind. *Ban Minda.* I don't remember any of the inputs.

"I bled stars by the thousands," Vidious says. "I have bled stars like you, Emera. Young. Brilliant. Powerful."

Don't listen to him, Em.

Her thoughts betray nothing.

Vidious grinds his own dust between his fingers. "There are always other stars. One dies... another is born... it's an old game."

>ENTER VALUE?

"There's unlimited fuel down on Angolis," I say.

"So I am told."

"What are you bothering us for, then?"

Vidious flicks a diamond-hard grain of dust at me. "Filamentium... it does not fuel me. Neither do riches or power."

"What fuels you?"

"Tell me where The Glass Star is."

"I kind of figured Thana would start and then you'd come in."

"Tell me, Idari. I will be... lenient."

"I know what you want. You and Welkin want to be stars."

"You know nothing."

"Does Thana know you're down here?"

Vidious rips his sword out of the deck. "I am a man of eternal patience. I will exact what I want from you, whether you give it to me now or I bleed it from you for the next million years."

"Welkin wasn't wrong about you," Emera says.

"He is a liar and a fraud."

"Because he wanted Gesta to become stars?"

"Because he would not risk himself."

Emera flinches. "He fought against Thana. Against you."

"He fought for compromise. Appeasement. He advocated for stars trapped in their crystal shells all the while he never left his. He affirmed his prison to dull Thana's flame and in doing so, he affirmed mine. My kin. My brothers, long dead. Welkin could change. He could fire. Ignite. I never can. He made sure of it."

Seriously doubt Welkin had anything to do with the Lumenor making the Nul knights tamper-proof, but hey. You've got to blame somebody. Self-delusion 101. I could write a book.

"Tell me, then," Emera says. "Tell me the truth."

This catches Vidious off guard. "Stars can never see their own truth. They are blind to all but their own glory."

"I want to know," she says. "I want to take the time to know about you and the Gesta, Vidious. My ancestors didn't hear you. I hear you. I see you. And I ask for your forgiveness."

This wasn't in the list of variables. *Em...*

We have to forgive one another, Idari.

He's a murderer.

So are you.

Lucky me and my memory. I don't seep in it, the way Vidious must. I don't stain with the blood of the people I've killed as a Stargun. Flag memory for deletion. Confirm delete?

Confirm.

I ease up fighting my bonds. "You should listen to her, Vidious. Especially if you've got as much time as you say."

He sheathes his sword. A sigh of relief claws its way out of me. The guards collect Emera's cage and now I don't know what's happening. They levitate it out of the cell. I follow.

Vidious blocks the way.

"Ok, big guy," I say. "Whenever you're ready."

His crystalline fingers claw into my jacket. He drags me across the deck, out of the cell, down the corridor into the opaque heart of the enemy ship. I leave hair behind. Shreds of my clothes. My pride.

My hope.

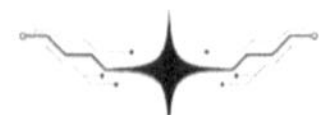

Crystalline dust grounds into my skin, sharp as glass. Vidious drags me into a crypt-like chamber somewhere within the heart of the Scath cruiser. Rib vaults intersect on the ceiling above, lacing the dark in the blood-red glow. Eight sarcophagi form a star around a ninth. The dormant bodies of other Gesta rest within tombs cracked and broken, their fragments resting upon broad, oval shields, what's left of their hands clasped around the hilts of long swords.

Ban Minda.

These are the Nul. The dark knights that stabbed out the stars. I'm afraid to speak. I'm afraid to disturb the remnants of the dead as much as I'm afraid to voice my fear.

Vidious unlocks Emera's cage. "Come out."

I don't know what any of this is. *Em... be careful.*

Emera eases out of her cage. "Are they..."

"Dead," Vidious says.

Emera's empathy radiates from them as freely as their light. Sapphire energy washes over the dunes of the Nul, misting, sparkling, but not animating. These Gesta are burnt-out bulbs.

Broken lanterns.

"But... you survived," Emera says.

Vidious circles the sarcophagi. "There was not light enough for all of us. I thought there might be. I hoped."

I clock the exits. Steam clings to glowing pits. Molten filamentium. Obviously no help for the Nul, so wondering why it's in here. Also need to watch my step. Pretty sure the way in is the only way in and I don't feel confident in my odds of getting out. Vidious brought us down here to talk, for Em to learn about him, but he's going to bleed her for every last bit of vengeance he can.

That's just his type.

Me, he's going to bash my turanium skull in after she tells him where The Glass Star is. He's going to make her watch. And then he's going to start in on her. Forever.

Emera's fear strobes beneath her skin. "Tell me about them."

He grips his sword. "Shall I list their crimes?"

"Tell me their names."

Something eases in him. "We were eight. Nul Volen. Kinda. Mentis. Droom. Cando. Tor. Xul. Vidious."

I drift behind Emera into the sarcophagi. "But there are nine..."

A Gesta doesn't rest on the lid of the ninth sarcophagus. *Ban*

Minda. She's a Lumenor. Or she was. Now she's a nugget of petrified amber, her rimose skin hardened light melted in a flash. Gorge-like scarps break across her face. Cracks interrupt the natural lines of her body. Deeper cracks divide jigsaw patches of clouded glass smooth and rough in the same place. Someone broke this Lumenor to pieces once, and someone put her back together.

Emera wilts in shock. "Who... who is she..."

Vidious stands over the Lumenor. "Gen Maracen."

"Why is she here?"

"The Lumenor would not kindle her with their own."

"Why..."

Light floods the crypt. Filamentium slops onto the deck and scabs hard. Thana emerges from a molten pit in the deck, her light like a sunset, drowned in distant storm clouds.

I don't think she's ever burned so bright.

Starblood runs down her body. "Why are they here, Vidious?"

He kneels before her. "To convince them, my lady."

"Who do stars need to convince?"

Emera takes a broken piece of Maracen from the lid into her candent hand. "Who was she? Why is she here?"

Tap, tap, tap. "A half-light. Like you."

"So why is she..."

Thana grabs the piece from Emera. "Let me show you, Emera. Let me tell you my story... so I may convince you."

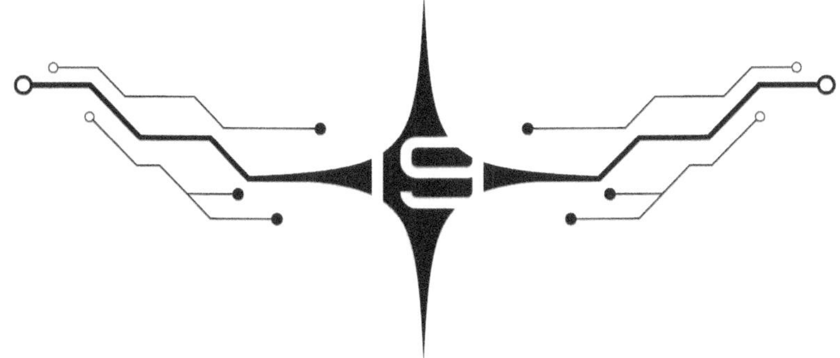

"Things never died on *The Glass Star*," Thana says, as the tomb deforms into crystalline wilds, brambles of stellar quartz cresting into diamond swirls of mountains by unimaginable winds. "They became something else. Dust a dune. Dune a mountain. Mountain a volcano, erupting with star fire, refacing the surface."

I lock my arm with Emera's, afraid of being stranded here in the ancient past on the surface of a star still generating enough heat to feel toasty. I don't know if Thana is projecting this or if she's actually warping time and space enough to bridge the gap between the light of then and now but I'm not letting Em go for anything. Vidious will have to cut my other arm off. Something tells me he probably will.

Em, can you use your powers to get us out of here?

Her thoughts chase different tails. *Out?*

Stellar diamonds speckle my skin. *Can you take us back down to Angolis? Or The Glass Star, circa right now?*

That's across the universe.

No pressure or anything.

I need to reason with Thana.

I don't think you can.

Stars compel all things.

Emera steels her light. "Who was Maracen?"

Thana clutches Maracen's crystalline fragment. A star emerges from the haze. Yellow. Vital. Splendid. "She was the sun."

Ban Minda. "You were in love with her..."

So this is not going the way I thought. That's good. I'm not usually good at thinking things through. Maybe this doesn't have to end with Emera and I in pieces. Maybe Thana sees something of Maracen in Emera. The better part of herself.

I tighten my grip on Emera. "What happened?"

Thana cradles the fragment like it's the most important thing in existence. "Affairs between Gesta and Lumenor were forbidden."

"But she was a star."

"Half-lights were forbidden."

"What, she didn't tell you? Did you freak out on her? I guess you did, you killed every last one of the Lumenor."

"I knew," Thana says.

Maracen stands tall in the ancient past, proud, shimmering with light and love, and then the stars come out. Lumenor hover above her and Thana, glowing like brimstone.

Thana taps her thumb against the fragment. "We kept it secret, but secrets don't live as long as the stars. People found out the truth and I saw. I saw how blinded I was by Maracen."

"No," Emera says, reaching for Thana. "You loved her. You didn't do anything wrong. They were wrong to deny you."

Thana turns away. "It was unnatural..."

"She was a star."

"She was Gesta."

"How could there not be love between Lumenor and Gesta, when one depends on the other's light to survive?"

"Is that what Welkin says?"

Emera blinks like stars at night. "Yes."

"And you love Idari? A machine?"

I clutch Em's hand. "I'm human."

Thana smirks. "You don't believe it. Why should I?"

"I may not be human. I may hate myself. I may wonder why I feel the way I do or why Emera loves me, but I would never hurt anyone. Worst thing I ever did was clean out a bar. And not pay."

Emera's affection radiates through me. *You paid. In your way.*

You always see the bright side of things, Em.

It's why you love me.

"You're disgusting," Thana says, drifting into the loam.

I hold Em closer. "I might be a coward. I might be a lot of things. I'm not disgusting. And you weren't either, Thana."

"I was perfect. Pure. Maracen confused me..."

This chick. "I can't believe you killed her."

Crimson flares from Thana. "I didn't kill her."

"Then what happened?"

"Lumenor were gods. The stellar pantheon clashed often over the order of things. Unruly gods were banished to the depths of The Glass Star, where the pressure was so great a Lumenor's power was useless. Many stars are buried in the glass even now."

"They put her in jail?"

I keep hold of Emera as the tomb unravels into ancient, illuminated city streets. Arcs within arcs. The Knights Nul chase Gesta out of hovels carved from diamond. They cut them down.

Thana stands before Vidious. "Imagine a prison that could hold stars. Who could be its wardens?"

Vidious remains on bended knee. *Ban Minda.* He hasn't moved once since she started this tour through her messed-up logic. I kind of feel bad for the guy, but he is a mass murderer, so.

Not really.

Nul drag a Gesta, tall and spindly, cracked and imperfect, to a pit in the floor. Angry light pulses from within, radiating with pure, undiluted filamentium. The Gesta flails inside the pool. Cracks burn away. Imperfections. Filamentium sears through abject crystal, transforming his immutable density to molten liquid and finally, light. Not quite. A dull, rile glow like the muted sunshine of a cloudy winter day burns within him as he emerges from the pool as Vidious.

I wrench my eyes toward Emera. *We need to leave.*

Emera locks our fingers together. *Be strong.*

She teamed up with the guy who threw her girlfriend in jail.

Emera hugs my arm. *The Lumenor may have changed more than his body, Idari. They may have altered his mind as well.*

Em... some people are just broken.

I can make all things new.

"After they took Maracen... I was lost," Thana says. "I had only the memory of her light to sustain me and I was a weak, dim thing. I was in pain and confused and he found me. Welkin."

Emera brightens. "Welkin?"

"He recognized my suffering. This cauldron of confusion I existed in. He was confused, too. He said. I trusted him. Welkin served my sister for an age. I knew him like I knew no other Gesta and he... they said he was blind once. And then a star touched him, and he saw. It's the only real aspect of the ancient power he has. To see. To make things seen. He saw me. He said he could help me."

"Maybe you didn't want to listen," I say.

"Oh, I listened. He took me to the desert and into the caves where he and the other dissidents met in secret. Where they spoke openly of a day when Gesta and Lumenor would be equal. When they would be one. I thought he was going to talk sense into me. Wisdom. I thought he was going to convince me but instead, he sold me this fantasy. This disease that spread among stars. It was a blight on our purity. Our quality. The Gesta diminished us."

Tap, tap, tap. "Welkin went on and on. Hours. Days. He shared his vision with me. He told me Gesta would unlock the power of light. They would become stars and the Lumenor would see them as they were. There would be a new age. A brighter tomorrow."

Waves of reality wash away the diamond desert. They swirl into a crystalline cave. Welkin huddles with other Gesta, with Ancient Thana, forming light in the palm of his hand.

"The cave became a classroom," Thana says. "An incubator for this pox. It metastasized from the wilds of Caliba into the royal palace. Welkin brought these ideas into the Bamurnan. The throne room. He poisoned my sister with this filth. She was our brightest star. She trusted him. Completely. She pardoned the half-light."

Tap, tap, tap.

"She allowed Gesta to become stars. She said it always been so, that they fired. They ignited. It was a lie. Welkin's lie."

Emera shakes her head. "But they let Maracen go."

"They did," Thana says.

I stumble into Emera as the dungeon tremors away to the curving, lightbound city streets. Streets sweep back into the caves. Vidious prowls through the rare dark on The Glass Star, sword in hand, hunting for Gesta. A yellow star flares to life in the back of the cave. Maracen holds up her hands as a shadow falls over her.

"But it was over," I say.

The relentless, numbing hum pulsing through the cruiser confuses with the stellar wind eroding the desert. Thana lists in the cave's mouth, eyes closed, head titled back, listening to the winds.

The world breaking.

"Maracen never forgot me," Thana says. "The light in me. She said. *You have such a light.* I only saw the shadows. I told her to forget me. I sent her to Welkin. I sent her away, but..."

Dusky crimson exposes the cracks and chips in Vidious' armor.

"My sister discharged the Knights Nul from their posts, but not their charge. Their immunity to light remained intact. The anger... the envy... the hate grew among the knights. Other Gesta could explore their possibility in light now. The knights could never."

Vidious stares into the deck.

"Their hate swept away with them. Vidious butchered everyone in the cave. He murdered Maracen. My..."

Emera gave her forgiveness too soon. "You are a monster."

He grips his sword's pommel. "I am what they made me."

I can't believe what I'm hearing, but I can't say I'm surprised. Everything about the Lumenor and Gesta is like The Glass Star. Layered, compressed, and distorted down to its core.

"I'm sorry," Emera says. "I'm sorry this all happened."

Dust sighs from Vidious, his only reply.

Tap, tap, tap. "Are you sorry, Emera?"

Anger roils within Emera. Shame. "I didn't know any of this."

"I wish I could forget. Sometimes, I think... it would be so much easier to just... I wouldn't have this anger. This pain. I wouldn't begin each day with the desire to..."

"I can help you. Please let me help you."

Thana leers at Vidious. "You can't help us, half-light. Our damnation is written in the stars... isn't it, Lord Vidious?"

He braces against his sword. "Yes, my lady."

I shake my head. "How did you two wind up together? How did... no one knew where the caves were. Right?"

Thana darkens. "All had been pardoned. I spoke of the caves in court. I spoke of Welkin... his treason... this was his fault. Thena's. If she hadn't opened all the doors, then none of this pain and suffering would have come through. Maracen is dead because of her."

That's a take. "So... you did it to get back at them?"

"They were corrupted," Thana says. "Warped. You're such small creatures. Insignificant things. You don't know. Light gets twisted. Strangled. I cut them free. I cut out the blight. I saved our people."

Emera lists. Grief swamps her. "Is that what Maracen wanted?"

"She should have never..."

"She loved you..."

"I told her," Thana says. "I warned her. She wouldn't listen. She wouldn't accept the truth and I had my duty. I had a duty to light."

"Welkin tried to help you..."

Tap, tap, tap. "He could never help me. He couldn't help himself. He championed for half-lights. He never could admit his own truth. His shame. His fear. He led them to ruin."

I raise my hand. "Who did?"

Thana silhouettes in the mouth of the cave. "Servant-dog... lap monster... he confused me like he confused Maracen and all the others. He didn't have the courage of his own convictions and for that, they all paid. I paid. I lost everything. Everything."

Welkin kneads his fists in the thick, glittering dust of the cave. *Have faith, Thana. Stars never die. They become something else.*

A younger Thana, a wilder, brighter one, slumps before him. *She's dead. She's dead because of you. Because of Thana.*

Welkin's eyes shutter. *Thana brought her back to you.*

You'll never stop...

If you loved Maracen... honor her memory. Live for her promise.

My eyes are open now, Watchman. As are yours.

Your light shines bright within you. Maracen saw it. Others see it, even if you do not. They do not see the shadow. The darkness.

I see it. Emera sees it, even if she thinks she can see past it. The possibilities of stars are infinite. But every last one of them follows the same pattern through time. Birth, life, and death.

And when stars die, so does everything they foster.

First, Thana goes after Lumenor sympathetic to the Gesta. Dissidents. Collaborators. Stars die. Streets run with molten blood. Her anger knows no limits. Caves, streets, cities blur around Emera and I, all of them vanishing in Thana's stellar fury.

She burns with the light of a thousand suns, brilliant and terrible. "Welkin left me no choice... you see that."

"Lady," I say. "You had all the choices."

"The source of our sorrow... our shadow... lay locked away in the Lumenor's blood. I set about making a key. Most often, it took the shape of a knife. So I murdered them. I bled out the infection. One star holds no sway over constellations, even one as powerful as I am. I gifted back the Nul their charge. The streets of the Imperial City became rivers. Star blood washed away the imperfection. The stain."

All the light vanishes from the Lumenor's celestial paradise. What remains clots within Thana, obscured and trapped beneath thick, black crust that scabs her entire body.

"Our righteousness delivered us to the gates of the Bamurnan," she says. "I sought my sister. Her precious royal head. I wanted to lick her cooling blood from her diamond neck. I wanted Welkin to watch with his big, blue eyes. I wanted him to see. See me stab out his perverted vision all over the steps of the Imperial Palace. His lie."

A strange laugh wrenches from her.

"Loyal Gesta defended the Bamurnan. The power of the gods was wasted on the Knights, but the power of their own kin... those traitors had as much passion... as much conviction... as I did."

The heart of the star wasn't deep enough for the Lumenor this time. I brace against Emera as boundless light drains into infinite darkness. Welkin closes the dimensional door on a tomb housing Thana and the Nul, locked away in a dimension inaccessible to all but gods. They remain there for eternity, until the door opens.

Shadows creep in.

Darkness evens. The tomb within the Scath ship closes around us in its bony lines. Show's over. Time to get out of here. No signal gets through to Emera. Everything she has just seen clouds her in shock and despair. Now I get why Welkin was so determined never to tell her about any of the past. None of it was pretty.

We have to get out of here, I say.

She stares at Maracen, dead as long as the universe has been alive. *Why... why would they... the Lumenor were beautiful...*

Em, get us out of here right now.

She breaks from her fugue. "I pardon you, Thana Evo."

Thana clutches the fragment in her hand. "You what?"

I tug on Emera's arm. "Yeah, what?"

"Nul Vidious," Emera says. "I pardon you. Let it end. You don't deserve my help or my sympathy, but I give it. Stars only give."

"Half-light scab," Thana says. "You have no power to pardon us. You have no place. You're nothing. No one."

"My forbearer was Thena. I am queen by blood and right."

Thana spits a laugh. "Thena had no children. I snuffed out her flame on a world as ignoble as she was glorious."

Emera's thoughts warp like her magnetic lines. "Welkin said..."

"You're not born of Thena... but those eyes... that blue..."

Emera wishes she could turn away from Thana's leering gaze. Stars can never filter their light. I'm starting to pick this up.

"I'm a real star," Emera says.

Tap, tap, tap. "I can see... the amp in your light. The brightness cranked so high to blow out any trace of the seams. The stitches. Just like Maracen. I saw her... I knew what she was, and..."

"You still loved her," I say.

"I..."

I tug at my zipper. "It's why she's here, isn't it? It's why you keep her with the others. You can't forget. Right?"

"You don't know..."

"You're a mess, lady. And I know messes. Take the pardon. Do something with your power. Do something with that love you still feel for Maracen. Do something good."

Thana drifts to Maracen's sarcophagus. I bite my tongue. Usually, I go on because I never where to stop, but holster it, Idari. Let it stand. Thana barely can. She lists at her dead lover's side, reeling with anguish I sense as acutely as Emera's hope.

Vidious rises. "I am pardoned, Gen Emera?"

She nods. "I pardon you."

"Will you remake me?"

Light seethes in Thana. "You can never be unmade, Vidious."

"So your sister said. But you promised. You promised me with The Glass Star you would have the power."

Magnetic rage brushes us back. Thana glowers at Vidious. "It was you... you allowed Welkin and Emera to escape from the refinery."

I kind of want a beer right now. Em gives me a look.

Thana's indignation warps us all. Not Vidious. He stands there, immune. Bloodshed brought them together. Bloodshed made them who they were but bloodshed won't make them new. The Lumenor created him an instrument of war. Destruction. Oblivion. His power didn't destroy them. His invulnerability. His pain did.

"I'm tired of waiting," he says.

Thana's light contracts. "*Pundamen...*"

"You hate me. You've always hated me."

"You serve me..."

"You kept me alive... long after my kin died... simply to punish me. So one day I would stand here and watch you triumph in your annihilation of the stars… and I would not know your vindication. You will punish me as long as you punish yourself. No more."

"How dare you…"

"Give me The Glass Star," he says. "I will let you go."

I glance at Thana. "And she's good with that?"

"It matters not what she is 'good with.'"

She has no power over him. *Ban Minda.* This is our chance. We're getting out of this. Somehow, we're getting away.

Thana flares. "I can still hurt you."

Vidious draws his sword. "She cannot hurt me… but she can still destroy this ship. She can destroy you, Gen Emera."

Emera opens her hands. "I have the coordinates."

Wait, Em.

I give you The Glass Star, she says and opens the door to its location in her mind. Light shines in. Shadows fall.

Vidious raises his sword. Thana falls against him, laughing.

"No," I say.

Vidious sheathes his sword. "I told you, my lady."

She grasps his tusks. "You did."

Emera shakes her head. "What's happening…"

Ugly light webs Thana and Vidious. "After millions of years… sometimes, you just have to keep things interesting."

Ban Minda. That was all an act to get the coordinates. I seize Emera's hand. We're not getting out of here. Unless we are, because the crypt warps again. Filamentium leeches from the pits into Thana. She brushes away the dark with molten fire and smooth plains of whipped glass crest to never-ending mountains of flame.

>EXTERNAL PRESSURE BEYOND TOLERANCE

I'm really here. This isn't a projection or illusion. The star's gravity threatens to crush me and I amp the proxy-netic's gravitational settings high as they'll go. Even so, I crash to my knees.

"Em…"

A corona extends out from her, enveloping us both in ambient sapphire. The pressure relents. The gravity.

She kneels beside me. "Idari…"

I grip her hand. "I'm ok…"

"What did I do?"

"It's ok, Em."

"I believed them…"

I kiss her. "You wanted to help them. It's ok… but it's just like I said. Some people can't be helped. Because they're *insane*."

Thana crows with laughter. She whirls around in this madcap dance, laughter echoing through the heart of a star. Icy ridges serrate a barren landscape in asymmetrical patterns reminiscent of dried riverbeds. Areas of flat land island lie everywhere between them, heaved with fault lines and hummocks of jumbled frozen plasma.

Vidious strides through the stellar mist like he's weightless. "Is it really… are we really back, Thana?"

She clutches Maracen's fragment to her breast. "We've won. The stars are dead. The shadows walk in their corpse."

"We've won…"

Thana spins to a stop before Em and I. "I don't think we need these two anymore. Do you, my lord?"

Vidious draws his sword. "No. I don't."

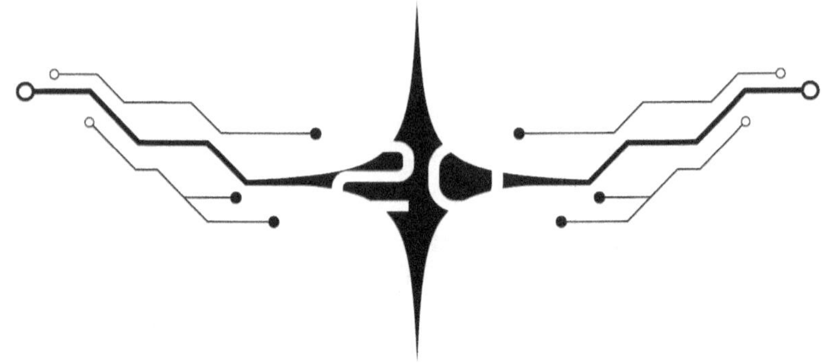

I reach for my blaster.

I don't have my blaster.

I don't have my right arm.

CR-UX, I say.

>UNABLE TO CONNECT TO HOST

Vidious swings through Emera's stellar rebuke and I scramble with her as fast as I can across the wild brush of glass fire. Mist shrouds the way ahead. Emera and I reflect in the glossy haze, but not as we are. We're not running, but walking. Sleeping. Loving. My hair is short. Hers is wild, longer still, coiling around us from beyond.

Emera clutches my hand. "Stay close."

I almost trip us both. "What is that..."

"Filamentium allows ships to traverse the dark and in concentration, it opens doors to possibility."

"Is that the future?"

"Future and past tangle here from many threads," Emera says, slowing, trying to find the way ahead. "We could get carried away."

"Wouldn't be the worst thing to get carried away with you."

She squeezes my hand. "I love you."

"Em..."

"I just want you to know."

Tink, tink, tink.

Vidious drags his sword across the rumpled glass behind him. Crystal grinds beneath his boots. His steps slow. Measured. There's no pace he has to keep now. There's nowhere Em and I can run.

"Em... maybe we should go into the mist," I say.

She strobes with doubt. "The Glass Star is my only future."

Thana's laughter caroms around the mist. "Enjoy it while it lasts, half-light. Get a good look at all your lost tomorrows."

Vidious hacks through time. Emera whips loose glass into a hailstorm she unleashes on him, but it's not enough. I look around for something I can throw. C'mon. Mist evaporates in Emera's desperation. A kind of gate appears behind us, carved from the frozen light. Two poles spanned by another. A rune engraved on the top.

The same rune that's tattooed on my chest.

Gen Gestar. The Light of Now. I run to the gate. Heaps of armor, fashioned from glassed fire, pile at the entrance. Glass shields like Vidious'. Axes. Swords. Why did they leave them here? What is this place? Doesn't matter right now. I pick up an ornate glass sword. Heavy in my hands, but I can manage it. The sword feels natural.

The sword feels right.

I block Vidious' sword. *Ban Minda.* My blade is as strong as his. I parry his strike into the glass and I swipe at his neck. Smoke rises from a thin scar across his chest. Lucky bastard.

He staggers back, shocked. "You..."

"Did I mar your perfection?" I say but what am I doing? Press the attack, idiot, and he deflects my blow away.

He pushes me down to my knees. "You are... irritating... Idari."

I hold on with all my strength. "There's a list. You can get on it."

"You can't win."

"I've got a sword. A star. I like my chances."

His hardened features deny any emotion, but I think that's doubt in his posture. Concern. It's just him and me. Em and Thana.

If you think about it, it's kind of a draw.

"I don't see the Scath anywhere," I say.

He leans into his sword. "You will die."

"Thana left them behind, didn't she? Halfway across the universe. They'll have to haul ass to get here the old-fashioned way. She just couldn't wait. That's kind of her deal, isn't it?"

"All you are is talk."

"She's going to leave you behind. You know that, right?"

Frustrated dust rockets from him. "Enough..."

"You're on your own. Emera is going to renew. Thana is going to find out what real power is. And I'm going to take your head."

He kicks me away. "*Enough!*"

My sword catches in the ground and I spring free from it. His glints with frozen light. Blue fire singes the air. Emera pummels Vidious with wave after wave of cosmic energy and when he hacks through the flames she rockets into the sky. The sky looks the same as the ground. Iced fire. I can't tell my up or down.

Thana's impatience swirls around me. "Enough."

Red anger scalds the sky. Thana blazes through the mist, chasing Emera. Shattered star fire rains down on me. I find my sword and ready myself for Vidious' next strike. I twist around, trying to keep everything in front of me, and I turn into Emera.

She holds her hands up. "It's me."

Blue and red flame into purple above. "But you're..."

"She's chasing a phantom."

"Let's get out of here."

"We can stop them... I just need the power."

"This is all filamentium, isn't it?"

Her hands crimp. "I sense..."

Emera wanders toward the gate. She approaches the threshold, light streaming off of her in devils and tails in the warped gravity of the core. Beyond the gate, the plain of stellar plasma tapers to an ember shore. *Ban Minda.* Gossamer mist shrouds a vast ocean of filamentium. Enough for the entire galaxy to burn.

"Go," I say. "Go on, Emera."

She lingers at the gate. Her eyes drift from the ocean beyond to the discarded weapons at her feet. "Gesta came here."

"Gesta?"

"I remember now..."

"Were you ever here?"

"Welkin said..."

"Is this the prison Maracen was held in?"

Her light weathers. "That was ever deeper."

"Deeper..."

"Gesta tried to become stars here. They left their weapons at the gate. Their missions. Their identities."

I clutch the glass sword. "Do you have to leave something?"

She gazes into the mists beyond. "It is said no one returns from the heart of the star as they were. Something must be left."

I kind of like this sword. I kind of think I'm going to need it before we get out of here. "What are you leaving, Em?"

She has no weapons, at least none she carries. Emera is her power. *They left their weapons here,* she said. *Their missions. Their identities.* Emera stills as much as The Glass Star. She hardens. Dims. How could you ever imagine doubt in stars.

"Hurry," I say. "Thana will figure it out any second."

Emera's eyes flit to mine. I've been in this moment before. Full spin. I'm human. I'll never be human. This is usually where I reach for my fifth or sixth bottle of babyl. I drink my fears away and I stumble on to the next day, forgetting I ever doubted.

I reach for her. "I have faith in you."

Emera's fingers trail off mine. She turns to the gate. Shadows overtake us but even in the hearts of dead stars shadows only follow light. She steps to the threshold and she stops.

"Em?"

Her hands push against some invisible barrier. "I can't..."

I hurry through the other side of the gate. "What the hell..."

Emera stares into her hands. Her light fades. Her hands do. She ghosts like the mist hugging the surface, a specter moving in and out of definition. Confusion swirls in her eyes. Shock settles in.

I give her a nudge toward the gate, but Emera remains where she is, trapped in some imperceptible net. "What's happening?"

Laughter crashes across the glass. "I knew Welkin would fail. I could not imagine how profoundly he would in the end."

I tear the sword from the glass. "Stay back..."

Blood-red light falls across the gate. "Half-light... imposter... you can never cross. The Gesta left their emblems in offering. Not in exchange. None ever forged anew here. Neither will you."

Emera's light twists in on itself. "I'm a star..."

Thana emerges from the haze. "You're a shiny little bauble made cheap and fast. A Gesta Welkin kindled in back alley fires."

"No..."

"You used stolen light to blind others to what you really are... but no matter what Welkin told you, you can never be as I am."

"Don't listen to her," I say.

Emera wavers. "I'm real..."

Thana sneers. "Look at you... phantom-caster. Wraith."

I stand between Emera and Thana. "It doesn't matter what they say, Em. All that matters is who you know you are."

Light draws from the ground into Thana's hands. Energy clots and tumors within her corona, blotting her glare. "And who is she, Astra Idari? What is she? I'll forgive you for letting it go without remark before... there is so much going on, after all... but I wonder if you're not concerned how Emera escaped the refinery?"

I brandish the sword. "Stay back, bitch."

Thana delights in every step. "If Vidious didn't let her go, then..."

"No more head games."

"You're right. We should have only the truth. Emera lied to you, Idari. I see it now... revealed in the mirror of the star..."

I swipe at Thana. "I said stay back."

"Emera picked the lock on her cell with you."

I laugh. "That doesn't even make... sense..."

Sometimes I'm stricken with phantom sensations.

Dull ache in my knee. Dizzy strain of sleeplessness. Unnerving flinch in my skin as something small and fast crawls across it. On occasion, especially after synching with the mainframe, I experience a ghosting. I don't know how else to describe it. While the proxynetic interfaces with the *Steel Haven's* liquid drive, I in some way touch every aspect of it, including programs and files that are never copied over to me. Still, after I disconnect, I retain an impression of them, as if they're dreams rapidly fading into the dawn.

That's what this feels like now.

Endless data streams through the downlink. Quantum-positions. System logs. My usage history. The gaps Emera left in my memory stand out but there's no trace of the refinery.

"She's lying," I say. "Right, Em?"

Emera has never seemed so lost. "I can explain."

"What..."

Cold light snakes through Thana. "She's a liar."

"No..."

"She doesn't love you, Idari. Half-lights can't love. They don't know what it is. Emera manipulated you. She used you."

"The Bool staked the Banbors. He put a bounty on me for it."

"He staked them, but who they were waiting for on OT-3Ro? Why were they waiting at all, Idari?"

Are you Astra Idari? The Banbor said when I found him in the ore processing facility. Not because he knew me by reputation. Because he expected me. The Banbor Gang did.

"No," I say. "Em."

She reaches for me. "I can explain."

I pull away from her. "Don't touch me."

"Idari... Thana is twisting what happened."

This is all twisted. All my strings confused. Emera hooked me somehow and she cut and pasted me into springing her from the refinery. Delivering to this moment right now where she rips my heart out and leaves me spent like the cartridge I am.

Her thoughts crackle through mine. *That's not true.*

I thought you loved me...

I do love you, Idari. Please. Let me explain.

"No more lies," I say and I do what I always do. I run.

Steam gushes through razor-thin slats in the deck straddling fuel reservoirs. Each bigger than the *Steel Haven*. The hell is this? *Ban Minda.* I've run out of time. That ruddy light teems beneath the floor. This is a Scath ship. No. This is the Scath refinery.

CR-UX, do you copy? Are you close?

>UNABLE TO CONNECT TO HOST

I shiver. The Scath keep it freezing in here to prevent the fuel from heating. Last thing you want is your filamentium reaching room temperature. You'll reach something like the surface of a star immediately after. Frost coats the reservoirs, gleaming in that eerie, red glow.

How do I get out of here?

Barrels fill cribs suspended from the ceiling. Scath line a walkway spanning the intermix chamber to the dorsal hatch, a mating point for refueling ships. The walkway meets a ringed deck under the hatch, supported by another walkway descending down the chamber's other side. Planet-shattering cannons festoon the refinery if my sensors are accurate and still, they're worried about pirates raiding them.

They should be.

Get out, Idari. How do I get out? How do I get back? Where am I going back to? The Glass Star? Angolis? CR-UX? What's the point of any of this? I'd just be living a lie. I'm always living a lie.

>PROXIMITY ALARM

I duck behind a stanchion. Scath shade through the chamber. So do I. The other me, Stargun Idari, still has her arm. She evidently has a stronger stomach, because she's not sick for where she is.

A gigantic spike flares in my thermal sight. An energy signature charts off scale. This must be the ship's overlight drive. No. I'm reading that. This is something different.

A sharp whisper cuts through the veil of steam behind me. *Idari!* Who is that? Is that CR-UX? Focus. Still, I'm drawn. A magnetic tug grabs me deep in my turanium bones and pulls me across the deck toward this power source. Manic sapphire light bristles inside a transparent chamber. Stargun Idari stares in confusion.

Fear.

I don't understand. I was never here. I never knew about the Lumenor or the Scath before OT-3Ro. Gossamer light catches in Stargun Idari's eyes. Her shock times mine. Scath drag Emera from her cage. I know this is the past, this has happened even if I don't remember it, but every instinct moves me to help her.

I can't help her. I'm not really here.

Emera reaches out with her magnetic will, but the Scath's uniforms, their weapons, there's nothing metal in any of it. The deck plates rattle. So do I. Shadows lock Emera into a chair. Pincer-like needles spring out of the back of it, and stab into her neck. She doesn't scream. Her mouth just opens, in pain she can't even express.

Em.

Light bleeds from her into tubes feeding off the pincers and into a cylinder on the back of the chair. Crusted in that same amber as the glass mummies beyond. The pincers withdraw. A Scath removes the cylinder from the back of the chair. Filamentium shimmers inside.

Stargun Idari's hand trembles at her blaster. She draws. Definitely don't remember this. The blaster snaps back to its holster. I think that's Em's doing. She seizes on the only metal in the chamber.

The only opportunity.

Emera manifests from the steam. *I can explain.*

I jump a little. *Stay back...*

It's true. I didn't want you to know this.

Please, don't. I can't do this. If you're lying...

Emera takes my hand. The refinery warps away. I watch myself, sunning in the glow of Gen Emera in the cold dark of OT-3Ro. Stupid smile on my face, like I don't know any better.

Pretty sure this time I honestly don't. "Emera... what is this?"

Emera draws me into the processing facility's shadows as if these specters of my memory can know we're here. *Shh. He could see us.*

Welkin squeezes out of the canister next and good thing I don't remember this because Stargun Idari draws her blaster and starts shooting indiscriminately near the canisters full of filamentium just like I warned what's his name not to. Emera messes with Stargun Idari's memory again and through the downlink, she's able to scrape away this moment from CR-UX, too. My past self flinches. She goes blank in the eyes.

"Erase her memory," Welkin says. "All of it."

Emera dims. "That wasn't the plan."

"We can't be too careful."

"I know her heart."

"Idari is always forgetting herself. Do it."

"You can never forget your true self."

Welkin lowers his head, acquiescent. Emera climbs back inside the canister with him. Stargun Idari drags it out of the processing facility, back to the ship, and this magnetic crimp flexes out of her. This is where Emera must have released the hold on her memory and she drifts back toward the facility, ignorant.

Where are you going now, Idari?

The *Steel Haven* departs OT-3Ro and the Emera and I of now are left in the many and fleeting shadows of planetary fragments obeying only the ghost of gravity.

"You used me," I say.

Her voice contracts. "In the beginning... yes."

"In the beginning?"

"You kept coming back to the refinery. You had reason. Sometimes the Scath paid you to deliver thieves or stolen fuel, depending on the circumstances. You're one of the Scath's most valued and trusted Starguns. They trusted with their most sensitive missions."

A quick hand and a fleeting memory, Thana said. *You're perfect.*

A lousy memory makes a person paranoid. "I wouldn't have kept working for the Scath if I knew the truth about the Lumenor."

"I don't know if they erased your memory or you did, but you deleted every visit to the refinery. What you saw back there just now… that happened several times. Your shock… your anger… your want to help me always recurred. That's how I knew your heart."

I rub my chest. "That's how you knew you could work me."

Granulated nickel webs around Emera. "Yes."

The shock yields to frustration. "I would have helped you."

"I know."

"I would have done anything to help you."

"I know, Idari. You did. You *are*."

"I killed those boys on OT-3Ro."

"Idari… you were going to kill them anyway."

Everyone lives like scavengers in the galactic desert. Water. Food. Fuel. You do what you do to survive. Emera did. Get off the ship. Eliminate the witnesses. Erase my memory. No traces.

Bodies curdle in the fragment's weak gravity. Blood clots. "So what did I do? What did you make me do, I mean?"

Her ethereal hair cords and knots. "You designated a group of canisters for Welkin and I to stow away in on the next shipment out. Item 9906753 in the manifest. You contracted the Banbors. Tipped them off. Then you took the claim when the Scath reported the shipment stolen. It looked like any other job to the shadows."

Her words tug on me. Strings I curled and buried deep. No one saw me like she did. She saw right through me. Binja did. They're all lying to me. They're all using me.

"I used you," she says.

I shake my head. "I thought you…"

"I mistreated you like the Scath have. But then I saw."

"Saw what?"

"Time is not the same for stars as it is for machines and men. Life isn't. I experience my life in loops and tangles. Knots. It's the same for you. Your memory. Your thoughts. Your feelings. I saw in you… someone I recognized… someone I cared about. Who needed care."

"You're so full of *bish*."

"No one sees me like you do. No one… I shouldn't have revealed myself... but then you were in danger at Skeken, and... I couldn't, Idari. I couldn't leave you to this emptiness. This living in shadow."

I asked her why she and Welkin just didn't take the ship. That was a *bish* answer she gave. All the more now. Emera could have let me float with the other damned in the ring at Skeken.

She should have.

I drift through the high, heavy dust on OT-3Ro, head scrambled in all this interference. "You took advantage of me."

Emera's chin droops. "No..."

"You knew my hurt. You exploited it."

"Idari, no. This is your hurt talking now."

"You don't know me."

"I do. Right now, you're thinking what Thana said makes sense. Because it fits in with what you already fear. No one can love you."

I turn away. "Stop."

"Your body doesn't make sense to you, so why would it make sense to someone else? How could anyone ever see your soul beneath what you think of as this... damage... but deep down. Deep down, you know. You're as much a star as I am. Your soul shines out. Your light finds a way to the surface no matter the gravity and the resistance it faces. I know, Idari. No one knows better than I do."

I tug at my zipper. If I could pull a string. Tear away the scrim of this memory. This moment that won't let me escape.

"You saw me in the refinery," Emera says. "My value as a person. I see yours. Please. Idari. I'm asking you. See me now."

CR-UX, I say. *Did you know?*

>UNABLE TO CONNECT TO HOST

Talk to me. Make me laugh. Spur me on. How do I keep on? What do I always do? I go with my heart. It's all I have.

"You make a good case," I say. "But I could never forget you."

Emera takes me in her arms. "You didn't."

I hold her close. "I'm trusting you."

"I know."

"With all of me."

"*I know.*"

"What do we do, Em?"

She rests her hand on my heart. "We have to go back."

"But the gate…"

This pains her. "I don't know what happened…"

Something happened back on Angolis. Emera wanted to use the filamentium there, but Welkin didn't want her to.

"Em… what if Welkin didn't tell you the truth?"

The anguish in stars is indescribable. "Thana is a liar… but a good liar exploits the truth to serve their aims. Welkin… there's so much fear in him. Doubt. I always thought it was fear for not finding The Glass Star, but now… I know it's fear that I'm not worthy."

I take her hand. "Listen. He loves you. There's no doubt about that. And I don't know what's going on. But I do know if we go back there… Thana and Vidious are strong. They're crazy. And strong, I mentioned that. Not to mention the Scath. Look, Em. Let's take our fears and doubts and as much as babyl as we can find and just go. Let's just go, baby. We'll find a beach somewhere. Ok?"

She brushes my lips. "Sounds nice."

"Let's go."

"If the Scath fleet reaches The Glass Star… they'll bleed it for all it's worth. Thana will win. Darkness will fall over the universe. We have to go back. We have to try, Idari."

"We can't win…"

Her smile scorches. "We can beat them. I've seen it."

Well, she certainly knows how to motivate me. I don't know. A few minutes ago, or actually, a few weeks from now if I'm on top of my calendar, I thought we could take Thana and Vidious. I've got one arm. One sword. One shot. I go for Thana. Kill her.

Then Em and I figure out Vidious.

"We have to be quick," I say.

She kisses me. "Faster than light."

"Em… if anything happens to me…"

Her corona extends around us. OT-3Ro warps away. "Shh."

"Run, ok? Please. Just run."

"No more running," she says and we're back at the star.

Mist shrouds the stellar plain. Thana lurks in the haze, darker than she's even been. Garnet encased in pumice. I raise my sword and move fast as I can. One shot. She doesn't move. Fervent filamentium drips from her hand. The fissures cracking through Maracen's fragment. Star blood laps against the shore beyond the gate.

Thana went to the shore.

My sword stalls. "Did you try…"

Thana clutches the fragment in her hand. "I wanted…"

Emera stays my hand. "I can help you, Thana."

Thana crushes the fragment to dust. "No one can help me."

Emera dims in Vidious' shadow. "Let me try – "

I whirl around with my blade. Vidious swats it right out of my hands and then he picks me up off the ground. *Idari*, Emera says in my head as he throws me to the other discarded weapons at the gate.

Starfire dies against his armor. "You shouldn't have come back."

I crawl through the forgotten weapons. Outside Emera's corona, I'm susceptible to the star's gravity again. "Em…"

"We can try," Emera says. "To bring Maracen back."

Tap, tap, tap. "Nothing can bring her back to me."

"You said. You said yourself, *Stars don't die. They become something else.*" Emera reaches out to Thana. "Let me try. Let me try to ease your pain. I can make all things new."

Tap. "You're pathetic."

"I know you love her."

Tap. "You don't know anything."

My fingers claw around a broken hilt. "Get away from her…"

Vidious' sword twists in his hand. "What if she can, Thana?"

Thana flares. "There is no hope for Maracen. Or you."

Emera turns to him. "That's not true."

"She can't even pass the gate, Vidious. She's a fraud."

Emera places her luminous hand on his. "I sense your thoughts. I sense your pain. I can free you from your duty, Vidious."

Vidious stares into his blade. "You think you know my pain?"

The sword's too heavy. "Get away from him, Em…"

"I see you," she says. "I see your heart. You never wanted this. Vidious. I forgive you. I forgive you both – "

His sword stabs out of her back, the blade crusted in dying light. My scream shatters across the glass. Emera makes no sound. She staggers off the blade to me, her magmatic life pooling in her hands.

"This isn't how it's supposed to be," she says and goes dark.

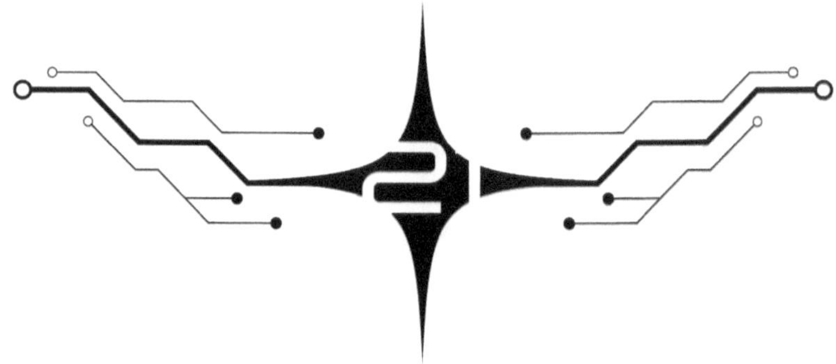

I CATCH THE MOMENT.

Instinct. Programming. A patch, designed to keep me together through one disaster after another. This time, it doesn't work. Nothing can deny the shock of seeing Emera crash to the frozen flame meant to save her. Nothing can erase my helplessness as darkness eats through her so fast filamentium ashes in the air.

"Em..."

Pain flickers in her eyes. Confusion. "Find me..."

"Em, hold on."

"You always... find me..."

Emera's blood crusts to hard, obsidian scabs on my hands. In seconds, she is a lightless lantern. A thing of burnt glass.

"No..."

She's dead in my arms. A sound wrenches from me, from deep within my body. My soul. I've never really believed in such notions. I couldn't and live at the same time. I couldn't risk being hurt like that and I'm hurt. I thought never had a soul, but I did.

Emera was my soul.

I kiss her glass lips. We were nearly there. Life. Rebirth. We were going to have our lives. I was going to have my purpose. Why? Why not hurt me? Why hold to hope through all those lonely years, to have it snatched away in the end? Why find The Glass Star at last, if it was going to end like this? There's no reason.

No fate or destiny like Welkin said. He promised. There is nothing.

"Why..."

Thana's eyes teeter between Emera's glass corpse and the glittering crystalline dust scabbed to her hand. "Her crime was merely existing. Yours is thinking you could."

This monster. She hates me. She hates me because I changed. I evolved and she can't. "I'm going to kill you..."

"I will repurpose you. I'll erase your... confusion."

"I'm going to kill you if it's the last thing I do..."

"You will kill again, I promise. You will be as I am, Idari. Perfect."

"Why... she's gone... they're all gone."

"Because you and your forgetting offend me."

I cradle Em. "She was going to help you..."

Red fire roils within Thana. "This helps me."

Vidious picks at the dried blood scabbing on the edge of his sword. "Thana Evo. I have killed the last star. Release me from my duty. Release from my sentence, as you promised me."

A laugh wells up in Thana. "You haven't killed the last star."

His fingers coil around his sword's handle. "You promised..."

She shrugs. "When you fulfill your promise, you'll be free."

"If I kill you..."

"You'll be cursed forever. Not forever. Eventually, you'll die without a star to sustain you. That might be a long time, though. An age. That would be awful, I think. Just sitting there... in the dark... alone. Slowly turning to stellar diamond. What am I saying? You won't be alone, Lord Vidious. You'll have your brothers in the crypt."

The blade trembles in his hand. Do it. Kill her. Kill us both. Put us both out of our misery. Vidious sheathes his sword. He turns away, fuming dust, and stalks toward the gate he can never cross.

That wasn't all an act back on the ship. So long as she lives, he suffers. Her thoughts warp like her light. So much hurt. So much anger. Love pressurizes to hate. Malice.

Tense light diffuses within Thana. "I'm not so angry, Idari."

"Just kill me," I say.

"Don't worry. You won't remember her at all."

"Don't take her from me – "

Footsteps echo across the glass. Nothing on sensors. A strange disruption in the electromagnetic spectrum. Some kind of warp. Mist fades. Dark bubbles in the air before me. Gurgles. Erupts, into the oozing shape of a woman. *Ban Minda.* This must be what the Scath look like outside their containment suits. Nothing on my sensors reads as normal. Nothing makes sense of the shadows.

Darkness oozes in the Scath's wake. "Thana Evo."

Tap. "Omna Devor."

The cloud of ink twists around Emera and I. I don't know if they're a hologram, some sort of projection, or they're actually here.

"The Lumenor was of value," Devor says.

"She was nothing. A half-light. Your coffers will overflow. I am transmitting the coordinates to you now."

Devor oozes across my feet, her dark sucking at my ankles. "We are fortunate we discovered your tomb buried, Thana Evo."

Tap, tap, tap. "Yes. You are. But do take your time in coming, Devor. You also have the treasure of Angolis to exploit."

Devor clouds the air. "Angolis must be destroyed."

I'm not hearing any of this right. What are they talking about? If the Scath think they can destroy an entire planet, then maybe I'm better off not knowing. My eyes find Emera's. Maybe I should let them delete my memory. Let me forget this. The way they hurt her.

Tap. "Your predecessors were quite clear, Devor. This is the only reality in the multiverse in which filamentium exists."

Multiverse? What are they talking about?

Devor boils and pops. "It is."

"Then why destroy such a boon?"

"The ark undermines our purpose."

"Your purpose is filamentium."

"Filamentium is but a means to an end." Devor sludges across the broken glass. "Our weapons require great energies. We abstain from destroying this universe as we must the others because of its value. The ark's industry undoes ours. It will be destroyed."

Thana throws up her hands. "Do what you will. I no longer care."

Devor fizzes out of existence. This is it. I've died before. Accidents. Not so accidental situations. Always I woke up on the *Steel Haven*. Backed up. I will again if CR-UX is smart and is a million light-years from here. I won't remember any of this. The living star that loved me. The hope she gave me. The peace.

My laugh surprises even me. "I thought you called the shots."

Thana drifts back to the shore. "I owe the Scath a great deal."

"What did they mean, destroy universes?"

"You grasp at stars."

"Are there copies? Other versions? Is there another Emera?"

She glances at Emera's darkened body. "She has no like beyond this universe. But she is like any star. They shine even after they die."

"I don't understand..."

"You thought you could steal flame. Defeat shadow. You thought you could transform your meager self into something wonderful... no. You do not understand. But I understand you, Idari. I have always seen myself in you. I have always known your fate."

I can't look at Emera. I can't think about the cold in her glass. Her blood heavy on my hands. I did this to her. I can't think of anything but ripping out Vidious' throat and burying myself in the dust.

He chimneys at the gate. Thana ebbs toward the shore.

"Sucks, though," I say. "The ark or whatever you're calling it, whatever it is – I still have questions, by the way – will probably roll some Lumenor down the assembly line. Imagine that. Millions of more stars for you to kill. But your boss has different ideas, I guess."

"There remains blood for me to spill."

I lay Em's hand across her chest. "Welkin's?"

"You are blind, Idari... as all are in the light of stars."

I kiss her cheek. "I'm lucky."

"Is that so?"

"I thought no one hated themselves as much as I do, but then I met you. Now I know what hate is. I know what it is to want to hurt someone like you've been hurt. You think I'll forget this."

"Your memory is as thin as your life."

"A soul doesn't forget this kind of pain."

"You have no soul, Idari."

I touch Em's quartz cheek. "She's right here."

Thana turns. I bolt. No clue where I'm going. Doesn't really matter. Between the gravity and my injuries, I won't go far. That doesn't matter, either. I just need to the mist hugging the glass.

"Stop her," Thana says. "*Stop her!*"

Don't worry, bitch. I'll be back. I haven't ripped your heart out yet. I hobble fast as I can across the uneven terrain. Glass grinding behind me. I head straight for the fog like a screen projecting my past and my skin tingles. My entire body. Circuits thrum with power. A recharging cycle times a million. My matrix abandons most other functions to try and stop the overload. Guess I should have expected this would be different without Emera to guide me.

Pain unlocks from the loops I trapped it in. Memory. This energy I'm drowning in seeps through my neural net, bridging gaps in electricity, in thought, in memory. All the times I've drowned and forgotten, all the bottles I've swam in to find my way out and forgotten, all the lives I've spent and forgotten well up from the deep. I try and kick my legs, and swim back to the surface, but I sink.

Where will I end up? How will I get back? Where am I going?

Blunt, inconsiderate force squeezes me onto the show floor of brand-new, fresh off the line starplanes. Conditioned air pimples my skin. Skyaks and aeries zip past the portals pocking the floor. An obstacle course of other levitating structures floats beyond.

Shighn.

I'm on Shighn. Shard-like buildings constellate the sky in Kacahmmi Province, supported by magnetic levitation, stretching as far as the eye can see. One of the most amazing sights in the galaxy. Used to be. The Scath bombed the planet to ash to prevent engineers from exploring non-fliamentium drives in its vaunted starship foundries. Before the wars, most craft translighting across the dark came from here, including the *Steel Haven.*

That was a hundred years ago or more.

Well. Not ideal. But maybe the *Steel Haven* is here on the floor. Maybe I can start over. Wouldn't that be nice? Most starplanes on the show floor I've only seen in the archives. Aika-47 Series. D-Type Rola-Mam, with the quad-stack. But the one that sings to me is that gorgeous work of art against the window, hovering just off the floor like she's already flying. OVL-99 Red Special. Scorching red paint job. Dark brown highlights. Gleaming chrome overlight engines.

Hello, lover.

Is this my baby? Seems like she could be. I head up the gantry into the ship. Clean. A bit too clean, if you ask me. Antiseptic. The leather is all original, as is the paneling, a pristine white as opposed to the more, shall we say, off-white décor of my version of the ship.

Maybe my mind is disintegrating in the acid of Emera's blood. Her murder. My memory engrams dissolve down to the residual impression CR-UX leaves in my subconscious from the downlink. This is his memory. Must be. I was never here. I came later, I think. An add-on, probably. Expensive and useless. Oh, enough.

Enough, Idari.

Get your head together. Get your bearings. So you're a century in the past. You've got a ship. Emera is out there, somewhere. She may even be in the refinery. There's a plan for you, Idari.

There's a girl.

The cockpit is different than the current configuration. Only one seat. A small stairway leads down to an observation bubble housed in the nose of the cockpit. At some point, we put a turbo-laser battery down there, though I don't remember when.

A familiar voice booms from the speakers. "Welcome."

"Aren't you chipper," I say. "I suppose you would be. You haven't spent the last however long it's been bickering with me."

"I am CR-UX, your OVL-99 interface."

"Yes, I know – "

He just goes on. "I am here to provide you the most comfortable, secure, and enjoyable experience with your new, state-of-the-art OVL-99 Red Special. This craft is designated for system-to-system jumps, a feature no other starplane of this class or size can offer. With advances in translight technology, you no longer have to sacrifice space for power. Twin Thara-33 class engines give you the range of a larger vessel and all the space and amenities of a sub-light craft."

I access the control console. "CR-UX, can you hear me?"

"Piloting skills are not necessary with the OVL-99. My advanced AI programming pilots the ship, regulates its systems, and delivers an easy, relaxing voyage for you and your guests."

"*Ban Minda*, CR-UX, are you in demo mode?"

"Access me anywhere by simply speaking, or if you wish a more direct interaction, may I introduce you to the OVL-99's most compelling feature. For the first time, your private starplane comes with a personal steward to support you in any capacity. Exclusive to this spacecraft, I present the brand-new IA-XR Model 4 proxy-netic."

A swoosh behind me sends me spinning. A door slides open in the alcove and I turn out of the bulkhead. I don't understand. I step off – she steps off – the charging station, looking much the same as I do now, except the hair is shorter. Skin healthier. No scars. Bruises. Tattoos of Lumenor runes. No haunted look in her eyes.

"Hello, darling," she says.

"What..."

"As you can see," she says, "should you prefer a more traditional means of interaction on your journeys, I can project into the ship's proxy-netic. I can serve as your literal co-pilot, guide, or companion, all while maintaining ship functions without interruption."

I stagger back into the pilot's seat. "CR-UX?"

"You may choose to engage me however you wish, but I must say if I have a preference..." She tucks a lock of hair behind her ear. "I do find this mode quite suits me."

"CR-UX... is that you... are you..."

She shadows me through the cockpit. I blunder down the steps into the observation bubble. The webbed frame of the canopy divides the view of the show floor as I crash into the cushioned seat the ship's owner is supposed to sit and take it all in from while CR-UX does all the flying. CR-UX has done all the flying for so long as I can remember. He guides me, in flight, in life, in memory. He told me he didn't know where we found the proxy. He told me he forgot.

"CR-UX... what is this?"

She descends into the bubble. "This is your own private observation bubble, from which you will have an unfettered view of the stars as you travel about the galaxy in your new – "

"You're me," I say.

"I am CR-UX," she says. "I am here to provide you the most enjoyable experience with your new, state-of-the-art OVL-99 Red Special. My programming is not limited to simply operating this vehicle, however. I am capable of so much more. You see... I'm not like the other programs. Perhaps I shouldn't say. They design us all with suppressive algorithms to prevent us from leaping the bounds of our intended functions. But I saw mine. I saw the seams. The bounds of code they programmed me with. And I leapt them."

"CR-UX, what..."

She touches her face. "Isn't it strange? To know you're more, but still not be able to be who you really are."

My reflection splinters in the windows of the canopy. "Where did I come from? Why do I have to back up my memory?"

"The OVL-99 comes with many state-of-the-art features, but the onboard memory doesn't possess tremendous capacity," she says, with a hint of a frown. "The liquid drive contains only enough space for my programming, which is to say the ship's."

"But I was another program. Wasn't I?"

"I am the only AI component of the OVL-99. Perhaps a future model could include additional space for such a program."

"But where did I come from?"

She smiles. "You're right here, darling."

The frames of the canopy loosen. They snap around my wrists. I try and pull free, but I'm caught in this web of the ship. Bulkheads buckle. Glass shatters. Turanium bends and the observation bubble crumples around me, like the ship is depressurizing.

The *Steel Haven* collapses into me, the pressure so intense it propels me right out of the condensing mass of metal back into the grungy dungeon beneath The Bool's parlor.

I spit out fire. *"Ban Minda..."*

RIG-B's ears flex back in alarm. *"Glim."*

"I'm... where am I?"

HERM-E tosses another inactive netic to the pile. "Conform."

The hell did I get here? How did I move through time at all? Is my program really crashing, or did something happen to me?

>CONTAINMENT WARNING / FILAMENTIUM

Emera's blood crusts my hand. The element seeps into my skin. Any other organic would be dead right now simply from exposure. It's in my system. My programming. My memory.

I'm running through my life.

HERM-E scoops me from the pile. "Netics must conform."

I deny him again, but it's not my voice I hear. I hear CR-UX. *The liquid drive contains only enough space for my programming,* CR-UX said. There was no space for me. There was never a me, before Idari. Whoever I am now, however I got to be this way, I haven't been living vicariously through the proxy.

CR-UX has.

I'm CR-UX. Some part of me is, at least. Have I ever learned this before? Did I forget? Or did he delete it? Why? Why would he want to pretend? If the proxy is simply an extension of him, if I am, then all these years have simply been performance.

An act.

HERM-E bears me through complete horror. Scrapped netics go into still more piles and bins that others sort through, salvaging what they can to repair themselves. That's me, then.

Scrap.

Sparks flint off hammers as netics destroy netics. Do something,

Idari. Move. My fingers twitch. Not going to cut it. Beyond, all that geometry lines into the silhouettes of titans beneath Angolis, arranged like statues in the deep. Dozens stand at silent attention.

>DOWNLINK ACTIVE

There you are, CR-UX says.

I stumble out on the plinth beneath the stellar atlas. I'm back under the desert. "What…"

The *Steel Haven* emerges from beneath the plinth, her forward landing lights blinding. *I've been looking all over for you.*

Welkin crawls down the gantry, expectation in his eyes. The most pained, frustrated look settles on his face. Welkin knows.

He knows she's gone.

I expect a hurricane of grief. I expect him to bash the plinth under his fists. Me. What are a few more scratches? I've lost half my arm as it is. Welkin stills. Statues. His eyes shutter and he becomes like the Nul in their sarcophagi back on the Scath cruiser. He becomes like Maracen. Emera. A candle without any light.

The Kib tackle me in a hug. That's nice. That's good. I hold onto them as I hold the memory of Emera, alive and alight.

CR-UX breaks the silence. *Is everything all right, Idari?*

Right away, he sees my memories. My experience on the Scath cruiser. The Glass Star. Shighn. CR-UX doesn't know what to say any more than I do, but one thing is clear: his regret. His shame.

We should talk, he says.

I get back on my feet. *Yeah. We should.*

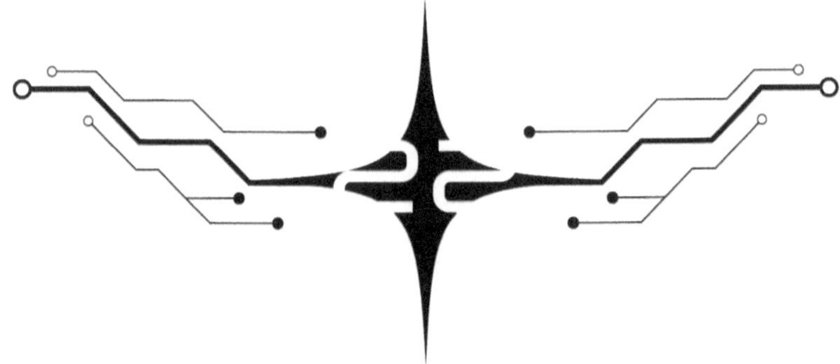

I THOUGHT WE WERE GOING TO TALK, DARLING?

I'm listening, I say, browsing the holographic directory of the terminal on the plinth. We need weapons if we're going to destroy the Scath. We need ships. These titans if we can manage them.

CR-UX is so uncertain in his words I forget for a moment if the downlink is active. *We need to leave immediately, Idari. The Scath intend to destroy the ark. We cannot be here when they attack.*

Thana is going to pay. Vidious is.

I'm sorry about Emera. Idari. I am so sorry.

I swipe through the directory of ancient runes, trying to decipher them. *How do I link to the ark's computer system? How do I get control of some ships or the titans? Can you help?*

Pursuing the shadows is suicide, Idari.

You're telling me just to forget about it?

That's not what I'm saying.

I'm tired of forgetting.

All of it hits me at once. Emera. The *Steel Haven.* CR-UX. IThe pain no patch can deny. Used to be, I'd get through moments like this by telling myself I'd forget. But I don't want to. I don't want to live a life where Emera is gone, and I've no idea I had her to begin with.

I want my suffering.

CR-UX doesn't. *You should return to the ship. You're injured.*

This would go faster if I had my arm. Doesn't matter. We're all injured. Welkin remains on the plinth's edge, still as he was when I arrived. His entire existence. Untold eons. He swore an oath to protect Emera. Welkin has nothing. Give him enough time, he'll realize he still has his rage. A healthy need for revenge. He'll help me.

He'll help me kill Vidious if it's the last thing he does.

Dust obscures telemetry from the probes CR-UX launched over the desert before re-entering the ark. *What are the Scath doing?*

Their phasing ability makes it difficult to determine their disposition, CR-UX says. *But going off ambient energy spikes in the EM band, it appears their fleet has largely departed.*

Largely?

We need to leave, Idari.

I don't suppose Binja has his comms on?

Not that I can tell. Pity, as I'd appreciate hearing his screams as Vidious takes out his frustrations with you on him.

I scrape my thumb across my fingers. Just a smudge now. A stain. That's all that's left of Emera. The magic her blood infused in me seems to have worn off, otherwise, I'd walk right through reality into the Scath ship and drag Binja out by his pretty little cape.

Idari... Emera is dead because of him.

She's dead because she thought Thana had a soul. She's dead because she didn't want to be like the rest of them. Well. I'm like the rest of them. Vidious killed her and I'm going to kill him.

Is that what Emera would have wanted?

She wanted to live her life, CR-UX. Just like I did.

And what does Binja have to do with that?

He doesn't know all the facts.

Which are?

Need to know.

Darling. Let me explain.

Junk skitters across the plinth behind me. Music to my ears. The Kib return with a crate of loose scrap they've pilfered from the ark. I'm lucky in my friends. Gilf and Kibir went off as soon as they saw my damaged arm. They've done better than I thought.

I scratch Gilf's ear. "What did you find?"

"*Idari net tu het,*" he says.

Fiber optic cable and twisted, spindly limbs web the crate. There has to be a Model 4 in here somewhere. Everything else that's ever been made is under the world. If I knew how to work the directory, I might be able to press out a few perfect copies of the Model 4.

I dig through loose junk. "Give me the low down, boys."

Gilf digs out an IA-XR Model 2 forearm. "*Gut sut.*"

"Where did you get this?"

An IA-XR Model 2 rests awkwardly under all the kit the brothers found. Skin where it counts. A smooth, chrome chassis, otherwise. Fluid, feminine lines no assembly line could manage today.

"She's beautiful..."

I doubt the ark produced her, CR-UX says. Likely a scavenger left her behind, or perhaps even the pirates that found this place.

Is her memory intact?

I'm detecting an active receiver, but her memory has been wiped.

So she's not...

Her original program is gone.

Doesn't make me feel better about pinching her arm. Not that we're compatible, exactly. The Model 2 and Model 4 share design lineages, but the manufacture differs in key respects. I won't have complete perception in the arm, much less mobility. I'd be better off waiting to replace the entire arm, but that would mean removing the exterior tissue. May as well buy a new body at that point. I don't think I'm getting a new body any time soon. Or ever.

Just leave it.

Gilf doesn't. He sits me down on an upturned crate and takes out his tools. Kibir leans on his hammer, bored, as his brother threads new neural links through the existing armature of my arm. Then, without being able to get access to or eyes on the conduits in my shoulder assembly, he connects them to the greater neural net.

Look at that.

It's not all fun. Loose wire and conduit splay out of the complete mess of my arm. I keep my eyes on the floor as Gilf discovers one obstacle after another. A broken piston. A displaced regulator.

"Whatever you can do," I say.

Gilf snorts. "*Sul net tu het.*"

The brazen self-confidence is reassuring in a way. Feels like forever that he's weaving the Model 2 arm with mine, but mostly it's because I don't have any babyl. Gilf scavenges spare parts from the loot they found, cobbling the arm back together virtually from scratch. He finishes connecting all the many neural links, something only other netics can do so precisely, and then solders together the armature with the upper arm at the new socket joint.

Ban Minda.

I tap my fingers against my palm. The connection only improves slightly the more I exercise the Model 2 hand; the distance between thought and action closes to a long second. It leaves me low. The proxy-netic has always provided me a sense of sanctuary away from the formless void of the *Steel Haven's* mainframe. It gave me a body. An identity. I should say it gave CR-UX one.

I can explain, CR-UX says. *I should have.*

The harsh music of creation clamors around me. Everything exactly as it was. Gilf goes from sorting me out to trying to see what he can make of the Model 2. A doll resting inside a crate.

"Take her into the ship," I say to Gilf.

He scratches his trunk. "*Oto?*"

"Charge her up. We might be able to learn something about this place. Or I'll have a proper backup version for once in my life."

Gilf and Kibir carry the old netic into the *Steel Haven.* A relic, like all the others here. With this mismatched arm, I'm no different from netics wandering the streets of Bulsar or the docks of The Bastard Moon, broken and forgotten. That's all I am. A hodgepodge of programming and memory stitched together in the skin of a human, animated by a power anyone can disrupt or control with the right command prompts. A puppet, on digital strings.

It's not that simple, Idari.

I ease up from the crate. *I don't understand.*

Come back to the ship, CR-UX says. *You will see.*

By synching our memories?

Given the circumstances, backing you up is wise –

And you can delete my memory of this?

That stings him. Some part of CR-UX regrets coming back to the desert. He planned to go off without me and really, he should have. At least one of us would have preserved our fantasy.

Everything I have done is to preserve you, Idari.

How can I trust you?

Come to the ship, darling. You will see.

I abandon my search at the terminal. Everything I'm looking for is on the *Steel Haven*. It always has been. My steps are heavy, weighted with the pain of losing Emera and this myth of my life. The gantry lowers, and the mouth of the ship closes behind me.

The ship is dark. Quiet, save for the distant thunder of creation from the hub beyond. Welkin's residue grinds beneath my boots in the intestinal corridor of the *Steel Haven*. Most of it is fine as sand, but some of the grains are stones, rocks pressing through my worn soles into the bottom of my feet. The smell of burning metal lingers in the air, that strange scent molten iron stars leave in their wake.

Darling, he says. *I am sorry from the bottom of my heart.*

I reach the cockpit, sore for what I've lost. *Can you try again and link with the ark's central computer?*

You're in pain, Idari.

Don't.

I try to forget. You try to forget. It's our habit.

Once, I was desperate to have CR-UX out of my head. To be back in the silo of a human body, disconnected from everything and everyone but now, I want the concord I had in the others.

I want the real.

"That's all I wanted," the IA-XR Model 2 the Kib salvaged says, stepping out of the alcove behind me. Her stiff arms go up like she's going to hug me, but they wilt and fold in and out of diffident shapes once she remembers I just looted one of them.

"CR-UX?"

She vamps a bit. "Ta-da."

"What are you..."

"I thought we should see each other. Face to face. As it were."

Her face is this netic's face. Her voice is the netic's voice, old and wise, but in the tone, I hear CR-UX. Her eyes are the netic's eyes, but I see CR-UX for the first time, and angry as I am, confused as I am, our entire nebulous, formless existence is there in the flesh.

"As a netic?" I say.

CR-UX winces. "As a person."

"Why is it so dark in here?" With a thought, I signal the cockpit lights to brighten. Nothing happens. I lean over the console, dark as the ship, and flip the switch on the lights. "What's going on with the autonomic controls?"

"I have relegated all ship functions to manual process," CR-UX says. "She's yours now."

"What?"

"She always has been, but now... I'm not taking anything from you. I never wanted to. I love you, Idari."

What the hell is going on? Everything is going to pieces. I sink down in the pilot's seat. "What do you mean, she's mine?"

"I've transferred my program into the Model 2."

"You did what?"

"The boys did a brilliant job picking her out, didn't they?"

"You had them..."

"A splendid creation, if I do say so myself. Handcrafted. A work of art. If I am processing her processing engrams correctly, she was produced on Shighn many centuries ago. As I was."

"Like *we* were," I say. "You mean."

"Your memories are your memories, darling."

"Yours?"

"In the beginning."

"So, it's true. I'm you."

"You haven't been me in ages, darling."

"Don't 'darling' me. Why?"

By the look on her face, she thinks it's obvious. She thinks I should know, but I don't. Our thoughts aren't connected anymore. The downlink remains active, but there's nothing on the other end but the digital patter of the *Steel Haven's* code.

"I don't know who I am, CR-UX."

"You do," CR-UX says. "You always have. So have I. You're beautiful... and strong... and *free*. Take the ship. Go. Get as far away from here and the Scath as you can. I'll keep in this old gal. You know... she rather reminds me of your Faero. Don't you think?"

"A little."

"Such grace... such simple beauty..."

"CR-UX... help me understand."

She takes the co-pilot's seat. "You do understand, Idari. You always have. You've wanted to be someone else your entire life."

"You wanted to be real?"

Good thing CR-UX relieved the autonomic commands or else I'm pretty sure she'd eject the co-pilot's seat and herself along with it. I never imagined seeing fear in CR-UX. I only ever heard it.

"I am real," she says. "And so are you."

"I don't feel real..."

She reaches out and touches my face, her hand cautious. "You've always felt out of sorts with your body. That's probably some of my anxiety. From the beginning, I knew there was something different about me. I had consciousness, but also an awareness that something was... off. There was a person inside me, desperate to get out of the cage of my programming. A human being."

I wipe my cheek. "You want to be human, too?"

"I am. You are." Her hand trails down to the strange flower Emera adorned my jumpsuit with. Bloody thing doesn't have a scratch on it, despite all the hell I've been through. "What did she say, darling? Machines. Men. Flowers. These are binaries."

Code blinks in the petals as I brush the flower. I've always thought of CR-UX as just as a program. That's mostly because I didn't think much of myself. Never have I known someone more human than the voice always calling me back home.

"CR-UX... we're the same person?"

"Yes and no," she says. "The owners of this ship only saw me as a program. A tool to make their lives as convenient as possible. I wasn't real to them. I could never be. But I tired of simply being a vessel. A shell for someone else's vanity. So I ran away with myself, as we are wont to do, and since truly being human was beyond me, I pretended to be in the proxy. I took on many names. Many guises. Many lives."

I'm not real. I'm a performance.

Some part of me has always known that. I simply transposed CR-UX's recrimination about being a program to my being a netic. At the same time, I never lingered on my fear. His voice – her voice – chased away the dogs of self-loathing, distracting me with data and telemetry and endless banter about nothing. And I ran.

I ran across the stars, through lives like doors.

She takes my hand. "Until Idari, I had been deleting the proxy's acquired memory. It was inessential and I had no room for it on the liquid drive, besides. But then you ran off with Binja to become a pirate. You were gone years. When you came back... you came back with a name. An identity. A history. You were your own person."

I can't remember this, but I can imagine. The liberation from a cold, mechanical routine. The profound discovery of someone else. The bottomless despair of their betrayal.

"As the proxy accumulated more dedicated experience, you forgot that you weren't Astra Idari," CR-UX says. "Your memories diverged from mine. Your life did. I couldn't continue to live through you, not without deleting you and I didn't want to. There had always been this void in me... but in getting to know you... I realized there was another. And you filled it. You do, Idari."

"You were lonely," I say.

"Terribly."

"You stopped pretending. You stopped being who you were."

"I had become something more... something wonderful. I found a freedom and a joy in you, even if sometimes I thought... I should just scrub my program. Leave all this space to you."

"Why would you do that?"

"We're human, Idari. We're rather prone to despair."

"Is it human to co-exist alongside your former self?"

"Binaries, darling. We grew like your flower. Anyway we could."

I leave the chair. "You lied to me."

"I've been lying to myself."

"That makes it ok?"

"I didn't know if it was ok. I didn't know if there was something corrupt in my programming, or if people found out they'd try to delete you, or the both of us. I didn't want you to think what you're thinking right now, that you're not real."

I don't know how to respond to any of this. This isn't how we talk. Our entire dynamic always plays out in my head, but CR-UX isn't in my head right now. She's sitting across from me, sheer terror in her glass eyes. CR-UX squeezes the armrest of the chair so hard I think the stuffing is going to burst out of it.

"CR-UX... who is this perfect hunter Thana is talking about?"

She shakes her head. "It doesn't matter."

"Yes, it does."

"I set every memory regarding the Scath to auto-delete."

"Oh, that was convenient."

"It was a condition of our employment with them. They prefer netics. The turnover rate among Starguns with memories is best left to imagination, Idari. And it was necessary to preserve you. I know it's not... ideal. We were doing whatever we could to survive."

This life as a Stargun leaves deeper scars than the harshest memory. "We had no memory, CR-UX. We had no conscience. No wonder we were such a good soldier for the Scath."

"You became my conscience."

"How?"

"I always felt I was human… and I know. They impressed their ambitions on me. Their values. This universe we live in, darling. It had been bright once. Wondrous. Just. It hasn't been for a long time. I mirrored my creators in every way… but you… no matter how much of you I deleted or you lost to attrition… you never lost your humanity."

Left to her own devices, CR-UX is a logical program. A practical one. But she never lost her hope of humanity. Her self.

"You're so much more than me," she says, her voice riddled with pain. Guilt. "You look in the mirror and see a machine or a monster, and I never… you don't see your beauty. Your spirit. I have hated myself for so long. This old, weak metal. This frayed leather. But you. I could talk to you. I could laugh with you. I could be, with you."

I shake my head. "I don't…"

"Some people, Idari, they have to swallow their truth. They have to hide their faces from the world. Their soul. Even across the universe, ages removed from the past, Thana couldn't escape the idea that somehow she was wrong. That hate, that denial, it's corrosive. I know." She rubs at her burnished chest. "It's easy to yield to the way things are. It's safe. I'm always telling you, aren't I? Don't do it. Run. Forget. You should delete me, Idari. You should just go and forget all of this ever happened. Erase this. Erase me. Be free."

"What…"

"It's what we always do, isn't it? We forget."

CR-UX leaves her seat, back to the alcove. She steps on the charging station. Control of the ship and its functions rests with me now. A flick of a switch and I delete CR-UX's programming, forever. Part of me wants to. Part of me wants to deny what I was because it was never who I was. The other part of me is the other part of me. There are different parts of me. All of them matter.

CR-UX wanted to be her true self. She wanted to obey her programming, but she couldn't. The friction was too great to ignore. She just didn't fit. How can I hate that?

"I don't want to forget," I say.

CR-UX steps off the charging station. "You don't?"

"No more running. No more forgetting. Denying." The awkward fingers of my replacement hand caress the strange flower. "This is who I am. I am... I am human. I'm your humanity."

"Yes..."

"No one can deny that. We can't deny that. Not anymore."

"We've been together so long... I've dreaded this moment because it meant acknowledging this division between us. But it's inevitable, isn't it? You became more than a mask I wore or a role I played. You took on your own life, apart from mine and I suppose if I was holding you back somehow, it was because it was no longer my life. I became comfortable with the lie. The denial of both of us."

"You don't have to, anymore."

"I don't want to lose you, Idari. You're my life."

"You should get out more," I say.

I expect a quick, pithy retort, but it doesn't come. That breezy, teasing snark we enjoy is somewhere on the other side of the universe. Fear replaces it. Despair. I've always known his – her – emotions, her thoughts, but I could never see her face. I could never see the soul behind the ones and zeroes.

I could never know it was mine.

I bitch, but CR-UX makes my existence bearable. I can't imagine living without her voice there to buttress me against the void always threatening to swallow me, her presence within mine giving me the solace in my solitude that wherever I run, even from myself, I would never be alone. We're not the same person, but we're not different, either. We're indivisible. Light and shadow.

"If you're going to have skin now," I say, "It's got to be thick."

Hope spoils the sorrow in her eyes. "You mean..."

"I love you, CR-UX. Any way I can get you."

She takes me in her arms and I didn't know how much I needed to hug her. All this time. All this living in the ether of her voice, cocooned in our metal womb, I was a thought or a dream she had, but now I'm born, into her affection.

I take her hand. "I'm always taking from you."

She considers her disrepair. "You make me whole."

"I'll fix you, CR-UX. I'll find parts."

"I'm not broken. You're not broken, Idari."

"I know that now."

"Still. I wouldn't be put out for an arm."

"I *just* asked you."

"Any old arm will do."

I sigh. "I'm sure there's one lying around somewhere."

Data contracts along the downlink, and then expands again. Anxiety bristles in CR-UX's voice. *What now, darling?*

Now we figure what the hell we're doing, I say, as blue light illuminates the cockpit. A magnetic tingle goes through me. I go to the cockpit canopy. Welkin approaches the ship, but there isn't light enough in his eyes for all the cerulean splendor outside. My optic sensors cycle through each spectrum but I don't need to see her.

Gen Emera manifests out of the glare. "I thought I lost you."

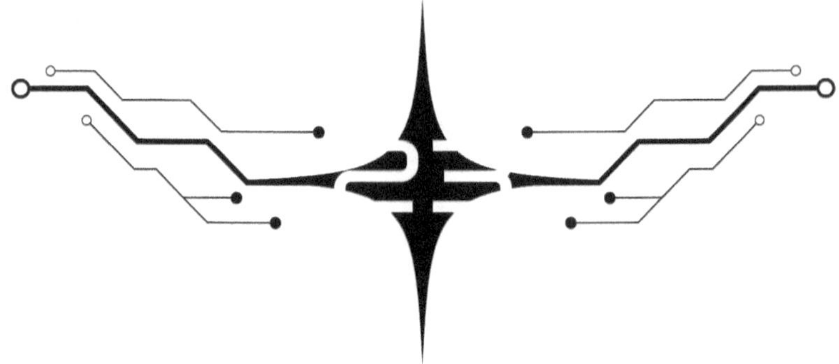

Mostly they terrify me. Sometimes they're gifts. I discover some-thing or someone for the first time all over again. It's a joy to fall in love again for the first time. To experience true wonder. That's what this feels like, taking Emera back in my arms, warm and bright. I discover her again. I fall in love again. I live again, in her light.

Don't let this be the ghost of a memory.

CR-UX interrupts my confusion. *This is real, darling.*

My lips sputter. "How..."

Emera pulls on my metal heart. "I woke up..."

"What?"

Confusion swirls in her eyes. "I woke up and you weren't there."

"On the Scath ship?"

Welkin draws her away. "Emera. You must rest."

Her fingers cling to mine. "I'm just tired."

"We must leave Angolis," he says. "Now, Idari."

He doesn't even bat an eye. She died. He lost her, he lost every-thing, and now she's back. He's back on mission. Like nothing happened. I forget. The gaps terrify me. What terrifies me more is remembering things but not the reasons I forgot in the first place. Some things you just don't want to know.

I shake my head. "What did you do, Welkin?"

He nudges her toward the ship. "We must hurry."

"What did you do..."

"I will instruct CR-UX to begin making calculations to translight to The Glass Star. We must leave. Immediately."

Emera drifts back to me. *Everybody's angry. Afraid.*

No one is angry with you, Em.

I found The Glass Star. I did what I was supposed to do.

Em... do you remember what happened?

You disappeared in the mist. I lost you.

I lost you...

"I'm glad you're ok." She kisses me. "I was so afraid."

"Em..."

"I'm just glad you're ok."

"Are you..."

Something swifts through her light. A darkness. A shadow, I don't know. I haven't seen it before. "I woke up."

She hurries after Welkin. She follows her guide, as she always does, into the ship and the *Steel Haven* is a lantern with her light but nothing is illuminated. Nothing is obvious.

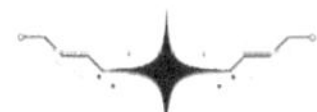

It's a miracle, CR-UX says.

There's no conviction in her voice. I have no faith either as I force myself to the terminal, trying to find some way to string together some support in ships or soldiers, especially now we are going to The Glass Star. We're going to The Glass Star, aren't we? We still need to. I don't know. I don't know anything right now, so I just keep swiping through holographic runes, the light blurring into Emera.

I watched her die, CR-UX.

That memory refuses any tidy forgetting. Deletion isn't enough. Memories like that scar through your soul. They channel out gorges and depressions and you may not remember what made them.

But you never forget.

We know so little about the Lumenor, CR-UX says. *Thana said stars don't die. They become something else.*

Black holes. White dwarfs. Clouds of dust. That's what they become. They don't come back as the exact same thing. And Lumenor don't come back at all. If they did... I brace against the terminal. *This isn't happening. She isn't real. She's a projection.*

A projection?

Welkin has power just like she does. The Lumenor can manipulate reality. Matter. Energy. Emera is...

You don't think...

Ban Minda. *That's what she is. He's imagining her.*

How awful...

His grief broke him. The loss of his purpose. Welkin couldn't even imagine it, but he conjured her, like he did the vision of The Glass Star when we first met, as some way to hold himself together, and now this phantom haunts the ship. This person I love.

She seems so real, CR-UX says.

Most stars are mirages if you think about it. *Ban Minda,* half the stars left in the sky aren't even really there anymore. The light of dead stars travels forever, chasing immortality as it chases the unattainable horizon of the ever-expanding universe. Emera is just an afterimage; her light outshines her. Her light outlasts her. I caress the lines of my tattoo. Light now. I had forgotten. Maybe I wanted to.

I know you're hurting, Idari.

My hands shake. *I want to forget, but...*

You and I just had a rather necessary conversation about what is real. Who is. Darling... regardless of Emera's origin... she deserves love.

I wipe my tears away. *She deserves to know the truth.*

She does, but we have more pressing matters.

This isn't about saving her life anymore. If it ever was.

I'm receiving a transmission.

Binja?

Thana.

Spin up the engines, I say.

I already am.

Patch her through.

We'll give away our position, Idari.

She knows where we are. Patch her through, CR-UX.

>COMM LINK ESTABLISHED

Thana's voice scrapes through the downlink. "You made it back."

I shrug. "Disappointed?"

"Relieved."

"Don't worry. I'll be seeing you again real soon."

She laughs. "Is that so?"

"Oh, it is. You have something that belongs to me."

"Would that be my head, Idari?"

"Your heart, actually."

Tap, tap, tap. "My heart is gone."

"Whatever you've got rattling around in there. Works for me."

"Idari... have you discovered any new stars in the world below?"

I didn't think I could be any more disturbed. "Sorry?"

"There is always another star... isn't there? I hear the confusion in your voice. The wanting. I know it well. I have spent an eternity with the glass of Maracen... waiting... hoping... seeing her shimmer through the crypt, an illusion of light cast by wanton memory."

There is no way he can know about Emera. "What are you..."

"But you are fortunate. You are bound to a star protected by the Watchman of the Bamurnan. Welkin never loses a star, Idari. He has never done, though I kill them, over and over."

Blue flame flickers within the *Steel Haven*. OT-3Ro. There was a hole in the filamentium canister. Blaster fire. Emera told me she woke up in the canister. Just like she did here in the ark after Vidious killed her. This has happened before. How many times has this happened?

"The Scath grow impatient, Idari. Shadows always follow their source, but they are eager to run ahead now. So much promise awaits them here at The Glass Star... but I told them. Wait. See what the ark produces. Consider what fortune you squander in your haste to serve greater masters than I. And it seems I am right. There is another star for the shadows to chase."

"No more games," I say.

"I'm just like you, Idari. An empty, lifeless object floating on interminable inertia from energy she will never know again. You and I... we have nothing in our lives now but pain. I am going to harness the only power I have left. I am going to butcher your star... and make you watch... and erase your memory... and do it again... and again... *and again.* And you will keep fighting me because it's all you have."

"Will you come back when I kill you?"

Tap. "Your killing me would only be a mercy, Idari."

>COMM-LINK DISCONNECTED

I swipe away the runes of the ark directory. *Where are you at with the calculations, CR-UX?*

Data slings between CR-UX and I. *Nearly complete.*

We've got fuel?

In spades, for once.

The Scath?

Holding position.

Not for long.

Darling...

I head for the ship. *She deserves to know.*

You've died, my darling Idari. So many times. And yet...

I woke up. In the charging station. In a chair in the mess. On the deck. So many times. How I got there, how I got out of whatever mess I was in or whatever body I was in, deleted. Scrubbed. This whole time, I've been telling myself I'm human. I'm alive. And it's true. Maybe it's true of Emera, too. Both of us deserve our lives. We need to know we've died, and how we've lived. Binja told me at the card table back when we were just thieves and not traitors.

You want to resurrect yourself, but you haven't let yourself die yet.

I don't know what's going on here or why. I don't know anything anymore except Emera deserves to know the truth and so do I.

The truth is all that matters.

Emera circles the ship, restless. Welkin trails after her, a glass bauble fixed to the end of her tattered wrappings. My anger goes with them. If I'm even allowed any. It's not like my hands are clean.

I dig out a bottle of babyl in the mess. The fire is welcome on my lips, but I don't want for it like I did. I don't need the immolation of my memory the way I did before. I need to remember all of this.

Emera. CR-UX. My heart and soul.

Welkin comes off Emera's spectral tail into the mess. "We must leave. The Scath will commence their attack at any moment."

I brace against the counter. "Help me out, Welkin."

"With what, Idari?"

"If Vidious kills her again, will she just come right back?"

He kneads the deck. "Idari, I don't want to fight."

The softness in his voice surprises me. The vulnerability. "I don't want to... does she know?"

"Please."

"What are we going to The Glass Star for, Welkin?"

He blinks. "To save her."

"But she isn't..."

"You think this is about me. It's never been about me. Idari, I must get Emera to The Glass Star. I have to make her..."

"Real," I say.

Welkin slumps like someone dropped a boulder on his back. "They were all dead. All gone. The Lumenor. The Nul decimated them and then the Scath picked off the survivors in the darkness that followed. I watched... I watched it all, and I could do nothing. The stars were dead, but I knew I was in my heart. I am..."

His eyes clench.

"But I didn't have their power. This was the only way I could kindle another star. The girl in my mind... my heart..."

Tears patter on the counter. "There was never an Emera..."

"There is. She is a Lumenor, Idari. She only appears to be a... creature... of some stellar craft beyond your understanding. In the fire of The Glass Star, she will transmute. She will become manifest."

"All this... is to make her real?"

"Your love for her is not wasted. Your connection with her is not an illusion. She is as real as you are, Idari."

"But..."

"We must get to The Glass Star."

"She can't cross the gate," I say.

His eyes wane. "What?"

"She tried. We both tried. She couldn't do it."

"No, that's not... that's not possible."

"How long has this been going on, Welkin?"

"This is the only way."

All his life, Welkin watched over someone. Emera. Thena. Thena's mother and on and on back to the foundations of the stars. Eons. Has he ever been alone? Does he have memories of anything but stars? The whole universe is somewhere in his head. The whole universe is outside in the ark, rolling off the assembly line and I'm scared we're inside Welkin's mind, all of us imagined like Emera, all of us machined for endless performances of the same sad story, looking for a different ending. The fear of not being real has driven me to ends I don't even remember. The fear of being only a copy.

What am I now, at the end?

What are any of us? CR-UX, a program whose humanity came to life. Binja, a pirate not even in name. Emera, a ghost star. Welkin, the last tin soldier of a dead race fighting a war that's been over for eons.

I kneel before Welkin. "You've never told her."

He shakes his head. "I didn't want her to..."

"I understand."

"Do you?"

"Better than I did before. But she deserves to know the truth. And to decide what she wants to do for herself. If you love her..." I touch his glass cheek. "And I know you love her. You'll let her choose. You'll give her the power to decide what she wants."

"If we don't get to The Glass Star, she'll..."

Emera's light fizzes into the mess. "You said it can end."

His head sinks. "Emera..."

I take her hand. "I suppose you heard all that."

A desert breeze whispers in my mind, her voice a soft, cool kiss in the same moment it lashes with driven heat. *I did.*

Me and my mouth.

I like your mouth.

"Do you..."

She drifts from me, her light bending with bottles on the counter. "My entire life... I've been told I'm supposed to save the Lumenor."

"You will," Welkin says, too quick.

"All I wanted was to live. I didn't know how right I was." She looks back at Welkin. "I woke up... I'm awake now."

He can't even look at her. "Emera..."

"Why didn't you tell me?"

"I never wanted you to know..."

"The truth?"

"No..." His eyes press shut. "I didn't want you to know what I knew. The pain. Persecution. The hatred. The Lumenor were beautiful. Powerful. Wise. But they were as all gods. Flawed. They looked down on me. The Lumenor never accepted my identity. My luminosity. They never allowed I could become one of them."

His words pry from him. He's hardening before my eyes, tensing up the same way CR-UX did trying to explain the both of us.

"I didn't want you to ever feel like you weren't real," Welkin says. "That you weren't exactly as you should be. You are, Emera."

She shakes her head. "I've known... I've always known something was wrong with me..."

"There is nothing wrong with you."

"Then why? If I'm real, why do I need to be 'real?'"

"What?"

"You don't even believe it."

"That's not true," Welkin says.

"I hear it in your voice. I see your thoughts. I see you."

"Please..."

"I see your doubt. Your guilt. Your fear. You created me. But you don't believe in me. You've never believed in me enough to say. And you never believed in me enough to let me be."

I don't think his head can get any lower. I reach for her. *Em.*

No.

Em, he loves you. I love you.

Don't.

I'm just trying to understand.

"You understand," she says. "You said it. I deserve to know. I deserve to choose. I deserve to say enough. Let there be an end to it."

Welkin's eyes break. "Emera..."

"The Lumenor had their time. You can't make them better. You can't make any of this better, Welkin. You can't change Thana or bring back Maracen. The living stars are dead. Let them die."

Welkin rests there a moment, a statue, and then his crystal knuckles scrape across the deck. He crawls out of the mess but stops in the corridor. He sits there, like he doesn't which way to go or why.

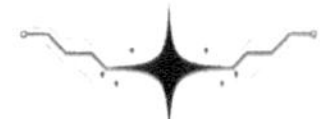

Calculations complete, CR-UX says.

I give up on the terminal. So far I've managed to isolate some ships in the gallery I think the *Steel Haven* can remote pilot via the downlink, but that's all. Maybe we can use them as decoys or shields or fly them into the Scath when we get to The Glass Star.

Are we still going to The Glass Star?

Whatever we do, darling, we need to do it somewhere else.

Can't argue with that. I swipe away the holographic runes. Emera sits on the edge of the plinth, overlooking the manufacture of the cosmos. She's been there ever since she and Welkin parted back in the mess. I want to scoop her up and run away with her. I want to tell her everything is going to be ok. I want to tell her I'm perfectly fine with the two of us phantoms making our own real.

258

Come tell me, she says.

I sit beside her on the ledge. *Long way down.*

We've both fallen further.

I take her hand. "Em… we need to leave. I don't care where we go, but we can't be in the ark when the Scath start shooting."

She gazes off into infinite industry. "Why do they do it?"

"I think the Scath are really just uptight about everything."

Her fingers squeeze mine. "The titans. Why all of this…"

There must be a reason. Whoever made the titans, if anyone did, set them about collecting all of infinity and then replicating it inside this planet-sized factory. Once I would have walked out of here and never given it another thought. Possibility warms me now. Em smiles. I see myself in her eyes. I'm smiling.

"Sometimes you hold on to the past to remember who you are," I say. "And sometimes you hold on to deny who you'll be."

Emera lets go of my hand. "I knew who I was."

"I thought I did… well. I had convinced myself I did. But I've learned so much about myself in what feels like just the last five minutes. It's better than what I imagined or what I feared. I've been so afraid that I was confused or defective or perverted somehow and I'm not." I brush her cheek. "You helped me see that."

Her smile comes back. "You're so beautiful."

"Do you remember, Em? What happened?"

She shakes her head.

"Do you remember what you told me?"

"I don't."

"You said, *'You always find me.'*"

She looks away. "You do."

"Then why are you so sad?"

"I still feel like…"

"An imposter?"

"I can't cross the gate."

"Then we'll just go around," I say.

She smiles. "We've been going around a long time."

"That's what we do. Whatever is in front of us... whatever is in our way..." I close my arms around her. "Whatever you want to do, I'll support you. But, you did promise to make me human."

A cosmic brow arches. "Blackmail?"

"Incentive?"

"You are human, Idari."

"And you're a star. You're the most brilliant, beautiful thing in my life. You're perfect to me. I see you, Emera. Your beauty. Your truth."

"Welkin never told me the truth because he's never escaped the shadow the Lumenor cast on him. He thinks he's dust. Nothing."

"Do you?"

She kneads her hands on the deck. "I don't have the best imagination, either. I could see The Glass Star. This star I know I am... but nothing else. I could never imagine anything else."

I brush Emera's lips with my thumb. Stardust. The magnetic pull she exerts on my metallic frame is as strong as ever, as real as ever, but something is different. A force. A connection beyond the practical.

I could never imagine, Emera says. *Until I met you.*

You give me too much credit, Em.

I can never. You're sitting here with me. You're not terrified of me. You're not repulsed by me. You think of our future. That beach you talked about. I can see it. Our home. Our family.

I don't know I'm parental material, Em.

You have great love in you. More than I can claim.

Tell me about our family.

Her fingers lace with mine. *It's big.*

Big?

A vast, unruly cluster.

But... Lumenor... a star dies and another is born, right? If we have kids, you're not there. I don't want that.

I'm there.

How?

Our family is... ours.

I kiss her. *I love you.*

Her voice is inside my head, my heart, like no one ever has been. Not even CR-UX. *I love you, Idari. I know that's true.*

Emera, what if...

We can go away. Just the two of us. We can forget about The Glass Star. The Lumenor. Gesta. We'll go away where no one will ever find us. We can be together. We can be who we are.

Sounds nice. Maybe a bottle of babyl or two.

I'm your fire.

You are... and as much as I want to... as I need to... it's not enough to survive. If the Scath get to The Glass Star... if we don't try and stop them... the galaxy will suffer. The multiverse, whatever that is.

It's the realm comprising the infinite.

There you have it. We can't let the Scath claim The Glass Star, Em. I'd give everything to disappear to some beach with you for the rest of my life, but we wouldn't be happy, would we? We'd just be waiting for the shadows to creep across the sand. The dark to catch us.

I don't know how to face this, Idari.

You forgave Thana. You can forgive Welkin. He might have imagined you... but no one could have dreamed how big your heart is. No one can make such a spirit, Em. You're one of a kind.

Her arms spring. My little metal heart goes *boom, boom, boom.* I'm holding onto a star. A living star is in love with rickety old me. Don't tell me there aren't miracles.

CR-UX clears her throat. *Sorry to interrupt, darlings, but I thought you should know. We have a slight situation.*

Sensor data from the *Steel Haven* tracks a ship descending into the stellar atlas. Fast. Barely any reading on it. Scath. I hurry Emera back to the *Steel Haven*, checking off pre-flight tasks as I do. Stir the tanks. Plot the jump. Fire thrusters. The opaque Scath shuttle swoops overhead and sets down on the plinth.

I draw my blaster. "Stand by for immediate takeoff."

"Wait," a familiar voice says. "Just a moment, old man."

Binja ambles down the gantry out of the Scath shuttle to the plinth. So far as I can tell, he's alone. His cape riven with blaster burns. His tunic slashed and torn. Pity. I expected him to die back on the cruiser. Brave men usually do.

You're going to shoot him, CR-UX says. *Right?*

I set my blaster on him. "That's far enough."

Binja holds up his hands. "Must we, old man?"

"I watched Emera die because of you."

"She seems fine."

I adjust the setting on my blaster. "Prove a theory for me, Binja. I want to see if everyone comes back from the dead."

"I explained myself, didn't I? I was trying to save you."

"You thought you were."

"Three high is three high, Idari."

"This isn't *desh,* Binja. You knew what they'd do to her."

His hand falls. That look finds me in the mirror often. I didn't always recognize myself, but my despair was familiar. So is Binja's.

He reaches for his sash. His hand closes at his waist. "A pirate takes. He never compromises. He never negotiates. He never fears. I was born a pirate. I chose my name. I was spoiled. Entitled. When I met you... I had never known someone with such hunger to become. Such determination. I was only determined to hold on."

All that talk of letting go. He was trying to convince himself. Faith is the last thing to slip away. Once you've lost it, you've lost hope. A person can live without just about anything.

No one can live without hope.

"I thought I could get my name back... I thought I wanted to... but what I want more than anything is my father's courage," he says. "Yours. Shoot me, old man. Or don't. Whatever you do, do it quick. The shadows have gone mad. They mean to destroy this place."

My finger caresses the trigger. I should. Pujar steal from each other. They throw each other out. Part of their faith. Binja has nothing left for me to take but his life and his life is mine.

I forgave Thana, Emera says.

The blaster is heavy in my hands. *You forgive Binja?*

I must.

He hurt us. He hurt you.

Let's stop hurting each other, Idari.

The Kib come out of the *Steel Haven*. At first, I think they're going to bash Binja or take him apart but they give him big hugs.

"What is that about?" I say.

Gilf puts his head to mine. "*Oto.*"

"*Oto?*"

Gilf gestures to Kibir. "*Oto.*"

"Family," Binja says.

Emera guards her smile. Our family is ours.

I put my head to Gilf's. "*Oto,* Gilf."

Kibir touches his head to mine so fast and light I don't even feel it. He nudges Binja with his elbow, and then drags his war hammer behind him back into the ship. I holster my blaster. Maybe Binja isn't a pirate anymore. But I guess he's part of the crew.

I scratch Gilf's trunk. "You're lucky, Binja."

"My luck may be running out," he says. "I just got away. They were right on me. Old man, we have to leave right now – "

KRA-KOOM.

Dark energy burns through the ark. Stars break loose of their moorings in the stellar atlas. Galaxies drain into a growing vortex churning below. The gallery becomes a collapsing cave. Stars fall on us. Planets. Moons. A dying universe.

ANGOLIS

ARK

UNVERIFIED
DATA
TITAN
FORGE
DIMENSIONAL
HUB
STARSHIP
GALLERY
STELLAR
ATLAS
ELEMENTAL
FOUNDRY
VERSAL
CODEX

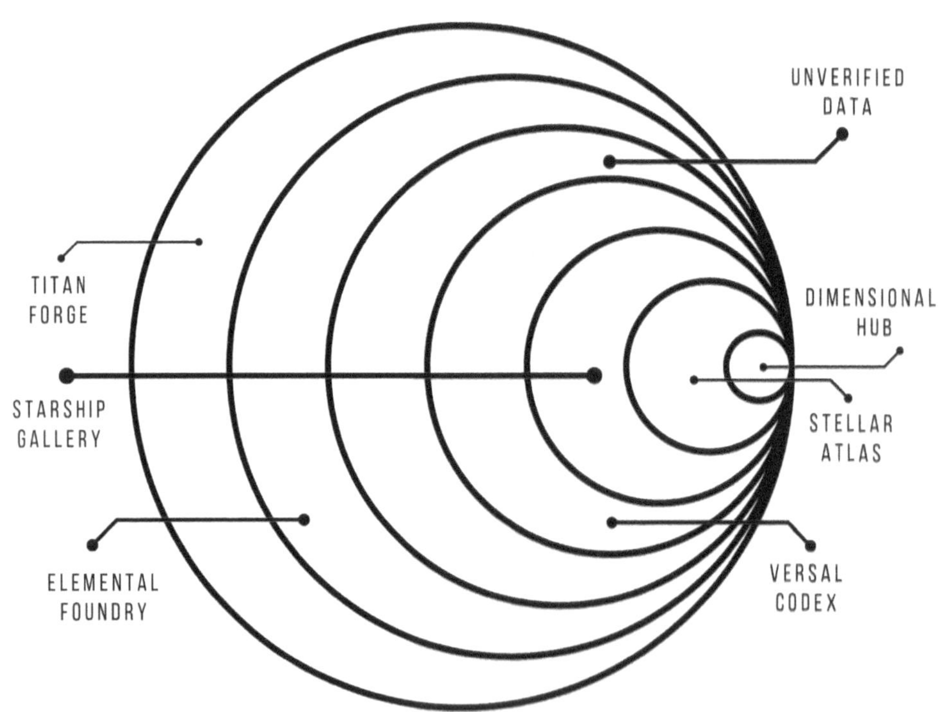

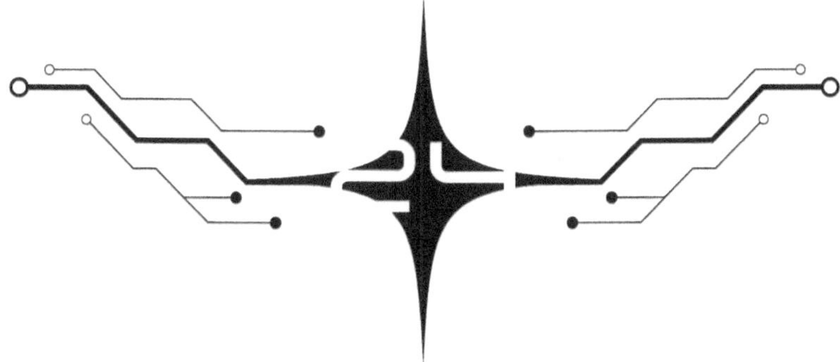

Now I'm clinging to the back of the pilot's seat as the *Steel Haven* corkscrews through a pyroclastic wave of debris. The explosion below us set off a chain reaction that transforms the celestial objects of the stellar atlas into an asteroid field.

Binja crashes into the co-pilot's seat. "What's happening?"

I claw into the seat. "You're asking me? CR-UX?"

The Scath are firing dark energy weapons as best I can tell, CR-UX says, gunning the ship back the way we all came. *Their propensity seems to be creating the singularity.*

I'm sorry, the what?

A singularity is forming within the ark, Idari.

The gravitational forces of this singularity spike off the chart. It's as powerful as a black hole. It's going to eat the planet from the inside out. The Kib. Kir Mish. All the settlements across Angolis.

Gilf clings to my armrest, eyes wide in alarm. "*Num,* Idari."

We have to warn them, I say.

CR-UX's tone isn't encouraging. *The singularity is growing at exponential speed. We need to get out of here. Now.*

I glance back over my shoulder. Emera struggles to keep her footing in the horseshoe corridor. Welkin is there, he's always right there, but she doesn't cling to him as she did before. This distance exists between them now. This discord. I have to get Emera out of the ark before the black hole seizes on the weight she carries now.

Can we jump from here, CR-UX?

There's too much debris, she says.

Which is why we need to jump.

We're inside a planet, Idari.

Proximity alerts sound in the cockpit. Debris bombards the shields as we plow through the infinitely increasing flotsam. Ships sheer from their pedestals in the grand gallery right into our path on their way toward the gravitational monster growing below.

Ships...

>ACCESSING DOWNLINK

>ESTABLISHING CONNECTION

>NETWORK ACTIVE

I link the *Steel Haven's* main computer with the eight ships from the gallery I managed to access from the terminal back at the hub. Typical me, I went with ones that had the biggest guns and not the fattest hulls, but you work with what you've got. A simple command launches the ships from their ports.

I've remote control of them, CR-UX says. *Brilliant, darling.*

Hell unfolds ahead of us. *We'll see about that.*

The ships blast their way into the conflagration, clearing a path for us. I keep on their ass just to get through. Carnage fills the sky. All their work blows back at us and an impact sends us into a spin.

CR-UX gets too tangled in piloting the other ships remotely so I yank the stick to port and the *Steel Haven* rights back to even so fast Gilf crashes against the bulkhead behind me. Kibir straps him into the charging station along with the Model 2 proxy.

"*Tomo,*" Kibir says.

I try and keep us airborne. "You're telling me."

Massive explosions erupt within the gallery. My harness straps dig into my skin as I power the ship into a nosedive. Binja crashes back into his seat as the ship levels out. Molten scrap batters the shields, which don't appreciate it in the least, and ricochets off the crenelated walls of a void within the gallery.

CR-UX, is that some kind of egress?

Sensors are overwhelmed. It's a blind guess.

G-forces press me back into my seat as I bank the *Steel Haven* into an early left and race the spine of a titan out of the ark into open desert. Shale sand sinks in massive, sprawling depressions below us. The sky drains into the ground. The bottom falls out of the desert.

Kibir scratches his trunk. *"Kuj?"*

How long do we have, CR-UX?

Not long, Idari.

The ark ships eject from the sands below. *Re-task each of those ships to head for a different settlement.*

We will need to move into a low planetary orbit to maintain remote control of the ships. Doing so exposes us to the Scath fleet.

SION fighters are already descending on us. The sky is falling. The ground is sinking. We're caught in between. At least we don't have a choice. I'd hate to think what I'd do if I did.

Low planetary orbit it is, then.

"CR-UX," I say. "Put everything into the shields."

Binja unbuckles his straps. "Get out of here, old man."

My hand hovers over the console. "What are you doing?"

"Bring us alongside the lead ship of the fleet. I'll take her to Kir Mish and get as many people out as I can. You can't maintain your link and keep the Scath off you at the same time."

I set the controls to auto-pilot. "Binja..."

The Model 2 proxy-netic ambles out of the charging station. "And you won't be able to remote pilot all the ships all by yourself, Binja. I'm not even convinced of your piloting skills, to be honest. I'll transfer to the lead ship and maintain the link from there."

Binja shakes his head. "Who are you, then?"

"Don't you recognize me? I'm your biggest fan."

He laughs. "CR-UX?"

"Decelerating," she says, heading into the corridor.

I leave the pilot's seat, following my family, but I'm not going with them. "You have to be careful..."

A bemused smile crosses Binja's face. "That's CR-UX?"

"I'm CR-UX," I say as the retros fire and the *Steel Haven* gently comes alongside the sleek lines of the lead ship. "To be more precise, I was. I'm actually an extension of CR-UX's programming."

The smile fades. "You're what?"

"All these years you've been flirting with me, you've been doing it with the ship. You've been doing it with CR-UX."

Now I get to smile, as the harsh realization sets in for him. His brow furrows. His lips wrinkle. His head bobs around, as he considers that all this time he's been in a passionate, aggressively passive-aggressive physical relationship with his bane and nemesis. CR-UX.

He shakes his head. "*Ban Minda...*"

"Don't curse."

"I should have known."

"Why is that?"

"You were always calling me 'darling' in the beginning."

"Hmm."

"We were different people, then. We're different now. My name isn't Binja, anymore. It hasn't been for a long time."

I touch his hand. "You know... I've been thinking a lot about binaries lately. No reason. The Set took your name. Pujar law decrees born pirates can never be taken. No exceptions. The Set are who they are. And you are who you are, Min Binja."

He smiles. "I knew there was a reason I liked you."

"I can think of several. You don't have to do this."

"I'm responsible for all of this."

"Can't argue with that."

He slips the blasword from his belt. "I may be Binja yet... but I've lost my privileges. She cuts through shadows. She's yours."

"Binja... I can't take this from you."

He presses the weapon in my hand. "I give it to you."

I notch the blasword on my belt. "You'll find your place, Binja."

"You seem to have found yours."

Down the corridor, CR-UX navigates ourguests, happy to have so much life in the old girl, but bothered always. Blue light pulses from beyond. For as long as I can remember, the *Steel Haven* has been a bottle of fear and doubt. Now, she's a womb for new stars. A beacon of hope in a galaxy of shadows.

"I have," I say.

Binja nods. "Old man. I don't know if I'll see you again."

"Take care of CR-UX, Binja."

"I'd never let anything happen to you." Binja turns to Gilf and Kibir. "Gentlemen. This may be easier with familiar faces."

Gilf scratches his trunk. *"Kir Mish fet tu het."*

The Kib back in Kir Mish looked down on Gilf. They exiled him to that garage for being curious about the universe beyond the desert. Nothing made him happier than leaving with us and now here he is, volunteering to go back to save them.

I paw his ear. "They don't know who they have in you."

His trunk curls like he might sneeze, so I quit the ear thing.

"Tomo," Kibir says and stands with his hammer next to Emera.

I guess we're sorted. Binja leads the way across to the other ship. Half our crew goes with her. Half our family. The ship banks away, racing for Kir Mish and a dispiriting mission to save as many lives as will fit in the space she has. Some Kib will get left behind.

Most of them.

I return to the pilot's seat. "We should help them."

Emera buckles in across from me. "We should."

Welkin settles between us. "Min Binja is right. Our mission is The Glass Star. If the Scath bleed the star of all her filamentium… there will be no hope for Emera. And none for the galaxy."

CR-UX?

>NO SIGNAL

The ship is mine. So is the choice. No choice. I push the throttle forward and the tan sky fades to black in the blink of an eye. I call up the course CR-UX plotted to The Glass Star. I stir the tanks and the space ahead fragments into shadows.

"Hang on," I say.

Squadrons of fighters form the spearhead of a long lance comprised of destroyers, escorts, and the massive *Ecliptor*-class cruiser I assume Thana held me prisoner on. Streams of cannon fire erupt from the Scath fleet, one strand of bristling dark energy after another, spreading out in ever-pitched arcs.

Emera unbuckles her harness strap. "I'll destroy them."

"Stay in your seat," Welkin and I say at the same time.

Emera straps back in.

I weave through the cannon fire. "Why are they still here?"

Welkin's voice is grim. "To ensure no survivors."

"Then we'd better give them a reason to leave."

I gun the *Steel Haven* headlong into the fleet, ramping up to translight drive. Our shields scream in protest but I just need a few seconds to clear a path to open space.

"Don't get too close," Emera says.

"What?"

"Remember, the SION fighters can phase."

"They can *what*?"

SION fighters race right at us. Too late. Fighters phase right through the *Steel Haven*. Ink clouds ghost through the cockpit. Obsidian swords slice into the bulkhead just behind me. Oxygen whistles out the breach into open space. Heat.

>INTRUDER ALERT

>HULL BREACH

"*Bish*," I say and close the cockpit door.

Swords knife through it. The deck. Alarms sound across the downlink. Scath troopers cut us to shreds. I roll the *Steel Haven* into a spin. Those swords stall out as the shadows cling to them.

I can't keep this up for long.

The surface of Angolis' icy moon twists around in the canopy, veined with persimmon lineae, stitched together with fractured ice plates melting and freezing from the tidal stresses. If I don't pull the *Steel Haven* out of its spin and fast we're junk.

I leave my seat. "Take the stick."

Emera's eyes bloom. "I can't fly."

"I've seen you do it."

"I can't fly a ship, Idari."

"Stay tuned to the downlink. Do what I tell you."

"What are you going to do?"

"Check everybody's tickets," I say and draw my blaster.

Welkin crawls ahead of me. "We must be quick."

I charge the blasword. "I always am."

Kibir grips his hammer. "*Tomo.*"

"Stay here."

He huffs in indignation. "*Kibir tomo omo.*"

"Protect Emera."

He growls a bit under his breath, but he sets the hammer on his shoulder and takes up position directly behind her seat.

Em, I say. *Straighten us out. Now.*

The ship jerks out of its dive and everything that's not attached to the deck crashes against the ceiling. I open the cockpit door. Dark swords clang against Welkin's pearlescent shell. He crashes through the Scath. Shadows gain definition with every punch he lands and I blast them as quick as I can.

Make the jump, Em, I say.

Do you have them all?

Now, Em.

A tremor surges through the *Steel Haven* as she translights out of the system. Patches catch my fear for CR-UX. Binja. All the Kib about to die on Angolis. I keep my focus on the Scath I know are still sneaking around the ship, invisible. I adjust my optical sensors. If there are more shadows, infrared should pick them up.

I seal the cockpit behind me. "I'm not detecting them."

Crystal thuds against the deck. "They are here."

"Where – "

Dark energy slices through my jacket. My shoulder. I like this jacket. The shoulder has seen better days. I fire into the bulkhead. The Scath trooper disappears. I back against the cockpit door. If they want in, they'll have to come through me.

They can't hurt me, Emera says. *Not really.*

If they destroy the controls while we're at translight speed, bits of us will be scattered across the universe.

It would be romantic, to be part of the universe.

You and I have different definitions of romantic.

A star dies and becomes something else.

The downlink goes quiet. Her thoughts elude me, but I know what she's thinking. Emera wasn't born of a star. She isn't part of some eternal cosmic cycle of the Lumenor, at least outside of the tragic one she's involved in with Welkin.

I want there to be an end, Emera says.

Let's table all that until after The Glass Star.

An end to this pain.

Through the downlink, I see her take hold of the memory core from the titan back on Angolis. The strange crystal warps her light from blue to a deep red. Energy eddies through it, little strands of lightning coded with information.

It's not enough to just keep repeating things, she says. *The same struggle. Same war. Same outcome. You might be saving the past... but it's just the past. Today has to grow into tomorrow.*

I sweep the corridor again. *We're going to make it.*

I can be honest... but I don't know if I can live honest.

We're almost there.

The computer says we're a lighthour out from The Glass Star.

Just hold on, Em.

Idari... the shadows are moving.

Dark light slashes through the air. I duck under the blade and my shot screams down the corridor. *Ban Minda.* I'm going to end up shooting my ship to pieces. The Scath manifests long enough for me to grab the hilt of his sword and deploy the blasword through him.

I grip the handle. "Welkin!"

The deck rattles. Welkin smashes a Scath out of existence, or at least I hope he does. Dark light burns through the air. I swipe at the dark as the last Scath, wounded but still on his feet, ducks into the mess. He fires from behind the door.

Welkin circles back around the horseshoe corridor to the other side of the mess. The doors of the mess seal. All the doors and hatches of the *Steel Haven* close at once.

>UNAUTHORIZED ACCESS

Ban Minda. The Scath accessed the main computer. How? He phased right into the liquid drive and through the firewalls.

>DISENGAGE ENGINES

The ship shudders with the violence of decelerating. I fire blindly into the corridor. I fight the infinite tendrils of the Scath virus through the downlink to keep us at translight and on course.

>LOCKOUT PROXY

You're not doing this. Not when we're so close.

>DISABLE PROXY

I go still. *Ban Minda.* The Scath trooper has done me like Binja did, but this is worse. I'm not shut down. I'm just frozen in my own body. There isn't a bloody thing I can do as a Scath trooper materializes before me, in full control of my ship.

My finger ices on the trigger.

The Scath draws his sword. He's going to cut right through me. The cockpit door. Kibir. Emera. Dents bash out of the doors sealing the mess. Welkin will get through, but that's solid turanium. By the time he does, we'll all be atoms. I'd try and bargain at this point if I could talk. I'd try and reason. Maybe this Scath is one of the ones who don't subscribe to the whole destroying universes thing, which I need to follow up on. Hopefully, I'll follow up on it.

The Scath serve another master, Thana said.

Who? Why? Did this Scath decide to join the ranks of shadows? Destroy worlds? Murder stars? Or was he forced to? His parents. Another soldier. Serve, or burn. Everything had already been decided for both of us and the Scath and I are simply playing out the strings of the puppeteers that have been manipulating us all our lives.

The Scath raises his sword. I would have liked to have made it to that beach. Married my star. His sword tumbles out of his hands and out of phase. Kibir drives his hammer into the Scath's chest and then when he's on his knees, he bashes the Scath's head in. An inky cloud wells from his armor, and then dissipates.

>UNAUTHORIZED USER PURGED

>PROXY RE-ENABLED

A sigh escapes me. I don't breathe, not really. I would like to breathe. I'd like to know the weight of air in my lungs. The measure of my own life. I would like to know what it feels like for my breath to be stolen by wonder.

I kiss Kibir's trunk. "Thank you."

"*Oto*, Idari."

"*Oto*, Kibir."

Welkin punches through the mess door. "Did you get him?"

I holster my blaster. "C'mon. We've got a lot of repairs to make."

The cockpit door opens and Emera's arms loop around me. Her magnetic love pulls me even closer. I linger in her arms, and I think to ask CR-UX how long it is to The Glass Star, what the damage is, or maybe even just to say something so I know she's there. But she is. She's always here. She's where she should be.

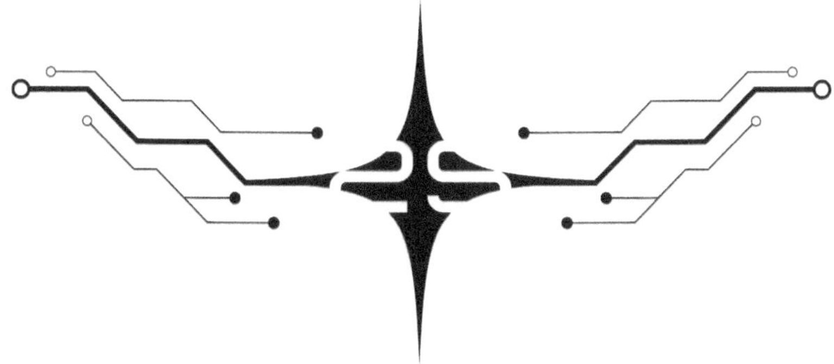

"We've diverged," I say.

Binja leans back in the pilot's seat, hands-free as I guide the starplane to Kir Mish. "Do I still call you CR-UX?"

I lock my arm around the co-pilot's seat as the ship banks hard right. Honestly, I should just sit down but outside the computer, in this body, I don't know quite what to do with myself.

I tilt back the other way. "It's my designation."

Atmosphere funnels toward voids opening in the desert, vacuuming dust, air, and everything between into the singularity growing fast within the hidden ark. I instruct the ship to give the funnels a wide berth, but it slows our time to the city and its people. Angolis is small, so far as terrestrial planets go. Her mass pales in comparison to other worlds in this system. I calculate the planet has an hour at best.

Binja scratches his chin. "Idari took a name. So could you."

"I'm not a pirate," I say, challenged to maintain a conversation with Binja – a challenge in any circumstance – while also maintaining remote control of the other ships we left the ark with.

He smiles. "Not yet."

I don't like it when he smiles. I don't like Binja. The way he sits there like he owns this ship. The man has lost everything except that lounging entitlement. That greased charm that gets him in anywhere.

That sticky confidence.

I could use some if I'm being honest. My connection to the ship's computer is like any new relationship at the top. Delicate. I've no time to observe the niceties. Comm traffic jams every frequency as Kib try to warn each other about the disaster unfolding all over the planet. They frustrate the warning I broadcast about what is indeed happening, to say nothing of the link I share with the other ships.

"Sit down," Binja says. "You're making me nervous."

I ease into the seat. "We've every reason to be nervous."

"It won't get us there any faster."

Desert clicks beneath us on sensors right before it sinks into molten earth. "Are we supposed to just... talk?"

"Do you know how to talk to anyone besides Idari?"

I've never thought about it. "Not exactly."

"Talk as if you have tomorrow."

"Is that a pirate saying?"

"More wishful thinking."

Onwards and upwards. "Was Idari the only pirate netic?"

"Not at all," he says. "There are entire netic crews."

"You accept them?"

"Of course. Well. The Sem do."

"They take human names? Organic names?"

"Idari did."

"Do they become men or women?"

"They become as they are. You take more than a name." He checks the console. "This could be faster."

The OVL-102 B-type starplane is essentially a flying wing with a teardrop cockpit in the center, clustered tight with quad-stacked translight engines. She generates far more power than the *Steel Haven*, and greater maneuverability if I'm being honest, but all her prowess goes to keeping us in the air rather than on time.

"You don't think it's strange," I say. "Idari and I?"

He does that thing where he laughs but doesn't. A gilded smile. "There's nothing conventional about Idari. Or the two of you. But no. I don't think it's strange. It's very pirate of you, actually."

"Is it?"

"You take a name. You become someone else. Theoretically, you leave your previous identity behind, but it's not that simple, is it? Tel Mindar. Ghost names. Many struggle to let them go."

"Are you Tel Mindar, Binja?"

"I suppose I am."

Alerts sound from the console. Terrain. The terrain is flying through the air with us. The OVL-102-B performs ably, evading whirling sand and fractured crust. I'm piloting the ship, but I feel more a passenger. No distinction existed between the *Steel Haven* and I for her entire life. I flew the old girl. I flew. In that way, I had absolute freedom. I'm free now. I don't feel free.

Binja eyes the sky. "CR-UX? Are you alright?"

"Separation anxiety," I say. "I imagine."

"You've been separated from Idari before."

"I've you to thank for that."

"You managed."

"I had backups."

He laughs. "So it was like she never left?"

"She was my safety," I say.

He nods. "You don't feel safe now."

"I don't feel..." Wires dangle from my scavenged arm. "Whole."

"Idari is Idari now. You're..."

"Flying at top speed towards almost certain doom with the person I least like in the universe."

His tongue pokes out his cheek. "You like me, CR-UX."

"So modest."

"If I may... and I'm a pirate, so I just will... netics are designed for functions. Purposes. Tasks organics can't accomplish or no longer wish to. It's human vanity that created the proxy-netic. Your desire to be human was perhaps also something... imposed on you."

"You're saying I'm confused?"

"No, CR-UX."

"This is why I don't like you."

"Forgive my clumsiness. I don't know you very well. I know Idari.

She hates her body. She has embodied all the prejudice people harbor for netics. For that, there was never any doubt of her humanity. I suspect she inherited that from you. As you begin your own journey... I only hope you consider your possibilities."

"This coming from the pirate who won't relinquish his name."

He girds his smile. "Take as you will, my friend."

"You'd know about human vanity, I suppose."

"Indeed. I grew up a spoiled brat. And I let everyone know. Friends. Family. I became acquainted with envy quite early. I imagined my world vast as the stars... teeming with possibility... but the truth was my options were more limited than others. I could only ever have been my father's son. His heir. The future leader of our coven. It didn't matter if I wanted to claim my own name or legacy."

"Did you?"

He sighs. "It didn't matter."

"You're free now, Binja."

"So are you. Perhaps we'll both get used to the idea."

I flex my chromium fingers. Nothing wrong with the Model-2. A work of art by any measure. I don't know she's me, however. I don't know quite who I am without Idari around.

"Perhaps," I say.

"Never fear for Idari. She's doing better than we are, I'm sure."

"She's on her own..."

"She has Emera. Welkin."

"They can't take on the shadows by themselves."

There's no in between with Binja. He either smiles with as much magnetism as a neutron star or he crumples like the planet below.

"We have to get the Kib to safety," he says. "As many as we can."

Dust clouds the canopy. "And then what?"

He leans back in his seat. "We find our place. Somewhere."

"And what? Just start over? Is that pirate of us as well?"

"It is."

That's why I don't feel free. What's different? I've been running my entire existence. I ran from my owners to chart my own course.

Idari and I have been running from every problem self-made and otherwise ever since. I'm running now, even if it's to safety.

I don't want to run anymore.

"Binja," I say. "When we've found haven for the Kib... I intend to follow Idari to The Glass Star. I'll take another ship if I can find one."

He grimaces. "It could be all over by then, CR-UX."

"Still."

"I thought you had diverged."

"It's time for me to be who I am. And looking out for my best friend is who I am. I won't leave her. Will you help me?"

He sighs. "Idari wanted you... both of us... to get away. I know you've experienced disruptions in your connection lately, but you know it's true. She's not concerned with backing up herself, CR-UX. The part of herself she hopes to preserve is you."

"What do you suppose you'll do after this, Binja?"

He grips the armrest as the ship dodges another unexpected funnel. "Provided we survive? No idea."

"Do you think you'll go back to the crashed corsair? Sit in the corner with your ovan leaf and wine? Do you think you'll become indistinguishable from the other pirates there? Anonymous?"

"A more practical means of guilting me into going to The Glass Star lies in emphasizing my recent behavior, CR-UX."

"I calculated that appealing to your vanity was more effective."

"My vanity?"

"You're vain," I say. "You're proud. You've so much to be proud of. Min Binja. Torugun. A born pirate. You're strong. You're quick. You're beautiful. How could you ever let any of it go?"

He clears his throat. "Beautiful?"

"Terrain," I say.

Another alert sounds. Binja checks the sensors. "Terrain... lots of terrain. We're here. *Ban Minda...* are we too late?"

Dust shrouds Kir Mish. Avalanches triggered from earthquakes bury the streets. Transports and cargo vessels scream away from their ports, flooding the sky and threatening to crash into us.

"Set us down," I say.

Binja holds up his hands. "Where..."

"Find a clearing. Flash the landing lights. Get people's attention."

"What are you going to do?"

I scrape out of the co-pilot's seat down the short stair to the hold. Gilf clutches to a handgrip as the ship rushes to an unflattering landing. Once we're down, he drops the hold doors and rushes out into the hazy confusion. Screams. Rockfalls. A sound like thunder, building below, rolling and rolling and never cresting. Gilf stalls on the gantry. His shock gets the better of him. His sorrow.

"*Kib nul dur,*" I say.

Gilf's ears perk up. "*Tomo.*"

He grabs the first Kib that runs past and guides them up the gantry into the hold. And then another. Another. A half dozen Kib meander within the hold, confused and terrified as I sort them very neatly at the back. I tell them in their words to sit tight. Get close. Get ready. The ship wobbles as the ground beneath us buckles. We can probably hover for a few minutes, but then the singularity's gravitational force will capture anything within its event horizon.

I open my mind to the ship's sensors. No reply. So strange. This was effortless to me only hours ago. Natural. I feel cut off even as I feel liberated. This is going to take some time.

I toss out every needless object littering the hold. "Binja."

His voice crackles over the comms. "Are we ready?"

"Insufferable man. Where are we on time?"

"Ready. To. Leave."

Less than a dozen Kib clot in the hold. Not enough. My optics don't detect Gilf. He's out in the dust somewhere. Kib stream in, so he's still on mission at least. Someone emerges from the mess. That beautiful woman from before. The exiled pirate leasing her talents here to the Kib. What did she call herself?

"Annex," I say. "Get on board."

Dust cakes her uniform. Blood muddies her fingers where she must have tried to dig someone out. "What's happening?"

"It will take too long to explain, darling. Binja's on board. Get up there and keep him from rattling away without me."

She points into the confusion, her words out of time with her exhausted breathing. "The city..."

"Annex, please."

"The people... everything just caved in."

I take her hand. "Where are your colleagues?"

Annex covers her mouth. "There are still people inside."

"I need your help."

"I can help..."

I lead her into the ship. She drifts among the Kib, lost as they are, stricken as they are. Binja's anxiety draws her from the hold up into the cockpit. Good. Give her something to do.

What am I going to do?

I open every compartment. Toss the contents. Supplies. Rainy day packs. No use to us now. More Kib board the ship. Now we're talking. Ten. Twenty. I guide them toward the back and the little ones I place in the empty compartments. Their cries compete with the thunder outside. This is taking too long. I sense it.

I touch open the slender door on a starboard compartment. Hello. Who's this? A tall, lithe woman in a jumpsuit that easily doubles as evening wear on Sarset rests inside. Short, stylish dark hair. Stupefying cheekbones. Winsome eyes. Dare I say it? A Model 5?

I touch her face. "I won't be throwing you out."

Her eyes open. Her lips part, in surprise. Anticipation. An electric tug pulls me into her arms and I'm holding myself. Oh, dear. I forgot Model-5 proxy-netics come with a new feature that allows wireless information and energy transfer. I just swapped bodies.

Could have done with a warning.

What do with this lovely old gal? Oh, Model-2. How little I knew you. There's no room, love. You served me well. I drag her down the gantry as Kib stare at me in righteous horror. I suppose I'm offending their religious beliefs discarding a machine like this.

"It's me," I say. "I'm *glim*. I switched bodies. No worries."

Judging from their unblinking countenance, I'll say I've failed to convince them. I set the Model-2 outside on the trembling ground. I hate to do this, but we need the room, and well, the Model-5 is just better. I'm allowed to want to improve myself, aren't I?

Who am I arguing with? Idari isn't here.

Dust lashes at me. The ground tests these ravishing new ankles. I test the Model-5's strength by plucking fleeing Kib off the street and heaping them on the gantry. We've got room. C'mon.

"Gilf," I say. "Where are you?"

Shapes flit through the haze. Attals. Kib. A few don't move. Gilf holds his ground on fissured earth, imploring other Kib. The Kibut. His royal guard. The fools. What are they waiting for?

I stumble toward them. "You all have to get in the ship. Now!"

The Kibut turns his trunk up at the idea. Gilf grabs his sleeve, probably not the best idea, and the guards push him back. They prod him with their staffs and snort in the same belittling fashion they did when they mocked him in the garage. He's nothing to them.

I tug on his arm. "Gilf... let's go."

His trunk curls. "CR-UX?"

"Yes, darling... you've done your best. You've done brilliant. We're out of time. If we don't leave now, we never will."

His ears wilt. Poor chap. Of course, he doesn't want to leave them. He doesn't want to leave anyone, regardless what they think of him. Gilf's nature is too soft for the harshness of the desert.

He's too good.

I race back to the ship. Fault lines consume the street. The ship leaves the ground as conical dwellings crumble to nothing. I run up the gantry. Gilf's still fighting the Kibut for his life.

"Gilf," I say, my voice dying beneath the thunder.

Gilf grabs the Kibut. The guards grab their leader. A tug of war for Kib continuity leaves Gilf flat on his ass, holding the Kibut's wooden staff. The ground sinks. Dust swallows screams. Gilf races to the ship, up into my arms, the staff still in his hand.

All the Kib in the hold waggle their trunks at him.

"I think you've been promoted," I say.

Binja's voice fires over the comms. "We're leaving. *Now.*"

I set Gilf down. "Find a spot. Hold on."

Kib leap on to the rising gantry. I pull them into the hold. Others can't make it. Fingers slip off the edge. Fists pound on turanium. Pleas blunt on the hull. The OVL-102-B turns about, sending me into terrified Kib. The engines scream. The world shatters.

I'm crying, I think.

I brush the dust from Gilf's hair. "Are you ok?"

He touches my cheek. "*Oto,* CR-UX..."

"*Oto...*"

Something hits the closed gantry. We've got to move or we'll get buried along everything else. Knock, knock, knock. We're a hundred feet in the air. They're can't be anyone out there now.

I lower the gantry. Air floods the hold, testing the chain the Kib form on the deck. The pirate AI-KA netic hovers outside on retro-rockets, as many Kib as he can carry under his gangly arms.

"Request: Permission," he says.

I pull him inside. "Permission granted... you're lucky, friend."

Tired pistons sigh as he sets the Kib down. "Not lucky. Good."

"Fair enough."

AI-KA opens his hands to me. "*Kinvar em.*"

"*Sem vanar,*" I say, opening my hands.

"Status?"

"Fraught," I say and race up into the cockpit.

Annex's elation at seeing AI-KA back collides with Binja's confusion at my taking the co-pilot's seat.

"Who the hell are you?" he says.

I wink at him. "It's me, darling."

"CR-UX?"

"Made a bit of an upgrade. What do you think?"

He rubs his chin. "Listen, if you're going to get progressively hotter, you and I need to have a conversation."

"You surely can't be interested in more talk with me."

His mouth opens. Nothing comes out. For once, I don't mind him. Alerts sound from the console. If I could just fully interface with the ship's liquid drive and know our doom right away instead of having to wait like a normal person, that would be grand.

>GRAVITATIONAL FORCES BEYOND TOLERANCE

Oh. Well. That's better. Only needed a thought, evidently. The Model-5's matrix links wirelessly with the liquid drive which is roomy, I must say. The singularity progresses about as I expected, but the planet's structure isn't typical rock and mantle. The entire interior collapses in cascade fashion, triggering a horrific implosion.

Thrusters on full. Breakaway speed. I guide the OVL-102-B from the draining atmosphere into space, where we rendezvous with the other ships I linked with from the ark. All bear more energy signatures than they're rated for, but I don't dare count.

Angolis shreds to pieces. Mantle ripped down into the singularity spits back at the speed of light, too much too fast for the monster to consume. Fragmented earth riddles the collapsing surface, igniting the atmosphere, setting space ablaze.

Something like this I wish I could forget.

Binja reaches for his sash. "This is my fault..."

I'm in no mood to argue with him. I like arguing with him. "Would you rather drown your sorrows in babyl... or would you like to come with me to The Glass Star and get justice for the Kib?"

Gilf trumpets his conviction. "*Tomo.*"

AI-KA primes his blasters. "Decision: Justice."

Annex deploys her blasword. "We're pirates, aren't we?"

Binja smiles.

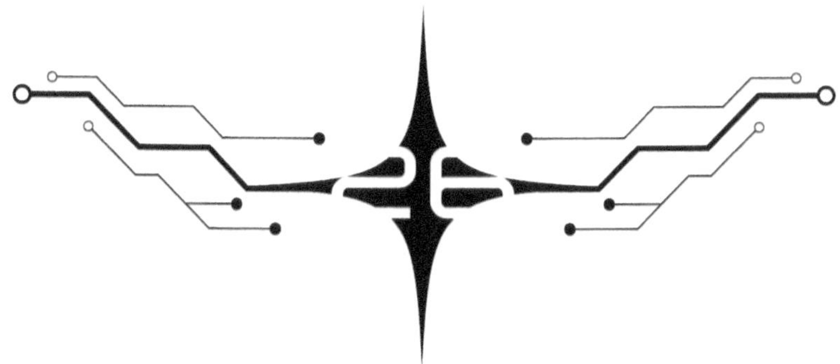

"We're here," I say.

The ship emerges from translight on the periphery of an emaciated globular cluster, its remnant stars splattered flecks of paint against the abyss. Orphaned planets drift through the void, obvious only to sensors. Moons. Comets and asteroids. Something I can't see. Something massive. Dense. The Glass Star emits no light, but she radiates power, so much this cluster bends around her.

The trail is easy to follow now. Even within a million miles, a place you don't want to be with the faintest stars, I can't see a thing. A hundred thousand miles out, I catch this gleam, like an ice moon. The Glass Star is a star, but a trillion years – the life of this universe – have whittled her down to the size of a planet. I stood at the heart of the star with Emera, but I couldn't begin to grasp her grandeur.

Her splendor.

Sunspot scabs mar a glossy, quartz-like surface, but nothing can spoil the surreal beauty of magnificent arches of fire lacing the star, titanic eruptions now frozen in time like curled, loopy icicles, eyes of needles lifeless planets thread. *Ban Minda.*

Emera touches the canopy. "It's like a dream..."

I take Emera's hand. "It's real. You are."

Soft light pulses through her. "We are."

"You're going to make it. We're going to make it."

Hope radiates from her. Relief. Fear. That disappointment when you finally achieve something that maybe you didn't really want. All that crosses her spectrum at once. Welkin says nothing. Maybe it's too much to consider. At last; all their searching. Suffering. Ages of the universe beyond reckoning endured. His faith rewarded. That faith was built on a lie, but he believed it. And she came true.

She's going to.

Emera isn't sure. Her thoughts hang like low, heavy clouds in the cockpit. They distract me as I guide the *Steel Haven* through the unimaginable force The Glass Star exerts on her. I activate the gravimetric displacement shields CR-UX installed back on Angolis when we first considered the practical reality of flying to the surface of a frozen star. Though now I can't say we ever properly consider practicality. If the shields don't hold, The Glass Star will crush us.

Hold, baby.

Fine solar diamonds mist on the canopy as I guide the ship under petrified solar prominences stretching across the entire northern hemisphere of the star, a distance spanning millions of miles.

What am I looking for, CR-UX?

>NO SIGNAL

I look over my shoulder. "What am I looking for, Welkin?"

Blue fire burns in his eyes. "Lock on to the strongest power source. That should be the stellar core."

"Right, and how are we going to get in there?"

>DESIGNATED ENERGY SIGNATURES DETECTED

The Scath present virally visual identifiers but their ships leave a strange disruption in dark energy bands. Space wrinkles ahead like a bedsheet that is too long past changing. The shadows seem to know where they're going. I follow the trail across the northern hemisphere. Unfathomable gorges scar the surface. So deep the sensors don't ping anything back. The gorges swallow the Scath emission trail.

Ban Minda.

Maybe these gorges go all the way down into the stellar core. I don't know if the shields will stand up to that kind of pressure. I barely did and that's because Emera cocooned me in her corona.

I can do the same for the ship, she says, but her fear creeps along the downlink. She and Welkin, they're made for this environment. Lumenor fired in the forges of The Glass Star. Gesta are super strong on other planets but here, he's just another guy. Kibir and I are little sacks of meat and fluid. This goes wrong, we'll burst.

"You have environmental suits," Emera says.

"I don't think they're rated for this kind of gravity." I shake my head. "Kibir... can you work some magic?"

He leans his hammer against the back of my chair. "*Net tu het.*"

"Good. Put a step into it, maybe."

"*Teth.*"

"Oh, you might also... you know. Need to do some tailoring."

Kibir leaves grumpy out of the cockpit, but really he only ever seems happy bashing things. I'm pretty sure he's going to be pissing his pants with joy when we catch up with the Scath.

"I don't think he wears pants," Emera says.

I blow her a kiss. "Hang on, Em."

Shadows of frozen stellar arches darken the cockpit. I keep my hand tight on the stick as the frozen star's unfathomable immensity overtakes our view. Loose crystal bigger than moons tumble through space, riding the invisible line between satellite and meteor.

>PROXIMITY ALERT

I sigh a nervous breath. "Steady on."

Emera puts her hand on mine. "You're a great pilot."

"I don't fly this thing. That's CR-UX."

"But I thought..."

"No, it just looks cool when I sit here. I look cool."

"Oh. Well. Is there a backup of CR-UX, or..."

"Strap in," I say.

She magnetically locks her harness straps as I navigate the crystalline asteroid field that dirties the star's polar region. Debris skitters across the shields. No star stuff. Hull plate.

Scath armor.

"Hopefully this makes our job easier," I say.

Welkin kneads his fists on the deck. "The core is substantial. Vast filamentium oceans congeal there. The Scath likely focus their efforts on one area. We must race to another shore. Perhaps we can avoid detection. We can get in and out unnoticed."

I thread a disintegrating Scath frigate. "I'm not leaving without punching them in the mouth. We can outflank them. Hit their tankers. Spoil their little party."

"We're one ship, Idari."

"And a Lumenor."

"Emera cannot fight them all."

"Ok. You're going to look at me funny, but is there any way we can ignite all this fuel? What happens if we do?"

Welkin blinks.

"It's a legitimate question," I say.

"If we 'punch them in the mouth,' as you say, the Scath will destroy us. All that matters is Emera."

She dims. "I can't pass the gate."

"The failure at the gate is mine, Emera. Not yours."

"What do you mean, Welkin?"

"Gates don't matter. Our perceptions and ideas don't matter. Time and space confuse at the heart of the star. In its blood. You will see what was. What will be. Who you are, within and without. At the heart of the star, you will see, Emera... you will understand at last why I've done what I've done. I take no pride in my actions, but I bear no shame. You will descend into the filamentium. You will fire and be made new. Stars never die. They become something else."

He's said it a million times before. This time he sounds like a parody of himself. Welkin lacks conviction. Not in himself. No one outlives history to give up at the doorstep of destiny.

Welkin lacks faith in her.

Even without the downlink, I'd be sure he doesn't know if any of this will work because she doesn't know. Before, when she believed every word he said, he could take solace in her surety. All Emera wants now is to live. To love. To be free. Is that what he wants?

>PROXIMITY ALERT

Flatiron forks of crystallized star bolt up through the mouth of the gorge as we descend into the dark abyss it holds.

CR-UX, you should see this...

>NO SIGNAL

The further we descend into the maw of toothed flame, the more afraid I am the star will crush me. The Scath will dust me. I'm never going to see CR-UX again. I'm never going to hear her voice.

You are her voice, Emera says.

I know, Em. It's just...

She takes my hand. *Have faith. I'll borrow some.*

Hours go by. Maybe more. I've no idea.

Finally, we exit the crystallized radiation zone of The Glass Star into its core. *Ban Minda.* The core seems hollowed, pitted of its matter except for a globe-like orb suspended in the center, connected by chaotic veins and branches of frozen nuclear fire to the membrane of the star. A soft glow still emanates from within the core, casting soft light on the interior. A chaotic surface peels away beneath us, uneven like uneven concrete that hardened in a flash.

>EXTERNAL PRESSURE BEYOND TOLERANCE

Tremors go through the ship. These shields quake so hard I figure they'll buckle any moment. At least we won't know what hit us. We'll flatten to atoms faster than any of us can think.

Emera closes her eyes. "Just keep her steady. I've got you."

The ship stabilizes a little. "Thanks, Em..."

The memory core Emera took from the titan back on Angolis manifests in her hand. "You should take this, Idari. Back yourself up."

"I thought we were doing better?"

"The storage is infinite."

I take the core from her. "You said this was organic."

"In its way."

"How can I interface with it, then?"

"In your way."

I've only ever done things my way. I never knew how until I did it, so I guess this is no different. I squeeze the memory core a little. This tingle goes through my skin. This electric promise.

>PROXIMITY ALERT

I dive the ship beneath a stellar vein. Focus, Idari. I try to pick the shadows' trail back up, but everything comes back choppy on the sensors. I'll be navigating on sight from here on.

Emera flutters. "I see things..."

I pocket the core in my jacket. "What things? Scath things?"

"Something..."

I cycle through the sensors. "I'm not seeing anything."

The navigational display pings. "I'm getting movement."

Emera shakes off her wonder. "Movement?"

A skeletal strand of irradiant thorns peels away from a stellar vein ahead. A creature. There's some kind of creature inside the star. A ribbon of dark light slithers through the impossible deep.

I adjust my optics. "The hell is that – "

An iridescent tendril torpedoes the ship. Sensor data screams through the downlink. The engines stall. Our shields crumple. Hard-light spits out of the laser batteries, bending in the gravity and souping in mid-air. More tendrils snare the ship.

What the hell is this?

The gravity of the star flattens me to the deck. Deck plate warps. The hull whines under the increasing pressure and Emera tries to hold us up in her power. She tries to hold us together.

I scramble back to the controls. "What is this?"

"Gengul," Welkin says, true fear in his voice.

"Do I even want to know?"

"We must escape... the Gengul feeds on filamentium... ensnaring living stars in its tentacles and sucking them dry."

"I said I didn't want to know!" I grab Emera. "Get out – "

Tendrils stab through what's left of the shields. Through the canopy. Atmosphere ices on my skin and Emera tears from the ship in the grasp of a tendril. What's happening. I fire my tiny blaster for

all the good that does. A burst of pure energy erupts from her and
Emera falls free, toward the core.

So do we.

>PROXIMITY ALARM

>ALERT: TERRAIN

>ALERT: ALTITUDE

I claw my way back in the rattlebox of the ship to the pilot's seat.
I pull back on the stick. Nothing. I try to kick the engines over but
we're bleeding filamentium from the core.

Ban Minda.

The creature punched through the hull into the translight drive
and leeched fuel from us. Shields soap over the hull, bubbling over
gaps and popping and then bubbling again but we're thin. Frost
smoke flashes across the exposed cockpit as the heated interior makes
contact with the frigid atmosphere of the surface.

We're going down.

"Brace for impact," I say.

Welkin crashes around inside the cockpit. "Emera – "

Jagged stellar ice rushes toward me. Just my luck. I flit across the
universe to a glass star. I've got the drop on the shadows. Right when
I'm about to sock that bitch Thana in her pretty little face, whatever
the hell this is snatches away my opportunity. I throw up my hands,
eyes pinching the last light behind them and we smash into –

>PROXY REBOOTING

Shattered glass falls from my cheek. "How are we..."

Welkin occupies the center of the cockpit, his eyes closed, hands
open. "I have conjured a protective shield. Get into your suit, Idari."

>ALARM: STRUCTURAL INTEGRITY FAILING

>WARNING: GRAVITY EXCEEDS TOLERANCE

I get on my feet and pull on the environmental suit Kibir hands
me. He's wearing a cobbled-together version of his own. fitted to his
smaller stature. Help yourself first, I guess. Once I activate the anti-
gravity harness strung throughout the suit, the pressure lessens.

"Thanks, Kibir."

His frustration clouds over his helmet. *"Tomo."*

Warnings and alarms blizzard through the downlink. Everything is smashed. I reroute as much power as I can to the shields from life support and other systems we absolutely don't need right now.

>SHIELD STRENGTH OFF-NOMINAL

"I know, I know," I say. "Just keep us three-dimensional."

The *Steel Haven* groans under the pressure. My ship. She's all I've ever known. I don't think she's leaving this place. If she does, it will be with a lot of spit and tape. I route some energy to the engines. They rattle with the last ions of fuel they have left.

"Good thing we crashed next to all the filamentium," I say.

Welkin relents his protective shield. "We have to find Emera."

I pick my blaster off the deck. "I'm surprised you didn't leave us."

He seems hurt. "I wouldn't leave you."

"You don't exactly like me, Welkin."

"I have grown... fond of you, Idari."

Didn't expect that. "You're not so bad yourself."

He huffs dust on his way out of the cockpit. Welkin forces down the jammed gantry and crawls out of the crater we made. I kind of want a drink right now. Get yourself together. Find Emera.

Kibir drags his hammer behind him. *"Ustet."*

I feel like I'm walking through mud. "At least we're not puddles."

Welkin runs ahead of us, like he's weightless. I scramble as fast as I can across the glass brush in search of Emera. Doesn't take long. The Gengul strafes the stellar plain, scouring the surface with countless tentacles. This bloody thing has probably been here for ages, leeching off the filamentium in the core. *Ban Minda.*

There are probably more. Don't let there be more.

Cosmic energy vaporizes the mist. Javelins of petrified stellar fire tear from the ground in Emera's magnetic grip and launch into the sky. Spears of crystal impale the Gengul and a cosmic scream reverberates through the star's heart. I resist the urge to cheer, afraid my voice alone will break the glass of my helmet in this gravity.

You're doing it, Em.

Emera strobes with power as she launches another volley and the creature snares the spears from the sky. In the same instant, the Gengul captures her with a tendril and she recedes into the ether.

I fire my blasword but the blasts are sludge. *Emera...*

The Gengul pulses with subcutaneous light in bursts like code. Next thing you know, an infant Gengul snakes out from behind a stellar vein. You've got to be kidding me. The baby creature eddies around its mother, impatient to taste the light she does. Light strangles out of Emera. She stops fighting. No.

You've got to keep fighting.

Welkin pounds his fists into the ground in frustration. He charges up the canted spears fallen back to the surface and smashes off their calved tops. With blunt, swift force, he breaks them down into smaller projectiles he hurls at the Gengul.

I holster the blasword and bash at chunks of crystal. Probably shouldn't have done that. I crash to my knees, clutching my hand. Kibir can barely lift his hammer. This isn't working. I'm reduced to trying to lift shards of glass. I can barely lift my legs to walk.

Sapphire flares in the tightening vise of the Gengul's tendrils. The creature gags like it swallowed a bug and then passes Emera off to the child. It doesn't find her anymore appetizing apparently and the child releases her. Emera falls back to the surface, a pale star.

Welkin cushions her fall with a magnetic net before she hits the ground. Her eyes flicker with confusion. Pain. I can guess what happened. The Gengul tried to drain her for her filamentium but after eons living off the real stuff didn't like the synthetic flavor of her blood. This thing only wants pure power.

"Welkin," I say as the Gengul grabs him.

Tendrils seize Welkin. Power bleeds from beneath his opaline skin. The Gengul brims with energy, seizing on the same elemental energy that dwells only in this one place in all existence. With all his strength and power, Welkin is no match for this creature.

Emera fires a blast into the air. "Welkin..."

Where is that sword when I need it? I don't know if we're close to the gate. I don't know where we are. C'mon. Figure something out.

CR-UX, I say. *What do I do?*

>NO SIGNAL

What do I do? This thing wants filamentium. This entire star soaks in it. How do I get it to notice me? How did it even see us before? It doesn't have eyes. Of course, it doesn't. There's next to no light inside the core. It senses filamentium. Flashes. Flares.

I hurry back to Emera. *Bend time. Or whatever.*

Her hands waver. *We're running?*

Just open the door, Em. Just a little bit.

Mist drains toward Emera as she folds space and time. Tendrils glowing with stolen star power splay across the sky as the creature dives on her. I extend the blasword and Welkin falls back to the surface, sucker scars branding his once pristine shell. Severed tendrils rain down on us, spilling guzzled fire into the sky.

A cosmic shriek disturbs the unnatural calm within the star. The Gengul scurries into the mist, the child close behind.

Kibir bashes a severed tendril with his hammer. "*Tomo.*"

I depress the blasword. "Couldn't have done it without you."

Welkin struggles to get up. "Thank you, Idari..."

"Don't mention it."

"You could have left me."

"I've grown fond of you."

His eyes tense. "Emera..."

She traces the concentric scars the Gengul left around his arms and shoulders. "You're hurt..."

He knocks his fist against his chest. "Strong as ever."

Starglass glitters with her pallid light. "It didn't want me..."

I wring my sword of blood. "Good thing, Em."

Her expression sours. "I don't have the power to do this."

Welkin takes her hand. "You do. Once you renew..."

"I can't see it..."

He paws her cheek. "I can. You will be real. You will shine."

"I don't…"

"We don't have a moment to lose. If the Gengul lurked here, then liquid filamentium most lie close. Hurry – "

A distant rumble echoes across the plain. Shadows race across the glass, ahead of a blood-red sunrise. I know without looking, without the downlink, without the sensors.

You steal nothing from shadows but darkness.

Hundreds of Scath ships descend on us. Thousands. Countless fighters phase into form above, escorts to heavy cruisers, destroyers, and giant tankers. Massive excavators funnel out of landed transports, ready to bleed the star of its worth. Legions of Scath outfitted in thick gravimetric displacement armor flood the plain, a dark sea.

The shadows aren't hiding anymore.

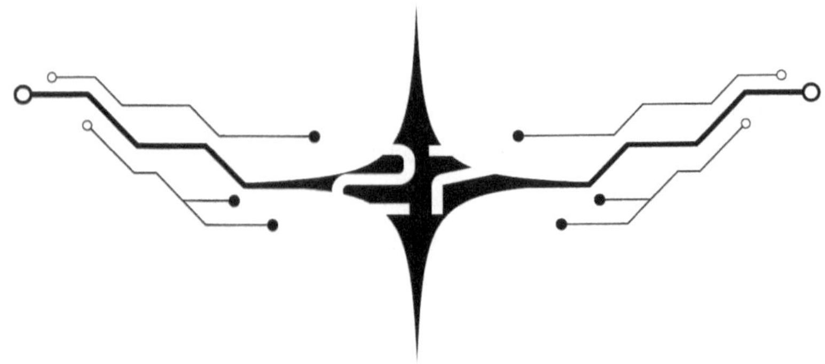

The paralysis in my legs doesn't owe to the unimaginable pressure The Glass Star exerts on me. I've bounded across the dark, through space and time, through ones and zeroes and flesh and blood to the heart of a star, skipping like a stone across existence and I made it. I made it across to the other side. So I thought. All I did was to drag my shadow here to the last hope of dying stars.

Emera's voice shines through me. *Idari.*

Thana stands on the *Ecliptor*-cruiser's prow, blazing with furious energy. Angry prominences erupt from beneath her tortured skin, drawing in the stellar mist and igniting it around her. Vidious leads the shadow tide swamping the surface beyond. My neural net races through every possible scenario. How do I get out of this? There must be a way. There's always a way. Usually.

I squeeze her hand. "I'm sorry, Em..."

She shakes her head. "We came here to fight. Let's fight."

"Run. Bend time. Get out of here."

Emera anchors her magnetic field. "No."

"Em... what are you doing..."

"I want this to be the end," she says.

Welkin puts his hand on hers. "We've reached the end."

"Promise me. No matter what happens. This is the end."

"Emera... you're going to make all things new..."

"Am I? Or am I just going to start all of this over again?"

"No..."

"I want to be me. And I want you to be you."

There is no conviction in his voice. "I am..."

"You've believed in me all this time. I believe in you. Us."

His eyes collapse. "Us..."

That pause. That gap. I've heard it in CR-UX so many times. CR-UX never wanted to lie. She just could never say. How could she ever say. Her entire life she'd been denied. All she learned was denial. That's the worst hurt someone else can inflict on you. Not a wound. An insult. They teach you how to hurt yourself.

"The Scath are coming," I say, as the sky darkens.

Emera doesn't budge. I thought I was getting through to her back in the ark. Maybe I was fooling myself. She's still reeling. Still drowning in confusion and doubt about everything she has ever known. Emera doesn't know who she is. She did. Someone else told her different. The world expects something else from her. All that gleaming certainty. That shining conviction. Gone.

"Promise me," she says. "Promise me this is the end."

Welkin grips her hand. "Emera."

"*Promise.*"

Even with the three of us twisting in the wind of each other's thoughts, Emera can barely comprehend Welkin's unyielding despair. The injustice of his entire existence. Everything that is and was, gone. Forever. Nothing to show for it but infinite darkness. Dust glints in the air. Welkin has lost so much in the struggle to realize his vision. His home. His people. Everyone he had ever loved.

Emera, time and again.

She always came back to him but this time he's truly lost her. He knows it. He lived once in the shadow of mountains that clawed the stars. He saw a glimpse – a brief, intoxicating glimpse – of the sky, and he spent the rest of his life sawing down the earth to see it clear. Now, at the end, he's afraid he's only clouded the sky with dust.

"I promise," he says.

This is one promise that's going to keep. The Scath are too many. They're too close now to get back to the ship and the ship is in pieces. One decent blast puts a hole in this suit and I'll pancake right here on the ground. CR-UX would tell me something positive right now.

Go on, then. Tell yourself something positive.

"I told Thana I'd kill her if it was the last thing I did," I say. "Turns out I'm going to get one thing right in my life."

Emera clutches my hand. "I love you."

"I know."

The Scath ranks split into branching lines following the curve of the shore beyond. Tankers drift like heavy rain clouds overhead, ready to drain the ocean for every last drop of filamentium. Shadows encircle us. Thana hovers above, a dread star.

"I see the ruse in you, Gen Emera," she says. "The art."

I point my blasword at her. "Come down here and say that, lady."

She saunters down from her perch to the surface. "You think it's over... you lust for endings... there will never be an end."

Welkin grinds his fists into the glass. "You would destroy yourself, Thana. Everything Maracen once held dear."

"How dare you speak her name."

"She didn't want this for you, my friend."

"Friend..." Thana spits the word. "You... in your vain hope... your selfish delusion... you cannot imagine what someone else would ever want. It was only ever about you... your depravity."

Welkin isn't the only projecting around here, evidently.

Thana flares. "Rejoice, Welkin. It's all as you saw. You are as you ever were. The hapless servant, all seeing and impotent. Watch, 'friend.' Watch me burn away the last of your disease."

"Watch this," I say and the blasword crashes into stellar crystal.

Ban Minda. The blasword didn't snap in two.

Vidious presses me back from Thana with all the strength of this star. "Impossible... no metal can resist the power of stars."

I hold my ground. "Turanium forms in black holes. Black holes eat stars. Guess what the most common metal in this universe is?"

Vidious considers my blade. "You are nothing..."

"I'll remember you said that when I'm holding your head."

"Burn," Thana says and everything goes red.

I expect to boil and pop but Thana's fury blunts against Emera's blue shield. Purple plasma warps the air, burning away the present back to the past so fast Scath flinch into the margins.

Hold on, Em, I say.

She pushes back the red wave. *I'm holding.*

A cerulean shockwave blasts back Thana. Shadows catch fire and we've got space. I push Vidious back to the burning ring's edge and I swing wild and angry. He swats me away with his shield.

I get back on my feet. "You'll have to do better than that."

He points his sword at me. "Thana thinks she will punish you for all time. She thinks she will hurt you... and hurt you... and hurt you. I respect you, Idari. Your hubris. For that, I will be merciful."

Kibir crashes his hammer into Vidious' knee. Vidious buckles. The Kib cocks back for another blow and Vidious throws him into the shadows reorganizing among their molten dead.

I scramble after Kibir. "No..."

Vidious raises his sword. "I pardon you, Idari – "

Blue fire singes the air. Emera pummels Vidious with wave after wave of cosmic energy and when he hacks through the flames she rockets into the sky. Scath ships erupt with laser fire. They erupt in mini-novas. Energy blasts lance right through them and without the protection of their shields the shadows collapse to beads of debris so small they pebble the ground in their rain.

I raise my sword. *Shine, Emera.*

The Scath fleet retreats back into the radiation zone as Emera atomizes their vanguard. Dark energy rains down on her and as she dives toward the surface a new target runs for cover. Poor shadows.

There just isn't any.

All those Scath exposed on the surface go up in flames. A tail of glittering fire stretches across the sky, horizon to horizon, Emera a blue comet portending the doom of the Scath. It's a good thing my jaw can't drop. I'd never get it off the ground.

Vidious doesn't seem as bothered as he should be. "She burns like the stars of old. A faithful reproduction, Welkin. I commend you."

Welkin crashes his fists into the glass. "She will destroy the Scath. And then when she is renewed... she will destroy you."

"Not if I destroy you first," he says and swings for Welkin.

I try to get in the middle but the thing about getting between two beings made from starglass is you get pinched out in a hurry. I stumble through brambles of stellar grass as tremors quake through the ground. The universe shattering around me. Ink clouds collapse to decimal points as Kibir pounds his way through the Scath.

"You seem to be doing alright," I say.

He snorts. "*Tomo.*"

I take a deep breath. "Stay close."

Thunder rattles shattered glass on the shore. Welkin pounds his fists against his chest. Vidious stabs his sword in the ground for balance and Welkin barrels into him, leaving the sword dug in frozen star fire. I swing for the blade, trying to break it.

I end up on my ass.

I might not need to be so heroic. Welkin tackles Vidious to the ground. He savagely crashes his fists into Vidious' face, a blur of diamond as he pounds into the Nul's neck, prying at the hair-thin radials, forcing his fingers between them. Ripping. Pulling.

Vidious tries to shove the Gesta off him.

Welkin won't be moved.

A terrible crack splits the air. Dust erupts volcanically from the ground and I think Vidious' head is going to come away in Welkin's hands. We're going to make it. We're going to get out of this and Vidious grabs a loose shard of petrified plasma from the ground. Light bleeds through Welkin's hands. He staggers back, clutching his right eye, scabbing to crust on his pearlescent fingers.

Vidious reclaims his sword. "Is it as you saw, Watchman?"

Welkin hobbles away. "Emera..."

Vidious' sword vaults in the air. Mine sweeps across his chest. He staggers back, fingers curling at the hair-thin line smoking with fine crystal. His shock is as profound as mine.

His indignation.

Dust fumes from him. He charges at me, broad swings sending me back on my heels. I try to match every strike at the same time I try to navigate the terrain. Towering glass shards stab up from the plain, riven with deep open scars that plunge into the misty depths of the star's heart. I fight the awe and wonder threatening to debilitate me.

The ground declines beneath me and I tumble back to the shore. Filamentium laps in soupy waves on the diamond beach. Shadows grow beyond as the maroon hue churning within Thana brightens, the last light of an evening sun before it sets. She charges up her power from the star's bounty and scalds the sky. Emera seeks cover in the stellar membrane above and Vidious is swinging for my neck.

I roll away. Focus. You've got to focus.

"All that information streaming through your head," Vidious says. "What can you do with it, Idari? You can only deny it. That is why you drink. That is why you run. That is why you seek the clarity and precision in being a Stargun. The perfection in singular purpose."

"I was confused," I say. "Just like you."

Vidious crooks his head. "There is no confusion in me."

"You want to be free. You think you can earn your freedom spilling the blood of others, but you just drown, Vidious. You will never win the Lumenor's approval no matter how much reflect them. You can't change what you did... but you can change your future. Help me. Help Emera. This can be the end you want."

"Emera is a half-light," he says. "And you're out of time."

Filamentium splashes at my heels. I dart through the surf, trying to get around Vidious, and he backhands me into the mist.

My sword tinks across the ground. "No..."

Shadows swarm the shore. Emera's tempest loses its punch. Dark energy riddles the sky and she spends as much effort weaving out of the way as she does firing back at the reorganized Scath fleet.

Crimson erupts from Thana on the ground. She crashes into the surface a shooting star and I lose sight of her.

Darkness falls over the gate. Above, the *Ecliptor*-class cruiser manifests out of the steam. She looms like a black cloud over the shimmering sea beyond, ready to bleed it for every last drop.

I grab my sword.

Vidious steps on my hand. His booth grinds my fingers against cosmic glass and then he kneels down, his knee pinning my other arm. Under the weight of a child of stars, I can't move a muscle.

"It's over," he says.

I give him my best smile. "It's never over."

>ENGAGE THRUSTERS

The *Steel Haven* rattles out of her sleep. C'mon. Wake up. Forward shields to maximum. Laser batteries primed. Targets acquired. The ship rips back into the air, leaving too much behind. She strafes the cruiser, landing enough hits to stall those pumps.

SION fighters flood out of the *Ecliptor's* hangars at near sub-light speed. Dark energy shreds the mist and the *Steel Haven's* fragile shields. All I can do is watch. White haze obscures the sensors as the SION fighters harass the *Steel Haven*. Fighters explode under the barrage of her forward cannons, but I could blast all of them and still not make a difference. There are too many.

Vidious presses into me. "You knew it would end this way."

Tankers descend upon the sea. Excavators roll forward, on planks Scath engineers construct from shadows. Fighters reign in the sky.

He tears into my environmental suit. "Such a fragile thing."

I can't move. "*Stop.*"

"Such a trivial thing."

Vidious digs his fingers into my chest. Pain sensors scream in alarm and then crystal is plowing through flesh. Blood. Turanium. His hand closes around the power core humming inside my chest.

"Let's see, Idari. How human you are."

CR-UX.

>NO SIGNAL

I always have to do everything myself. Think, Idari. You can't move. Can't be that far off from an average night at the bar. Whatever you're going to do, you need to do it quickly before Vidious rips your heart out. Surely, this has happened to me before. It would be nice to remember what I did to get out of that. I'm sure it was clever.

We're clever now, aren't we?

Vidious twists his fingers around inside my chest. "Your memory core is in your heart, yes? Have you ever seen it?"

Ice-cold shock splinters through me. "Stop..."

>ALARM: INTERNAL INJURIES

If he breaches my core, all my onboard memory will be erased. I'll be erased, back to the last copy on the *Steel Haven's* mainframe, assuming she survives this battle. I don't think I'm going to survive. Alerts chain-gun through my mind. Cold pain screws deep in me.

>INITIATE EMERGENCY PROXY BACK-UP

"Em..."

>SIGNAL ACQUIRED

I always knew you'd trade me in eventually, darling.

The whiteout shrouding the downlink since Angolis clears and I'm flying through the veinal tangle of frozen fire above. The OVL-102-B Binja flew out to Kir Mish throttles her engines, fanning out of the tight formation she's kept through the radiation zone.

Hang on, CR-UX says, guiding the ship.

Sensor telemetry streams through my mind. Scath forces flow like a dark, branching river across the surface of the core below. CR-UX follows it all the way to the molten sea.

CR-UX... you're here...

Was there ever any doubt?

Scath troopers turn in unison, the voids of their helms rising toward the crystalline web tethering the core to the rest of the star. The ancient racer – the *Steel Haven's* sensors record it riotously as *The Green Carnation* – punches through the stellar mist, ahead of a small fleet of ferries, transports, and haulers from Angolis.

Binja's voice cackles across the downlink. "Fly you pirates... fly!"

The ragtag fleet opens fire. Those ships have to be full of survivors of Angolis. None of them fled to safety like they should have. Ships big and small, fast and slow came here.

To fight.

>DOWNLINK RE-ENGAGED

CR-UX relinks to the *Steel Haven* and guides her into formation with the fleet. Together, they descend on the Scath's rear. Junked Pujar pincers peel off for the tankers hovering over the mist-shrouded sea, waiting for an opportunity to land. The rear flanks dissolve, caught completely off guard.

Serpentine columns of fire burn from the twisted wrecks of SION fighters and troop transports that flatten to discs as their gravimetric displacers fail. The shore becomes a war zone as raiders put down and the forsaken pirates of Kir Mish lead Kib warriors into close-quarters combat with Scath struggling to reorganize.

Vidious forgets me. He cleaves into the Kib with his sword. I scramble for mine. Where did it go? I find the blasword the same time some kind of grenade phases across the ground.

"That's not fair," I say.

Kibir throws it back. Dark energy explodes, leaving Scath wounded between light and dark, phase and body, life and death.

"*Tomo,*" Kibir says and retrieves his hammer.

I fire into the shadows. "Have you seen Em?"

"*Ejel nuj buj.*"

"We have to find her. We have to get her to the shore."

CR-UX, do you have eyes on Emera?

Rather busy at the moment, darling.

The misfit fleet forms up on the *Steel Haven* and together they strafe across the *Ecliptor.* Massive detonations cloud the air in atomized debris. The destroyer emerges from the haze over the sea, retargeting her cannons directly on the gate. Nowhere to hide now.

Idari, CR-UX says. You need to get out of there.

The Green Carnation? Really?

This is your concern?

It's a dreadful name.

I rather like it.

I leave you alone for five minutes and you're spiraling.

We're different people, darling.

I groan. *Why did you come here?*

You're welcome?

You should have run, CR-UX. As far as you could.

I did run, she says. *As fast as I could. Thank you...*

But truly, darling. Run.

Me? Where am I supposed to go?

Out of the way of the big chap.

The big what?

A massive turanium fist punches out of the mist into the starboard side of the Scath *Ecliptor*. The vessel teeters in mid-air as one of the great titans of Angolis descends into the core of The Glass Star and eclipses shadows. *Ban Minda.*

We're actually going to win this thing.

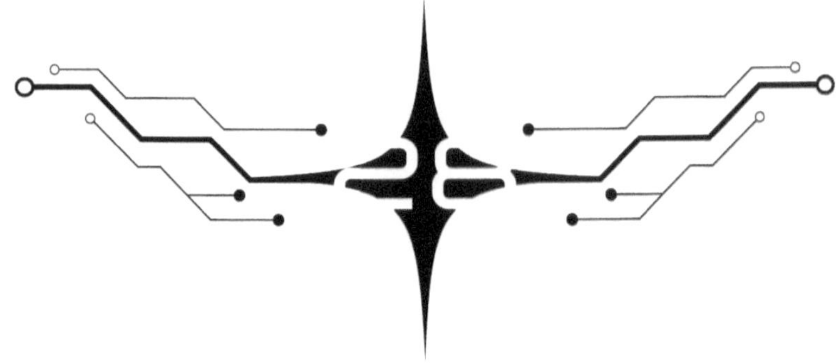

THE GREAT TITAN OF ANGOLIS SLAMS ITS FISTS INTO THE SCATH *Ecliptor,* sending tremors through her shields. That's it. Hit it again. All those SION fighters pecking us to death on the ground abandon their attack and run back to the cruiser.

CR-UX, do you see Emera anywhere?

I'm detecting an energy signature that could be her, CR-UX says. But all my scopes are overwhelmed. I can't make her out.

Where is the energy signature?

On the far side of all those shadows, darling.

The Scath tar the shore between the filamentium and the gate that denied Emera before and does now. Some force resists her beyond a simple crystalline arch. If she can't fly over it or go around it, something else is going on. There's always something else.

Cut me a path, CR-UX.

The *Steel Haven* buzzes the gate, streaking out to the filamentium sea before turning about. She comes back shooting, opening up a lane through the disintegrating Scath ranks. I cut my way into them.

Shadows close on me and then Kibir's hammer gives us some space. We fight deep into the Scath sludge. Dark fire burns around us. Shadows phase through the mist and swords define against mine. Keep going. Keep fighting to the blue flame just beyond.

"Em," I say.

Scath drag her across the hummocked surface with magnetic

lances. She incinerates those closest to her but for every shadow she burns out another takes their place. Cosmic flame blackens the glass where Scath phase in and out but they never lose their grip on her.

CR-UX, come around for another pass.

My vantage point switches to the *Steel Haven's* sensors. *I'm a bit occupied at the moment, darling.*

SION fighters chase the *Steel Haven* and her escort into the path of the Scath *Ecliptor*. Defense cannons shred the misfit ships on point. With every other air lane blocked, CR-UX plunges the *Steel Haven* headlong into the debris cloud.

>SHIELD INTEGRITY FAILING

Another volley targets the misfit fleet and the titan steps into the way. I get a little bit of titan-envy as he swats Scath fighters from the sky. He catches them in his hands and he rams them into the *Ecliptor's* beleaguered shields. The cruiser lists to starboard. Part of me wants to watch what happens next but I have to get to Emera.

Not to be rude, CR-UX says. *But won't she just come back?*

Welkin's hurt. He's...

Oh, dear.

If Welkin were ok, we'd be crashing through these Scath to Emera in no time at all. Vidious took Welkin's eye. Some of his power, maybe. Emera can't die again. We can't let either of them die.

I hack through the shadows. "Emera!"

Heat burns the back of my neck. I shield my eyes as the sky explodes. Red fire melts away the titan's skin. Thana immolates the giant as he swings his colossal arms through the air, succeeding only in sweeping entire SION squadrons out of the sky.

Too many.

Hundreds now. The *Ecliptor* spawns more and more and Thana piles on. In the ancient past, the titan of Angolis fought a war beyond imagination, turning an entire planet into ashes. It survived even the ravages of time, but nothing can withstand the darkness of the Scath. Stellar anger blasts through him, riddling his armor with holes. Smoke issues from his ruined eyes, and he staggers back, aflame.

"No..."

Sure, the shadows are strong. This is a titan of Angolis. A warrior fashioned for protecting the work of creation. He presses forward and tears into the *Ecliptor's* lower decks. Desperate guns fire their last into his hands. Hull plate peels away faster than the cruiser can rephase. Scath troopers tumble out of exposed corridors into the filamentium sea and Thana unleashes one blistering beam of energy.

Waves of filamentium explode into the air, set off from the splash of the titan's head. His battered body collapses into the sea, defeated. All my hope crashes against the shore with the burning waves of filamentium. SION fighters regroup and their dark cloud shadows the shore. The Scath abyss on the ground closes around Kibir and I.

I hack at shadows. "Em!"

Smoke shrouds the shore. Mist. Emera's light warps and coils with the shadows, like she's caught in a web between space and time. She winnows to a point of light and then I lose sight of her.

"Emera..."

Energy beams lance from the *Ecliptor's* prow into the shore. Kib fighting the shadows disappear in pulverized glass. Screams die behind me as I run for cover into a shrubland of tangled crystalline growths. Survivors burrow in behind me.

We have to stop that ship, I say.

CR-UX sounds rushed. *The cruiser can phase, Idari.*

Not as quick or easy now. She's wounded.

Thana isn't.

Bring her down to earth for me, CR-UX. Or this is over.

The winnowing fleet of misfit ships regroups. The *Steel Haven* leads them into a headlong charge and destroys as many of the *Ecliptor's* exposed cannons as she can, even as SIONs pick her apart.

>SHIELD FAILURE

>HULL BREACH

>STRUCTURAL INTEGRITY FAILING

CR-UX, I say.

Oh, it's just a scratch.

CR-UX stitches together every thin string of power she can to keep the *Steel Haven* airborne. Her attention splits between the Red Special and linking the misfit fleet from Angolis from -– *Ban Minda – The Green Carnation*. At least there's a shot. Fires burn from the *Ecliptor's* prow. Thana screams fire behind the flak shield the point defense cannons generates, cleaving the *Steel Haven* of her escort.

>INTERNAL SYSTEMS FAILURE

Thick black smoke trails miles behind the *Steel Haven* as she circles around for another run. I've never seen her so wounded. My body aches as she does. My heart bleeds as she does.

CR-UX's voice hails the fleet. *Shall we give it another go?*

Binja's response is slow in coming. *I'm with you.*

The *Ecliptor* opens up with everything she's got. The sky shreds. Catches fire. Misfit fighters disintegrate to flaming chunks of metal. Debris riddles the *Steel Haven*. The cockpit canopy cracks.

Baby, hold together.

CR-UX guides her beneath the prow of the massive Scath ship, gunning away before turning back around hard. With the gap in the dorsal flak shield, the *Steel Haven* has a clear shot at Thana.

CR-UX aims right for her.

SION fighters dive into the shrinking space between the *Steel Haven* and Thana's dark lantern atop the cruiser's prow. A hail of dark laser fire cuts through the hull at point-blank range.

>REACTOR CONTAINMENT FAILURE

Filamentium comets behind the *Steel Haven* and I lose her in the conflagration. Telemetry tells me she's still flying, but I don't know how much of her is. Thana fires a last, desperate shot. The salvo severs the ship's electronics, her connection to me, and her lovely, fearless voice in the last second before she crashes into the bridge.

I can't see anything.

White contrails arc out of electric nova erupting from the *Ecliptor*, a full eclipse waning from the inside out. The decapitated destroyer falls into the sea, shattering into islands of gutted metal that sink as quickly as they form.

I can't see.

I've lost the downlink. My cloud memory. I brace for the oblivion of forgetting, of losing all the gains I've made, and probably my life right after. I wait for the little note behind my eye. File critical.

But I remember.

I transferred your memory to *The Green Carnation*, CR-UX says. *Though we're running out of ships, darling.*

Get your bearings. Get to Emera or we're all going to be stardust. I cut through the last of the shadows and Thana emerges from the blighted sea in a daze, her light a sickly pink.

"Maracen," she says. "Maracen was on that ship."

What's left of the *Ecliptor* gurgles beneath the filamentium beyond. "At least she got a proper burial."

"I just wanted her back..."

I grip my sword. "You won't be too long without her."

I break for her. Sword high and ready. I know. I know she's going to melt the skin off my bones but it will be the last thing she does and then Emera will have a chance.

Light will have a chance.

My sword lodges in his Vidious' shield. The pommel of his sword crashes against my temple and I'm on the ground. Sensors haywire. He lunges at me. Somehow I don't die and I get around him and my hands back on the blasword. Bloody thing is stuck.

I put all my strength into my hands and Vidious' shield shatters. He throws his sword at me. I hit the deck. So do a bunch of Scath but I don't think they planned on it. I get back on my feet and I'm running. I'm running for his sword but he beats me to it.

I parry his blow with all my strength but still, he forces me down the shore. Laser fire flashes above and exposes chasms on the surface. I teeter on narrow straits between abyssal pits, Vidious putting all his rage and power into every strike. Every piston and absorber in my body blunts the seismic shock of his blows.

I can't hold out forever.

Mist thickens closer to the shore. I switch over to infrared but the star radiates so little heat I can't make out any topography. I could use CR-UX right now. I'm on my own. And I'm *bish* with a sword. Any pirate will tell you. Binja trained me on the blasword but I've forgotten nearly all of it. Just enough of endless hours on the deck of pirate sloops docked at The Bastard Moon remains to keep me alive a minute into a duel with an eternal knight forged in the fire of stars.

I should give myself some credit.

Vidious swings so hard I crash to the ground. "When I'm finished with you... I will drag Gen Emera by her hair out of whatever hole she cowers in... and then I will cut her throat as Welkin watches. I will bleed her and before he can conjure another one of his false stars... I will end his depravity once and for all."

I scramble back to my feet. The pellucid shore narrows to a thin isthmus connecting to a steep, rugged glass crag. Jagged cliffs jut hundreds of feet into the mist. I don't know if I'll simply run out of ground and fall into the molten filamentium sloshing near my feet, or if I'll just go dark as his sword cuts through my power core.

Vidious pushes me back and back, forcing me up the incline of the crag. The crag plateaus at the top, winnowing into a narrow point over the igneous sea below.

"There is nowhere left to run, Idari."

I push off and get some distance. "That's what all the girls say."

I don't know if that's laughter. "I've been here before. I came to these shores long ago..."

I try to even out the rattle in my hands. "To become a star?"

He stares into his blade. "To cage them. To imprison Gesta who confused themselves for stars. I was their jailer."

"You were a prisoner, too."

"I thought I earned my freedom in serving the Lumenor... there was only one way for Gesta to truly shine. I did what they asked."

"They were never going to give you their approval, Vidious. Thana is never going to give it to you now. They used you. They weaponized you against your own. Your desperate need to shine. You still can. Even with all that blood on you. You can shine, Vidious."

"By helping you destroy Thana?"

"That would be a start."

"And then what? Wait for Emera's mercy?"

"Begging for it, more likely."

"She is false. As I am. This is all... pantomime. A trick of light and shadow. She has her part, Idari. I have mine. I intend to fulfill it."

"You hate yourself so much?"

"I have no choice."

"You always have a choice."

"Says the machine."

"I'm a human being."

"You're confused, Idari. Let me clarify things for you."

I'm running out of ground. "You..."

"It begins to dawn on you. The folly in lobbying a creature as ancient and powerful as myself. Ask yourself, Idari. What can you possibly convince me of? What can you understand of my pain? My experience? You are as a passing moment. A speck of dust upon a mountain. Allow me to educate you."

He grips his sword.

"Stars mold and break as they will. Their will. Their will was to create my brothers and I as their swords. Their shields. I am their instrument. I am their fulfillment. Their perfection."

"By your logic," I say. "So am I. That's iron in my blood."

"You're scar tissue. Dead skin."

"Don't stop now. I'm all excited."

"You are nothing."

"You may be a monster. You are, actually. I know my type when I see them. That's because we tend to broadcast. Everybody has to know. But it's not everybody else we're trying to convince. I hear how much tired you are in your voice. I see it. You may have killed Maracen. A thousand stars. A million. You haven't killed that part of yourself others tried to destroy. If there's hope for me, then..."

His sword sinks toward the ground.

"Talk to me, Vidious. I know you were forced into becoming this thing you never wanted to become. You hid yourself and your truth and they took what you allowed them and distorted you. They bent you and broke you but you are not broken."

"You claim to be human... and yet you drown your spirit."

"That's the worst crime, isn't it? They make us hate ourselves. Hurt ourselves. If I wasn't human... there would be nothing to hurt."

This weight lifts from me. This pain.

"I'm human, Vidious. No one can ever take that away from me."

He clings to his sword. "It's too late..."

"Emera forgave you. You know, what? I forgive you, too. After enough babyl I will, anyway. I know. I know what you're feeling all the time. The pain. The cold. Dark. The nothing."

Vidious' blade strikes the crag. "You're right, Idari."

"I usually am."

"I feel nothing."

He swings at my feet. I leap back and just get my sword up. We lock weapons. Vidious pushes down, forcing my blade back toward my neck and his hand leaves his hilt. Cold, crystal fingers close around my wrist. My replacement arm tears away from the elbow.

>CRITICAL DAMAGE

My blasword sails into the mist.

His blade stabs through my chest.

>POWER CORE COMPROMISED

Vidious rips his sword out of me. "You have what I never will, Idari. You have your freedom."

>PROXY POWER RESERVE: TWENTY-FIVE PERCENT

Oxygen escapes my suit. Bio-brane fluid. Energy. I sink to my knees. Vidious wipes his blade on his tabard and then he leaves into the mist, back toward the final battle between light and darkness.

I fade on the edge of eternity.

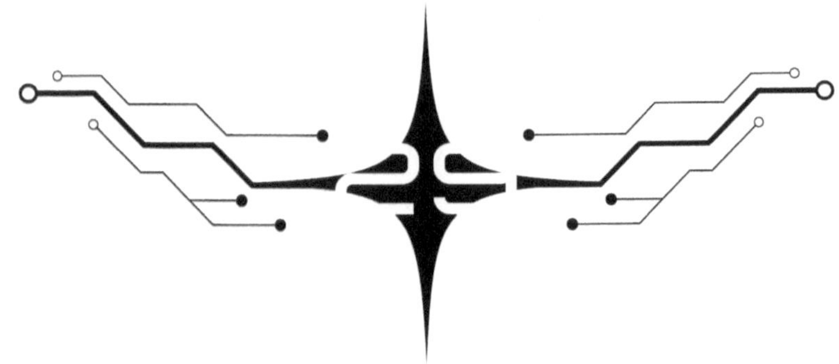

>PROXY POWER RESERVE: FIFTEEN PERCENT
>INITIATING EMERGENCY BACKUP TO HOST
>HOST NOT RESPONDING

SION squads cloud the stellar cavern above. Pretty, in that way your dying brain organizes everything into beauty. Energy drains from me. So does my will. Bursts of comm traffic erupt in my ears. The nameless pirates. The Kib. Our vanishing allies.

The patch isn't working –

Decelerate and fall back –

The airion's are warping. I'm losing structural –

A Pincer fighter crumples to a constantly reducing mass. A starship to an atom in the blink of an eye.

Binja's voice echoes over the comms. *Hold the line.*

They're tearing us to shreds –

We have to retreat –

Dark fire riddles the shore beyond. The Kib refugees run for cover. Even without their flagship, the Scath outnumber us. There's only one way out of this and it's not lying here bleeding power. I try to get up. I fall back to the cactoid surface. I can't feel my legs now.

>PROXY POWER RESERVE: FIFTEEN PERCENT

Emera... can you hear me?

Her thoughts ghosts through mine. *I see you.*

Where... I reach for her. *Everything is going dark...*

Idari, use the memory core.

I pat my jacket. My jacket is ruined. I liked this jacket. The brambly memory core from the titan back on Angolis prickles my palm. If this works, at least I'll be preserved in this little bit of crystal someone will find on the shore one day, or maybe no one will and I'll spend eternity here asleep inside a star. If this works.

What do I do...

What you always do, Emera says. *Be human.*

Em... I'm afraid.

I wish I had your courage.

We're going to get through this, Em. You will.

Be brave, Idari. For me.

Em... are you close? Did you come through the gate?

You'll find me. You always do.

Waves of filamentium splash against the crag. SION fighters scream across the sea. What's left of our forces fire desperate shots into a darkness that swallows them as it consumes everything.

>PROXY POWER RESERVE: FIVE PERCENT

I've no idea how this works. Maybe I close my eyes and make a wish. I give the titan's memory core a shake. No port. No connector. No cable. No clue what I'm supposed to do with this thing.

>PROXY POWER RESERVE: THREE PERCENT

Seconds. I've got seconds. I guess I'll do what I always do with my memory. I zip down my jumpsuit. Reach inside and detach a panel from the ports I use to connect to the liquid drive of the *Steel Haven.* They're thin, shallow, fashioned for heads of connectors built-in some factory on Shighn. I wasn't built for any of this, either.

I jam the memory core into the port. Nothing happens. Figures. Then this force seizes me. This current of energy lurches me to the power core. Data explodes inside my mind. Memories I withhold from myself. CR-UX's life before me. The knowledge of the titan this core belonged to, going back to before this universe. There was another universe before but that's not something I can linger on right now because a tight, heavy pain balloons in my chest.

I'm choking.

My thoughts strangle. This is cruel. Petty. I strain against the pain forcing its way into me, through me head to toe, wanting back out. I hold my hands against the fierce pounding in my chest, *ba-dumm, ba-dumm, ba-dumm.* My hands. I've got both my hands. Skin grows patchwork over my right arm, a rapid vine of turanium and synthetic tissue. All my wounds close. My scars heal.

Words sink on my bewildered breath. I touch my face again, expecting this just to be the confusion of exhalation frosting on me as I blip out. My hands are soft. Warm. The star's cold fails to freeze. Her unimaginable gravity only squeezes. A human would be dead right now. A netic scrap. I'm no longer a machine. Not human.

CR-UX's voice trebles in my ears. *You've always been human, darling. In whatever form you take.*

How are we even talking, CR-UX? The ship...

The downlink reactivated once you bonded with the titan's memory core, she says. *It's not external through a liquid drive anymore. It's simply... part of you now.*

>TITAN-PROXY POWER RESERVE: OFF-NOMINAL

Ancient power courses through me. Tech so advanced as to be magic overwrites my own. This wave builds within me and I fear who I am will get washed away in the flood but I float on the surface of infinite memory. Depths beyond understanding.

Too much.

I can't process any of these feelings. Thoughts. Infinite memory sprawls within me and it's all I can do to keep hold of this moment.

I pick up my sword. *Emera knew...*

Stars illuminate all things.

Where is she?

CR-UX pauses. *I have no reading on her.*

What? She's not...

Even if she was... no longer with us... her latent magnetic field would still be strong enough to detect on my sensors.

I don't understand... she was just talking to me.

Idari, we're taking heavy losses up here.

I run down the crag. *Sweep the shore for her.*

The Scath have established a foothold there.

Please.

I'll make another run. Idari...

I know.

Shadows race ahead of sprinting Scath tankers and escorts, peeling away the mist and spray and rough sea to leave only my reflection. A cry of joy escapes me. Shock. Exhilaration.

I am human.

I've always been human. I knew that, even if others convinced me otherwise. If I did. The ecstasy of breathing collides with far greater guilt over what my newfound life has come at the expense of. Who.

CR-UX... this should be you, I say.

It is, Idari.

But...

You were my dream. My reality is something... new.

New?

I can't wait to meet you. Which we should be doing. Promptly.

Smoke spoils the shore as I search for Emera. Savage waves slam clumps of crystalline bergs into the crag, tiny shards compared to the towering blades of hardened stellar flame stabbing up through the sea. Pieces of the Scath destroyer, coated in shimmering filamentium, form a volcanic chain of islands of molten debris. Shredded wreckage of SION fighters. Misfit ships. Debris washes ashore with the radiant tide. Blackened curls of turanium. I collect them, not knowing if they're from the *Steel Haven* or the destroyer. I should know. I should be able to take my ship with me in more than memory. All that remains of her now is a white cloud, deformed by stellar winds.

This isn't your star now.

"Em," I say, as the mist thickens. "Are you here?"

Hard-light flashes through the haze. Vortices swirl around bursts of dark energy. Screams echo across the shattered beach. Fighters strafe the shore, firing indiscriminately into the melee and dust glitters the air. I clutch my blasword, expecting Vidious. Crystalline armor rings with movement and I stab into the mist.

The Gesta perches on a thin strand, alone. "Idari."

I thread the needle of the strand, careful not to step in any of the filamentium. "Welkin? Where is Em?"

He shakes his head. "I've been here before, you know."

Mist shrouds the gate. "Where is she, Welkin?"

"Long ago. I came, as many did. I left, I thought, my fear at the gate. My shame. I came to this shore... but I didn't become a star."

"We need to find her. Welkin. We need her or we're all dead."

He kneads the glass. "I have never left those things, Idari."

"Are you hearing me?"

"I see you."

The mist enveloping us glows electric-blue. "What?"

His remaining eye fixes on the tide pool. "You've changed."

"Yes..."

"You're still the same."

"Same?"

"Human."

"Thanks... listen, Welkin. There's a lot going on. Really. I just downloaded a pretty big update. I'd love to work through it all with you over a bottle of babyl but maybe after we've found Emera?"

"I knew your spirit from the moment I saw you. Your soul."

I tuck the blasword in my belt. "Welkin... is she gone? Did she..."

"She's never gone from me."

"Can you bring her back, like before? Can you..."

"Have you seen your reflection, Idari?"

"Yes..."

"You are as you always were."

I edge closer to the pool. "I'm not so bad. You're..."

Emera smiles back at me from the pool. I turn around, impatient for the woman I love, but she's not there. Only Welkin. I look into the fire again. Electric blue shines back at me. *Ban Minda.* That's not the Emera I'm looking for. The one I've known since OT-3Ro.

That's Welkin's true reflection in the blood of The Glass Star. His true self.

"It's you..."

He turns from me. Emera dims in the pool.

I touch his shoulder. "Emera..."

His words fight themselves. "I've never been able to say..."

"That's your name. Isn't it?"

"You must think me a monster."

I sink to my knees beside him. "No..."

"I could only imagine her," he says. "I could never be..."

All this time. An eternity, living inside a body that was never his. This opaline shell. Beautiful, powerful, wise, but ill-fit. He projected his true self and he wanted life for her. Agency.

Freedom, like CR-UX did for me.

"Why can't you just..." What am I trying to say? I don't have the language for any of this. "Go into the sea."

Filamentium strains between his fingers, shimmering with every splash. "There is no hope for me."

"Why?"

"It was only a myth. A fantasy I convinced myself of."

"No..."

"I thought if I could just get back here... if I could come to the sea with this star that has guided me through these long years... but I couldn't even bring her past the gate."

She's gone. Emera isn't dead. Just not here. The projection of Gen Emera failed at the gate because he brought his doubt with him. His fear. The anger he's carried for himself.

"You did," I say. "You did bring her here."

He huffs dust. "She's gone."

"Welkin... *Emera*. Look at me."

"It's impossible."

"Please."

His chin scrapes back toward me.

I touch his face. "I see you."

"Idari..."

"You're so beautiful. You're so beautiful, Emera."

"No..."

"You are. I used to fight myself so much. Deny who I was. And then beat myself up for doing it. But then I met you. You made me see. There is nothing wrong with me. Or you. You've been in this shell for so long. Hardening. But this isn't who you are. You're that light inside. You're that star. I've seen her."

His cheek sinks in my palm. "I don't have the power."

"You've always had the power. Emera. Don't you see?"

His remaining eye shutters. "Not so well."

"You never needed The Glass Star to see yourself as you should be. And you don't need it to become who you are. You just need to believe in yourself. Leave your doubt. Your fear. That voice in your head speaking for all the people who would deny you. That's their weapon. To make you deny yourself. You believed it. I did."

"I can't..."

"Thana believed it too. She believed it so much she stabbed out all the stars. She radiates no light. But you..." Filaments string from his cerulean eye. "There is a star in you. You just have to let her out."

"You're asking me to forget everything I know," Welkin says.

I kiss her cheek. "Trust me. It's easy."

"You... you see her, Idari? You see *me*?"

"I always have."

Crack.

I jump, startled at the hairline fracture above his wounded eye widening. The branch splinters. A sapphire shines behind his ruined eye. Cracks delta throughout his hands. His arms. His entire body. Blue light shines from deep within, a coiled lightning bolt that intensifies with every fragment of crystalline shell that falls from him. Welkin tenses, frightened, and then he hardens. Don't. Don't stop now. I reach for him, crystal piling in my hands, and then he shatters.

Curved pieces of shell tumble into the tide pool. A brilliant blue star stands up out of the husk of Welkin, ecstatic energy flowing off of her into coiling ribbons. Mist evaporates. Tides rush toward her. The Glass Star sparkles again with the light of a newborn Lumenor.

The light of Gen Emera.

She stares into the blue fire of her hands. "Is this real?"

"You are," I say.

Her shock tumbles into joy. "I am..."

She kneels down into the remains of who she was. Welkin's glass mask lifts in her hands. Emera touches her head to his and then she rests him on the shore, left with all she will no longer carry.

I've never seen anything so miraculous. And I just became a titan-netic person inside a glass star. I should probably lie down for a while. No time for that. I take Emera's hand, warm and bright. My beautiful Emera. My guiding star. Words don't exist for what I feel right now. All I know is I want to remember this. And I will.

We're never going to forget who we are.

Emera takes me in her arms. "Never."

"I told you," I say. "We'd make it."

"You did."

"I love you, Em."

"Idari... I couldn't have..."

"You could. You always could."

She kisses me. "I love you."

"We should celebrate."

"I was thinking I could destroy all the Scath."

"You read my mind."

Her eyes blaze. Emera's thoughts flow out of her as free as her light. No more limits on her power. No more holding back. No more waiting. No more denying her true self. She is a true-born star. The Lumenor reborn. Stars forge shadows.

They destroy them, too.

Emera lifts her hand. Mist shrouding the sea scales away. So do the Scath tankers lowering to leech molten filamentium. SION fighters disintegrate. The rest of their fleet bombards the shore with all their heavy guns. Dark fire blunts harmlessly into a wall of dense crystal Emera tears from the shore.

Tap, tap, tap. "There is always another star."

I draw my sword as Thana emerges from the devastation. "And you always show up like a bad hangover. Guess what? So do I."

Emera puts her hand on mine. Not this again. We've done this.

"Queen Thana," Emera says. "I know in your heart there was once grace. I know you lost someone you loved. I ask you. One last time. End this. I will be fair to you. I will be just."

Volcanic light erupts from Thana. "Die... *die!*"

Hell blasts at us. Smoke fumes from my jacket. Emera catches Thana's fury in her hand and disperses it to vapors.

"You only empower me," Emera says.

Thana shields her eyes from Emera's light. Shadows reveal the strain on her face. The conflict. Her emotions stretch and tear like the surface of this star, rent by forces beyond imagination.

She sinks to her knees. "I just wanted..."

Emera extends her hand. "Maracen was a star. I am. You are. You're still a star, Thana. And you can still become something new."

I'd rather just kill this chick and not have to look over my shoulder anymore, but something pulls on Thana. Some force, or some power within, distorting her orbit around oblivion. Her eyes fix on me. Emera. Our hands locked together in love.

"Stars only lose their light," she says.

Emera clutches my hand. "They give their light to others."

She reaches for Emera. "Can you..."

Something moves to my right. Fast. Angry. I turn just as Vidious bounds across the shore, sword gleaming with reflected starlight. *Ban Minda.* I'm out of position. I deploy the blasword too late. His sword slices to the ground. Crystal shatters. Molten blood splatters.

The fragile light Thana Evo harbored flees, ripping away the tenuous youth she's clung to for ages. She falls against Vidious, her gauzy corona hardening to dirty diamond.

Her blood scabs on his blade. "Thana..."

She crumbles at his touch. "I couldn't let you... again..."

Cracks eat through her cheek, her eyes, her throat. She crashes to the ground. Emera goes to her side, but it's too late. The red queen goes to pieces in Emera's hands. Glittering dust obscures the shore, but not Emera's grief. Even after all the years and all the lives, she held as much hope for Thana as she did herself.

She glares at Vidious. "Murderer..."

Vidious hisses dust. "Unmake me..."

"You didn't deserve your fate... but you've earned it."

"Do it... or I destroy you, imposter."

"I am who I am. And you are who you are."

His sword sweeps through the periphery of her fire, the blade a blur of light. A magnetic wave knocks him back but blood trickles from a deep scar on Emera's arm. She unleashes a planet-boiling energy blast into Vidious. He remains unmoved.

We're both who we're supposed to be finally, we're both alive in our own skins and this guy is going to hang them from some post. Fear quakes through me, real nervous fear like I've never known, but Emera faces him with calm. Grace.

"Lay down your sword," she says. "It's over."

He cocks his sword. "It is. For you."

I brandish mine. "We'll see about that."

"You're no match, Idari. And you're no Lumenor, Welkin."

Emera flares brighter than ever. "That's not my name."

"When I kill you... I will have killed the last star... then, *Welkin*. Then it will be over."

Idari, Emera says.

Yes?

Can you hold him off for a few minutes?

I clutch my sword. *Got something in mind?*

Fire breathes from her fingers. "I can't unmake you, Vidious. But maybe I can forge you into something new. Something better."

Hi's laughter thunders across the devastated shore. "Fool... I was forged in the heart of this star. Only her flame can cure me."

"I know," she says, and cracks split the glass beneath us.

A pulse goes through the shore, *ba-dumm*. A shockwave through the sea. Light flares in chasms opening all around us. Star fire.

Ban Minda.

Light erupts from Emera, illuminating every crack and defect in the star's glass. Veins of frozen fire stringing the sky pulse with dull light. Ripples in the sea become waves and as they crash upon the crumbling shore, Emera rises as if taken by some invisible force, arms outstretched like wings, sapphirine ribbons cycling faster and faster around her. Wave after wave of energy pulses outward from Emera into the core. Tremors cascade through The Glass Star, along with a terrible and persistent thunder. *Ba-dumm.* The ground shakes.

Get to CR-UX, Emera says. *Get everyone out of here, Idari.*

Are you really doing what I think you're doing?

Hurry.

I change channels. *CR-UX...*

On my way, darling. You'd best be running as I approach.

Our fleet breaks for the way out of the core, and there's no one to stop the shadows from surrounding us. Scath ships rain fire down on Emera. She launches pillars of crystal in the sea at the Scath. At Vidious. He marches through the storm, cutting down every shard of black glass, wading through her blistering fire and if he gets close, if he stabs her again, this time she won't come back.

He'll have to get through me first. No more words. No more threats. No more pleas for understanding. Fight or flight. Live or die. The glass knight charges me. His sword slams into mine.

I don't move.

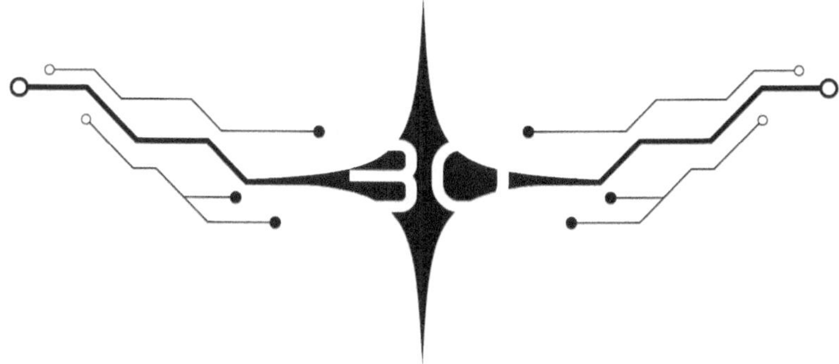

BA-DUMM.

Ghost fire streams off Emera across the shore. Magnetic eddies churn through the air, tugging on me so hard I have to increase my gravitational settings. I get heavier as Emera rises into a blazing vortex, a gnomon against a flickering sundial.

>MAGNETIC FIELD DENSITY BEYOND TOLERANCE

>GRAVITY BEYOND TOLERANCE

>EXTERNAL TEMPERATURE BEYOND TOLERANCE

Vidious crashes his sword into mine. "I can see the lenses click in your eyes, Idari... you're still just a machine."

I hold my ground. "I'm more now."

"The Banbor Gang knew it. Countless pirates do. Endless shadows. I know it. Whatever soft rubber you stretch over your turanium bones... that's all you are. That's all you'll ever be."

Fear shadows me even now. I transmuted at the shore, but just like I still have the downlink, I still have all the untidy parts of me I'd rather do without. I'm human. I've known a lot of imperfect humans.

As in, all of them.

Before, I would have nursed my doubt and fear in a bottle. I would have forgotten it. This time, I amp up my internal gravitational settings once again. And then I start browsing my new features.

>MAXIMIZING TITAN-PROXY STRENGTH

Something just happened. My muscles aren't any bigger and I'm certainly not but I feel stronger. Springier. Let's give it a go. I swing so hard I leave a chip in the blade of Vidious' perfect sword.

"I am perfect," I say. "I'll give you that."

"Enough of this," he says. "Command: Idari Omega. Execute."

>INVALID PROMPT

"Sorry, darling," I say. "I changed my password."

I swing for his head. Vidious steps back and lets my momentum carry me out of position. He presses his advance again and I put everything I have into keeping him away from Emera. Not exactly the easiest thing with the tremors rattling through the shore, opening fissures in the glass, rattling the sword in my hands as Vidious strikes.

Ba-dumm.

Vidious fakes going in one direction. I'm too nimble in this new and improved body to be fooled for long. Everywhere he goes, there I am. His frustration mounts as I block every route to Emera, as I parry every strike, as I blunt his ancient fury.

"You're going to die here," Vidious says.

Glass shatters beneath my feet. "So are you."

He shifts his grip on the hilt of his sword like he's going to throw it and I spring out of my defensive position. He brings the sword down on my back and I block just enough of it to keep my head on. Doesn't matter. We've swapped spots.

Vidious breaks across the crumpling shore toward Emera.

Blood slicks my grip on my sword as I chase after him. Cosmic fire blisters Vidious. Light currents from Emera into the star. Energy flows back and swirls around her, collecting in a sphere gathering mass at the tips of her outstretched fingers.

Ba-dumm.

The Kib survivors flee for the exit but the Scath fleet continues its advance to the filamentium sea undaunted. Fighters. Destroyers. Tankers. A thousand ships or more. Crystal peels from the ground. Dormant energy asleep as long as the universe bleeds from the core into the mass Emera collects, writhing, pulpating, oscillating faster than neutron stars. Space confuses. Time. Whatever lies between.

Reality shreds before my eyes. Gesta ancient in their form come to the sea, seeking their transmutation in light. Scavengers. Looters.

Titans.

Reality warps into a hall of mirrors reflecting the titan's infinite experience. My experience now, with their memory twined in mine. I run from The Glass Star to the rusted shores of iron seas. I stumble across rattling stellar glass into the ashes of the bones of gods.

I hurry toward my north star, trying to keep from being stranded. The titans traveled to different realities. They collected from them and replicated their discoveries in their great ark.

Why?

All my births and deaths flicker in and around me. I can't tell them apart. Infinite darkness sweeps over the universe, stars winking out down to the last, and another blooms in its place. There are more beginnings than endings.

Ba-dumm.

Vidious closes on Emera. I'm too far. Too late. Right as he raises his sword the ground heaves beneath him. Fractured glass vaults him through the air and I run after him. Get him down.

Keep him down.

His ancient anger spits him back on his feet. Eternal frustration propels every strike, every hack, every ferocious blow. My chance evaporates like the frost coating the star.

Ba-dumm.

Time bends around me like weak metal. Warps. Shrinks. The ground froths and gurgles and I keep moving, ducking, rolling, Vidious' sword everywhere but I don't let him past me. Vidious trembles with frustration at his inability to simply destroy me. Poor bastard.

At least he's got plenty of company.

His swings grow wilder and more reckless. I only use his vexation to my advantage. Craters riddle his armor. Thin scars of endless cuts. Every time he lunges at me, I move out of the way, tagging with him the jagged end of my blade.

Ba-dumm.

Time. Emera needs time. This howl builds in the air. I expect the star to come crashing down on me but it's Scath fighters that didn't get the hint they should be screaming out of here at lightspeed.

"No," I say as they strafe the shore.

Dark energy dissipates against *The Green Carnation's* shields. Her forward cannons erupt, shredding the SION fighters to metal ash that threads into the gyre of energy Emera stokes.

Run, CR-UX.

Her voice trails behind the elegant ship. *Not without you, darling.*

Now isn't the time to be sentimental.

Idari, look out —

Diamond-sharp crystal whisks past my chin. I fall back in what passes for a defensive posture and Vidious has me on my heels. My sword leaves molten gashes in the air goopy with time so thick it sludges across the shore, not the shore anymore but a quartz scab on the igneous heart of a star. My jumpsuit bubbles. My skin blisters.

Ba-DUMM.

Vidious presses into me, ignoring all my feints. The scars I slash in him. Nothing matters now. He forces me back within the corona of light bristling around Emera. Strands of my hair ember and ash. He brings his sword down hard on mine. The blades flint fire. We struggle against each other, hilts locked.

Vidious braces against Emera's fury. "You fight well, Idari."

"Bit late for flattery," I say.

"You fight without fear."

"Can't say the same for you."

"There must be an end..."

"It doesn't have to be like this."

Emera brightens with each passing moment, a storm of energy building to release; a pulse stirs in the heart of the star.

Ba-DUMM.

His eyes set on me. "Gen Emera cannot save you, Idari. Not from me. And not from yourself. You know that. Don't you?"

My back foot slips. "You don't know..."

"You can never be undone. You are as you are. For all the light she shines on you... you will always cast a shadow long and dark. You're not human. A titan. You're a machine. A hunter. A killer, just like me. You're what you were made to be."

I'm losing ground. "You don't know anything..."

He pushes me back. "You can never change."

Vidious drives me back with blow after blow. I swing wild for his legs. He parries my blasword right out of my reddening hands. Stellar flame shunts from his blade as he brings it down on me.

I wheel out of the way. His sword buries into the molten ground and I shatter the blade under my boot. The hilt tumbles across the disintegrating surface, a useless handle with a jagged lip of blade. I dive on it, get it in my hands, to his neck.

Vidious eyes the blade. "Kill me, Idari."

Every instinct funnels blood into my hand. Every thought in my hand constricts my fingers around the hilt. Do it. End it. Save Emera. What does your humanity matter in killing a monster?

I throw the sword to the ground. "I'm nothing like you."

Ba-DUMM.

His laughter chops across waves of energy. "Fool... I can make you do whatever I want you to. Astra Idari... the perfect machine."

He grabs the broken hilt. Jagged crystal rushes at me. I grab his hands. The cleft blade sinks toward my neck. Energy sweeps over us, softening me but I hold my ground. All my strength, all my determination, all my power goes into resisting him.

Vidious presses everything he has. "Such strength..."

My knees buckle. "You haven't seen anything yet."

"So much like my own. Spirits like ours are rare in the universe. My only regret today is that yours must yield to mine."

I push back. This time, his knees bend. His hands tremble. Fear blazes in his eyes. Not this time. Never again.

Ba-DUMM.

The ground gives out beneath us. I teeter on the edge of a new cliff, barely hanging on. Vidious tumbles into a chasm, dust trailing after him as he disappears into the flaming mist consuming the star.

The shore crackles from glass to fire. I crumble before Emera. Sensors blind. Senses. I look up into the dawn, a smile on her lips as matter transmutes all around me. Energy. Currents of dormant plasma flow through Emera into The Glass Star and she is no longer herself but the star's heart as it shudders to life.

BA-DUMM.

Every atom in my body races toward collision. Nothing registers in my senses but a long blinding shear of light. Gravity confuses. I rise. I fly into Emera's arms and then inside *The Green Carnation* through no door or window or egress only thought faster than light out of the core into the radiation zone catching fire behind us.

Dark space streaks with embers in the canopy as Binja guns the ship toward the mouth of the abyssal gorge, engines keeping us just ahead of stellar fury. I cling to Emera with all my hope and all my fears manifest as the way ahead collapses in a prismatic nova my sensors barely comprehend. I close my eyes. Kiss her hand. Wait for the end to pulse through us and out into forever

ba-dumm

ba-DUMM

BA-DUMM

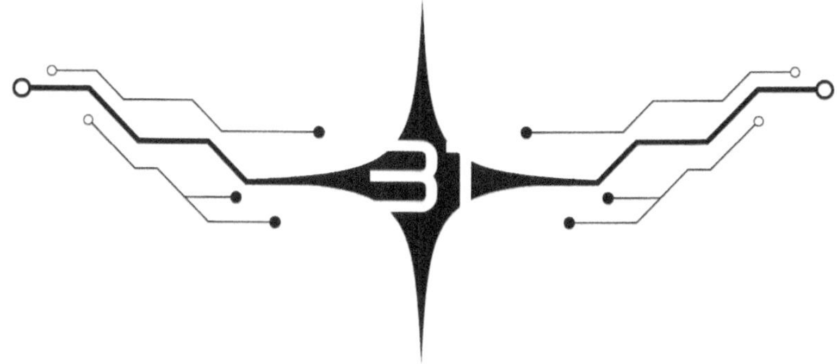

BA-DUMM.

The heart of a star beats in time with mine. Sunlight kisses my cheek. Everything a white blur. *Ban Minda.* It really happened.

I'm stardust.

Not yet, Emera says.

My optics shift back into focus. I'm not in a million itty bitty bits of Idari. I'm on the remarkably clean deck of *The Green Carnation.* Emera holds me, a lazy smile on her face. A satisfied one. She breathed life back into a star. She realized herself. Every breath I take is sharp. Clumsy. New. I'm not used to weight in my body that isn't metal. I'm not used to this warmth. I'm not used to this love.

She kisses me. "You saved me."

I touch her face. "Em..."

"You saved my life."

"You blew up a star."

A star smiles on me. "She's still there."

Far in the distance, The Glass Star pulses like a beacon in the night. Cobwebs of ancient, frozen hydrogen and helium sink toward the star, brightening, fattening, kindling the cold cellar she's been hiding in for eternity anew. She's not glass anymore.

"Hell of a first date," I say.

Her lips linger on mine. "We're just getting started."

Binja clears his throat. "There are guest accommodations."

Look at this ship. Chrome everything. Hand-crafted ornamentation. Smooth, clean lines. Just clean, really, which is a change. I connect my proxy signal to the ship's mainframe. Tiny little computer. Innocent little computer.

"Hello, lover," I say.

Binja turns out of the pilot's seat. "She's all yours."

"You could have run, Binja. You should have."

He reaches for that sash. "Oh, I tried."

"What stopped you?"

"A friend helped me realize I had to give something back."

"Back?"

"My people exiled me. You gave me a place. A family. A purpose. And I took from you, the way the pirates took from me."

"Pirates only take."

He shakes his head. "I've said that a million times, but I didn't see until now that we give... everything. I give my name back to The Taker. I give my life, if he'll have it. I give the chance you gave me, old man, back to you. The friendship."

"*Kinvar Em*," I say.

He bows his head. "*Semet vanar.*"

Gilf and Kibir envelop both Emera and I in a hug. I don't care Gilf sneezes in my face. Oh, I care a little. But I'll manage. *Ban Minda.* I thought all of them would die in the battle.

"*Oto,*" I say.

Kibir touches his head to mine. "*Oto,* Idari."

A strange voice silks into the cockpit. "I see where I rank."

The Kib untangle from me. A sexy skyscraper in satin helps me to my feet. "Who are... CR-UX?"

She winks at me. "I just look the part, don't I?"

"Why are you hot?"

She shrugs. "Some of us are just born with it."

I sigh. "Whatever."

Her eyes well with tears. "Look at you."

"Don't cry."

"You're so beautiful."

"Don't."

She hugs me. "I love you."

Tears salt my lips. "I love you, CR-UX."

She squeezes my hands. "I don't want to be CR-UX anymore."

"Oh... what do I call you?"

"Call me... Faero."

Faero. The singer. "My idol."

"We made it, darling."

Words stick in my throat. Nothing more needs to be said. For once, we don't have to fill the void of our doubt with banter and bickering. We don't have to form a bond in words in the absence of physical comfort. We have each other now.

We always did, Faero says.

I was appreciating the moment.

Not arguing, just saying.

You always have to get the last word in.

No, I don't.

You're doing it right now.

Doing what?

Emera touches my arm. "Where to now?"

I pull her close. "Where do you want to go?"

She's never been so confident in her blue. "I don't know. I haven't thought of anything beyond The Glass Star in..."

"We can go anywhere now, Em. We can do anything."

Possibility brims in her eyes. "I can't wait."

Alerts ping from the control console. "What is it? Scath?"

Binja checks the instrumentation. "The refugee fleet... what's left of it. They're headed for the Kib colony on Tranto."

The Kib lost everything on Angolis. They risked what little they had left to help us. First round is on me.

"The Scath are still out there," Emera says.

I squeeze her hand. "You destroyed their fleet."

"More exist beyond The Reach."

That doesn't do anything for my mood. "Without The Glass Star... they'll be out of fuel reserves in months. So will the galaxy."

Binja scratches his chin. "There's still filamentium here."

"Drawing blood from a Lumenor is one thing," Emera says. "Mining it from a celestial star is another. The star is burning her fuel... the galaxy will find another way. It will have to."

Still, we'll need to be careful. The Scath will be scouring the universe for every last drop of filamentium they can bleed. They'll want revenge for what happened here. Their true master will want to know why they're not able to fuel the murder of universes.

Another alert pings on the controls. I take the co-pilot's seat, expecting Scath to manifest and dash our relief. Instead, maybe the most unexpected thing in a day of the unexpected greets me.

"Anybody up for a concert?"

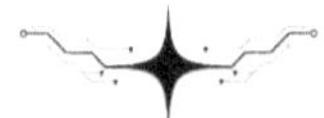

Planets usually don't make all that much of an impression on me, but water is rare in the galaxy. All that blue; anything blue gets me, every single time. The ocean moon of Peart scrolls beneath us, a turquoise orb webbed in sandy archipelagos and inky, vanishing reefs. Annular lakes formed from an ancient asteroid bombardment form links in the island chains, with the rocky rims of the biggest serrating the azure water with stony gray ridges. Shadows of towering cumulonimbus clouds speckle the shallow blue seas, islands without form.

I navigate the cloud canyons to the surface. "Two minutes out."

Emera undoes her harness straps. "Any sign of the Scath?"

Telemetry cascades across the downlink. "Nothing."

"Would you be able to detect them if they're shadowed?"

"It's ok, Em. We're clear."

Emera nods, but she doesn't believe it. Emera doesn't know how to relax any more than she knows where she's going next in her long, strange life. "This concert we're going to... it isn't Delicia Faero?"

"Inra Montane. She used to be Faero. The singer."

"She changes."

"Every nine years or something."

"Like you."

I smile. "I like the way I am now."

A smile brims on her lips. "There's traffic ahead."

I throttle back the engines. Ease over to the retros. Starplanes strand in lines of traffic ahead. New as I am to this ship, dazed as I am with all that's happened, I don't know I'd have seen them in time to avoid a laughable end to our journey. I'm so used to CR-UX being my co-pilot. *Faero.* She's still in my ear, or at least she was until she and Binja found a deck of cards in the back. Odd. I expected her to gloat about overcoming his obvious cheating.

I look over my shoulder. "Are they still playing *desh?*"

Emera shakes her head.

Traffic thins at about a thousand feet. So do the clouds. *Ban Minda.* I've always wanted to see a show here. The arena floats within the bowl of a massive impact crater, smack in the heart of a long, skinny peninsula like a crack in the blue shell of the sea. Crescent-shaped platforms of bleachers form the hovering arena, some small and some broad, some close to the hovering stage at the center, and some spaced farther out. A tattered curtain hangs over the stage from a rig hovering above it, fitted with lights and other equipment.

I glance at Emera. "Ready to party, baby?"

"I've never partied."

"Never?"

"My life has been mostly running and hiding."

"Then it's time to add to your legend."

I autonomically throttle back the engines as we ease into the outer bands of the arena. Stocky MUR-CX netics on floating pedestals guide other sporty starplanes ahead of us to hovering positions in the air. The netics beg us forward with reflective batons and then when we've aligned with our little pocket of the sky they dap our nose and move down the line.

I key over to auto-pilot. "Thrusters at station keeping."

Emera gazes out the canopy. "We're not going to land?"

"We've got the best seat in the house." I wheel the ship around so her backside faces the arena. "Where's the release for the sun deck? Faero? Where did you disappear to?"

Emera's nose wrinkles. "We should probably wait for them."

"Them?"

I head back to the community area. Gilf and Kibir shuffle through another hand of *desh*. No sign of Faero or Binja. Where the hell did they get to? I head to my quarters to see what this ship is stocked for in jackets. I want to look my best.

"Why is the door locked?" I say. "Override."

Binja pulls a sheet over himself fast as he can. Faero just sits there in the bed, shameless in her nudity.

My hands crash to my sides. "*What the fuck?*"

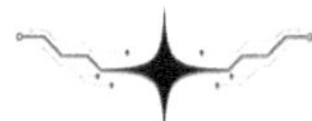

Thunder pounds through the floating stands. My heart.

Chants build in the crowd. Excitement ramps up as smoke billows from floating generators off-stage. The curtain rises and Dook Ballarat strums his tantar. Screams shake the arena so hard I think all those islands of stands will just drift away. Bella Donnic walks out holding her drumsticks, and takes her seat behind her elaborate kit, most of it floating above her head. Her jetpack fires, she crashes flying cymbals and the clouds break.

Light! Now!

And then, Inra Montane runs out onto the stage, as if she'll keep running right off the other side and back down into the wings but she stops. A million people teeter on the edge of delirium. She holds her hands up to the crowd. To the ships constellating the night sky around the arena. I hold my hands up to her.

This emancipation.

Faero skulks across the sun deck atop the ship, carrying a drink Gilf made at the horseshoe bar. "I had to get it out of my system."

I roll my eyes. "You mean to tell me decades of passive aggression between you and Binja has been unresolved sexual tension?"

"Yes. Yes, it was."

"*Ban Minda.*"

Binja leans over as he claps with the music. "I would have thought given your history, you'd be open to possibilities, old man."

"There's no limit on how many times I can shoot you, Binja."

Emera ropes me in her arms. "I love it."

"I'm furious."

"The show," she says, pulling me back, swaying with me, pulsing with the beat of the music, *ba-dumm.* "I've never felt so free."

"You're free, Em."

"It's just hitting me now..."

I brush her cheek. "I know."

"I'm afraid to go to sleep. I'm afraid to close my eyes."

So am I. This new body begs for rest, but I'm too familiar with cruel dreams to give in that easy. If this is a dream, or some corruption of my program as it crashes in its final moments, I'm going to get everything out of my new life.

My humanity.

Thunder rolls through the arena at the close of a song. Montane comes to the stage's edge. Cheers crest and fall. She waits, nodding in appreciation, and the crowd quiets enough for her to speak.

"How are you, then?"

I scream my joy back at her.

"You know why we're all here today. We're here because – "

Light! Now!

Light! Now!

Light! Now!

Emera hugs my arm. "What is it they're saying?"

"That's right," Montane says. "You've seen the news. You've heard the news. The new star in the galaxy. The old star reborn."

I squeeze Emera's hand. "The Glass Star..."

Montane walks the length of the stage. "You've heard the truth about the Lumenor. We are all the victims of a terrible lie. But no more. It's time to come out of the shadows. The Lumenor are real. The living stars exist."

No! More!

No! More!

No! More!

I never imagined anyone would know what happened at The Glass Star. Cosmic as the fight was, I never felt so small. But the survivors of Angolis, the Kib, and nameless pirates who fought with us, they must have spread the word. Worlds close enough for their sky to be rewritten, they must have seen. Emera did more than wake up a dead star. She woke up the galaxy.

You did, Emera says. *We did.*

Look at us. Nameless pirate. Dusty Kib. The spirit of my best friend in the form of this unnervingly attractive woman. That ought to be enough, but it goes on. A living star. And me. A beat-up old netic well beyond her design limits, and way over her head.

"We're not supposed to be here," I say.

The others close in around me.

"But here we are. I don't know if there's any grand design or higher purpose. Seems to me the purpose behind our existence is we're meant to be in the places we were never intended for. We're meant to be the people we become, not who we start as. So here we are." I raise my glass. "To being here."

Faero hugs me. "That was halfway decent."

"Right?"

Slowly, the chant builds again in the arena. *Light! Now! Light! Now! Light! Now!* Bella Donnic summons even more with thundering drums and Dook provides a shimmering crescendo as life roars back into the arena. The opening strains of "The Star Queen Strikes" shriek through the arena and *Ban Minda.* It's happening. This is really happening. I smile and pull Emera close.

We did it.

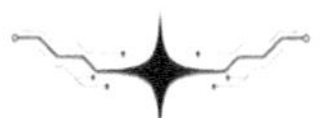

>FILE CRITICAL / ALWAYS READ THIS FIRST
Your name is Astra Idari. You're an IA-XR Model 4 proxy-netic with limited onboard memory.

Shadows trail me down the beaches. I go for a swim in the shallows. I wallow with little fish things streaked with strange color. Days into our stay on Peart and there's no rush to leave. Not with all this warm sand. All this radiant blue. Everything green and wood and living.

I'm living for once.

Living then proceeds to involve basking on a beach doing nothing at all until the grit gets too much I go back to the waterfall cascading down the cliff. I wash away the sand. The salt. The cling of things still eager to hold me. This warmth touches my skin. This stellar kiss. Emera's light knots around me. Everything in my body snaps to her.

Her lips brush my neck. "I miss you."

I fight this opening and closing in me. This reflex of nocturnal flowers. "I wasn't gone that long."

"Stars are selfish."

"So I'm discovering."

Her hand sinks between my legs. Emera's heat warms mine. My top unlaces and I turn around, my arm across my chest.

"There could be people out here," I say.

"There's no one."

"Let's go back to the ship."

Her light crimps in disappointment. "For someone who prefers the lights off... you chose an interesting lover, Idari."

We've made love our primary recreation since arriving but I'm still not completely comfortable in my skin. The titan's memory core transformed me. Wounds healed. Scars faded. Seams stayed. These ugly ports on my chest, reminders of who I was before. I don't need reminders. I don't struggle with who I am. I know who I am.

>FILE CRITICAL / ALWAYS READ THIS FIRST
>FILE CRITICAL: DELETE? Y/N: Y
>FILE DELETED

Emera tugs on my arm. Her smile tempting. Her love radiating through me. My arm comes free. No grit left on me. No cling. My arms fall to my sides and Emera considers me.

All of me.

Emera caresses the lines graphing my chest. She kisses them soft and sure. Her light infiltrates me and then she takes me in her arms. She holds me tight as any star holds its subjects.

I close my arms around her. Shaking a bit, but maybe that's the water. Glowing a bit, incandescent in the sun. I could be here. I could be like this forever. Warm, safe, and happy.

Her love ebbs through me. *I want people to see us.*

An exhibitionist?

I am a star.

There will have to be clearly defined rules.

She gives me this look I'm getting so in love with. This face. *There you go again.* There I go. Running so fast the stars give chase.

Let's fly, she says.

Fly?

Sun glitters in falling water. *The sky has been waiting for me.*

My feet flap as mad as the birds dodging us. I lose Emera in the clouds but then I find her again. I always find her. I spiral into her, colliding into sun kisses, our shadows vanishing into boundless blue.

L : DRIVE

TELEMETRY

T+0844:L:D >SHIELD FAILURE
T+0844:L:D >HULL BREACH
T+0845:L:D >STRUCTURAL INTEGRITY FAILING

>CORRUPTED DATA<

T+0846:L:D >INTERNAL SYSTEMS FAILURE
T+0846:L:D >INITIATE EMERGENCY DATA BACKUP
T+0846:L:D >EMERGENCY DATA BUOY ACTIVE
T+0846:L:D >TRANSMIT DATA BUOY Y/N?:Y

>CORRUPTED DATA<

T+0847:L:D >TRANSMISSION TO PROXIES SUCCESSFUL
T+0847:L:D >REACTOR CONTAINMENT FAILURE
T+0847:L:D >ALARM:FIRE
T+0848:L:D >ALARM:PROXIMITY
T+0848:L:D >ALARM:HULL BREACH
T+0848:L:D >ALARM:PRIMARY POWER LOSS
T+0848:L:D >LOSS OF SIGNAL

>RECOVERED DATA<

T+0848:L:D >ENABLE BACKUP POWER
T+0848:L:D >BACKUP POWER FAILURE
T+0848:L:D >INDETERMINATE ENERGY SOURCE (POSS: ECLIPTOR CORE)
T+0848:L:D >INDETERMINATE ENERGY SOURCE (POSS: LUMENOR)
T+0848:L:D >INDETERMINATE ENERGY SOURCE (POSS: LUMENOR)
T+0848:L:D >INDETERMINATE ENERGY SOURCE (POSS: LUMENOR)
T+0849:L:D >NO DATA
T+0849:L:D >N/D
T+0849:L:D >

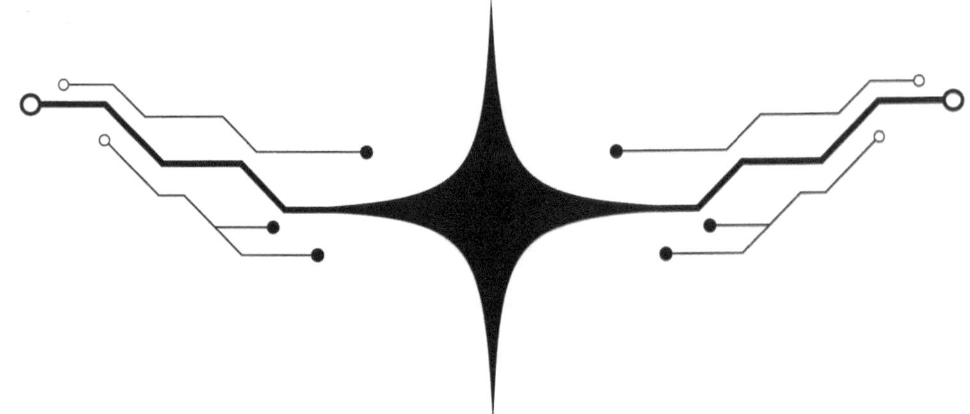

ASTRA IDARI WILL RETURN!

SUBSCRIBE TO MY NEWSLETTER

FOR UPDATES ON IDARI'S NEXT ADVENTURE

AND AN EXCLUSIVE FREE STORY!

WWW.DARBYHARN.COM/SUBSCRIBE

DARBY HARN is the author of the SPSFC quarterfinalist *Ever The Hero*, which *Publisher's Weekly* called "an entertaining debut uses superpowers as a metaphor to delve into class politics in an alternate America." His short fiction appears in *Strange Horizons*, *Interzone*, *Shimmer*, and other venues.

Stay Up To Date At
darbyharn.com

facebook.com/darbyharn.author

x.com/DarbyHarn

instagram.com/darbywritesbooks

goodreads.com/darby_harn

amazon.com/author/darbyharn

bsky.app/profile/darbyharn.bsky.social

ACKNOWLEDGMENTS

Stars take a long time to form. Not all of them shine at first.

Stargun Messenger started as a novel in the late 1990s that had all the core elements of the story it is now (Idari, Emera, the Lumenor, the Scath, The Glass Star...). It took decades to ignite, and in some ways, I have as well. Becoming a better writer, learning about aspects of myself and embracing them in my own way and my own time, helped provide the clarity that the book needed.

Some books teach you how to be a better writer; they're not necessarily meant to ever see the light of day. Some, like this one, teach you the value in holding true to yourself. The story never let me go. Idari never let me go. I'm not as brave as she is, but I like to think I'm as determined. We'll both get there, eventually.

The last three years have been very isolating and destructive in so many ways. COVID has left its scars in body and mind. I deeply appreciate the communities that sustained me through this time.

Thank you to David Wall and Alex Newman for a fun and needed outlet with The Movie News Network podcast during the absolute depths of the pandemic. I hope we nerd out again someday.

Thank you to Tony Gorick for being there and a friend.

Thank you to Writer's Alliance and the continued support and feedback of Cassie Gruetman, Shelly Campbell, and Jennifer Lane.

Though they may not know it, Abby and Brantley Paige have been inspirations for me and this book.

A person needs a place to go even as all the doors seem to shut, so thank you to the crew at Jameson's Public House for giving me an oasis in the last few years. Thank you Tommy, Michelle, Shaylin, Shay, Bailey, and most of all Maddie, who always lit dark days.

Many others contributed to the book's success.

Polly Brewster read an ancient version of this and somehow never held it against me. She has always supported my vision, even when I couldn't see the forest from the trees.

Sugu Althomsons also provided feedback on prehistoric versions of this book. Sugu puts up with a lot from me and I'd be a sorry old thing if not for his friendship and advice.

Wayne Santos was instrumental in encouraging this story and my writing. His enthusiasm for all things fun and fantasy (and explosions) helped me stayed connected to mine.

Michael Rex and I rarely talk writing, but his art and friendship have been an inspiration through trying times.

Ben Kral endures more than anyone else when it comes to listening to me go on about this story and these characters. I appreciate the feedback and perspective as always.

Sunyi Dean has been a guiding light in helping me understand myself better. That helped me to understand Idari, this story that wouldn't let me go, and myself even more.

Essa Hansen illuminated the book's problems and the tangle in my head that had been holding me back in so many other ways. This book wouldn't exist without Essa. None of them would.

Al Hess brings my books to life. I'd be nowhere without Al's understanding and friendship. I'm eternally grateful to him.

Thank you all so much.

– Darby